SNOW
ANGELS

BOOK YOUR PLACE ON OUR WEBSITE AND MAKE THE READING CONNECTION!

We've created a customized website just for our very special readers, where you can get the inside scoop on everything that's going on with Zebra, Pinnacle and Kensington books.

When you come online, you'll have the exciting opportunity to:

- View covers of upcoming books
- Read sample chapters
- Learn about our future publishing schedule (listed by publication month *and author*)
- Find out when your favorite authors will be visiting a city near you
- Search for and order backlist books from our online catalog
- Check out author bios and background information
- Send e-mail to your favorite authors
- Meet the Kensington staff online
- Join us in weekly chats with authors, readers and other guests
- Get writing guidelines
- AND MUCH MORE!

**Visit our website at
http://www.zebrabooks.com**

SNOW ANGELS

Cherie Claire
Phoebe Conn
Victoria Dark

Zebra Books
Kensington Publishing Corp.
http://www.zebrabooks.com

ZEBRA BOOKS are published by

Kensington Publishing Corp.
850 Third Avenue
New York, NY 10022

First Printing: October, 1999
10 9 8 7 6 5 4 3 2 1

Printed in the United States of America

CONTENTS

THE LETTER

Cherie Claire

Chapter One

*"Well has it been said that there is no grief
like the grief which does not speak."*
—*Henry Wadsworth Longfellow*

"Read it to me one more time, Fiona. The part where they find each other."

Fiona Riley sighed and stared down into the haunting blue eyes of her best friend, eyes that would not see much more of the world. "You must rest now, Mattie," Fiona implored. "No more stories tonight."

"Please," Mattie answered. "One more time. Just the part where she finds Gabriel."

Fiona detested Mattie's choice of reading materials. Since immigrating to New Orleans to escape the Great Hunger of Ireland, Mattie insisted on reading Louisiana stories, "to become more American," she explained. But "Evangeline" was not Fiona's idea of romance. While Mattie wept at the story of a young Acadian girl separated from her true love during their exile by the English from Canada, Fiona hated the tale of unrequited love. Evangeline spent her life in search of Gabriel, her intended, only to find him long enough to watch him die in her arms in an eastern hospital. Fiona had seen enough of dying, of roads leading to more despair, more heartbreak. If she was to read an American story, let it have a happy ending.

But that was the trouble. She and Mattie had ventured to America in search of a better life and found death at the end of their travels. Mattie's husband had perished on the boat from Ireland, and Mattie had turned ill as soon as they reached New Orleans. When the baby came, Mattie took to her bed and never regained her strength. Now, eight months later, Fiona knew her friend's time had come.

"Please, Mattie," Fiona begged, trying to keep the emotion out of her voice. "Don't leave me. Not here. Not now."

"Do you think I'll find him at last?" Mattie whispered.

"Who?" Fiona asked.

"My Gabriel. My Patrick."

Tears Fiona had struggled to keep inside flowed relentlessly down her cheeks. "You're not going to die, Mattie." She had meant it as a command, a defiance to God, but Fiona knew her wishes were futile. The soft-spoken woman who had been her lifetime companion and confidante had not eaten in days.

"Take care of my angel, Fiona," Mattie said, her voice weakening with each breath. "Keep her safe."

"Of course, Mattie," Fiona answered, gazing over at the soft whispers of red hair peeking out from beneath the woolen baby blanket. Since the two women had entered the Crescent City, Fiona had worked every available job to keep them all alive. "You know I will do everything in my power."

"You're the survivor," Mattie continued, her eyes closing from the fatigue. "Take her away from here. Somewhere where the air is clear, where you can grow a little garden, where things are green."

"Yes, Mattie."

Suddenly, Mattie regained an ounce of strength, leaned

forward and grabbed Fiona's sleeve desperately. "Promise me, Fiona."

"I promise, Mattie," Fiona replied, retrieving her friend's hand from her shirt and placing it lovingly back within the warmth of the covers. "Now, get some rest."

Mattie's breathing relaxed, and she closed her eyes. Still, she waited for Fiona to speak, to tell Henry Wadsworth Longfellow's story about a love so powerful nothing could keep the two lovers apart. Fiona began the epic poem as she had done almost every night since they arrived, this time from memory.

> *Vainly he strove to rise; and Evangeline, kneeling beside him,*
> *Kissed his dying lips, and laid his head on her bosom.*
> *Sweet was the light of his eyes; but it suddenly sank into darkness,*
> *As when a lamp is blown out by a gust of wind at a casement.*

When Fiona uttered the last phrase, a slight draft blew across the back of her neck, that small line of skin left precariously exposed between the top of her collar and the edge of her hairline. Fiona shivered and at the same time witnessed the candle's light beside her flicker and wave. When she looked up again, Mattie was gone.

"I'll keep her, but it'll cost you plenty."

Mrs. Watkins held Mattie's child up by the arms, inspecting her as if she carried the plague about her. Fiona didn't know which to fear more, the fact that she had spent every last penny on Mattie's funeral, the rent was due and there was little food about, or the panicked look on the young baby's face the moment Fiona handed her to the old woman. Since she had been born, Mattie's child had never allowed anyone except Mattie and Fiona to hold her. A minute hadn't passed before the baby girl broke into sobs and reached her arms out to Fiona.

"I will be paid today," Fiona said, trying to brace her heart against the entreating blue eyes of the baby who now belonged to her. She couldn't tolerate leaving the poor child with such a monstrous woman, yet how was she to work and keep from being evicted from their home?

"I want the money tonight, in advance for the week," Mrs. Watkins said. "Or there is no deal."

"I will pay you tonight," Fiona replied, quickly kissing the baby and hurrying down the stairs. But not before the baby's shrieks echoed through her head and ever so painfully pierced her soul.

Fiona's employer, Mr. Walter Peterson, lived in the Garden District of New Orleans, the wealthy American section of town that was a good distance from the roach- and rat-infested tenements of the Irish Channel where Fiona lived. His house took up an entire city block and contained all the latest furnishings.

Fiona felt fortunate to be hired by such an illustrious man. The pay was no better than other Irish immigrant girls were receiving, but she hoped to advance to a position that paid more. Vividly remembering the anguished cries of her adopted baby daughter, Fiona knew today was as good as any to ask for an increase in salary and position.

She cautiously made her way to the front study, an enormous room dedicated solely to the pleasures of the house's male occupants. Fiona knocked softly, her courage suddenly leaving her. To her great surprise, Mr. Peterson threw open the door. "What is it you want?" he demanded.

Fiona stammered, her heart thumping loudly in her chest. "I wish to speak with you, sir."

Mr. Peterson moved his gaze slowly down the length of Fiona's dress, pausing in places a woman in a different situation would slap him for. She instantly wished she could retract her request.

"Come in," Mr. Peterson said, closing the door behind them and turning the key. "What is it you wish to speak to me about?"

Fiona rotated back toward the door and found her employer too close for comfort. She stumbled backward to allow space between them until she felt the pointed end of the side table, the one, she had noticed earlier, with the doilies of Irish lace. "I wish to make more money," she blurted out before she had time to think.

"Do you now?" Mr. Peterson answered seriously, slowly moving his hand down her arm.

"My companion has died and I must raise her child," Fiona continued, moving slightly to avoid his touch. "You have not replaced Sylvie as your upstairs maid. Perhaps you would consider me."

Again, Mr. Peterson evaluated her physique, as if her body contained clues as to whether she would qualify for the job.

"You will have to perform more duties than before," Mr. Peterson finally said.

"Of course, sir." Fiona swallowed hard to keep her emotions stable. "I will do anything you ask."

At this, Mr. Peterson smiled, the kind of grin her landlord offered every time the rent was late. Fiona recognized the game right away. She instantly knew what duties Mr. Peterson was implying. The same ones her landlord had suggested, before he thrust a hand down her blouse.

Fiona gazed over her employer's shoulder and knew she could not bolt past him to the door without being caught.

Feeling like a rabbit trapped in a hunter's grip, she tried talking her way out. "You don't understand," Fiona said, smiling. "I will be glad to do the duties of a *maid*."

"Then, let me show you what those duties are." Mr. Peterson firmly placed two hands about her waist and pulled her so close she could smell the whiskey on his breath. Before she could react, he forced his mouth on hers and pressed his tongue aggressively between her lips. Fiona groaned in defiance and fought his encroaching hands which were moving up the front of her bodice. Finally, she managed to pull her mouth from his and push far enough away from his embrace to be heard. "I'm not that kind of girl, sir. You have mistaken me."

Mr. Peterson roughly drew her back against his chest and began kissing her neck. "Relax," he replied tartly, when Fiona wouldn't stop resisting. "This is what you asked for."

"No," Fiona implored, still pushing and fighting with all her strength. "Please, stop."

Having to work too hard for his pleasure, Mr. Peterson drew back and thrust Fiona back against the table. "Don't play that game with me, *lassie*. I know exactly what you Irish girls want."

"Please, sir," Fiona said, hoping to let reason win her argument. "I only wanted the extra position. I need the money."

"I'll give you more money," he answered, leaning in close again, backing Fiona tightly against the table's edge which pinched the back of her legs. "And you'll give me what I want."

Mr. Peterson grabbed her breasts roughly while his mouth descended again. Fiona didn't have time to fight. She remembered Father Ryan's instructions when he placed her on the ship that cold November morning, the list of survival tips he had parlayed that she had thought inconsequential at the time. Now the message was all too clear.

Fiona thrust her knee upward and gave her employer a stiff jab to the groin. His hold on her breasts immediately lessened, and he backed away with a startled look. Then his eyes glazed, rolled back in his head, and with a cry he doubled over and fell to the floor.

Fiona raced to the door, but in her panic couldn't get the bloody thing unlocked. While she struggled with the key, she heard her employer threaten her from behind.

"You're fired," he tried to yell at her, but the threat came out mostly as a hoarse whisper. "You'll never work anywhere in this town."

It was then that Fiona spotted the wallet. Mr. Peterson must have removed it from his waistcoat when he retired to the study for his afternoon drink and newspaper. Without thinking, she seized it, rotated the key in the lock, and threw open the door. She raced down the hallway, stopping only to grab her threadbare coat before exiting the Peterson household, a long parade of startled employees staring after her.

There was more than enough money in the wallet to cover the rent, pay Mrs. Watkins, and survive for a few weeks without a job. But as soon as Fiona retrieved the baby from the upstart, she knew it was only a matter of time before the police would arrive. Fiona gathered up her meager belongings, wrapped the baby tightly in a series of woolen blankets, and left the tenement through the back stairway to avoid meeting the landlord.

She rounded the corner and immediately caught sight of a policeman standing on the building's stoop asking the tenement's owner of her whereabouts. While she hid in the late afternoon shadow of the building, she listened as the landlord all too happily supplied information, since he hadn't been paid in two weeks. Fiona waited until the two men entered the building, then hurried down the street, not caring which direction she took, for she hadn't the slightest idea where to go.

She wandered the dirty city streets of the Channel for hours until the cold afternoon turned into frigid night. While drunk patrons staggered out into the street from bawdy taverns and pubs and tired workers made their way home from the river's docks, Fiona kept walking, her eyes downcast so as not to attract attention. When darkness settled, the night turned so biting cold that the humid air seemed to permeate the marrow of her bones.

Fiona's fears intensified. How would she survive in such a city without a job? How would she take care of an infant, when the winter had been labeled the coldest to date?

She felt her resolve falter, her hope diminish. Father Ryan had called her "The Survivor," the only one in her family who had lived through the potato famine and the rage of typhus that had consumed her brothers and sisters. She had watched Mattie's husband wither away from two years of malnutrition, followed by the dearest friend she had ever known. Yet, here she remained. And now she was to mother a child who continually gazed up at her with eyes the color of the sea at Kerry, as if Fiona held the secrets to the universe.

Her feet aching from walking the streets, and the frigid air getting the best of her weary lungs, Fiona sought refuge in the only place she knew, St. Alphonsus Church, the church of the Irish. Since New Orleans was a major port town, people of many nationalities had poured into the city since its inception. Although these separate groups of people hardly socialized together, in the one block where Fiona now stood there were three Catholic churches— one each for the Germans, the French and the Irish.

The inside of St. Alphonsus was hardly an improvement to the streets; the cold drafts of air invaded every corner of its bright interior. Yet, Fiona made the sign of the cross and maneuvered down the aisle to the altar of Mary, hugging the baby to her breast as she knelt down and prayed.

"Mary, Mother of God," she pleaded to the benevolent statue before her, the altar where miracles supposedly occurred, particularly in the case of children. "Help show me the way to go."

The wind howled around the stained glass windows portraying the mysteries of the Rosary, beating at their lead mortar as if to demand entrance. The prayer candles flickered with the cold drafts, and shadows played across Mary's serene marble face silhouetted by a golden crown. Above her, the archangels Michael and Gabriel stood guard.

"Please, Mary," Fiona implored, "give me a sign. Tell me what to do. I am lost and I can't find an answer."

The silence that followed literally made Fiona's heart ache. Was this how it ended, surviving the Great Hunger to die like so many of her country's people on the shores of their new home? Would she be forced to surrender to the police in order that her child be given something to eat? If she was caught, would she ever see her baby again?

"Pardon me," an accented voice sounded from her immediate right. Fiona turned and found a small man tightly bundled in a thick coat, a woolen cap covering most of his face. "I wish not to disturb you, madame, but I am looking for the parish priest."

Fiona couldn't place the accent, but it sounded similar to the French who walked the streets of New Orleans. "I haven't seen anyone here tonight," Fiona said, hoping she hadn't given the man ammunition to molest her. "The priest, I mean," she quickly added, slipping a hand inside her bag to find the knife hidden within.

The man at first appeared visibly irritated that he might

have to wait, then shrugged, as if resigned to the matter. "I'm supposed to deliver a letter to the parish priest," he said with a sigh. "Aristide Dugas passed away in Bayou Paradis, near Loreauville. He had no family there, but word has it he may have distant kin in New Orleans who will inherit his property. I am to deliver this letter to the priest of the French church."

Fiona knew that the man searched for Notre Dame, the French church the next street over, but something stilled her tongue.

"I am in need of assistance," the man continued. "I promised to deliver the message when I arrived into town, but we were delayed because of ice on the river. My family will be worried if I do not return soon to home, and I must catch the next boat upriver. Is there someone here I can . . . ?"

"I shall give it to the priest for you." Fiona couldn't believe she uttered the words, until the wind sent another draft through the building. With the resulting shadows cast by the prayer candles, Mary almost looked as if she were smiling.

Was it a sign from God or was she making the biggest mistake of her life? Fiona wondered. Still, she accepted the grateful man's letter and headed for the riverside. She knew where she would sleep that night. On a steamboat heading west to a town called Loreauville.

Chapter Two

"Every man has a paradise around him."
    —*Henry Wadsworth Longfellow*

"I don't understand," Emile Dugas said, staring down at the freshly made broom in his hands. "Why are you giving me a broom?"

Emile understood the broom's meaning all too well. Remote Acadians, like himself, who didn't have the luxury of a nearby priest to perform a marriage ceremony, would *saut le balai*, or jump the broomstick. But if his *marraine*, his godmother, would be as clever as to make him a broom to entice him to marry, then he would make her work for its explanation.

"You know well what that broom is for," exclaimed Claudine Marie Breaux, known affectionately to everyone in Bayou Paradis as "Nana."

"You don't approve of my housekeeping?" Emile countered with a sly grin.

"I don't approve of who you keep house with." And with a swift movement of her tiny hands the petite woman pushed Emile, a full-grown man whose chin easily rested on the top of Nana's head, into a nearby kitchen chair. Before he could ask who this mysterious person was that he was living with, Nana had poured him a cup of dark, drip-roasted coffee, dropped a teaspoon of sugar into the black aromatic liquid, and settled into her own chair. Quietly she poured her own cup and began to drink as if nothing had passed between them.

Emile sighed. "All right, Nana. Who am I keeping house with?"

Nana eagerly placed her cup down. "No one. That is the problem."

Feeling like the bayou animals caught in the tight jaws of his metal traps, Emile could only brace himself for another lecture on the joys of married life.

"You're too old to be a bachelor."

"I'm twenty-four."

"You need someone to cook and clean for you."

"I cook and clean fine."

"It's not healthy for a man to sleep alone."

Emile placed his cup in its saucer and smiled. "You got me on that one."

"Emile," Nana said, placing a maternal hand on his arm. "I worry about you running around in that half log you call a boat, making a living with your head in the trees. If you had a wife, *I* could sleep better at night. What if something happens to you like it did to your father?"

Emile's smile faded as the painful subject was broached yet again. He didn't want to discuss it, not now, not ever. Why couldn't anyone in his family understand that? "I don't want to talk about that," he answered much too harshly.

Nana removed her hand from his arm, but she refused to let the matter die. "It's not good for you to keep this inside you, Emile," she said, her hurt feelings apparent. "We should talk about it."

Emile leaned across the table and lovingly caressed the small, withered face he had known since birth, the woman who had patiently taught him to read, to write and to learn the ways of the church. Besides his mother, he had never loved a woman more. "Please," Emile pleaded, "can we speak of something else?"

Nana's large brown eyes, once dimmed with anxiety and the overabundance of caring that women carried about them, suddenly brightened. "Then let us talk of marriage."

Emile knew he was cornered. He would not emerge from Nana's house without a commitment to court some woman of Nana's choosing at Saturday's *fais do do,* Bayou Paradis's weekly dance. He decided to be honest. "There is no one who interests me," he said. "They are all wonderful women, all destined to make wonderful wives, but . . ."

"Seraphine Comeaux?"

"She talks too much."

"Josephine LeBlanc?"

"She has her eye on Hypolite Aucoin. Besides, her only interest in life is standing behind a stove."

"She does make a good gumbo," Nana added while one eyebrow lifted suggestively skyward. "With Aristide gone, who are you going to cook for anyhow, *hein?*"

"Despite the myth, the way to my heart is not necessarily through my stomach." Emile grinned as he added, "Besides, I make a better gumbo."

"Scholastique Barbier?" Nana asked, ignoring his last remark. "She will inherit a nice piece of land."

Emile's smile disappeared when he realized the conversation would not end. "She will want to live on that land," he countered. "I'm no farmer, Nana. I've got my home on the bayou now, and I plan to stay there."

Nana threw her hands up to heaven. "What is the way to your heart, *mon ami?* Must this woman be an angel?"

Sensing Nana's acquiescence to defeat, Emile made his move. He grabbed his new broom and headed for the door, placing a sweet kiss on Nana's furrowed brow on the way. "I want a simple life, Nana," he whispered to the top of her gray head. "Just like my father's."

Nana grabbed his wrist as if a sudden thought had come to her. "Maybe she will come to you."

Emile didn't know if it was the constant grilling, the incessant worrying or the silly broom he held in his hands, but he began to laugh at the gentle, eager face beaming up at him. "If she does," he said with a smile, "I have my broom ready."

Before Emile could make it to the door, Nana had the last word. "Maybe someone will answer the letter," she said.

Emile paused with one hand on the door knob. "Nonsense," he said. "Aristide told me himself he had no relatives. I only sent that letter to appease Widow Pitre, who's always confusing our family with the Boudreaux's. Pierre Boudreaux is the one with New Orleans family."

Nana stared out at the bayou, its normally placid waters reacting to a bitter wind blowing hard from the north. "Perhaps," she said softly. "But we can hope."

Emile grunted. Marriage was one discussion, his land quite another. "Hope all you want, dear Nana," he said as he placed his hat firmly on his head. "That land is mine now."

The land of opportunity, Mattie had called America. The land of a million languages was more like it, Fiona thought as she stared at the confused faces around her. She had stopped at a place called Franklin, a booming American town on the sleepy Bayou Teche, where she heard all sorts of accents. When she asked for Loreauville and Bayou Paradis, an American had pointed the way, calling it a "Cajun" village, whatever that was. Another nationality and another language, no doubt.

Fiona rubbed her eyes in a vain attempt to ward off the weariness she had accumulated during her week-long boat travel from New Orleans. Trusting no one, she had rarely slept, keeping one eye on her bag, the other on Mattie's precious child. Now, with a dozen curious eyes pointed in her direction in the only store—possibly the only building—of Bayou Paradis, she wanted nothing more than to find a place to sleep.

She held up the letter one more time, which brought another round of remarks, all in what she figured was French, but slightly different from the French she heard in New Orleans. This language was slower, less formal perhaps. If she thought hard enough, she could decipher a few words, but fatigue was getting the upper hand.

The older man behind the store counter kept insisting on something to do with the stockroom. The short, balding man to his right repeatedly pointed to the baby, and Fiona could have sworn he mentioned milk. Another man, mumbling away in his native language, grabbed Fiona's elbow and tried to move her in his direction before she promptly put an end to his intentions. In another moment, she feared she would lose all control or collapse on the spot.

The chorus of indecipherable voices halted when a gust of frigid air poured in from the direction of the bayou. While a chill slivered up her spine, Fiona heard a door close and saw a man throw a batch of skinned animal hides onto the counter. She couldn't make out his face, for the other men were busy crowding him and most likely updating him on the arrival of Aristide Dugas's non-French-speaking relative.

When the men finished explaining their story, the room became eerily silent. This man—they had called him Emile—was of some importance, she suspected. She prayed he spoke English.

Too curious to stand still, Fiona inched her way forward.

At the same time, several men moved aside. When a path was cleared and the man finally came into Fiona's view, he glanced up, his enormous brown eyes meeting hers.

In that second, Fiona felt exposed, that her deceptive identity had been discovered. The man gazed at her with a look that wavered between accusation and astonishment. Worse, he stood there speechless, as if the sight of Aristide's long-lost relative was cause for alarm instead of joy.

But you're not a relative, she reminded herself. She swallowed hard and commanded herself to breathe. If she had eaten that morning, she was sure she would have been sick.

"I wish to go to Aristide Dugas's place," Fiona said, barely above a whisper. "Do you speak English?"

The man finally moved, his long legs slowly erasing the distance between them. The questioning look never faltered, however. When he reached her, he towered over her menacingly.

"I have a letter," Fiona said. She held the open envelope and papers up to his chest, but the man ignored the correspondence and continued staring, as if searching for the truth, as if reaching into her soul to retrieve what remnants remained of Fiona Riley, an Irish resident of County Kerry. *God help me if he finds it,* Fiona thought.

"What is your name?" the man finally asked.

Fiona had never once considered a name, and a sudden panic seized her. Glancing madly about the room, she searched for a clue, wondering what kind of names French people in the swamps of southwestern Louisiana would fancy. Her mind a blank from fatigue and hunger, she could only resume staring back at the man, at a loss for words.

Suddenly, the baby laughed, forcing them both to break eye contact. The man looked down at the child, surprised, as if it was the first time he had noticed the baby in her arms. To Fiona's amazement, the child laughed again, then held out her arms to him. The man picked the baby up and brought her to his chest where she quickly made use of the drawstring at his shirt's collar.

"She doesn't take to strangers," Fiona said, immediately realizing the absurdity of the remark. Clearly, the baby was enjoying herself.

"Eraste says you can stay in his stockroom until the weather clears," the man replied, his eyes glued to the baby's affectionate smile and curly red hair, a slight grin appearing at his lips' edge.

"I must go to the house now," Fiona said, relieved to know that someone could understand and speak English. "I don't wish to wait until the weather clears."

The man looked back toward her, and the now familiar harsh look returned. "There is a winter storm coming in from the north. The roads are washed out and the only way is by boat down the bayou."

"Can someone take me there?" Fiona asked.

"You don't understand," the man said, a little louder, as if her hearing had something to do with her lack of understanding French. "There is a storm coming."

"I'll pay," Fiona insisted. "If it's a matter of money . . . "

The man began to shake his head, until the baby grasped his cheeks and pulled him close. When the child rubbed her forehead against his, Fiona saw his countenance change. "It has nothing to do with money," he said more gently. "The storm was on my heels as I was coming in."

"Please," Fiona said, glancing at the dozens of strange eyes still staring at her. She had to find her home; she had to be safe from the constant eyes and advances of men.

The man sighed, and Fiona could only hope that was good news. But he handed the precious bundle back to her, and her hope faded.

"You and the baby and one bag," he said. "Anything else you are carrying must stay here."

Fiona's heart leaped. "I only have one bag."

The man frowned at the sight of her travel-worn carpetbag, but he tightened his coat at the neck and returned his wet felt hat to his head. "Follow me," were the last words he uttered before leaving the building.

What was he thinking? Emile wondered as he plied his paddle down the bayou, praying he would outrun the oncoming storm. Clearly this woman wasn't a Dugas. With that accent and those freckles, she was hardly an Acadian. Something in her lilting intonation rang a bell. Irish perhaps? The child, sporting red hair more natural to a horse, was as far removed from his dark-haired relatives as Canada was from Louisiana.

Most definitely an impostor. Which was why he should have insisted she make her claim before the sheriff. Still, the way that baby had held his cheeks, smiled so lovingly at him, looked at him as if he were a beacon of hope, he couldn't bear to throw the skinny woman and her child into Eraste's stockroom on the coldest night of the year.

"What's the baby's name?" Emile asked.

The woman frowned and resumed her usual guilty look. Was this another secret? Emile wondered. A baby out of wedlock? Clearly the two had nothing physically in common. The baby, at least, had some substance to her cheeks.

"She's not my baby," the woman replied. "My best friend died ten days ago, and I promised her I would raise her."

Surprisingly, it was the first thing the impostor had uttered that fateful afternoon that appeared sincere. "Then, what is your best friend's baby's name?"

"She doesn't have a name," the woman said quietly,

tightening the blankets around the child nervously. "Mattie was ill since she gave birth; we didn't have time to christen the baby. Mattie used to call her her angel."

Emile stole another look at the angel's face, a soft, round glow of rosy cheeks and incredibly sharp aquamarine eyes. The scarlet hair curled endlessly about her forehead, and she giggled when she realized she had captured his attention once again. Emile dipped his thumb into the bayou and lightly brushed the pink skin above her nose. "Angelle Dugas," he baptized her and grinned down at the child who was now laughing with delight.

"And your name?" she asked.

For a moment Emile had forgotten the skinny Irish woman sitting in the bow of his pirogue, the woman about to steal the only thing he held dear in life besides his family, the land bequeathed to him by his old friend and business partner, Aristide Dugas. A man who had assured him he had no living kin besides Emile, a very distant relative. Waiting for an answer, the woman who looked as if she had not met with a good meal in months stared at him with a mixture of boldness and anxiety.

"Emile Dugas," Emile finally said, watching her expression change into one of doubt and fear.

"Were you related to . . . ?" she asked sheepishly.

"Oui," Emile said, not wanting to disclose that he and Aristide were *very* distantly related, connected by relations before the English exiled the Acadians from Nova Scotia one hundred years ago. Still, Emile had helped Aristide work his land, improve the house and construct a new well. That property was his and his alone.

"What is your name," Emile asked, watching her countenance change as he added, "cousin?"

Fiona swallowed and uttered the first thing that came to her. "Isabelle," she said. *Where had that name come from?* Fiona wondered, hoping against hope that Aristide's distant relative wasn't called something else that people remembered. Isabelle was a French name, wasn't it? It sounded as such. "Isabelle Dugas," she repeated with more authority.

Emile appeared to accept it, but his puzzled, accusing stare never faltered. She was making a grave error posing as this "cousin," Fiona knew, but she couldn't back out now. She could see, through the cypress trees, the storm's low-lying dark clouds threatening to explode at any minute. Large raindrops began to pelt them, and a cold, biting wind caused massive wrinkles in the bayou.

Fiona tightened her meager jacket at her neck and pulled the hem of her skirt down further over the baby's head. Angelle, as the man had named her, giggled freely as if the sun were shining.

"Is it always so cold down here?" Fiona asked.

"No," Emile answered, paddling harder in a race against the rain. "This is the coldest I've seen it in years."

Since he appeared more agreeable, Fiona delved further. "What language was everyone speaking at the store?"

"Pardon?" Emile asked, and Fiona had her answer. It was French, after all, and this "cousin" was being smart. Her instincts demanded she stay quiet so as not to disclose more of her ignorance, but there were so many questions.

"An American in St. Martinville called Bayou Paradis a 'Cajun' town. What did he mean by that?"

For a moment, Fiona swore the man smiled. "Americans can't pronounce *'Cadien.* Cajun is their word for us."

"I don't understand," Fiona replied.

" *'Cadien,"* Emile repeated. "It's short for *Les Acadians."* When Fiona still didn't make the connection, Emile leaned forward and pronounced the word in his best English pronunciation. "A-ca-dee-an," he said slowly and succinctly.

The realization hit Fiona with the force of the brutal wind bearing down on them from the north. *Mother Mary and Joseph,* she thought with astonishment, *I'm in a boat with Gabriel!* As much as she later regretted uttering the words, Fiona couldn't help herself. "You'd be an Acadian?" she asked incredulously.

Emile never answered, just continued to stare that penetrating look that made Fiona shiver. When it began to rain harder, he paddled furiously until he landed abruptly on the left bank.

"Get out," he commanded, reaching for the baby. Fiona looked around and found nothing along the bayou. She began to fear that this man, this apparent cousin, was out to do them both harm.

"Allez," he shouted as the wind increased its descent on the trio. "I'll hand you the baby."

She could always run, Fiona thought, glancing around at the endless forest of cypress and tupelo trees. She stepped out of the pirogue, landing on the muddy shore. *Please God,* she found herself praying, *let there be a house above this bank.*

Emile deftly handed her the baby, exited the boat, then pulled it up and over the small incline. Before she could intervene, he quickly grabbed her bag, his supplies, and a homemade broom, then placed a firm but gentle hand on her elbow and practically dragged her up the bank and through an opening in the trees. When she finally looked up and attempted a protest, Fiona saw the house.

The small wooden cottage offered a couple of windows, a large back porch with steps leading down to the yard, and possibly an attic, for the roof pointed skyward to where a brick chimney kissed the menacing clouds. As Fiona came closer, she made out some sort of stairway leading up to the roof from the back porch, and alongside the house an honest-to-goodness cistern sitting ready for action.

Besides the seashore at Kenmare, it was the most beautiful sight she had ever seen.

"Dépeche-toi!" she heard Emile yell as he literally pulled her up the back stairs and onto the porch. Just as her foot reached the dryness of the porch's broad cypress planks, the storm unleashed its furor, and the wind howled around the sides of the house, blowing rain into their faces even though they were feet away from the edge of the roof.

Emile unlatched the door and pushed Fiona inside, but the cold humid air permeated every inch of the meager one-room cottage. Emile shut the door and immediately went to work on building a fire at the enormous fireplace to the left of the house. With the storm upon them and dusk approaching, the dank, shadowy house would soon be in total darkness. There was little time to spare.

Angelle had been agreeable throughout the trip down the bayou, but Fiona could tell she was becoming both tired and hungry. She fidgeted in Fiona's arms and moaned as she threw her head from side to side. A blood-piercing cry was imminent.

Fiona sat down at what appeared to be the kitchen table and reached into her bag for the last of the apple slices and the bottle of milk she had paid dearly for from a farmhouse on the way to Loreauville. With the storm bearing its weight down upon the house, pounding at the windows as if demanding she return to New Orleans, Fiona wondered when she would be able to buy supplies again.

"Is that all the food you have?" Emile asked.

The fatigue Fiona had fought off all day returned, and she longed to collapse in the bed that lined the far wall to Emile's right. Once that starter fire he had made erupted into something of substance, she would curl under those sheets and forget about French-speaking bayou men, American employers and landlords with greedy fingers and seductive smiles, and whether or not she pronounced

"Acadian" correctly. For a moment, before she drifted off to sleep, she would forget that everyone she had ever loved had died and left her alone with a baby without a name.

"Isabelle," she heard a voice say, but for the life of her Fiona couldn't remember where she was and who was speaking. She felt her head drop and a wave of fatigue envelope her.

"Isabelle." The voice was louder now.

Suddenly, hands at her shoulders were shaking her, waking her from the delightful sleep that had briefly overpowered her. "What?" she asked, looking up at the strange brown eyes of a man silhouetted by a red fire's light. "Gabriel?" Fiona whispered.

"You need some sleep," the man answered, and Fiona instantly knew where she was and who was calling her. She brushed off his hands and sat up straight, tightening her hold on Angelle.

"I'm fine," Fiona answered tartly. "You can leave now."

Emile resumed his familiar stare. Was this a common trait of Acadians? Fiona thought with irritation. If he wanted an argument, why didn't he speak his mind?

"I'll feed the baby while you get some rest," Emile offered, but it was clear he was not pleased.

"I'm fine," Fiona reiterated. "How much do I owe you?"

Emile's anger finally surfaced, and a long string of French expletives emerged. Fiona would have recognized them anywhere. If there was one thing she had learned living in New Orleans, employed in the company of two obstinate French cooks, it was a wide vocabulary of colorful French words.

"Where do you expect me to go?" he finally asked in English.

"I don't care," Fiona insisted. "You can't stay here."

Emile closed his eyes as if to calm his anger. "Have you

not noticed the storm outside?" he finally asked. "Has the rain and cold escaped your attention?"

Fiona certainly could see the wind and rain beating at the windows. Did he mistake her for a fool? But she was a woman and he a man. He couldn't stay there. He wouldn't stay there. Not unless he killed her first.

She reached inside her bag and retrieved the one weapon she possessed, her meat knife salvaged from her tenement apartment. Fiona held it high in the fire's light so Emile would have no trouble making out its shape. To her surprise he laughed.

"What do you propose to eat, *cher?*" he asked. "Arrogance?"

Fiona had no idea what the man was implying, but he had to leave, and he had to leave now. "Get out," she stammered, the tears of intense fatigue pooling behind her eyes. "I want you gone, now."

Don't cry, she commanded herself. *Don't let him see you weak.* Yet, despite her valiant efforts, the tears poured down Fiona's cheeks, leaving trails of moisture in their paths.

Emile sighed, dropped his head to stare at the floor, and pulled his hair through his fingers. "I'm not going to hurt you," he said, and for a moment Fiona wanted to believe he meant it. Still, he was a man, and men were not to be trusted.

"How do I know that?" she asked, still fighting back the sobs.

Emile looked up then, his immense brown eyes appearing so plaintive and gentle Fiona almost dropped the knife. "I would never hurt a woman and child," he said quietly and with intense emotions. "I'm sorry you do not trust me."

Emile turned and opened the sack of supplies he had carried from the boat. He deposited a few items on the table, then retrieved a few more and put them inside his coat pocket. "There's food here if you're hungry, and I suspect you are. I'll check on you in the morning."

Before Emile made it to the door, Fiona had to settle the argument. "That's not necessary," she said, assembling as much authority as she could muster.

Emile gazed back at her solemnly as the wind howled through the thin cracks in the house walls and rattled the pane glass windows. "Oh, *oui, madame*, it is very necessary."

And with those final words, the Acadian was gone.

Chapter Three

"How can I tell the signals and the signs
By which one heart another heart divines?"
—Henry Wadsworth Longfellow

Through the floorboards Emile could hear the baby's incessant cries and Isabelle pacing the cabin. He wondered who was worse off, the overtired, half-starved impostor with her fussy baby or himself, freezing in the cabin's *garconnière* with only the sides of an attic fireplace to keep him warm.

The cabin followed a typical Acadian style, one large downstairs room for parents and their daughters and the *garconnière*—an attic for growing adolescent boys with access by a porch staircase. Emile loved moving up to the attic as a youth, gaining both freedom and room to stretch at the same glorious time. Now, the *garconniere's* sloping ceiling threatened to suffocate him, and the frigid temperature kept him at a constant shiver. He had lived there as a guest of Aristide, but now that the cabin was his, he had gotten used to sleeping in comfort by a roaring fireplace.

Aristide had no relatives; he told Emile so when he dictated the Will, signing over the property, livestock and cabin to Emile. The letter had been fruitless, a gesture. No one was supposed to answer.

Emile furiously turned onto his side, irritated that the movement caused another round of shivers. God, but it was cold. The wind whistled through every weak spot in the mud-and-Spanish-moss-plastered walls to provide a steady stream of drafts upon his head. She wasn't his kin, Emile reminded himself. Letter or no, the skinny woman claiming to be Isabelle Dugas was fresh off the boat and it sure as hell wasn't from Canada.

He should have left her at Eraste's stockroom to ride out the storm. Instead, he delivers her to the cabin in question and practically hands over the deed to his land. "You'd be an Acadian," she had said in that lilting accent of hers. The woman didn't even know the nationality of her own relative, the man who supposedly left all his worldly possessions to her. She couldn't possibly plan to get away with this scheme.

The words Nana had spoken that morning came rushing through his thoughts. "Maybe she will come to you."

Emile sighed with frustration, turned onto his back and stared at the ceiling, now covered with cobwebs from disuse. It was too much of a coincidence, as if the woman and child had fallen from the heavens in answer to Nana's prayers.

"What is the way to your heart, *mon ami?*" Nana had asked him only hours before. "Must this woman be an angel?"

She got that one wrong, Emile thought. He wondered if Nana had prayed for a child as well. Thinking back to when Isabelle had said the child was called angel sent a shudder up the entire length of his spine, but he had to smile. The charming baby was a joy to behold. Angelle was clearly the reason the impostor enjoyed the warm confines of his cabin and not the smelly, cold floor of Eraste's stockroom.

The baby sent up a fresh wail, and Emile thought to go

downstairs to offer his help; but remembering the look in the young woman's eyes when she brandished that knife at him, Emile knew it was best to stay put. She would never learn to trust him if he appeared out of the dark stormy night half-dressed, unshaven and shivering like a crazed man.

The baby fell silent, and Emile prayed they would all finally get some sleep. Tomorrow, he would determine the next course of action—for all of them.

The dream began as it always did. Fiona's father screams from the direction of the fields, waking everyone in the household as a retched smell infuses Fiona's senses. She rushes to his side as the sun rises over the nearest hill providing enough light for them to see that the potato blight has returned. Brown spots appear on some of the plants' leaves; others have turned completely black. Fiona's father yells for her to retrieve the few stalks that appear healthy, to collect those potatoes not touched by the disease. But Fiona knows it is too late. They have lost everything.

While Fiona's father falls to his knees in despair, Fiona notices Father Ryan's dark cloak at the back door of their cottage, and she knows why he has come.

"No!" she screams, but the words refuse to emerge from her lips.

Fiona begins to cry, running to the cottage door to witness one last look of her mother's face before the homespun blanket, lovingly created by her grandmama, is pulled up and over her lovely countenance. Fiona screams again while trying to reach her siblings lying helplessly in their own beds; but Fiona's legs won't move and she watches from a distance as their bodies, too, are taken away.

"Do something," she implores Father Ryan, but he only shakes his head and walks away.

The grief is so intense it knocks the breath from her, and Fiona begins to shake from the heartache. This time, the agonizing pain of her soul is heard.

The dream's overwhelming emotions jolted Fiona awake, and she sat up in bed with a start. But it was the large, masculine hand on her forehead that scared her the most.

"What are you doing here?" she asked as she grabbed the blanket and pulled it tightly against her chest. "Get out now."

"Are you feverish?" he asked, ignoring her command and standing too close to the bed. "You feel a little warm."

"I'm fine," she answered, brushing her hand against her cheeks that were, to her embarrassment, streaked with tears.

Emile nodded. "A bad dream, then."

Fiona refused to acknowledge the horrific dream that continually haunted her sleep. "What are you doing here?" she asked again, trying to regain some semblance of composure. "Why haven't you gone home?"

For the first time since they had met, Emile smiled at her, but Fiona found it anything but friendly. "This is my home, *chèri*."

He moved toward the kitchen, pulling an assemblage of pots and pans on to the rough kitchen table. Fiona reached for the knife wedged between the mattress and its wooden frame.

"It's on the mantel," Emile said.

"What is?"

"Your knife. I thought it best to keep it out of reach of Angelle."

Fiona looked up to see the ivory handle protruding from

the edge of the mantel. "It was safe with me. She doesn't crawl yet."

Emile laughed. "Then, how did she get over there."

Fiona gazed in the direction of his gesture and found the blue-eyed baby sitting in the far corner of the cabin, quietly gnawing on the leather laces of a man's boot.

"I would have taken it away from her, but she seems to be enjoying herself," Emile said, pouring water into an upright pot that was filled with a dark, grainy substance. "Has she cut any teeth yet?"

Teeth? The man wanted to discuss baby teeth while she sat in bed in a swamp cabin that he suddenly claimed as his own?

As if sensing her thoughts, Emile turned. "Why don't we eat and I'll explain."

"And how am I supposed to dress?"

Emile's gaze moved down to the collar of her blouse peeking out above the sheet. Fiona suddenly realized she had fallen asleep fully dressed after walking the floors with the baby all night. Feeling rather foolish, which only fueled her anger, she brushed the sheet aside and went to retrieve the baby. When she attempted to separate the child from her beloved boot, the baby let out a piercing cry.

"Why not let her play with it," Emile suggested. "They're my good boots, hardly used."

"She's hungry."

Emile turned his back to the fireplace and began dipping large slices of French-style bread into a milky mixture, then dropping it into a skillet lined with lard. To his left the upright pot made a noise that sounded like dripping. The aroma was tantalizing. "I've already fed her," he said.

"When?" Fiona's fears were intensifying. How long had this man been inside the cabin?

"This morning, about an hour ago. I didn't want to wake you since you had such a difficult night."

Fiona's mind whirled. How did he know what kind of night she had? Had he been spying on her all this time, watching her from some secret hiding place? "Where have *you* been all night?" Fiona asked, trying hard to keep the panic from her voice.

Emile appeared deep in thought, then raised his fork toward the roof. "I don't know the English word. We say *garconnière*. The room above." Again, he pointed to the ceiling.

"The attic?" Fiona asked, wondering how anyone could access the attic since there was no opening inside the cabin.

"Oui, the attic," Emile agreed. "You get there from the porch."

Fiona remembered the stairs on the back porch. Maybe that was what he meant by the cabin being his home. Aristide had lent this man use of his attic. "You sleep in Aristide's attic?"

"No," Emile answered with a slight sarcastic tone. "I live here, inside this warm, comfortable cabin. I sleep in the cold *garconnière* when long-lost cousins arrive claiming to own my property."

Fiona felt the hairs on the back of her neck rise. "I have proof."

"So do I." With that final remark, Emile placed a plate full of fried bread, sprinkled with sugar and cane syrup, in front of her. He then proceeded to pour a cup of black liquid from the upright pot.

"What is this?" Fiona asked.

"Pain perdu," he said as he placed a side plate of figs before her. "It means lost bread. We use everything on the bayou. When the bread becomes stale, we fry it for breakfast." When she hesitated, he pushed the plate closer. "Eat," Emile said. *"Ça c'est bon."*

Fiona sat down, cut a slice and soaked up the heavy syrup before taking a bite. The soft doughy bread smothered in sugary delights was a rich taste sensation she had never experienced before. She couldn't remember when she had enjoyed eating something so delicious.

Emile placed a cup of the hot liquid before her. "Coffee," he said.

Fiona had seen and smelled coffee before; the cooks at the Peterson household drank it like water, with plenty of cream and sugar. "Do you have any tea?" she asked Emile.

Emile stared at her hard, the way he had the day before when almost every comment Fiona uttered caused him to bore his eyes into hers. They were enormous eyes as well, the pupils a dark, solid color like massive drops of ink on a page, only brown. As accusing as those eyes appeared to be, Fiona couldn't help feeling safe within their gaze. The soft yet stern countenance of his handsome face told her that Emile was not a man to take advantage of a young woman and child in the middle of the Louisiana swamps. Still, Fiona refused to trust her instincts.

"All Acadians drink coffee," he finally said, more as a point of information than a retort, as if passing on a secret to someone who wouldn't know better. Someone like herself.

"May I have some cream and sugar then?" she asked.

Emile produced a sugar bowl and a small cup of milk. *He must know,* she thought. *He has to know.* Perhaps that was why he thought he could take the property away from her.

"Aristide Dugas was a friend of mine," he finally said, placing several more pieces of the bread into the skillet. "He left me this cabin, a barn, some livestock and the property in his Will when he died." He pulled a large piece of parchment from a side desk next to the fireplace, then placed the paper on the table and returned to his work at the fireside. "This property belongs to me now."

Fiona forked up one last bite of the toast, managing to

scoop every last drop of syrup on the plate, then pushed the plate aside to get to the parchment. The contents were in French, but it was clear it was a legal statement of some sort.

"I can't read this," she said to Emile. "I have no way of knowing what this says. But I have a letter."

"I know," Emile said.

"You don't understand," she continued. "There was a letter sent to—"

"I know," he repeated. "I wrote it."

Emile placed several slices of bread on her plate before Fiona could refuse. Secretly she was glad to have more of the sticky, delicious breakfast—even the coffee was tasty— but the discussion was causing her stomach to tighten into knots. "What do you mean, you wrote it?" she asked nervously.

"Aristide had no relatives," Emile said, sitting across from her with his own full plate. "That was why he left the land to me. I sent a letter to New Orleans because an elderly woman in town who's a little . . ." Emile touched the tip of his index finger to his forehead. "What is the word?"

"Senile?" Fiona offered.

"Yes, senile," Emile said. "She had Aristide confused with another family. But to appease her and the sheriff, I sent the letter."

Fiona jumped up from her chair and grabbed her bag from beside the bed. She pulled the letter—actually letters since there was one in English and one in French—from its envelope and quickly gazed down at the bottom signature. When she spied "Emile Dugas" at the letter's end, her heart fell to the floor. "But Mary sent me," she whispered.

"Who's Mary?" Emile asked.

In that one instant, Fiona absorbed every aspect of that meager cabin, its large blackened fireplace with the rudely carved mantel, the lumpy stuffed mattress that had felt like heaven itself when she had lain down last evening, the sky blue cotton curtains gracing the front windows and the homemade broom by the fireside that reminded Fiona of home. Everything she had ever wanted. The green spot of earth where she could be safe from the Walter Petersons of the world and be a proper mother to Mattie's child. A place she could finally call home.

"Why should I believe you?" she said. "For all I know your French paper could be a shopping list."

Emile took a deep sip of his coffee and sighed. "You're right. We will go into town when the weather clears, into Loreauville, and ask the sheriff to determine who gets the land."

Fiona huffed. "French sheriff, no doubt."

Emile sliced a huge chunk of the bread with the back of his fork, then pierced it, but he left the tempting bite in midair. "Why should that matter, cousin, since we're both Acadians?"

The dark recesses of those eyes stared again as he slipped the oversized bread into his mouth. He knew she was lying; why didn't he say so? Perhaps he was hoping to corner her into a compromising position.

"I won't lie with you, if that's what you be thinking," Fiona said with all the strength she could muster.

Emile looked as if he would choke. He grabbed his coffee, threw back most of the contents of the cup and swallowed hard. "What has happened to you," he finally said, "to make you so distrustful?"

"What do you expect?" she retorted. "I'm a young, single woman with a child in the middle of the Louisiana backwoods. I'm the target for any man hoping to take advantage, including, it seems, you."

Emile stared at her solemnly. "I don't know what you're accustomed to in New Orleans, *cher,*" he began softly. "I suspect that may be true in the city. But in Bayou Paradis, we do not take advantage of women and children."

For a moment, Fiona almost believed him, but her guard was too hard a wall to tear down easily. "I know what you're thinking," she said, looking over at Angelle, who was now crawling along the far wall in search of a new toy. "You think I made an error in judgment with a man, that I had a child and my family threw me out. That I came here out of desperation. Well, it's not true."

"Which part?" Emile asked.

Fiona thrust her chin up defiantly. "Angelle is not my child."

"All right," Emile said evenly.

"You believe me?"

Emile placed the last bite into his mouth and followed it with the remnants of his coffee. "I believe you for two reasons," he said, rising to put his plate on the side board. "One, the child looks nothing like you. Second, I can't imagine you trusting a man long enough to have a child."

She felt insulted, but at least he didn't assume she was an unmarried woman running from scandal. She had resorted to lying and stealing, but she hadn't stooped so low as to lie with a man out of wedlock.

Oh, God, she thought when she realized the hypocrisy of it all, *what have I done?*

She must have appeared ready to faint, for Emile grabbed her firmly by an elbow and led her back to her chair. "You're much too thin, Isabelle," she heard him say as she choked back tears. "You must eat."

"Why?" she asked in a fog, recalling the famine before she could consciously send the painful memory away. "It'd be one less tenant in the world."

"What?" Emile asked, now squatting beside her to get a better look at her condition.

"Something my English landlord said. Doesn't matter."

Emile leaned over her then, cutting her food into small squares as if she were a child. "Maybe we're related after all," he said solemnly. "I do believe an Englishman said the same thing to my great grandfather."

When Emile finished slicing her food, he placed the fork into Fiona's hand and picked up her coffee cup. "I'll get you some fresh coffee," he said gently.

Fiona wanted to whisper her thanks, but fatigue or guilt or a combination of both got the best of her. She heard Angelle crying to her right and immediately moved to pick up the child, but Emile's hand pushed her back into the chair.

"I'll tend to the baby," he commanded. "You either eat or get some rest."

"And then what?" she whispered.

Emile retrieved the baby, who giggled with delight at being the subject of his attention. He sat down and placed Angelle in his lap, speaking to Fiona but smiling at the bubbling child. "You have nothing to worry about," he told her. "We will let the sheriff decide. If you must find another home, my *marraine* will help you. Uh, *marraine* means ..."

"Godmother," Fiona finished for him. "I speak a little French. I lived in the Irish sector of New Orleans, which is why I sound the way I do, but I know a little of the French language."

Emile said nothing, and Fiona prayed he accepted the explanation she had rehearsed repeatedly since her departure from New Orleans. Her heart told her he believed nothing. Even for a man speaking another language he must have recognized her for what she was, an immigrant fresh off the docks.

"Eat," he commanded without looking her way. "Worry about this later."

He placed Angelle on the edge of his knees and began

imitating a frolicking donkey. Angelle burst into laughter as the donkey moved from a slow gait to a romping gallop.

He had a nice face, Fiona decided, lightly tanned like wild honey. His cheekbones rose high framing a regal nose, and his chestnut hair hung loosely to his collar, blown wild most likely by the cold wind howling around the cabin. He possessed strong forearms; she had noticed that when he expertly plied the boat down the bayou the day before. Definitely a solid man, one who worked off the land. And tall, with hands so large they had covered her cheek that morning when he tested her for a fever.

Her mother would have said Emile contained the three sparks that ignite love: a gentle face, a good demeanor and proper speech. For all his disheartening words, Emile's romantic accent was as enticing as his cooking.

"There is something else," Emile said, breaking her from her thoughts. "The pirogue was washed away last night by the storm. The roads have been washed out from all the rain we've had over the past few weeks, so the only way to town is by the bayou. Until I find my boat, we cannot leave the cabin."

The fear that had previously sent her neck hairs to attention returned. "What do you mean?"

Emile looked at her startled expression, and sighed. "I mean to cook Angelle here into a gumbo and use you as my personal slave." When Fiona didn't answer, he mumbled a few obscenities in French. "It's a joke, no?"

"It's not funny."

"Neither is you believing me to be some monster out to harm you."

Fiona threw her fork down, reached over and grabbed Angelle, who promptly voiced her disapproval, and moved to the opposite side of the cabin. Fiona turned and faced Emile defiantly with what little strength remained. "What do you expect me to do?" she asked, her voice trembling.

"Why should I believe you to be any better than the men I have met so far?"

Emile silently rose, pulled his coat from the back of his chair and put it on. "There's plenty to eat in the cupboard," he said softly. "You're welcome to anything. I milked the cow this morning, so there's fresh milk for the baby. In the bureau over there is a collection of Aristide's clothing and blankets. Please use the material as you wish."

Emile grabbed his hat from the post on the wall and headed for the door. This was what she wanted, Fiona thought, to finally be rid of the imposing man. But something inside her wanted him to stay.

"Where are you going?" she asked meekly.

He turned then, staring at her with those walnut-sized eyes that seemed to speak to her soul. "I'm going to tend to the animals and search for my boat," he said.

"Will you be back for supper?" Fiona couldn't believe she had spoken the words.

For the first time since earlier that morning, Emile grinned at her. Only this time, it was genuine. *"Oui,* Madame Dugas. Someone has to fatten you up."

Fiona wanted to smile back, pleased that she hadn't insulted him, that Emile would come back and dish out more of his delectable cuisine and make Angelle laugh again. But she still couldn't trust him. Not fully.

As if sensing her thoughts, Emile's grin disappeared. He placed his hat firmly on his head, tipped the rim and left the cabin. As Fiona watched the tall, sturdy Acadian head for the bayou, she wondered what divine plan Mary had in store for her now.

Chapter Four

*"There is nothing holier in this life of ours
than the first consciousness of love . . . "*
—*Henry Wadsworth Longfellow*

Emile had risen with the dawn, milked the cow, fed the chickens and searched relentlessly for his pirogue, the whole while amazed that the evening's storm had left behind a thin layer of snow. It was beyond his memory when the last snow had fallen, and he stood fascinated by the icy white substance that covered everything in sight.

It was a magical morning, the cypress and oak trees draped in the rare precipitation that glistened like the Gulf waters on a breezy day in summer. The icy Spanish moss floated mystically in the cold wind as if celestial beings were using it for some form of recreation. The bayou's edges were laced in ice, another first for Emile. Touching his boot to the glassy sheets, Emile watched entranced as the ice broke beneath his weight and slid down the muddy bank.

The bayou was a grand and glorious place, a land full of mysteries and abundance. To Emile, it was paradise, just like its name.

Leave it to a woman to cause trouble in paradise, Emile

thought, feeling his temple burn recalling his earlier conversation with Isabelle. He didn't know what was more irritating, her insistence on being Aristide's heir or her fear of being alone with him. Actually, he did know. The latter pained him. Pained him tremendously.

"Why should I care that a crazy, lying woman who wants to take my land thinks ill of me?" he asked the placid bayou, rippling only by the occasional burst of wind.

"So what do I do?" he asked aloud, hoping his father would answer back. Like so many mornings before, the wind was his only companion.

"What would you do?"

Certainly, his father wouldn't have thrown the woman out or let her freeze inside Eraste's stockroom while they fetched the sheriff. Isabelle looked as if a strong wind would blow her away. And those fathomless emerald eyes so unsure, so scared. Her meager clothes would barely warm a body on a balmy day, let alone the coldest day in his memory. He had the power to change her circumstances, didn't he?

Emile smiled, feeling satisfied, as he had so many other times when he stood by the bayou's edge, even if the answer wasn't the easiest one. "Thank you, Father," he whispered.

"There are no rocks here," Emile heard someone say to his rear. When he turned, he found Isabelle in her thin coat standing behind him. When he looked around her, he found her alone.

"She's asleep," Isabelle said. "I wanted to see the bayou now that the storm has passed. It's beautiful."

"Yes," Emile said. "It's a remarkable place."

"Who were you talking to?" Isabelle asked.

Emile had lived alone for so many months now, he forgot that he had spoken aloud. "No one," he answered. "No one living."

He instantly regretted his choice of words. This was the

moment when women always inquired about the death of his father. So many questions. So many accusations. How did it happen? It's rumored you were the one who found him. Is it true you stopped talking for two years? How can you possibly live out here alone with those painful memories as company?

But Isabelle said nothing, just stared silently at the trees. "It's amazing," she finally said. "So green, even in the middle of winter."

"That's the live oak trees," Emile answered. "They lose their leaves in the spring."

"The spring?"

He couldn't help but be charmed at the incredulous look on her small, oval face. Her green eyes, now devoid of fear, sparkled in the sunshine. She wasn't a classic beauty like the rich Creole French women Emile had seen gracing the streets of St. Martinville, but she was the cutest thing he had ever laid eyes upon.

Then he noticed the streaks of perspiration on her forehead beneath the curly tendrils of auburn hair.

Emile raised his hand to cover her cheek, and Isabelle instantly pulled away. But this time he wasn't giving in to her fear. He raised his hand again, and while she stared hard as if he meant her harm, he gently placed his hand against her cheek to gauge a temperature.

"You're warm," he said, amazed that the touch of her brought forth myriad reactions, one of which was reminding him he had been without a woman for a very long time. He meant to move his hand as soon as he determined whether or not she had a fever, but the pleasure of their contact made him hesitate. Surprisingly, Isabelle didn't object.

Finally, she blushed and turned to escape his hand. "I've been sitting by the fire. 'Tis nothing."

Emile removed his coat and placed it around her shoulders which brought an instant objection. "It's not necessary," Isabelle said. "I have me own coat."

"You have a garment more suitable for a veil," Emile answered, wrapping his coat about her. "And I'll not have you dying on me before I serve you my famous gumbo."

Isabelle reluctantly grabbed the sides of the coat to hold it in place about her shoulders. "That would solve your problems," she said softly.

Emile rubbed his arms as the frigid wind bore down upon him. "Perhaps. But then I would have your smelly remains to deal with."

Isabelle stared up at him with that familiar look of shock.

"It's a joke, no?" Emile asked with a sigh.

"You have a strange sense of humor," she muttered.

"It's better than none at all," he retorted.

Isabelle frowned, handed Emile the coat and headed back toward the house.

"Would you like some company?" Emile asked her back.

Isabelle didn't turn around, just shrugged her shoulders. But after a few moments, she turned to see if he was following.

"The woman needs me, Father, doesn't she?" he whispered, as the wind howled its reply. Emile sighed once more, then made his way up the bank to the secluded house he hoped forever to call home.

Fiona felt the fire burning in her cheeks, but she knew it had nothing to do with fever. She couldn't remember the last time a man made her blush. But then, no man had ever touched her out of concern. Lust, yes. But concern over her welfare?

She glanced over her shoulder to see if Emile was following. To her satisfaction, he moved up the bank several feet to the rear.

Why should she care? She came out in the cold in the hope of *not* finding him, so she could safely take a bath. Now she would have to endure his company, his questions, his accusations, and feel guilty every time those soft chestnut eyes turned her way.

Still, his presence was soothing in some inexplicable way.

When Fiona reached the door, she turned to hold it open for Emile, but he had disappeared. She glanced around the corner of the house and found no one. Not wishing to chill the house and wake Angelle, she jumped inside and began banking the fire.

Finding herself alone once more, she settled herself on the bed with her legs crossed before her. While she waited to see if Emile would reappear, she glanced around the sparse, yet immensely comfortable cabin, absorbing all of its tender details: The oak chest at the foot of the bed with the worn leather straps. The old gun hanging above the wooden mantel etched with indentations of every shape and size. The enormous kitchen table held together by wooden pegs and equally marked with use.

The cabin was, as the name suggested, a slice of paradise.

Fiona heard Emile approach before he threw open the door; she assumed the heavy footsteps landing on the porch were meant to alert her that he was near. Unfortunately, his forethought woke Angelle, who immediately burst into tears.

All the fatigue, all the fear and worry of the past few weeks, fell on Fiona's shoulders when she realized her brief respite from motherhood had ended. She needed that baby's nap. She needed it bad.

"Dear God, I'm sorry," Emile said, hurrying over to attend to the baby.

"Don't bother," Fiona said too harshly as she picked up the child and placed her on her shoulder. "Once she wakes up, she never goes back to sleep."

The baby continued to howl at having her nap interrupted, and Fiona could feel her own tears welling up in the back of her eyes. She was so tired. So incredibly tired. And Angelle slept so very little.

"How can a woman possibly care for a baby who refuses to let her rest?" Fiona asked Emile, her voice betraying her emotional state.

Emile walked over and tenderly took the baby from Fiona's arms. "That's why God made *parents,*" he said softly. "Why don't you get some rest?"

"And who will take care of Angelle when I do?" Fiona asked as if the man had gone dumb.

Emile emitted the now-familiar sigh and frown. "I will, of course," he said between gritted teeth. "I helped raise two brothers, both of whom were heathens and much more work than this sweet child. If you wish to rest or bathe, I'll be glad to watch her. I'll show her the animals in the barn. We'll go for a walk."

"It's freezing outside."

"I'll wrap her up tight," Emile said, then gazing down at Angelle asked, "Want to see the cow?"

He shifted the baby and retrieved a pocket watch from his trouser pocket, opened the watch, and compared its time with the clock above the mantel. "I'll be back in thirty minutes. Is that time enough?" he asked.

Fiona's spirits soared, and her instincts urged her on. "Yes," she answered eagerly. "I can bathe in that time."

"Then I'll come back and make you lunch and help some more with Angelle."

"You don't have to feed us," she protested. "I am perfectly able to—"

"Yes," Emile interrupted. "I know you can. But what else is there for me to do in this weather without my boat?"

Still holding Angelle, he pulled three peculiar-shaped

potatoes from his pocket and threw them at the edge of the fire. "These should be well cooked by the time I return," he said. "I'll get some eggs and make you an omelet."

"There's no need," Fiona started.

"You like omelets?" he asked, ignoring her last comment.

"I don't know what they are," Fiona answered.

Emile grinned, the kind that made his dimple appear. "Omelets are my specialty," he said, then grabbed up the baby blanket, wrapped it tightly around Angelle's body and head, and left the cabin.

Fiona struggled to catch her breath. Thirty minutes. Alone. Could it really be true?

Not wishing to waste one minute Fiona slid the metal tub toward the fire, then grabbed the pail and headed to the cistern to fill it. The pipe took a few pulls before the water broke through, but she soon had enough for a bath.

While the water heated over the fire, Fiona hesitantly removed her clothes, one article at a time. What had Emile said about Aristide's clothes? How wonderful it would be to wear something else besides her one filthy, threadbare dress.

To the left of the bed stood a primitive bureau from which Fiona removed a man's shirt and trousers. She would wear them temporarily, she assured herself, until she could clean and dry her own clothes.

Fiona slipped into the tub of steaming water, exhaled deeply, and felt her muscles relax. She slid farther down inside the tub until her tangled hair fell into the now tepid water. She closed her eyes and tried to remember swimming in the sea at Kenmare, while her da held her afloat and whispered encouragements in her ear.

* * *

Angelle reached out her hands to the cow's oversized nose.

"La vache," Emile said tenderly. "It's a cow."

Her sweet, angelic face rosy from the cold and her bright, sea blue eyes enchanted by the bovine touched Emile's heart in a way he hadn't known before. He pulled her close and kissed her sweetly on the cheek. She even smelled sweet, if that was possible.

Maybe Nana was right. He needed to marry and start a family. Hiding out in Aristide's cabin would get him nowhere. Aristide Dugas was a prime example of that. The man had lost his wife to the yellow fever eight months after their wedding, and he had refused to remarry. He had lived a solemn, finicky bachelor's life, despising change and most people. It was a wonder he had offered Emile his cabin, even when he knew he was dying.

Angelle, still tired from the loss of a nap, turned and placed her head on Emile's shoulder, her soft curls resting against his cheek. The gesture touched him deep into the core of his heart. Planting more kisses on the top of her precious head, Emile knew he wanted this. Home. Hearth. Family. Trouble was, a woman usually came with it.

Angelle shifted, and Emile deftly moved her onto his other shoulder and began to walk the barn, softly patting her back and singing an old French lullaby. Angelle had lost her parents, Emile thought, and God only knew what horrors Isabelle had seen to make her so distrustful. He recognized that darkness in her eyes, that aching look that accompanied intense heartache, that pleading stare secretly begging for help even though pride refused it.

He wanted her to trust him. Despite what motives she had in coming to Bayou Paradis, for some reason, known only to God, he had to win her confidence.

The tiny fingers pulling at his hair stilled, and Emile strained his neck to get enough of a glance to see that Angelle had fallen asleep. With his free hand, he pulled out his watch and noted that at least thirty minutes had passed. If he kept Angelle warm enough, he could bring her to the cabin's bed without waking her.

Emile carefully walked from the barn to the cabin and this time knocked softly at the door. When Isabelle opened it, he hurried through and gently placed Angelle on the bed, cozy and warm by the blazing fire. The baby stirred slightly, but remained asleep.

Emile sighed and stretched to untie the knot formed in his lower back from carrying the baby. He turned and found Isabelle freshly clean, her hair untied and loose about her shoulders, clothed in Aristide's shirt and trousers which, since Aristide was a much smaller man than Emile, fit her well. She seemed more relaxed, more comfortable, a brighter light shining in her eyes. Despite the masculine clothes, she was infinitely more beautiful bathed in the fire's soft orange glow.

Isabelle must have read his thoughts, for she immediately crossed her arms in front of her bosom. "I washed my clothes," she said self-consciously. "I didn't have anything else to wear."

The blush she exhibited earlier returned, a gesture Emile found amazingly attractive. "It suits you," he said.

"You don't have to be kind," Isabelle said, fingering the cotton ties at her collar.

"I like being kind," Emile answered with a grin, but Isabelle's stern countenance never faltered. "Do you ever smile?" he asked.

Isabelle frowned and began removing the remnants of her bath. He realized he had overshot his mark, like luring a deer to bait only to shoot prematurely. But he didn't want to harm this doe. He wanted to hold her close and plant kisses on the top of her soft auburn hair.

Emile abruptly stood up from the bed as if struck by a bolt of lightning. Where did that thought come from? he wondered with horror.

"Is something wrong?" Isabelle asked.

"Yes," he wanted to shout. "You are." But instead he silently grabbed the pail of water from her hands and left the cabin to dispose of it, this time ever so quietly.

Chapter Five

*"Love keeps the cold out better than a cloak.
It serves for food and raiment."*
—Henry Wadsworth Longfellow

Now where the devil was Emile? Fiona wondered. It was close to dinner, and he was nowhere to be seen.

For several days Fiona had been served an enormous variety of food created by the large, eager hands of her Gabriel. She had never seen so many different types of food: Wild turkey served with corn *macque choux,* stewed okra and rice. *Les gateaux de syrop,* cakes made with cane syrup, served hot from the fire for breakfast. Omelets flavored with what Emile called the "Cajun Four Seasons," onions, green peppers, garlic and celery. For dessert, *oreilles de cochon,* fried dough laced with thick, sweet syrup and dotted with pecans which curled up in the frying pan to resemble pig's ears.

Fiona awaited each meal, then watched as Emile delivered more food than she had seen, let alone eaten, in years. She craved the next opportunity to sit at his table and watch the amazing creations he would place before her. She never imagined a country such as this, a land teeming with wildlife, an earth rich from the overflowing waters and snow a rarity. And a man who loved to cook.

Most mornings Emile served a heaping breakfast, then left to check his traps and search for his boat, but always he returned by suppertime, if not before, his arms burdened with fresh vegetables from the barn and some wild game or seafood he had caught. The previous day, Emile had spent the entire afternoon fabricating what he called a duck and *andouille* sausage gumbo, the finest soup that had ever passed Fiona's lips, accented by a dark *roux* laced with an herb called *filé*.

But who was she fooling? Yes, the gumbo was delicious, but it wasn't the reason she tingled every time she thought back on the day before. It was his cheerful company she longed for, those endless hours of watching him cook, explaining how to make coffee or start a *roux* of flour and oil, the basis for most Cajun dishes. Emile filled the afternoon with stories of his childhood on the bayou and his recent years in Franklin where he lived with his mother, brothers and a couple of entrepreneurial cousins who had amassed a small fortune in horse racing. He talked well into the night of his days gathering moss from the bayou's cypress trees, of communal gatherings in the evenings with his godmother and friends when the weather was agreeable, of a simple life that reminded Fiona of home.

If she didn't know better, Fiona would swear she was falling in love.

Glancing at herself in the faded mirror above the bureau, Fiona knew just how silly that notion was. She was a skinny, penniless immigrant with no family, no land and no looks to offer a man. Even if she did care for Emile, he would hardly consider her. Most likely he was now consorting with the sheriff to have her thrown off his land.

Angelle murmured and stirred in her sleep, taken to bed early after a dinner of the peculiar orange potatoes

Emile had called yams. What a rare treat to have an evening quiet and alone. Fiona imagined Emile returning and the two of them eating in peace, perhaps playing that French *bouré* card game he had taught her the night before.

Perhaps that would be the time to tell Emile the truth.

Dusk began to settle, and Fiona walked onto the porch to see if Emile was near. She soon spotted him, in the least likely of places.

For the fourth consecutive day, Emile searched the bayou for his pirogue, but still the boat refused to turn up. He knew it was a matter of time; if the wind had dislodged it from its muddy prison, a resident of Bayou Paradis would spot it in his travels.

Emile held mixed feelings about finding the handmade pirogue he had owned since childhood. He would finally be able to resume his neglected work, but it meant the return of Isabelle the impostor to the outside world. The thought of coming back to a solitary house, a cold hearth and the absence of female company made him wish another winter storm would blow through the bayou and keep the pirogue at bay. He dreaded watching her leave, even though he knew she would be well taken care of at Nana's house or by another caring family on the bayou. More importantly, he dreaded seeing that fearful look return to her eyes. Not to mention that he still hadn't served her his catfish *court-bouillon*.

Emile laughed thinking back on the expression on Isabelle's face when she had tasted the gumbo the night before. He didn't know what surprised her more, the tasty thick soup stocked with succulent wild duck and home-made sausage or the fact that a man cooked it.

"Why do you cook?" she had asked him sheepishly.

"Why not?" he had answered with a grin.

She had almost smiled then, a light emerging in those usually cautious emerald eyes. God, how Emile wanted to see her smile, hear her laugh. It was a constant challenge.

"I live alone," he explained. "Me, I could eat poorly cooked food or I could eat well. Which would you choose?"

Maybe the way to a *woman's* heart was through her stomach, Emile thought with a smile. He hoped it was working.

The pirogue could wait, he finally decided. He would reheat the leftover gumbo and follow it with sugared pecans, since Isabelle favored them so. Mashed sweet potatoes with brown sugar for Angelle. Hot drip coffee, maybe a swallow of whiskey for himself.

He quickened his step. Through the outline of the trees he spotted the bayou-side corner of the house, the fire's light glowing through the windows, and Emile could smell the sharp fragrance of cedar wood burning inside. He wanted to hold his Angelle, hear her squeals of joy at his arrival. And he wanted to be welcomed home by a woman who haunted his dreams nightly.

Three restless nights he had stared at the *garconnière's* all-too-close ceiling and remembered the way Isabelle's chestnut hair fell about her ivory shoulders, or the sparkle he would create in those green eyes if he managed to tell a good joke. He would recall how the two of them delighted in watching Angelle laugh while playing with the leather ties on his boots or the way her lips pursed while she slept. The fresh smell of Isabelle's hair. Her inviting lush lips.

"*Merde,*" Emile mumbled, fighting the now familiar tightness in his trousers. The woman was taking over his mind, in addition to trying to confiscate his land.

Shaking his head at the absurdity of it all, Emile suddenly caught a movement in the rushes on the far side of the bayou. His pirogue had slipped free of a fallen cypress branch and begun to slowly move toward him, as if the wind was calling his boat home. Emile moved to the edge of the bank, holding on to a nearby tree branch to steady himself.

As if the boat saw him coming, the wind shifted, and it began drifting toward the center of the bayou, out of Emile's reach. Emile followed it along the bank, pausing while the wind shifted again and held the boat steady, then watched in exasperation as the boat slowly drifted farther down the bayou.

There was only one way to solve this problem, Emile realized, and he quickly discarded his coat. The weather had warmed only slightly during the past three days, and the continuous wind howling around every corner kept the temperatures well below freezing. Emile knew he had to be quick. A few yards into the bayou and he would have it; then he could safely return to the warm cabin.

He plunged into the frigid water and felt an instant chill travel up his spine. The water was too cold, his common sense told him, but his eyes insisted the pirogue was close enough to reach. He tried to move quickly toward the drifting boat, but the cold permeated his bones, and a harsh shiver began at the core of his being.

Emile gritted his teeth and headed toward the bayou's center, reaching a depth where his feet no longer felt the bottom and his head submerged several times while he tried to stretch his arms in a swim. The pirogue was so close. He spotted the bow rope floating teasingly within a yard's reach. Emile stroked an arm's length, far enough to reach the boat's side, but a gust of wind pushed it back toward the far bank.

His common sense should have intervened and demanded he return to shore, but Emile couldn't give up. The shivers returned, this time in a ferocious wave, and Emile struggled to kick his feet to remain above water. While he swam farther out toward the boat, the pirogue shifted once again, moving just beyond his reach.

I can do this, Emile thought, but his movements became clumsy and lethargic. Just one more stretch, he concluded as he followed the boat down the bayou, but again the wind pushed the boat away.

His eyesight now foggy and the shivers unbearable, Emile couldn't fully comprehend the jaws that had clamped on to his back. For a moment he imagined alligators, but the giant reptiles disappeared at the least sign of cold weather. Still, something large and sharp was grasping his suspenders and shirt and pulling him back toward shore.

When Emile's feet touched the bayou's floor, he felt an arm wind around his waist and an angelic voice sound from behind. But this angel was anything but saintly, spouting words more familiar to a sailor.

"Are you out of your mind?" the angel sailor demanded, pulling him backward up the bank like a child.

Emile wanted to right himself, turn to this person who had refused him the retrieval of his boat and give him a few choice words of his own. But he found his legs buckling and the words emerging from his lips in an incoherent slur.

"Put your arms around me," Isabelle directed, and for the first time Emile fully realized where he was and what was happening.

"My pirogue," he muttered through violent shivers. "I must get it."

"And lose ye life in the process?" she retorted. " 'Tis savage weather. A fish would be hard pressed on a day like this."

For some reason, Emile's legs had quit working, and had it not been for Isabelle moving her shoulder underneath his arm, his face would have made quick communion with the mud.

"Lean on me," Isabelle said, and they slowly made their way up the bank toward the house.

"It was so close," Emile muttered between shivers.

"Always is," Isabelle answered somberly.

It seemed an eternity before they made it inside the cabin, where a roaring fire brought welcome relief to Emile's frigid limbs. As much as he wanted to rid himself of his wet clothes, clinging to his body like a death shroud, his hands couldn't part the buttons for the shivering.

"Let me," Isabelle said. "Lucky for you, I've cleaned you a new set of clothes. They be sitting on the table there." She quickly unbuttoned his shirt, pushing away his suspenders to remove the drenched garments underneath. She rushed through her work, disgarding his clothes with abandon onto the hearth, but when she reached his trousers, her cheeks blushed a bright crimson.

"I'll take it from here," Emile said, inwardly wishing she would complete what she had started. "You should get out of your own wet clothes."

Isabelle nodded and moved toward the far side of the cabin. She began an instant disrobe, then straightened as if remembering she was not alone. When she glanced back, Emile realized he was staring and turned toward the fire, but not before he noticed the outline of her trim figure beneath the soaked clothes, the shape of her small but plump breasts, their nipples fully erect, and the full, sensual curves of her generous hips. Suddenly, his chill abated.

Fiona knew she should have felt intense discomfort and embarrassment undressing herself in the confines of a one-room cabin with a man not ten feet behind her. A flash of alarm crossed her mind, yet as quickly as it emerged, Fiona dismissed it and began to unbutton the bodice of her dress. Not only did Emile stand helplessly shivering behind her, unable to remove a simple set of trousers, but for the first time in three days she trusted him.

Fiona glanced over her shoulder—to check on Emile's progress, she assured herself. To her surprise and wonderment, Emile stood naked, his long, rock-hard legs glistening in the firelight from the lingering moisture and graced by the nicest set of . . .

Just as Fiona's gaze paused at Emile's taut and dimpled behind, he turned sideways to wipe the wetness from his right thigh. Her cheeks ablaze with shame, Fiona whisked around. "Mother Mary and Joseph," she whispered in awe of the sight she had witnessed for one brief, but oh-so-amazing moment.

Knowing Emile was recovering and well on his way toward dressing, Fiona rushed to remove her own wet clothes and replace each damp garment with Aristide's clothes. After carefully pulling on a dry piece of clothing while slipping off the wet one underneath, Fiona finished, and shyly turned toward the fireplace.

"All done?" Emile asked, and Fiona found him fully dressed opposite the fire. Just what had he seen?

"Are you crazy?" she asked, changing the subject. "A person can die swimming in water in such weather."

Emile's round brown eyes glistened in the fire's light, but the usual twinkle was absent. His uncharacteristically glum behavior unnerved Fiona. "It's a family tradition," he said softly, without emotion.

Fiona joined him by the fire, rising onto her toes to place a cotton blanket around his shoulders. "What is?" she whispered.

Instead of answering, Emile pulled the blanket up and over his shoulders, then gathered Fiona in his arms, wrapping the blanket's warmth about them. At first Fiona was shocked by the male arms encircling her, causing her chin to rest upon his left shoulder and his fine, shoulder-length hair to brush against her cheek. But regardless of his large hands at her back, their bodies barely touched, and the lack of connection signaled to Fiona that the contact was plainly therapeutic. He was simply trying to get warm. The disappointment that welled inside her was more shocking than their close proximity.

Nothing was more astonishing, however, than Fiona's own actions, as she wound her arms around Emile's waist and settled them at the small of his back.

He immediately sighed and pulled her closer, stretching his hands across her back. Fiona could feel the shivers still raking his body as one hand pushed her tightly against his chest and their bodies melded together.

She knew she was near dangerous territory, inviting passion that lurked too close to the surface in a man. If a landlord or employer could react aggressively from an innocent request, what would Emile do now that they were tightly wound? She should have been alarmed; she should have wanted to move away. Instead, Fiona let go of her held breath, closed her eyes and leaned her head against his cheek, absorbing the warmth of his broad shoulders and solid body, the smell of manliness about him and the gentle caress his hand applied against her back. She was being held, she suddenly realized. Dear God, someone was finally holding her close.

"Oh, Za'belle," Emile whispered in his familiar lilting accent, his voice betraying the longing of a solitary man.

Fiona wanted to answer, to reply that she knew exactly what he meant, that the need to be close to another human was like starving for nourishment, a hunger that could only be sated by the touch of another. Instead, Fiona silently treasured the feel of his chest, the muscled arms wrapped tightly around her, the slight whiskers scratching at her cheek.

They could have stayed there forever, Fiona dreamed, never moving an inch, each absorbing the warm affections of the other. But Angelle stirred on the bed. Emile loosened his hold, and Fiona pushed herself away from his embrace. Before she left the blanket's cocoon, she paused at his chest, her hands lingering at his waist, hoping to lock the moment to memory before it was lost for good.

Emile placed a finger at her chin and tilted her head upward until their eyes met. When his chestnut eyes made contact with hers, a bolt of lightning traveled down the length of her spine, and she shivered violently. It was true, after all, she thought. She had fallen hopelessly in love.

"Still cold?" he asked in a husky voice.

"Say yes," her inner voice instructed her, but the protective mother in her won out. She shook her head, left the blanket's confines and moved toward the bed. With a flood of relief, she found Angelle peacefully asleep. Fiona lightly touched her forehead for fever.

"Is she well?" Emile asked.

Fiona nodded and turned. "Are you?" she replied.

The shivers had abated, but the light that perpetually shone in Emile's eyes had diminished. It reminded her of the ominous phrase in Longfellow's poem: "Sweet was the light of his eyes; but it suddenly sank into darkness." Fighting off the memories of Mattie's death, she asked, "What did you mean it's a family tradition?"

Emile sat down on the fireside bench, leaning his elbows on his thighs and rubbing his forehead with one hand. "Like father, like son," he answered quietly.

She joined him on the bench, wanting to touch him, but afraid of the desire she felt stirring inside her. "Your father drowned out there, didn't he?" she finally said.

Emile stared for a moment as if wanting to discover how she knew. It was simply a guess on her part, derived from comments he had made and a feeling that his past lingered about the house and the bayou.

"He died when I was twelve," Emile finally said. "We were collecting moss from the trees for mattress stuffings when a storm arrived."

He paused and stared into the fire's glowing embers.

Fiona watched as the flames danced inside the pupils of his eyes. "The wind suddenly came upon us," Emile continued. "I wanted to go with my father, but he insisted I stay on the bank. You see, there was this massive cypress tree we had been trying to find all summer, and we had finally found it. She held more moss than we had ever seen before. My father refused to turn back, not wanting to lose a day's work. So he left me there, safe on an embankment, and took the pirogue on his own."

Emile paused again, and Fiona saw the guilt wash across his face. "I should have gone with him," he murmured. "There was lightning everywhere. I should have been with him."

Fiona pulled her arm through the crook of his elbow, sliding her hand down his forearm until it reached his hand. "It wasn't your fault," she said.

Emile shook his head, still staring vacantly into the fire. "I should have gone with him. I could have saved him."

"You don't know that," Fiona urged.

"I found him facedown in the bayou." Emile winced at the thought. "He hit his head somehow. I could have been there, could have stopped him from drowning."

Fiona pulled her fingers into his palm and held it tight. "You could have both been drowned, Emile."

It was then he finally looked at her, and she could see the pain of his adolescent youth still burning strong despite the years. Fiona felt her heart aching for this man, pained that he carried his father's death about his shoulders. She knew what he was feeling. She knew it well. How long had she felt guilty for being the only one to survive?

Emile then looked beyond her, staring at the enormous hearth. "She was standing right there," he whispered, the intense hurt emerging in his voice.

"Who was?" Fiona asked, looking in that direction.

"My mother. I had to tell her that the man she had loved all of her life was lying dead in the yard."

Fiona pulled herself to him and rested her head on his shoulder. "Oh, Emile," she whispered.

Emile bowed his head at the admission. "I never wanted to cause that much pain to anyone ever again," he said through clenched teeth.

"It wasn't your fault," Fiona repeated.

"I stopped talking after that," he continued quietly. "My mother was so worried, she sold the property and moved us to live with a pair of bachelor cousins in Franklin. She lost her husband and her home because of me."

It was then that the reality of the cabin being Emile's from the start hit Fiona with a striking blow. "This was your home?" she asked incredulously, raising her head and moving away.

Emile nodded. "My father built this house," he said, then pointed to the frayed wooden beams surrounding the fireplace. "I cut my teeth on that wood."

Fiona felt the breath leaving her lungs as she viewed the gnawed wood a foot above the floor. *Dear God*, she thought in horror, *what have I done?*

As if hearing the alarm inside her mind, Emile turned toward her as Fiona raised her right hand and lovingly caressed his cheek. "Your mother might have lost more than this house," she said. "She could have lost her first-born son as well. Your father was right in leaving you on the bank. Can't you see that?"

Without breaking eye contact, Emile grasped her hand in his and kissed the inside of her palm. He wrapped his fingers around her hand and rested her knuckles against his lips. His large brown eyes gazed at her in the now familiar stare that she had come to welcome, the warmth of his personality blanketing her with a peace she had never known before.

"Where is *your* family, Za'belle?" he asked so quietly Fiona wasn't sure she heard him right.

Then the words sank in.

She could feel her breath catch inside her chest. Suddenly, the wretched smell of potatoes filled her senses. She closed her eyes and fought to erase the painful image, but the screams echoed through her mind.

"Don't do that again, *chéri,*" she heard a soft voice call to her through the darkness.

Struggling to regain her senses, Fiona opened her eyes and tried to concentrate. "Do what?" she asked nervously.

Emile placed a finger at her chin and lifted her gaze to his. "Retreat under that cloud." Emile cupped her face within his broad hands and gazed deeply into her eyes. She felt the ominous clouds lifting. "You're safe now, *'ti monde,*" Emile whispered. "You have nothing to fear."

For that instant, Fiona believed him. She grasped one hand at her face with her own and held it tight as if his palm on her cheek held back all the terrifying memories and nightmares.

Then he kissed her. He lightly brushed the hair from her forehead and placed a brotherly kiss in its place. Fiona closed her eyes and sighed.

When Emile began to move away, Fiona placed a hand on his chest, grasping his shirt tightly between her fingers. He was her lifeline, and she couldn't let him go.

Emile tilted her head up so that their eyes met once more. Neither one spoke while they gazed into each other's eyes, and Fiona could hear the beating of her heart.

Then, without speaking, Emile pressed his lips to hers.

Chapter Six

At first, his lips tenderly brushed hers, then nipped at
the corners of her mouth and softly teased her lips apart.
Then Emile moved his hands to her waist, sliding one hand
up the length of her back, pulling her tightly against him
while he deepened the kiss.

Fiona felt herself falling into a lazy state of bliss as his
kisses devoured her lips and his tongue delicately explored
the soft reaches of her mouth. When his lips left hers
and began an investigation along her cheek, beneath her
earlobe and along the soft skin of her neck, Fiona sighed
and slid a hand up the front of his shirt, reveling in the
feel of his thick, solid chest.

Emile moaned and murmured something in French.
Fiona almost giggled. She liked this lovemaking, she
thought as she plied her fingers through his rich brown
hair and leaned her head against the warmth of his shoulder. After so long finding men the enemy, she was shocked
to learn how pleasant kisses could feel along one's neckline. And heaven help her, there were feminine places

reacting to his touch, as if nature was urging her to the marriage bed.

Trouble was, they weren't married. Yet, Fiona dismissed that fact as soon as it announced itself, and eagerly met Emile's lips when he circled back to her face.

He kissed her with such ferocity, Fiona moaned herself and lost all control. As Emile pulled her even closer, her breasts brushing against the tautness of his broad chest, she slid both hands around his shoulders and practically dragged herself into his lap.

Time seemed to stand still as Emile offered one deep, enormously sensual kiss after another. She was his, Fiona concluded as his fingers caressed her hair, then slid down her nape and across the length of her back. Shivers of pleasure vibrated through her. Heaven help her, lovemaking felt nice.

But instead of continuing, Emile pulled back, looked into her eyes briefly, then gently rested his forehead against hers. Fiona saw the heated flame of passion in his eyes, but the light faded fast. Fatigue was quickly replacing desire in her beloved Gabriel.

"Je regret, 'ti monde," he began.

"No, I am sorry," she said, regaining some semblance of her former restraint. "You need to rest."

Looking over his shoulder at the blazing hearth and the innocent face of the sleeping child, Fiona imagined a life like this, a warm home, food on the table, safety from the harsh urban world, and a man who loved her. Did he love her, though? That was the question. And would he still care when he learned the truth?

Emile softly tucked a strand of her hair behind an ear, brushing his knuckles lovingly against her cheek as he did so.

"Good night, Za'belle," Emile said, and the sound of her fraudulent name reverberated inside her mind.

When Emile rose to leave, Fiona thought of the cold attic, ravished by the brutal winds that refused to let up these past few days. She had sent Emile, owner of this cabin and son of its creator, into the frigid air on three nights while she and Angelle slept warm by the fire. Before he could leave her side, she grabbed his hand. "You must sleep here," she told him, feeling too guilty to meet his eyes.

Emile paused and slid his thumb across her hand. The gesture sent sensations coursing through her body. "That's not necessary," Emile began.

"Of course it is," Fiona softly replied. "This is your cabin."

He said nothing, but Fiona could feel him staring, probably wondering, she thought, if her admission meant she was agreeing to bed him. After the kisses they had just shared, he must think the worst of her. Sooner or later he would insist on being repaid for the food she had consumed. Fiona doubted he was the kind of man to ask, but since leaving Ireland, most of the men she had thought better of had disappointed her. Why shouldn't he?

"It's not proper," Emile finally said.

It took Fiona a moment to consider what Emile had said, then to realize the absurdity of the remark, since they had acted *very* improperly only minutes before. Her cheeks began to flush, and she saw the familiar sparkle reappear in his eyes. "You almost smiled just then," he told her with a grin.

She lowered her eyes. "I don't think it would be any more improper than . . ."

Emile murmured an agreement, then whispered as he caressed her hair, "It isn't safe to put two lonely people in a cabin together, yes?"

Fiona looked at him then and saw something new in his stare. Could he need her as much as she needed him?

Without thinking, Fiona stood and led him to the fire side of the bed, pulling the blankets down to give him room. When he started to protest, she placed a finger at his lips, still warm from their kisses.

"I don't think you'll do much harm in your condition," she said, "especially with a wee baby between us."

Emile smiled in agreement and climbed into bed, throwing an arm about the child, who happily snuggled into his embrace. "If I'm not mistaken, Madame Dugas," he said, sending a sly glance her way, "you just said something humorous."

Fiona wanted to smile back at that infectious grin, topped by two haunting brown eyes that sent shivers through her every time they looked her way, even though now their lids were drooping with fatigue. But the sound of her deceptive name on his lips sent a cloud over her heart. She wasn't Madame Dugas. And more than likely, she was never going to be.

Through the haze of first awakening, Emile knew somehow he was not where he should be. But when two tiny hands grabbed his cheeks and squeezed, he realized exactly where he was.

"Angelle," he whispered to the baby. "Let go."

Instead of releasing his cheeks, the baby leaned forward until their foreheads touched and began to chew on his nose. He might have been shocked to find a child gnawing on his face first thing in the morning had not his younger brothers done the same. When Emile felt the hard mounds of teeth just beyond Angelle's gum line, he discovered the reason Angelle wasn't sleeping well. She was teething.

Emile gently lifted the child and placed her on his chest. Before Angelle could protest, he offered her a finger, which she immediately grabbed and stuck in her mouth.

"You're going to be a pistol," he whispered, "just like your mother."

Emile peered to his left and found Isabelle asleep, leaning slightly toward him, one arm lazily arched above her head. Her silky hair fanned out on her pillow, and for the first time Emile noticed her eyelashes were the same color as her auburn hair. Even lying there in Aristide's clothes, she was the most beautiful woman he had ever seen.

"I could get used to this," he whispered to Angelle, but Angelle had more important matters on her hands. She bit into his forefinger with abandon. "Not so hard," he added. "Leave me a hand to make breakfast."

Suddenly, Isabelle twitched and murmured in her sleep. Her body tensed, and her brow creased in anguish. She appeared as she had that first morning when a dream caused her to bolt awake in terror, tears streaming down her face.

Emile moved his free hand to her and lightly touched her cheeks. He whispered soft, encouraging words, and it didn't matter that they were in French since he was speaking to a dream. "Sleep peaceful," he said as he gently stroked her hair and placed a loving kiss to her forehead. "Tell the demons Emile Dugas said to go away."

Isabelle spoke his name, but she didn't wake. Instead, she sighed, snuggled close to his shoulder and returned to a restful sleep. *Yes,* Emile thought, *I could definitely get used to this.*

Angelle released his finger and began to stare off in the direction of the front door. It was then Emile noticed the man at the window. Hypolite Aucoin, his mother's first cousin and stock clerk at Eraste Boudreaux's store, gazed into the cabin wearing the largest grin Emile had seen on his face since the spring *boucherie,* where families from miles around gathered for the communal hog butchering and ate and danced until midnight.

Emile bolted upright, grabbed Angelle and rose from the bed. With one arm holding the baby, he pulled on his coat and boots, then slid a blanket around the baby's shoulders. Snatching Isabelle's shawl from the kitchen chair, he emerged on the porch.

"Is that your cousin?" Hypolite asked wide-eyed, trying to peer inside the door. "The one from New Orleans?"

"Hold her," Emile said, thrusting the baby into the bachelor's arms. With two arms free, Emile quickly wrapped the shawl around Angelle's head and retrieved her before she could belt out her disapproval.

"She likes you," Hypolite said when the baby smiled coming into Emile's arms.

"No, she just doesn't like you." Emile gave him a grin, but inwardly he felt aggravated at having a private moment interrupted. What had Hypolite seen anyway?

"What did you do," his cousin continued eagerly, "jump the broom?"

Emile thought of Nana and her crazy broomstick and laughed. *"Oui,"* he said sarcastically. "I jumped the broom. Now, how did you get here?"

Hypolite's smile never faltered. "The roads are clear. What's her name?"

"Angelle," Emile answered, gazing into the sparkling blue eyes of his young charge, who was busy devouring his collar.

"Not the baby," Hypolite answered, staring back inside the cabin. "Your cousin."

Emile followed his gaze to Isabelle's angelic sleeping face, the same face he had showered with kisses the night before. For some unknown reason, he wanted to sock Hypolite in the jaw. He wasn't ready to introduce Isabelle to his friend and the community. He wasn't ready for the questions they would ask.

And he wasn't ready to let her go.

"Why are you here?" Emile asked much too brusquely.

Hypolite reacted as if slapped, and Emile instantly regretted his tone. It wasn't his cousin's fault that he had arrived the one morning Emile and Isabelle had slept together in an effort to keep warm.

"I brought back your pirogue," the young man finally replied, his smile gone.

Emile turned and saw the familiar boat lying on the bayou's bank. He placed a hand on his friend's shoulder and squeezed. "Forgive me," he said. "I am not myself."

Hypolite instantly brightened. "Of course not," he said as he nudged an elbow into Emile's ribs. "Women will do that to you."

Emile let out a heavy sigh. He had a feeling that spending five days and four nights with the mysterious "cousin" named Isabelle Dugas was going to require a lot of explanation. And for the life of him, he had none to offer.

When Fiona awoke, she found Angelle gone from the bed. She sat up and quickly searched the one-room house, but there was no sign of either Emile or the baby.

From the porch Fiona heard sounds of people talking—two men if she wasn't mistaken, speaking in French. She threw her legs over the side of the bed and slipped on her stockings and shoes. Grabbing her coat, she emerged onto the porch to find Emile jostling Angelle in his arms and talking to a bright-eyed stranger who resembled Emile in his features but not his stature.

Emile turned and caught sight of her, and Fiona's heart skipped. The memory of his embrace and the passion of his kisses made her feel giddy. He, too, seemed to recall the night before, for his eyes held a special sparkle and his lips turned up in a mischievous grin.

"*Bonjour,*" said the man to her left.

Fiona turned to greet him. *"Bonjour,"* she repeated. Was this it? Would one announcement that she was a fraud conclude her days of peace by the bayou's side in the arms of a man she had come to love?

"Isabelle," Emile said, breaking her thoughts. "This is Hypolite Aucoin. He helps run Boudreaux's store."

Fiona vaguely heard the man's name, something sounding like hee-po-lee o-qwan, but all she could think of was the prospect of leaving Bayou Paradis. When she saw the pirogue resting on the bank, her fear intensified.

The man began a long stream of French sentences until Emile interrupted and informed him she did not understand French. "I'm sorry," the man offered awkwardly in English. "I speak bad English."

Fiona nodded. "Coffee?"

The man brightened at the mention of the word and eagerly entered the cabin. Emile, on the other hand, appeared unhappy that Fiona had invited the man to breakfast. He handed Angelle back to her and glumly crossed the threshold. When Fiona reached the fire in an attempt to brew the coffee, Emile gently pushed her aside, even pulling out a chair for her to sit in. As he prepared the makings for *pain perdu,* he never cracked a smile.

What did she interrupt? Fiona wondered. The man sitting across from her seemed too cheerful and small to be a law officer. He continued to speak even though Fiona never understood a word. *"Anglais,"* Emile reminded him, a word Fiona did understand.

"Are you a friend of Emile's?" Fiona asked, hoping the man wouldn't spring out a badge. Emile translated the question, and the man nodded.

"Emile, *moi,* work together." The man pointed outdoors.

" 'Polite and I build boats together on occasion," Emile translated.

The man then began a long conversation, and all Fiona could think to do was nod. When she began to remove her coat, one arm at a time while holding Angelle, the man stopped talking and stared. Looking down, Fiona remembered she was wearing Aristide's clothes. How was she going to explain this one?

Just then, Angelle caught the loose tie at her collar and began to pull. Hoping to ease her embarrassment, Fiona turned her attention to the child. "I look like a da, don't I?" Fiona asked the baby.

Angelle kicked her legs playfully and smiled. "Da!" she exclaimed.

Fiona couldn't believe it. "She said her first word," she cried to Emile.

Emile put the skillet of hot French bread on the table, sat next to Fiona and looked intently at Angelle. "What did she say?"

"Da!" Angelle repeated, still looking at Fiona.

"No, I'm not a da," Fiona said, then pointed to Emile. "He's a da."

Before Fiona realized what she had done, Angelle turned to Emile, grabbed the front of his shirt and repeated, "Da!"

Emile gazed up at Fiona expectantly. "What does it mean?"

All Fiona had to do was meet those gigantic brown eyes and a flush burned across her face. Emile had to have guessed what the word meant, for he silently returned to dishing up breakfast. Angelle, however, refused to let the word go and continued saying it to Emile's back. The friend joined in the fun, playing with Angelle's hands while he repeated the word. Angelle, however, wanted nothing to do with him. She immediately let out a piercing yell.

"She needs changing," Fiona said and excused herself. As she passed Emile at the fireside, he suddenly turned and they collided. Emile caught Fiona by the elbow to keep her from falling, and their eyes met and lingered. "Da," Angelle said once more, and Emile smiled, kissing the top of her head.

"You're the only man she's known well," Fiona whispered apologetically to him, acutely aware of how close he stood and the tantalizing aroma of coffee, burning cedar and cane syrup about him. He looked and smelled good enough to eat.

"And what about you?" Emile asked seductively, his rich brown eyes searching hers as if peering into her soul.

Fiona felt the blush return, burning wild across her cheeks. Emile took the opportunity to brush his thumb across the soft spot in the cove of her elbow, and the slight action sent goose bumps across her arm.

Behind them, Fiona heard a chair scraping across the floor and Hypolite clearing his throat. When she turned, the man was gulping down his coffee and pulling on his coat with his free hand. He said something to Emile, and the two instantly erupted into an incomprehensible conversation. Finally, Emile turned back to Fiona. "I must go now," he said, placing the leftover breakfast on the table and grabbing his own coat.

Panic seized Fiona. "Where?" she asked a bit too loudly and a bit too anxiously. It stopped both men completely.

"I have lost days of work, *cher*," Emile said, apparently surprised at the question.

Fiona looked at the friend, expecting him to insist upon dragging her into town, but he said and did nothing. Fiona grabbed Emile's sleeves, leaned toward him and whispered, "What about him?"

Emile straightened, asked Hypolite a few questions, and the friend offered up some answers. "I'm going to take him to the store in the pirogue, save him the walk," Emile said with a shrug. "Is there anything you need while I'm there?"

Emile placed an arm about her shoulders. "I have to check my traps," he said softly. "I'll be back by lunch." With a twinkle and a grin, he added, "I have yet to make you my *court-bouillon.*"

While Fiona watched in amazement, the friend tipped his hat and exited the cabin, followed by Emile. She watched as they made their way to the banked pirogue, loaded it up and moved it toward the bayou.

"Flour," she shouted to them, feeling every bit as crazy as Emile. "I need flour."

Fiona spent a good part of the morning washing the clothes they had discarded by the fire the night before and sewing playclothes for Angelle from some of Aristide's remnants. Angelle was content to sit by the fire, chewing on her latest present from Emile, a strip of leather containing an odd assortment of animal teeth. If Fiona didn't know better, she would swear they once belonged to an alligator. Now, if only Emile would make her a cradle so Angelle wouldn't have to sleep on the bed, Fiona thought, feeling a girlish smile creep over her face. Too bad Emile wasn't here to see it. The poor man had tried everything to make her smile, and here she was grinning at the thought of him.

Fiona should have felt ashamed for the way she had acted the night before, but for the life of her she could only feel elated at her newfound love. Her common sense urged her to reconsider, to guard her heart against this man who could very easily be planning her removal from the warm hearth she now sat beside. But if Emile was that kind of man, he would have left her at the store the first day they met, she reasoned. He took them in because it was the proper thing to do; he fed and clothed them because he cared.

He did care, didn't he? Were the kisses he offered just a lonely man's need or did Emile feel as she did? In the grand scheme of things, were Fiona and Emile merely ships passing in the night, soon to separate and never meet again or was there a greater force at work bringing them together?

Fiona placed another log on the flame. The smoldering embers reacted by sending up a burst of sparks, while the new damp log hissed and sputtered.

Standing and wiping her sooted hands on her apron, Fiona caught sight of the letter, the fateful parchment that had led her to Bayou Paradis. Lying next to the envelope on the mantel were the papers Emile had produced legally proving he was the heir and owner of Aristide's property. Fiona reached out and touched them gingerly, still amazed at the power those three papers held.

"What difference does it make if I love him or not," she whispered to no one. "I have wronged him."

The old doubts and guilt returned, and Fiona turned away from the hearth, searching for something new to do, anything to keep her mind off the fear of leaving her beloved home. She spotted the broom and eagerly grabbed it. She would give the cabin a thorough scrubbing.

Starting with the filthiest corner, Fiona began to sweep, repeating with each stride a vow not to cry. It was in mid-stroke, as she was swallowing down the largest lump, that the first knock sounded at the door. A tiny, wrinkled face topped by a dark, thick braid of hair peered inside the front window.

"Bonjour," a tiny voiced cried out, followed by the deep timber of Hypolite Aucoin. "Bonjour," he echoed.

"Bonjour," Fiona answered, wondering what fate was in store for her on the other side of that door. When she pulled it open gingerly, broomstick still held tightly in her hand, she found the morning visitor smiling broadly beside a petite, elderly woman who barely reached Fiona's shoulders. Both seemed amazingly happy to see her.

The older woman instantly took her hand and squeezed, staring into her eyes with a warm intensity Fiona had not witnessed since leaving Ireland. She murmured something in French, patted Fiona's hand reassuringly, then surprised her by planting two kisses on each cheek while firmly grasping her shoulders. When the small woman finally pulled back from her embrace, she astonished Fiona even more by leaning forward and kissing the broomstick in her hand. Behind them, Fiona heard Hypolite laugh, and she wondered what odd Acadian custom revolved around brooms.

Chapter Seven

*"Ah, how skillful grows the hand
That obeyeth Love's command."*
—*Henry Wadsworth Longfellow*

Emile dipped his paddle through the emerald algae that floated on the top of the bayou's waters and watched the assortment of birds in a variety of colors dart from his path. The sun beamed down through the grove of cypress trees and evergreen pines and palmettos, warming his shoulder. So much color, so much life in the dead of winter, he thought. But no matter what crossed his path that day, all Emile could focus on was Isabelle.

He could feel her now, so warm and soft in his arms, the smell of soap in her hair, the taste of spices on her fingertips. They fit so perfectly together, as natural as the moss hanging from the branches of the bayou's trees. They belonged together. Two lonely exiles, cast off by the English, making their way to this remote corner of the American frontier, two grieving people offering comfort in each other's arms.

Was it merely loneliness? Emile wondered. The need for companionship? Was it only to satisfy the natural desires every young bachelor suffered? Or was he finally falling in love?

He could picture the tilt of her curious face and the cautious light of her emerald eyes when he would place another culinary creation before her. Or how her eyes studied him when he told a joke without cracking a smile. The way the edges of her lips would rise ever so slightly when she knew she was being joshed. How she listened to every word of his stories, correcting his English here and there.

Then there was Angelle. Darling Angelle.

Emile closed his eyes to ward off the now familiar tightness in his chest. If this wasn't love, then the real thing was a killer.

He had to tell her, confess his feelings, make her stay. It would solve their problems—and certainly please Nana in the process. Isabelle could stay with Nana until a visiting priest arrived or they could travel to Franklin and marry at the church there with his family present.

His mother, who was as eager for him to marry as Nana, would approve of Isabelle; he was sure of it. Despite the language barrier, they shared a lot of similarities. What a sight those two would make, Emile thought with a grin. His mother talking non-stop in French while shy Isabelle would only be able to smile and nod politely. Well, at least maybe someone would make her smile.

But marriage? Emile dug his paddle deeper and hurried his stroke. What was he thinking? He enjoyed his solitude, his simple life on the bayou. He answered to no one, came and went as he pleased. Marriage was not a step to consider lightly.

"Is this a conspiracy?" he asked the quiet bayou. "Father, are you and Nana behind this?"

The bayou became eerily quiet. Even the migrating robins, wrens and blackbirds were hushed. Silence and solitude could strangle the most cautious of men, Emile thought as the absence of noise reminded him just how isolated he was. He enjoyed it now, but how would the remote bayou and woods appear a year from now? Or ten? Besides, he had learned something important last night, and Isabelle had helped him see the light. A man need not grieve alone to ease his suffering.

And what of her pain?

Emile plied faster, eager to return home. He would solve this mystery. For some concealed reason Isabelle— or whatever name the impostor was called—was drawn to Bayou Paradis and his home. She needed him. And whether he wanted to admit it or not, he needed her.

The cabin emerged through the trees as he rounded the bend, and Emile found himself smiling. Tonight was the *fais do do,* the weekly house dance at Eraste Boudreaux's home. He would introduce Isabelle as his cousin, suggest Nana take her and Angelle into her home (which his god-mother was sure to do), then court her properly like a well-mannered suitor.

Emile banked his pirogue, gathered his things and headed for the cistern. He needed to wash before entering the house. He would be asking a woman to accompany him to a dance, and he had to look his best.

Despite the brisk weather, Emile removed his shirt, opened the faucet, leaned over and let the icy water pour over his neck and head. The chilly water stunned him as the bayou had the day before, but he threw his head back and laughed, shaking the moisture from his hair. Grabbing a bar of soap by the cistern's edge, he vigorously washed, then immersed himself in the cold water once again. He felt invigorated and began to hum an old French tune his father had taught him during their long stretches in the wetlands.

It was then he noticed the shadow pass over the sun.

He squinted his eyes to make out the image, but not before the fist struck his face and knocked him off his feet. Emile grabbed his injured chin and immediately glanced up to face his enemy, only to find Isabelle standing before him, her hands angrily planted at her hips.

"How dare you?" she shouted. "How could you do such a despicable thing?"

Before he could retaliate, Isabelle stormed inside the house, the door slamming in her wake. She hadn't hit him hard, although a small throb was beginning along the perimeter of his jaw, but Emile was stunned.

He grabbed his shirt and followed, relieved to find the roaring fire in the hearth and a grinning Angelle welcoming him home. "Da!" she exclaimed, and Isabelle turned from her place at the fireside and aimed another strike his way. This time, Emile was on his guard and grabbed her wrist in time.

"What is the matter with you?" he demanded.

"You know well what the matter is," she answered, jerking her hand from his grip. "How dare you do this to me? To Angelle? How could you be so heartless?"

What his married friends had said was true, after all. Women made no sense. "I have no idea why you are angry at me," Emile said, rubbing the side of his jaw. "Why don't you start by telling me what I have done."

Isabelle folded her arms across her chest and stared at the bed. A selection of clothes and a wedding circle quilt were lying there. "What is this?" Emile asked.

Isabelle huffed. "As if you didn't know."

He was tiring of this mystery. Nothing made sense. "Isabelle, would you please tell me what's going on?" Emile demanded.

Isabelle sat down, arms still defiantly locked in front of her. "You told your friend this morning that we were married," she said through gritted teeth.

Emile stared back dumbfounded, while his mind raced. "What?" he asked, all the while recounting what he and 'Polite had discussed that morning.

"You told him we were married," Isabelle repeated. "He and your Nana showed up later with presents and congratulations."

This time Emile sat down, rubbing more than his jaw. What had he said to Hypolite? His friend must have caught them in bed together, but did he admit to as much? Out of the corner of his eye, Emile saw the broom resting against the sideboard. Suddenly, he understood. *"Merde,"* he said, closing his eyes and rubbing the bridge of his nose with his thumb and forefinger.

"You told him, didn't you?" Isabelle insisted, her tone softer this time. "You told him we were married."

Emile opened his eyes and saw the hurt in hers. He reached over and grabbed her outside hand, then unfolded her arms so that both her hands could be held inside his. "I joked about the broom," he assured her. "It was a misunderstanding."

She didn't believe him. Her eyes stared at him accusingly.

"We don't have priests out here," he continued. "When a couple wants to marry, they jump the broom. It's a tradition, admittedly a silly one."

Isabelle tried to remove her hands, but Emile held them tightly. "So you told him we jumped the broom," she said stiffly, watching as he brushed his thumbs over her knuckles.

"It was a joke," Emile insisted. "He misunderstood." Emile reached up and tilted her chin so that their eyes met. "Tonight is the *fais do do*. Everyone will be there. I'll explain."

Isabelle's eyes softened. "What's a *fais do do?*" she asked.

Emile leaned back in his chair and pulled out his pocket

watch. "A dance. One that starts very soon." Replacing the watch, he added with a smile, "Madame Dugas, it would give me great pleasure if you and your darling child would accompany me."

Isabelle turned away and swallowed hard, and for a moment Emile thought she would cry. "It was a joke?" she practically whispered. "You and me jumping the broom?"

Women were a puzzle. First she was angry for being thought of as his wife; now she appeared upset that she wasn't. "It wasn't a joke, *cher*," he said softly. " 'Polite saw us together this morning, and I didn't know how to respond. I was being . . . what is the word?"

"Sarcastic?" Isabelle offered.

"Oui." That was the word, wasn't it? Emile sure hoped so. God help him if it meant something else.

Isabelle reacted positively, which gave him confidence. "Why don't you wear the clothes Nana brought over and I'll go upstairs and change," he said. When Isabelle glanced at his bare chest and blushed profusely, he added with a smile, "I would have been properly dressed to meet you, madame, but my bath was rudely interrupted."

He hoped for a smile, but Isabelle looked as glum as ever. "I can't wear those clothes," she said sadly. "They're wedding presents."

It was then Emile took a good look at the garments laid out on the bed—a white cotton shirt and petticoat, a brown full skirt and a sky blue vest and *garde de soleil,* or sun bonnet. Beside the ensemble were cotton stockings and leather shoes and a pair of silk ribbons to wear in her hair. It was the standard Acadian dress for women, an enormous improvement over Isabelle's threadbare clothes and one she must have been wishing with all her heart to wear.

Emile took her hands once again. "Nana would want you to have these, regardless of whether we're married," he said seriously. "We're Acadians. We take care of each other."

"She will think badly of me," Isabelle whispered, staring into her lap. "I couldn't possibly accept such kindness when she has been deceived."

Emile softly placed a finger at her chin and tilted her face upward so that their eyes met once again. "We take care of each other," he repeated slowly and succinctly.

Volumes of words seemed to pass between them during those few silent moments. For the first time since she had arrived, Emile was convinced Isabelle Dugas—or whoever she was—trusted him. He slipped his hand against her cheek and lovingly caressed it. For an instant he could have sworn she smiled.

"Now we must get ready," Emile insisted. "I will go upstairs to dress, and you will knock with the broom on the ceiling to let me know you are finished, yes?"

"Oui," Isabelle answered, the edges of her lips turning skyward ever so slightly.

The effect made Emile feel weightless as he bounded up the stairs. He was greeted with his own ensemble of clothes laid out neatly upon his bed, everything meticulously cleaned and pressed by the woman who had most definitely stolen his heart.

"Look, Angelle." Fiona threw the petticoat into the air so that the yards of material fluttered about her. "A new petticoat."

While Angelle gurgled with delight as she chewed on the new shoes, Fiona slipped on each garment, each time admiring the smooth yet sturdy cotton fabric and the majestic depth of color of the indigo-dyed vest. Looking in the mirror atop the bureau, Fiona swore it was another woman's reflection staring back.

Could it be possible to live a normal life? Fiona wondered. Without a doubt, she knew she dearly loved Emile, even if she wasn't exactly sure she trusted him.

Fiona tapped the ceiling with the now famous broomstick, and in an instant, he was at the door. The astonished look on his face mirrored her own thoughts. Someone else, a prettier, healthier girl, was wearing these clothes.

He murmured something in French, then smiled, not his usual carefree grin she had grown to know and love, but a slow, appreciative one. "Madame Dugas," he said admiringly. "You are quite a lovely sight."

Fiona blushed and felt the semblance of a grin steal across her face, for she was thinking the same thing of Emile, dressed in his clean cotton shirt, vest, trousers and coat and newly shined leather boots that reached up to the knee.

Emile's eyes grew brighter, and he stepped so close to Fiona she could smell the store-bought tonic. "Did I see a smile on those lips?" he asked.

Fiona blushed again and looked away. "Should I wear my coat or would the shawl Nana brought be enough to keep me warm?"

Emile leaned over, picked up Angelle and raised her high into the air, which made her giggle. "Wear the shawl," he said. "If it becomes cold tonight, I will give you my coat."

Fiona wanted to argue that his suggestion was gentlemanly but imprudent, but Emile was headed for the door. She quickly placed her shawl about her shoulders and seized the basket containing a blanket for Angelle and followed them onto the porch, still warmed by the late afternoon sun. Emile hesitated and held out his free arm for her to take, and the three made their way down the bank to the sleepy bayou and the waiting pirogue.

As Fiona looked up at her Gabriel, a wave of anxiety

washed over her. "I can't believe that only yesterday it was bitter cold," she said, hoping the small talk would relieve her worries.

Emile helped her into the boat, then followed, still holding Angelle as if she weighed no more than a feather. "Louisiana is a mysterious place," Emile said, as he pushed the pirogue off the bank. "Tomorrow may be as hot as summer."

They talked little as they made their way down the bayou, remarking only on the birds and plants they passed and reacting to Angelle as she gleefully sang a chorus of incomprehensible sounds. It wasn't long before they heard the music of a fiddle, its owner sending forth a tune so mournful that the notes seemed to glide upon the bayou's water.

"That's Ozide, Hypolite's father," Emile explained. "He loves the sad love songs."

As they made their way toward the house, Fiona saw a large group of people standing on the bank, looking in their direction. If it hadn't seemed so absurd, she would swear they were waiting for her and Emile to arrive. Emile shifted, glanced toward the house and stopped paddling. When he turned back and his eyes caught hers, his gaze spoke of alarm. The whole town could know by now, Fiona thought as she anxiously clutched the soft shawl wrapped about her shoulders. Emile must have read her mind, for he reiterated, "I'll explain."

They banked the pirogue next to an assemblage of other like canoes and made their way toward the house. In the meantime, the residents of Bayou Paradis approached, large grins on all their faces. Emile put up a hand to stop their offers of congratulations and began to speak, but was quickly interrupted by a large man who spoke French while patting him affectionately on the back. Emile began again, but another man shook his hand while another offered a toast and the rest of the group cheered. One of the women approached Fiona, but she couldn't understand a word the nice woman was saying. Emile looked back at the exchange, sighed and made what Fiona guessed was an introduction, for she heard "Isabelle Dugas" being spoken. The rest of the women approached then, asking questions, admiring Angelle. Fiona felt her throat constricting, at a loss for what to do. When she caught Emile's gaze, she knew he was suffering the same fate.

Suddenly, a hush fell on the group, and a path was cut through its center. Nana, dressed in her Sunday best, marched down to where Fiona and Emile stood.

"Nana," Emile began, then launched into what Fiona assumed was an explanation, but he never got the chance. Nana silenced him with a stern look, then kissed him once on both cheeks, turned and did the same to Fiona.

"Nana," Emile tried again, but Nana simply grabbed Fiona's arm and led her toward the house, sending Emile a stiff maternal look when she passed. As she was being paraded through the crowd, Fiona looked over her shoulder to Emile, now surrounded by talking, laughing men, one placing a drink in his hand, another throwing an amiable punch to his arm. When he looked up at her, he owned the gaze of a defeated man.

Nana led Fiona and Angelle into the warm house, divided into two sections by a fireplace. On one side, most of the furniture had been moved to the back porch so that there was ample space in the middle of the room. On the other side, Fiona could make out a collection of blankets placed upon the floor and several cots and beds lined against the wall.

All of the women had followed them inside, and there was much conversation among them. Fiona could understand nothing. One thing she did understand. Nana was extremely pleased she had worn the clothes, visibly amazed they fit her so well. She clapped her hands together and looked skyward as if in prayer.

"Nana." Fiona heard Emile behind her and turned to find him still surrounded by jovial men who appeared pleased by his obvious discomfort. "Nana," he repeated louder, but was quickly interrupted by the man holding the fiddle. Ozide Aucoin, she surmised, approached the group and proclaimed something in French, which sent up a round of agreement. The only person who didn't seem to enjoy his suggestion, whatever it was, was Emile.

Nana held out her arms to Angelle, and much to Fiona's surprise, the baby agreeably left her arms for Nana's. She then felt a push toward the center of the room. When she turned back to find Emile, he was standing next to her, voicing his disapproval to whoever was pushing him.

"What is it?" Fiona asked him in a whisper.

"They want us to dance," he mumbled as Ozide performed a slow, rhymic tune. Emile retrieved a red handkerchief from his coat pocket and wrapped it around his hand. "It's a tradition," he added glumly as he placed his covered hand at her waist. Fiona gingerly accepted his outstretched hand and placed her other on his shoulder.

"What kind of dance is this?" Fiona asked, hoping she wouldn't embarrass herself and Emile.

"It's a waltz," Emile explained. "Three steps, with an accent on the first. Follow my lead."

They slowly made their way around the room while Ozide performed a lovely tune and one of the women sang. Emile counted out loud until Fiona perfected the steps; then he grew silent, as every eye watched them circle the floor.

"I'm sorry, Isabelle," Emile finally said. "I tried to—"

"I know," she interrupted. The two grew silent again as

they danced among a host of smiling faces. Fiona couldn't help wishing their marriage waltz was real.

"They're excited I finally got married," Emile offered. "They have been trying to marry me off since I moved back."

"Why haven't you?" Fiona felt a surge of hope run through her. Maybe there was no other woman who had caught the eye of Emile Dugas.

"Never met the right woman," Emile answered, and Fiona's breath caught.

"What is the right woman?" Fiona couldn't believe she had uttered such a thing, yet she couldn't help herself.

Emile pulled back just enough to look into her face. His friendly brown eyes sparkled in the candlelight. "Honest?" he asked.

"Yes," Fiona said, although she feared what honesty he might impart.

"Someone like you."

Everything in the room faded, the music, the smiling Acadians, the young children darting through the door. All she could comprehend was the man before her, leading her through a waltz through heaven.

"What kind of man do you wish to marry, Isabelle?" Emile asked, unsmiling, breaking her from her thoughts.

Fiona almost laughed then, but she still wasn't convinced he meant to marry *her*. "A good father to Angelle," she began and noticed Emile's countenance relax. "Someone I could feel safe with," she continued. "Someone who could make me smile."

Again, Emile pulled away and gazed into her eyes seriously. "Isabelle," he whispered, "would it be so bad if you stayed married to me?"

Before she could respond, the music ended, and Ozide announced something loudly to the group, who responded by sending up a collective voice of approval. Emile objected in French, clearly upset, which made everyone laugh and continue to push the subject.

"Now what?" Fiona asked.

Emile grinded his teeth and folded his hands across his chest. "They want us to kiss," he muttered. "Since we didn't allow them the pleasure when we jumped the broom without them."

Fiona blushed, and Emile grabbed her hand and moved closer. "I have their attention now," he whispered hot against her ear, which sent goose bumps racing up her arms. "I could explain now."

Fiona turned toward the group where two dozen friendly faces stared back. These were nice people, her kind of people. A community who took care of their own, who reveled in the pleasure of another's happiness. She could see by the smiles that they loved Emile and were thrilled that he had found a woman to share his life. And then there was Nana, beaming at them both with Angelle happily cooing in her arms.

It reminded her so much of home, Fiona felt the familiar grief choking her. This was everything her parents had wished for her, what she had promised Mattie on her death bed. A slice of heaven where the air was clear and the land was green.

And then there was Emile.

She looked up into his enormous brown eyes and wondered if Mary had indeed answered her prayers by sending that letter at that particular moment to the wrong church. Could it be possible to be so blessed after years of such hardship and pain?

She wanted this. She wanted it all. Most of all, she wanted Emile. Every day. Every night. For the rest of her life.

"Well," Fiona finally answered with a slight smile. "You still haven't made me your famous *court-bouillon*."

Emile's brow tightened, clearly puzzled at her joke and her grin. But before he could react, Fiona raised herself onto her toes and planted a kiss on his lips before God and the entire population of Bayou Paradis.

Chapter Eight

*"Every house was an inn, where all were welcomed
and feasted;
For with this simple people, who lived like brothers
together,
All things were held in common, and what one
had was another's."*

—Henry Wadsworth Longfellow

Emile stood at the periphery of the dance floor, his shoulder leaning against the door frame as he watched Isabelle dance a mazurka with Eraste Boudreaux. The man seemed to be telling her his life story—or worse, flirting—while Isabelle smiled as he led her across the floor.

She was smiling! He had spent days trying to bring mirth to those precious lips and here she was bestowing on Eraste what he had hoped for himself. Eraste hadn't been the first either. When the men took turns at the dance of the four corners of the handkerchief, where each participant would dance at one corner of the handkerchief spread out on the floor, then leap to dance at the opposite corner, Isabelle had actually laughed when she proclaimed Matthew Landry the winner. The reel was her favorite, though. She took to it instantly.

Despite his jealousy, he marveled at the way her face lit up, spreading a crimson glow about her cheeks and making her eyes dance with merriment. She seemed reborn, brought back from the depths of despair, and he was happy for it.

Still, he couldn't help wonder if it was he who made her smile. She had offered that fateful kiss, that silent pledge of affection and matrimony that sealed their future together. He should feel trapped, much like Isabelle had that morning when she learned she had been cornered into marriage without her approval. But he had asked for it. He didn't know who was more surprised at that moment when she perched herself on her toes and kissed him, Emile for getting his answer with a kiss or Isabelle when he had instantly placed a hand at her waist and deepened the affection. Looking at his smiling wife, he could still feel the power of that kiss, a moment he would remember all his life.

"She's a darling girl," said Nana as she joined him at the threshold.

Emile turned toward his godmother, relieved that they were finally alone together. "What did you do, Nana?" Emile asked. "Did you put a *gris-gris* on that broom?"

Nana huffed. "How dare you suggest such a thing. I don't practice black magic."

Emile smiled and took her petite hand. "You did something."

Nana reached up with her other hand and touched his cheek lovingly. "Silly boy. I did what we all have been doing since you arrived here two years ago, praying that you find a soul mate and stop grieving in solitude."

Usually talk of Emile's father ended all conversation, but tonight, for the first time, Emile was ready to discuss it. "It wasn't my fault," he said, surprised at how that simple statement lessened the weight of the guilt from his shoulders. He breathed deep and exhaled.

"Of course not, *'tit chou.*" Nana squeezed his hand. "Your father took too many chances. He never should have been where he was that day."

Emile had always thought as much, but felt he betrayed his father for thinking such a thing. He knew now that it wasn't the grief that had silenced him as a youth and kept him guilt-ridden for so long. He was angry with his father for gambling with his life and hurting the ones who loved him. And that was the hardest guilt of all.

Emile thought to voice his feelings, but when he looked at Nana, he found her smiling, tears running down her face. She knew he had found peace at last.

Brushing the tears and the emotions away, Nana turned toward the dance floor where Isabelle was thanking Hypolite for their turn at a polka. "She's not Acadian," Nana stated matter-of-factly.

"No," Emile answered, surprised that she knew. "Does it matter?"

"Can she swim?"

Emile had to laugh. Nana would always be concerned for his welfare. "As a matter of fact," Emile began, "she dragged me out of the bayou yesterday when I foolishly chased my pirogue into the freezing waters."

Nana made the sign of the cross, and her eyes filled with tears once more. "She's perfect for you."

Despite his efforts to remain single, he couldn't agree more. "*Oui,* Nana," he said, taking her hands and kissing them. "I'm afraid I'm in love."

Nana squeezed his hands once again, this time unsmiling. "Just beware, Emile. We know nothing about her."

"I thought you said it didn't matter."

"It doesn't. She's a wonderful girl; I knew it the moment I saw her." Nana paused and glanced at Isabelle attempting a contre danse. "But a person's past can sometimes be like a sly alligator. When you least expect it, it will reach up and bite you in the rear."

Emile followed Nana's gaze and watched as a grinning Isabelle stared at her feet and counted, hoping to follow the other dancers in their steps. He thought of the scared, fearful look she had exhibited when she first arrived and how long it had taken for her to trust him. And he thought of Angelle, his precious snow angel. "No one will harm my family," he asserted firmly, feeling a sense of pride flow through him. "No one."

What next? Fiona wondered when the fiddler started up another tune. She swore she had danced with every man in the house that evening, all talking incessantly in French about God knew what. But heaven help her, she was having fun. She hadn't danced like that since the spring festival in Kenmare, when her mother had decorated her hair with a collection of dainty ribbons and she had at least three suitors begging for a dance. Three young boys who were dead now, all victims of the blight.

Fiona closed her eyes and wished the memory away. She wouldn't think about that now, not on the first happy night in years. Shutting out the painful recollection, she concentrated instead on the fiddler's song, a ballad that reminded her of Ireland. For a brief moment, she was home, dancing to Michael McKernan's fiddle at a *cuaird* with her family and friends, while her father offered tales as old as the burial stones on the hill. The song sounded so familiar a rush of shivers overtook her before she opened her eyes and realized she was still in the southwest bayous of Louisiana.

None of the men had since approached her, and the women were tending to their young, unmarried daughters hoping for a dance or preparing for the midnight gumbo. Could it be possible she had danced with every man present, as was the custom for a bride? Fiona quickly took the opportunity to retreat to the porch for some fresh air and to hopefully find Emile alone.

What was he thinking now, she wondered, married to a woman who had dropped out of the sky hoping to displace him from his home? He believed himself married to a distant cousin who had a right to live among these kind people. Fiona rubbed her forehead. Then there was the fact that they weren't really married. She was in a pickle, to be sure.

From the children's room came a soft baby's cry, and Fiona rushed inside to see if the source was Angelle. To her surprise, Emile had beaten her there, gently touching the sleeping child's forehead for signs of fever. Nothing could possibly have affected her more than the sight of her Gabriel caring for her adopted child, lovingly stroking her hair as if she were his own. If God had granted her wish for a home and family, he had delivered the finest of men.

Fiona silently reached his side and took his hand. "Emile," she whispered, emotions threatening her voice. "There is something I have to tell you."

Emile gazed down at her, his bronze eyes twinkling in the moonlight pouring in from the window. "Let me guess," he whispered back. "Your name's not Isabelle. You're not Acadian. And you come from a foreign land across the ocean."

Fiona tried to talk, to explain why she had lied, but the words wouldn't pass her lips. To her surprise, Emile didn't seem the least bit concerned about her falsehoods.

"How they call your name, *cher*?" he asked sweetly.

Fiona wanted to explain, to recite the story she had rehearsed repeatedly since her arrival, but she was entranced by the lilting tone of his seductive voice and his unique expression asking for her name. "Fiona," was all she could muster. "Fiona Riley."

Emile smiled and cupped her cheek with his hand. "Fiona," he repeated in the Cajun accent she had grown to cherish. "Fiona Riley."

Before she could adequately digest what had transpired, Emile lowered his lips to hers and kissed her. It was a soft kiss, gentle and unobtrusive, sending tingling sensations all the way to her knees. After several moments, he pulled back slightly and gazed into her eyes as he stroked her cheek with his thumb.

"Emile," Fiona began, trying not to be seduced by the gentle hand caressing her face. "You don't understand. I'm not a Dugas."

Emile smiled his familiar grin. "You are now."

He kissed her again, this time more passionately, pulling her close with his other hand at her waist. There was still so much to discuss, so much to explain, but Fiona abandoned all reason and slid an arm up the front of his shirt until it reached his neck, where she threaded her fingers into his dark, silky hair. Emile moaned and drew her closer, deepening his kiss and flooding her being with feelings that reminded her of the ocean at Waterville: wild, startling and invigorating, yet pulsating and soothing. After what seemed like an eternity of bliss, Emile pulled away and rested his forehead against hers, the light of passion shining in his eyes. "Fiona," he whispered seductively. "Will you marry me?"

It was spoken so unexpectedly, Fiona couldn't help herself. She began to laugh. First a soft giggle so as not to wake the babies, then a louder chuckle that forced her to cup her hand over her mouth. While she fought to control herself, Emile stared, clearly disturbed by her lack of decorum at such an intimate moment. "I finally get you to laugh and it's at the thought of marrying me?" he asked, unsmiling.

Fiona lovingly brushed her knuckles against Emile's tanned cheek, touched by both his proposal and his fear of her rejection. "No, my darling," she assured him. "I would be honored to be your wife. It's just that everything happened backwards. First I inherited a baby; then I was given presents, a wedding reception and a husband, and I'm not even engaged."

Emile's eyes resumed their usual twinkle as he placed his hand over hers, turned his head and passionately kissed her wrist. "I can remedy that," he whispered as his tongue traced her life line, sending a delicious shiver through her. "As long as you don't hit me again," he added with a grin.

"Emile, I am so sorry—" Before Fiona could finish, Emile silenced her with another kiss, finishing it off with a gentle bite at her lower lip. With her hands free, Fiona circled her arms about his shoulders and hugged him tight, entranced by the feel of his hair against her cheek and his body pressed hard against hers.

"We could go to Franklin and get married there at the church," Emile said, nibbling at her neck. "You could stay with Nana until the wedding."

Fiona drew away abruptly and searched his eyes. "Must I leave you?"

"Mon amour," Emile explained in a brotherly tone, "we're not married."

Fiona frowned and began to play with the button at his collar. "But we have the broom," she whispered.

The smile that overtook Emile's face was blinding. She could almost feel the warmth pouring from his eyes. "I was hoping you would say that," he uttered before once again taking possession of her lips.

Their kiss was instantly interrupted, however, by the sound of a woman clearing her throat. They turned to find

Nana standing before them, uttering a command in French with Fiona's shawl and basket in her outstretched hands.

Fiona looked up at Emile for a translation, hoping Nana was suggesting what she thought she was suggesting. "She says we should leave," Emile said, gladly accepting Fiona's things and kissing Nana in the process. "It's time for the gumbo, and if we leave now, they may not know we're missing."

Suddenly, Fiona thought of the nice people who had made her welcome in their home, the women offering their wishes and presents, and the men so eager to dance with Emile's wife, and she felt guilty for wanting to be rid of them so quickly. "We must say our goodbyes," she insisted, but Emile grabbed her elbow.

"Tomorrow," Emile said and gently retrieved Angelle and headed for the door.

Fiona followed him out of the *parc aux petits* where the many children were sleeping peacefully, but stopped at the threshold, turned and rushed back into Nana's arms. Hugging her close, she managed one of the few French phrases she knew. *"Merci,* Nana. *Merci beaucoup."*

Nana pressed a hand to Fiona's face and held her close, then kissed her cheek and nudged her away. *"Allez,"* she whispered, and Fiona left to join Emile at the bayou's edge.

The paddle home seemed twice as long, but infinitely more relaxing. Fiona rested her back against Emile's long legs with Angelle sleeping comfortably in her lap. Emile spoke of his family in Franklin, of his talkative, lovable mother who, believe it or not, was a better cook than he, he explained with a laugh. Then there were two brothers, both unmarried and wilder than a Gulf storm in August. And cousins. Lots and lots of cousins. Just about everybody for miles around was related to him in some sort of way.

"Which will make for a big church wedding when we finally make it to Franklin," Emile explained.

They banked the pirogue and carefully moved Angelle into the house so as not to wake her. When Fiona spotted the bed, she instantly remembered the night before when Angelle had slept between them, and wondered how they would master being husband and wife with a baby in the middle. As if he read her mind, Emile emitted a sly grin and removed one of the bureau drawers and placed it next to the hearth. He quickly rearranged the garments inside, creating a makeshift pillow and bedding for the child. Fiona was amazed. She had never thought of such a simple yet ingenious thing.

Fiona kneeled and placed the sleeping child into the makeshift cradle. When she returned to a standing position, Emile instantly engulfed her in his large, powerful arms and held her tight. Fiona shut her eyes and enjoyed the feel of his broad, strong back and shoulders, the soft cotton fabric which held a masculine scent brushing against her cheek, and his comforting arms holding her close. She prayed that this was no dream. That she would open her eyes and her Gabriel would still be there.

"Shall I get the broom?" Emile whispered into her ear, his hot breath sending wild vibrations through her.

"Oui," she answered, then added with a mischievous grin, *"dépeche-toi!"*

For the second time that evening, Emile's face exploded with delight. "I shall hurry, indeed," he said, then quickly retrieved the broomstick from the corner of the kitchen and placed it on the floor before them. He held out his hand to her, and Fiona happily accepted. They stood side by side, gazing into each other's eyes, both grinning profusely.

"Fiona Isabelle Dugas Riley," Emile started. "I promise to be a good father to Angelle. I promise to keep you safe. And I promise to try to make you laugh all the days of my life."

Fiona grinned broadly and felt a wild, fiery blush color her cheeks. "Emile Dugas," she answered. "I promise to learn French. I promise to keep *you* safe. And I promise to eat everything you put in front of me."

Emile's smile deepened, and he leaned down to kiss her. "Wait," Fiona commanded him. "We must jump first."

"On the count of three," Emile said. *"Un, deux, trois."*

The couple jumped across the broom and landed a bit too hard on the other side. While Emile grabbed Fiona's arm to resume her balance, they both glanced toward Angelle to see if she had awakened. To their relief, the baby slept peacefully.

When they looked back toward one another, they stared silently into each other's eyes for several moments. Then slowly, Fiona placed a hand on Emile's shoulder, and Emile gently slid his fingers into her auburn hair, slipping it free of its ribbon. He lightly brushed his lips across hers, then with one smooth movement grabbed her waist and pulled her tightly against him in an ardent embrace.

Fiona was thankful for the strong arm wrapped around her waist, for she doubted she could have stood on her own with the urgent kisses he delivered. When Emile began a slow descent down her neck and beneath her ear lobe, Fiona felt her knees go weak.

"Emile," she whispered. "The bed."

Emile didn't have to be asked twice. He effortlessly scooped her off the floor and carried her to the bed, kissing her all the while. When he placed her on the moss-filled mattress, finally giving her a chance to breathe, Fiona laughed. "Your kisses take my breath away," Fiona said as she gently pushed the fallen hair out of his eyes. "I've a reeling in my head from it all."

Emile answered with a seductive grin that made Fiona's insides feel like the syrup on his *pain perdu*. "I've been dreaming of this for days," he said heatedly.

To her amazement, instead of continuing the delicious kisses, Emile leaned back on his heels, far from her touch. But the separation didn't last long. He picked up her booted foot and placed it in his lap, then began the slow process of unlacing the shoe. After discarding both boots, Emile moved closer and surprised Fiona even more when he slowly slid his hands up the length of her legs, pushing her dress to her thighs and the garter that held her stockings in place.

His gaze never left hers as he slid first one finger then another inside the tight band and circled it slowly toward the inside of her thigh. As he pulled the garter and the corresponding stocking downward, Emile leaned forward and began kissing the places once covered by cotton.

Fiona gasped—loudly—as Emile left a trail of moist kisses along the inside of her thigh, the inner arch of her kneecap and the round curve of her calf. When he finished one leg, depositing the garter and stocking on the floor, he leaned forward again and began to kiss the other thigh, this time fanning his fingers out higher toward her inner femininity which was reacting quite profusely to his touch.

Mattie had always said lovemaking was enjoyable, but Fiona had no idea it was this exhilarating. When the French sailors had whistled at them on the boat, Mattie had giggled and relayed a rumor she heard that the French were liberal in the bedroom. "It's called the French way," Mattie said, alluding to something about tongues and kisses in places men shouldn't be kissing. But Fiona didn't mind.

After finishing with the second stocking, Emile straightened and gazed up at Fiona thoughtfully. "Are you scared, 'ti monde?" he asked sweetly.

Fiona ran both her hands through his hair and kissed him on the forehead. "No," she whispered, which gave him incentive to circle her waist and pull her legs around him while his tongue explored the deep, soft reaches of her mouth. The "French way," Fiona thought as she cautiously touched her tongue to his and felt a bolt of lightning race down her spine, was turning out to be quite nice.

Again, Emile left her mouth and nibbled at the tender skin along her cheekbone and the soft, ticklish spots at her nape. Fiona giggled, but leaned her head back for more. While Emile sent his kisses toward her neckline, he began unbuttoning her vest and the connections at her waist. Within minutes, the vest slipped off her shoulder, and she felt his hands softly caressing a breast, his flat palm massaging the awakening nipple. When his thumb found the pert nub and squeezed it gently, Fiona covered her mouth to keep from gasping for the second time that night.

The overwhelming emotions that swept through her gave Fiona courage, and she quickly untied the strings at her neck and removed her shirt while Emile did the same. He was bare-chested when they embraced once again, but she still had a corset and camisole to contend with. Emile tried to kiss her and remove the awkward garment at the same time Fiona wanted to run her fingers through the hairs on his chest. They stopped and began again, but their hands and kisses kept interfering with one another.

Emile sighed, something that sounded between a laugh and frustration. Fiona placed a hand on his cheek and kissed him deeply. "If you turn around, I'll undress," she whispered.

Emile instantly turned around on the bed, facing the other direction, and Fiona almost laughed at his eagerness. She quickly removed the corset, camisole and skirt, then slid herself underneath the covers. Without turning, Emile removed his trousers discreetly and joined her.

In a matter of seconds they were back in each other's arms, kissing, touching, exploring. He was so warm, so strong, so hard. And his lips were everywhere, driving her to a pinnacle of passion. When his kisses descended upon her breasts and lingered, his tongue teasing, his teeth nipping, racing her to the brink of ecstasy, she knew the time had come.

Emile gently entered, slowly bringing their bodies together. The pain was sharp at first, but dissolved quickly as they sought a mutual rhythm of pleasure. All his tender caresses had brought forth fervent sensations, but nothing equaled their coupling. Fiona felt a rush of desire building inside her, flowing through her veins with an increasingly wild ferocity. As their movements became more heated and faster, the desire increased until an enormous burst of elation enveloped her. While her body reacted in waves of passion, she called out exclamations in Irish. To her surprise, Emile shouted out similar thoughts, only his were in French.

Chapter Nine

*"Look not mournfully into the Past. It comes not
   back again.
Wisely improve the Present. It is thine. Go forth
   to meet the shadowy Future, without fear,
and a manly heart."*
                              —Henry Wadsworth Longfellow

Emile wrapped his arm around Fiona as she nestled into the curve of his shoulder. He couldn't remember a time when he felt more at peace. Breathing in the sweet feminine scent of her hair, Emile sighed, thankful at last that all their problems had been solved.

Or had they? There were still so many questions.

"Za'belle," Emile whispered, gently caressing her hair. When she looked up, Emile realized his mistake. "Fiona," he corrected himself, which made her smile. "Isn't there someone I should talk to, a family member to write about our marriage?"

The now familiar cloud passed over Fiona's eyes, darkening the sparkle their passion had produced, but Emile continued to lovingly caress her hair. "Where is your family, *cher?*" he insisted.

Fiona soberly laid her cheek against his chest. "I don't have any," she whispered.

Being one of literally dozens of cousins, Emile couldn't imagine a life without family. "Are you orphaned?" he asked. "Is there a brother, an uncle?"

When Fiona didn't answer, Emile wondered if she had been abandoned. He had heard that such atrocities occurred in large cities such as New Orleans. But there was Mattie. Surely, there was another friend or family member somewhere.

"Someone in Ireland?" Fiona still said nothing. She was so much like him, Emile thought, burying her grief deep within her soul, afraid that spoken words would only increase the sorrow.

"You must tell me, Fiona." Emile softly stroked her hair, wishing that she would feel comfortable enough to share her pain with him. "It won't help suffering alone. Trust me. I know."

"We lost everything," Fiona said quietly, then fell silent. It was a tidbit of information, but at least she was talking.

"When?" Emile softly prodded.

"When the blight returned," she continued. "It wasn't like the first time when we saved some of the potatoes. We had nothing to eat. Nothing. It was such everywhere in our county. Everyone was starving."

So he was right about Fiona having suffered dreadfully. "What happened to your family?" he asked again.

The silence that followed was so acute Emile could hear Angelle's breathing from across the room. Then Fiona continued.

"My baby brother and sister were the first to go," she said. "They were so small and frail. Their cries of hunger and pleading eyes begging for mercy were so hard for us to bear, but devastating to my mother. She died of grief two days later."

Fiona shivered, then sighed, the kind of exhalation that accompanies a wellspring of emotion. "My da tried to help by joining the public works project. He labored all day on a road that led nowhere, to return home exhausted with tenpence, hardly enough to keep us fed. I don't know when he died. The typhus overtook the household." Fiona swallowed hard and closed her eyes. "When I awoke, the rest of my family was gone."

Emile gently brushed the hair from her face while he kissed the top of Fiona's head. He slid his other arm around her and pulled her close. He wanted to build a fortress around her with his love, to chase the demons away, to let her know she was safe.

"I went to live with the nuns," she continued solemnly. "My priest, Father Ryan, raised enough money for me to come to America with my friends Mattie and Patrick Fitzgerald. Mattie was with child, and I was to help with the baby once we landed in New Orleans. Only Patrick died on the voyage, and Mattie became ill after Angelle was born. I promised Mattie I would take care of Angelle, bring her some place green."

Fiona grew silent again, and Emile wondered if she would finally tell of how she came in possession of the letter.

"I didn't mean to deceive you, Emile," Fiona whispered.

"I know, *mon amour*," he said, kissing her again and sliding his fingers up and down her arm in a gentle caress.

Fiona looked up again, resting her chin on his chest, the cloud still hovering in her emerald eyes. "I had no where to go, no place to live," she explained anxiously. "I sought solace in the church, and there was this man, with a letter, saying Aristide Dugas was dead and had no kin. I thought it was a sign from God. I didn't know you were . . ."

Emile placed his hands on her cheeks and silenced her

with a kiss. When he finally released her, there were tears streaming down her cheeks. "Can you ever forgive me?" she asked softly.

Emile turned on his side so that he could look down upon her face. He kissed the tears from her cheeks and brushed her hair off her forehead. "How could I not forgive a gift from God?" he asked, tears beaming in his own eyes.

"I love you, Emile," Fiona said, raising a hand to touch his face.

Emile kissed the inside of her palm. "I love you too, *mon amour.*"

Leaning back in the pirogue, letting the late winter sun warm her face, Fiona could scarcely believe only three weeks ago snow had fallen. She squinted when the light shone through the moss-covered branches of the overhanging cypress trees, smiling at the beauty of the clear Louisiana sky and the warm breeze blowing up from Lake Fausse Pointe.

"*Repetez,* Madame Dugas," Emile instructed as he plied his paddle effortlessly down the bayou.

Fiona sat up and smiled at her family, Emile with his haunting brown eyes always sparkling when he looked at her, and Angelle playing in her lap, still consumed by the necklace of teeth her "da" had given her. "What was the passage?" Fiona asked, too busy reveling in her happiness to have paid attention to her daily lesson.

"Evangeline was saying goodbye to Gabriel on the Canadian shore."

Fiona opened her tattered copy of "Evangeline" and turned to the proper verse. Learning English at Father Ryan's knee had been hard enough, now she was to learn French. Oddly enough, the more she heard French spoken by Emile and the other residents of Bayou Paradis, the more she comprehended. But translating poetry was another matter. "Gabriel!" Fiona read. "Be of good cheer! For if we love one another, nothing, in truth, can harm us, whatever mischances may happen!"

Emile translated the passage as best he could, but even he had difficulty finding the right words to the poetic verse. "Don't you have anything else to read?" he finally asked.

"Emile Dugas." Fiona slapped the book closed. "This is your story."

Emile slid his paddle across his lap so the pirogue could coast up to the landing adjacent to Boudreaux's store. "My story is sitting next to me in this boat," he answered with a grin. "And I certainly don't want to end up like Gabriel."

For a brief moment, the cloud returned, blocking out her sun, reminding Fiona that everyone she had ever loved had been lost to her. "You will be careful," she asked Emile, her smile long gone. "You won't go chasing some giant tree filled with that gray stuff you put in the mattresses."

"Moss," Emile corrected her as he helped her out of the boat, then handed Angelle into her arms. When he exited the boat, he slid an arm about her waist and pulled her close while delivering a long, tender kiss. Just like every day they had been together, Emile's kisses sent a flurry of butterflies racing through her stomach. "I will be home before sunset," he promised her. "I'll bring home a duck or two."

"Bring home yourself," Fiona uttered before grabbing his shirt and planting a kiss of her own.

Sandwiched between the two, Angelle began to laugh and squeeze her adopted parents' faces. Emile and Fiona pulled back long enough before delivering kisses on either side of the baby's face, which made her laugh even more.

"You will have enough to do today," Emile reminded

Fiona. "Now that I have sold my winter pelts, you can buy enough material to be wed like the queen of England."

Fiona huffed and placed a fist at her waist while she displayed a sly smile. "The queen should be so fortunate."

Emile traced her delicate face with his fingers, then delivered another kiss. Only this time his lips were wild and hot. The butterflies turned into shafts of lightning, shooting all the way to Fiona's toes.

"Enough," the couple heard Nana shout from behind. When they broke apart, they found the elderly woman marching down to the water's edge, a semblance of a smile betraying her words. "Let that poor girl breathe," she shouted to Emile. "Not to mention that poor child."

Emile greeted his godmother with a hug, then kisses on both cheeks. "Yes, Nana," he obeyed.

"Don't you have some work to be done?" Nana placed his palmetto hat upon his head and turned him toward the bayou. "We have shopping and sewing to do. *Sans* men."

Before he moved into the boat, he lovingly cupped Fiona's chin and placed a kiss on Angelle's forehead. "Take care of my family, Nana," he instructed his *marraine.* "And remember to speak slowly. She's learning, but . . ."

"And I'm doing quite well," Fiona answered proudly in French.

Emile beamed and shook his head. "Always full of surprises," he said. As he deftly entered his boat and sent it skimming downstream, he shouted back to Fiona. "Sundown."

Nana took Fiona's arm and began a long story regarding pecans, wedding dresses and what sounded like a broken wagon wheel. Fiona instantly doubted she was comprehending as well as she had thought. When the subject turned to trees growing out of soap, Fiona's head began to spin. *"Parlez lentement,* Nana, *s'il vous plait,"* she pleaded.

Nana had promised to act as her mother, to purchase material for a wedding dress and serve as her foster parent at the ceremony, but little good it would do if they couldn't communicate.

Nana smiled reassuringly. "I will speak slowly," she succinctly said in French, with perfect pronunciation.

"Merci," Fiona answered, her hopes returning.

Nana began again, this time more slowly, and Fiona managed to understand at least half of what was being said. The word was *barbe,* meaning beard, not *arbre,* meaning tree, and she gathered Nana was remarking on the stubble on Emile's face. One of the items Fiona was to purchase that day was a new shaver for Emile. When she recounted her confusion to Nana, the two began to laugh heartily.

They were still enjoying the joke when they entered the store, oblivious to the half dozen men scattered about the building. Fiona was so tickled by the misinterpretation that she failed to immediately notice the well-dressed gentleman standing at the counter, planked by a lawman sporting a five-pointed star. When the realization finally hit her that Walter Peterson, her former employer and the man she robbed of twenty dollars, was standing before her, Fiona gasped loudly, then covered her mouth with her hand to keep herself from screaming.

"Well, well. If it isn't Fiona Riley." Peterson moved away from the counter and strutted toward her with a smirk gracing his thin lips. He stood so close Angelle began to cry. "Thought I wouldn't find you, eh lassie?"

Fiona's breath caught in her chest, and she thought she might faint. "Is this the woman you have been searching for?" Fiona heard the sheriff ask in English with a Cajun accent. "The one who committed the crime?"

Peterson slid his gloved hand along her cheek, wrapping a lock of hair between his fingers. "Of course she is," he muttered with contempt, jerking her hair as if repulsed by the feel of her. "She's the bitch who assaulted me and stole my money."

Everyone was staring, including dear Eraste Boudreaux, who had welcomed her into his home, and Matthew Landry, who had taught her to dance the mazurka. She could feel their eyes burning into her, soon to condemn her as the impostor that she was. She wanted to run, to bolt into the woods, but she couldn't bear the thought of them thinking the worst of her. When she started to speak in her defense, Nana grabbed her arm and whispered heatedly in French, "Say nothing!" To her rear, Fiona heard Nana instructing one of the boys to fetch Emile; then Nana turned her irate attention to the sheriff.

"What is the meaning of this?" Nana demanded. "How dare you let him treat Emile's wife in this fashion?"

"Emile's wife?" the sheriff asked; then the two launched into a conversation too fast for Fiona to comprehend. While they discussed her fate, Peterson continued to stare, taking in her physique as he had done that horrible morning, gazing at her body as though she were a piece of beef on display at the market.

"You've fattened up," he said with a grin that reminded Fiona of the leering sailors on board the ship she had sailed on from Ireland. "Perhaps we can make an arrangement for you to pay back the money without having to go to jail."

Fiona moved to speak once more, to say that hell would freeze over before she would ever let him touch her again, but Nana squeezed her arm. Instead, Fiona responded nonverbally by spitting in his face.

Peterson jerked his head up, clearly outraged. "How dare you?" he shouted, then raised his hand to strike her.

Fiona closed her eyes, waiting for the imminent blow. Instead of a gloved hand at her face, however, she heard an ominous voice from behind. "Touch my wife and I'll break every bone in your body."

By the time it took her to think to turn around, Emile was at her side, wrapping an arm about her shoulders. Fiona wanted to feel relieved, but despite all she had told him, Emile knew nothing of her crime. How would he react when he learned she had deceived him yet again?

"I doubt that," Peterson began in a patronizing tone. "This woman is in my employ. She threw herself on me, and when I refused to be party to her sinful ways, she assaulted me and stole my wallet."

Amazingly, Emile's countenance never faltered. He gazed at Peterson as if the man had lost his mind. "My wife?" Emile asked incredulously. "In your employ?"

"Monsieur Peterson is from New Orleans," the sheriff interjected. If Fiona wasn't mistaken, there was a hint of sarcasm in his voice. "He claims he was robbed by his Irish maid, who was seen boarding the Elysian Fields bound for Loreauville. We traced a woman of his description to this area."

"That woman is she," the American announced triumphantly. "And if you'll step aside, sir, we'll be returning to New Orleans."

"She'll be going nowhere," Emile said sternly. "You have the wrong woman."

Peterson transferred his weight so that his height advantage was accentuated. He literally looked down his nose at Emile. "I believe, sir, that it is you who have been wronged."

Emile folded his arms and smiled, not his familiar cheerful greeting, but a look that announced he could not be bested. "You say my wife was in your employ?"

"That's right." Peterson shifted, but his gaze never faltered.

"And when was this?"

The American paused, clearly trying to discern where the conversation was heading. "More than a month. Three weeks before the snow fell is my guess."

Emile's sly smile broadened. "A month?" he exclaimed. "Why, my daughter is close to a year old. How would it be possible for my wife to have been in New Orleans a month ago?"

The sheriff slapped his hands together and placed his hat on his head. "Well, that solves that," he announced and headed for the door. "Why don't we try the next town."

Peterson, however, was not as easily convinced. "I'm telling you this is Fiona Riley and she stole my money," he bellowed.

The sheriff sighed and turned back toward the American. "He done told you, the baby was born a year ago. A trip to New Orleans takes a week. Wouldn't a man notice if his wife and child were missing that long?"

Peterson resumed his haughty stance. "That baby isn't his," he challenged them. "She looks nothing like him. Besides, the woman said she had inherited a child. That's why she needed the money."

A thought hit Fiona in a flash, and she softly whispered in Angelle's ear, "Where's da?"

The baby instantly brightened and thrust her arms toward Emile. "Da!" she called out to him, and Emile scooped her up and held her close, kissing her bright red curls in the process.

"Those are fighting words, monsieur." Emile stared unblinkingly at his foe. "Do you wish to settle this matter another way?"

Dear God, no, thought Fiona. She couldn't let her beloved husband be killed on account of her crime. She reached for Emile, ready to admit her guilt to save his life, but

Nana still held tightly to her elbow. "Say nothing," the elderly woman stated firmly. *"Rien!"*

The two men stubbornly refused to back down, both staring menacingly at the other. Finally, Peterson laughed and slid a hand nervously through his hair. "Fine," he said sarcastically. "I understand what's going on here."

The American hastily replaced his hat on his head and exited the store. As the door slammed in his wake, Fiona felt the blood rush from her head and her knees go weak. Emile quickly handed Angelle to Nana and caught her before she hit the floor. Fiona grabbed his arm, but she refused to look him in the eye, afraid of what lingered there. "I'm fine," she whispered.

She wasn't surprised when Emile stood, spoke a few words to one of the men and left the building. Now that he knew what she had done, what she was capable of being, there would be no question as to an annulment. She was a lying, stealing impostor. And now he knew the truth.

Emile emerged on the store's porch and found the American and the sheriff readying their horses. "One moment, if you please," Emile called to them.

Peterson refused to turn around, to acknowledge Emile, so Emile spoke to the sheriff. "How much did he say the woman stole from him?" Emile asked the sheriff in French.

"Twenty dollars," the sheriff answered in his native tongue. "But he's an American. Who's to say he's telling the truth."

Emile pulled out his earnings from the winter pelts, counted twenty dollar bills and thrust them into the American's hands. "I hope this helps to alleviate your inconvenience," Emile said, then added sternly, "but I never want to see you around here or bothering my wife again."

"This resolves nothing," Peterson said, turning and star-

ing down at him menacingly. For a moment, Emile
believed the man would take him up on his offer to dual,
until the sheriff interceded.

"It resolves everything," the sheriff countered. "And
I'm the law around here."

Peterson crumpled the bills and thrust them into his
trouser pocket, then mounted his horse and kicked him
into action. As the two men watched him ride away, the
sheriff placed a friendly hand on Emile's shoulder.

"Congratulations on your marriage," he said. "It's
about time. Although you could have picked one without
a criminal past."

Emile smiled and shook the sheriff's hand. "Thanks for
your help."

The sheriff placed his hat on his head and mounted his
mare. "If we don't look out for each other, who will?" he
asked before galloping away.

Emile headed back toward the store and the confused
conversation going on inside. Ignoring the questions from
almost every man present, Emile kneeled before Fiona,
placed a finger at her chin and lifted her head up. Still,
she refused to meet his eyes.

"Fiona," he said in public for the first time. "Look at
me." While the tears poured down her cheeks, she shook
her head. "Fiona," Emile said again.

"I stole that money," Fiona finally said. "But not the
way he said. He tried to molest me and he wouldn't pay
me my wages."

"I know, *'ti monde.*"

"I didn't mean to do it," she continued through her
tears. "But I had nothing to eat."

"Fiona . . ."

"I was entitled to some of it. He did owe me two weeks'
wages."

Emile couldn't stand another minute. He slid a palm

against her cheek and forced her to look at him. "You're safe now," he assured her. "He's gone back to New Orleans. He won't bother you any more."

Fiona stared at him, puzzled. "But I stole his money," she said softly. "And I tried to steal your home."

Emile delicately brushed the strands of hair from her face. "You were trying to survive."

When the room became quiet, Emile realized everyone was staring. He stood and offered Fiona his hand. After a moment's hesitation, she accepted it and rose. "Everyone," Emile announced in French to the store's congregation. "This is my wife, Fiona Riley Dugas."

Fiona slowly lifted her eyes while Emile explained how she had come to Bayou Paradis. He spoke of the famine, of the letter delivered to the wrong church and the meals he had created to win his wife's heart. Of their first trip down the bayou, when she had announced in her thick Irish accent that he must "be an Acadian." Of his prolonged dip in the bayou and how Fiona had pulled him out, suspenders first. At the latter remark, the group howled.

None of the light conversation relieved Fiona's anxiety. She stood clearly frightened, gazing at the smiling faces as if they had lost their minds. Nana wrapped an arm about her shoulders and hugged her close, while Angelle tugged at her sleeve. Eraste Boudreaux recounted how Fiona had valiantly spit in the American's face, which won her two friendly slaps on the back. Matthew Landry's youngest boy shyly brought her a flower. After several minutes, Fiona began to relax, but was still obviously confused.

Emile took her hand and squeezed it. "You're with friends now. We take care of our own."

Fiona appeared as if another round of tears were eminent. "But I'm not Acadian," she whispered.

Emile threw his head back and laughed. "You are now." The joking and the warm affections continued until finally Fiona began to smile. She retrieved Angelle, then inched her way over to Emile and leaned into the warmth of his body while he circled his arms about them.

"Welcome to paradise," Emile said to his family. "Welcome home."

TEXAS LULLABY

Phoebe Conn

Chapter One

"Oh, Papa," Alex cried. "You can't marry that ostrich woman!" Shocked clear to the marrow, Alex's heavy silver fork slipped from her hand and fell to her gold-rimmed dinner plate with a noisy clatter.

Frank Howard set his knife down with exaggerated care, but his gentlemanly control was sorely strained as he replied to his only child's outburst. "Willabelle may have a fondness for feathered hats, Alexandra, but I absolutely forbid you to speak of your future stepmother in such uncomplimentary terms."

Huge tears welled up in Alex's eyes and blurred her vision, but not before she had seen their guest turn away to hide an unmistakable smirk. "Who are you laughing at, Dr. Burnett? Me, or the old fool who actually believes Willabelle Dupré will make him a fine wife?"

Clay Burnett shifted uncomfortably in his chair. "Now, Alex, honey, your daddy is only forty-seven, which is a long way from being old, but I'd just as soon you left me out of your family disputes."

"Why? Because you've no excuse for not taking a wife yourself?" Alex challenged.

"Alex!" Frank cautioned sternly. "Clay isn't the problem here. You are. Now, your dear mother's been gone nearly ten years, and while I never expected to remarry, Willabelle is, well . . ." He struggled to find a suitably effusive adjective, and finally gave up with a shrug and slow smile. "Let's just say I'm honored that she's agreed to become my wife.

"We've both been widowed, so we'll have just a small ceremony, but I want you to help me plan the reception afterward. It's been years since we had a big party with music and dancing, and you'll need some fancy new clothes. It's high time you were married yourself, Alex, but you'll never attract a man going around dressed in pants like one of the hired hands."

Alex wiped her eyes on her faded shirt sleeve and hung on to the last of her pride. "Is it Willabelle who thinks I'm in the way here, or you, Papa?"

"I didn't say that," Frank exclaimed. "But most girls are wed by nineteen, and you've yet to receive a single proposal."

Alex had been too busy helping to run the ranch to care about having beaux, but for her father to make such a pointed observation in front of a guest was downright cruel. Unwilling to suffer any further humiliation, she shoved her chair away from the table and sprang to her feet.

"I know I'm not nearly as pretty as Mama was, but I didn't realize how badly I'd disappointed you. You'll have to excuse me, doc. I've lost my appetite."

As she fled the dining room, sunlight streaming in the windows turned her bright red curls to flame, but it was the length of her slender legs Clay noticed, and he thought it would be a damn shame if she ever traded in her tight-fitting pants for long skirts.

Perplexed and dismayed, Frank shook his head. "I've never compared Alex to her mother. Where would she get such a ridiculous notion?"

Despite his best intentions, Clay had been sucked into an embarrassing situation, and having lost interest in the noon meal, he pushed his plate away. "We've been friends since the war, Colonel, but you know better than to ask me for advice about women."

"Damn it all. I'm not suggesting a philosophical discussion on women. We're just talking about Alex!"

Clay leaned back in his chair and tilted his head slightly as he appraised his old friend's troubled frown. "Maybe that's the problem right there. You've raised Alex as your heir, and she's made a mighty fine son. Now you've ambushed her with your wedding plans and demanded that she start acting like a lady. It's no wonder she was hurt; but she's wrong. She's every bit as pretty as her mother was."

Latching on to that hope, Frank broke into a wide grin. "I've always thought so, but your opinion would mean a whole lot more to her. Will you tell her?"

"Oh, no, you don't," Clay swore. "I won't make the mistake of trying to reason with a woman. I swear I've never understood any of them."

"But you're a physician. Weren't females part of your training?"

"Their anatomy, of course, but that's not the same as knowing how a woman thinks, or glimpsing her soul."

"Oh, for goodness sake, I don't expect you to look that deep. Just go find Alex and tell her she's pretty. That will do for a start. I'll leave it up to Willabelle to talk her into wearing a nice dress for the wedding."

Clay opened his mouth to argue against relying on Willabelle where Alex was concerned, then thought better of it. "I really ought to be getting back into town."

"Your horse is tethered by the barn. You're sure to find Alex out there, too. Come on, Clay. You owe me a favor."

"Any favors I owed you have been repaid ten times over, Colonel, and you know it."

"Then, do it for Alex. She's always liked you."

As Clay hauled his long, lanky frame out of his chair, he tried to think of a compelling reason to avoid Alex. Unfortunately, none occurred to him. "All right," he agreed, "I'll see what I can do, but I'm not making any promises."

Frank walked Clay from the dining room down the wide hallway to the front door. Thick adobe walls kept the house cool all year round and lent the men's voices a faint echo. "I want you to be my best man, Clay. Won't being nice to Alex be part of your duties?"

"You don't need to prod me any further. Besides, I've always been nice to Alex."

Anxious to leave, Clay grabbed his hat from the hall tree and left the Howards' sprawling ranch house. He hoped Alex would be nowhere to be found, but when he reached the barn, she was standing in the shade of the open doors, brushing out her stallion's long mane. The big black-and-white pinto snickered a greeting but looked no happier to see Clay than his mistress did.

Clay wished an emergency had kept him in Fort Worth that day, but he had given his word and, after clearing his throat, made a sincere effort to help his friend as best he could. "Alex, I just wanted to say—"

Alex turned toward him and gestured with the brush. "Did my father send you out here to apologize for him?"

Embarrassed by how close she had come to the truth, Clay glanced down at his boots. Then he had to rake his hair out of his eyes as he looked up to meet Alex's accusing gaze. "No, ma'am, but I'm sure he didn't mean to hurt your feelings."

"Now there's a comfort. I'm so relieved that he didn't intend to be as mean as he sounded."

A cloud crossed the sun and for a brief moment darkened the day to the unusual blue-gray of Alex's eyes. Then the cloud dissolved as quickly as her tears, and left Clay drenched in uncomfortably bright light.

"What I came out here to say," he repeated more earnestly, "was that I remember your mother, and you're every bit as pretty as she was."

Alex responded with a derisive snort that could just as easily have come from her stallion. "Better put on your hat, doc. The sun's gotten to you."

Clay turned the pale gray hat in his hands rather than place it on his head as ordered. "It's just a matter of attitude, Alex. Alexandra," he corrected himself quickly. "Your mother was an exquisite creature, who was all lacy ruffles and shy smiles, while you—" Too late Clay realized he had gotten himself on very dangerous ground.

Alex's eyes narrowed as she moved toward Clay. He stood a couple of inches above six feet in height, but she was also tall and in boots needed to crane her neck only slightly to look up at him. "While I'm what, doc?"

Her skin was a lovely golden shade with a light dusting of freckles across the bridge of her nose, but her long, dark lashes again focused Clay's attention on her eyes. Rather than affecting a lady's demure glance, Alex's gaze was as direct as a man's. Rightly taking her question as a clear challenge, Clay took a step backward.

"Wild," he blurted out, then immediately wished he could take it back. "What I mean is—"

Alex swung back around to her horse and continued brushing his mane with long, sure strokes. The air was very still, and the brush made a soft scraping sound each time she pulled it through the stallion's flowing mane.

"I understood you the first time," she replied. "You better watch out, though. Once my father marries the ostrich woman, he'll start looking around for a wife for you."

"We were talking about you, Alexandra."

"No, we weren't. You were. There's a big difference between the two."

Clay was positive he hadn't improved things one bit, but he hadn't meant to offend her. "I'm sorry. I really do think you're pretty, and you'd make a fine wife for a rancher."

Alex rolled her eyes. "Thanks so much. If a rancher ever asks me for a testimonial, I'll send him directly to you."

Clay stared at her a long moment. She had still been a little girl when he and her daddy came home after the Civil War, and her mother had died while he was away at medical school. He had been dimly aware that she had grown up; but he usually saw her father in town, and he could not even recall the last time he had seen her.

"I hadn't realized how long it's been since we talked," he remarked absently.

Alex shot him a quick glance over her shoulder. He was a handsome man, with glossy brown hair and dark eyes, but so serious an individual she could not recall ever seeing him laugh. What she did recall, however, was the gentleness of his touch when he had stitched up a deep cut in her knee the time she had been thrown and landed on a sharp rock.

Blushing slightly at the memory, she turned slowly to face him. "We've never talked, doc. You're my father's friend after all, not mine."

Her mouth was perhaps a trifle too wide, but with a faint dimple in her chin, Clay doubted anyone noticed. "Your father's fifteen years older than I am," he heard himself say.

"Is that a fact?" Alex tossed the brush aside and grabbed her stallion's trailing reins along with a handful of silky mane. With an agile leap, she pulled herself up on his back.

"What sort of sound does an ostrich make, doc? Do you suppose they cluck like a chicken or quack like a duck?"

"I've really no idea," Clay admitted.

"What a shame. I thought you knew everything." Alex tapped her heels against her horse's ribs and sent the graceful animal dancing in a tight circle around the startled physician. "I guess you'll just have to keep a sharp eye out for the feathers."

Alex laughed as she rode away and left Clay choking on dust and feeling like a damn fool. He waved his hat to clear the air, then jammed it on and walked around the corner of the barn to fetch his bay gelding. José Blanco, the ranch's foreman, was leaning against the hitching post and holding his mount's reins.

Clay took one look at José's cocky grin and was doubly insulted. "Do you spend much of your time eavesdropping on Alex's conversations?"

"Only the amusing ones," José admitted with a deep chuckle.

"I'm glad someone was entertained. Tell me something. Does Alex often go riding alone?"

José was a small man with a tough, lean build. His deeply tanned skin had a leathery sheen, and his dark eyes shone bright. He threw back his shoulders as he replied. "I taught her to ride when she was no more than three. She handles that stallion as easily as you would a pony."

Clay mounted his horse without comment, but while José might be proud of how well he had taught Alex to ride, Clay considered it a real tragedy no one had taken the time to teach her how to behave like a lady.

Challenging the wind, Alex rode toward the Trinity River. As always, she reveled in the sheer exhilaration of her horse's strength and speed, but wisely reined him in long before they had outrun her angry tears. No horse had that kind of endurance, and she rode home at a lazy, meandering walk. The soft spring grass was dotted with bluebonnets, but Alex couldn't appreciate the beauty of the landscape when her mood was as dark as the fertile soil.

She blamed herself for not noticing how much time her father had been spending in town lately. The first couple of years after her mother's death, he had seldom left his study, let alone the ranch. Those years had blurred in her memory to the shadowy gray of the Confederate officer's uniform that still hung in the back of her father's closet, but somehow they had survived them. Now her father had become so damn sociable he wanted to get married again.

Alex didn't go into town much herself, but she had known who Willabelle Dupré was. Willabelle was a petite woman with fair skin and hair the color of pale cream, but it was her outlandish hats that had first brought her to Alex's attention. She owned a quiet little boardinghouse, but never ventured out without a huge hat festooned with bright plumes.

"How many birds have been sacrificed to feed that woman's insatiable desire for plumage?" Alex wondered aloud. She patted her horse's neck and, grateful for his devotion, took especially good care of him when they reached the barn.

Then, when she could not put it off any longer, she went into the house to look for her father. She found him seated in the parlor, reading the *Star-Telegram*. She stopped at the doorway and leaned back against the jamb, but didn't hesitate to speak.

"Couldn't you have waited until we were alone to tell me about Willabelle?" she asked. "Or was Dr. Burnett here because you anticipated one of us needing medical attention after you announced your wedding plans?"

Frank tossed his paper aside, left his comfortably worn leather chair, and came toward her. "I'd mistakenly believed you'd be on your best behavior with company present. I sure hope you apologized to Clay before he left."

Sincerely puzzled, Alex straightened up. "Apologize to him for what?"

Frank's auburn hair was streaked with silver at the temples, but his brows were still dark and accented the depth of his frown. "Haven't I taught you any manners at all, missy?"

Alex stepped into the room, spread her feet wide, and shoved her hands into her hip pockets. "You haven't called me missy since I was a child."

"Well, maybe I should have. Seems like only yesterday that both you and your mother would ride with me down to the river on my horse. She'd just climb up behind me, and I'd bounce you on the saddle horn. Those were the good times," he recalled wistfully, "way back before the war."

"I remember us all going fishing," Alex added softly.

Frank nodded. "We've had a lot of fun together, haven't we?"

Alex felt as though her father were saying goodbye, and her throat tightened in a painful knot. "We sure have," she whispered.

Frank clapped her on the shoulder as though she were one of his male friends, then began to pace excitedly.

"Well, I want to have a lot more. You left the table before I could tell you we've set the wedding for the second Saturday in April.

"That's just three weeks away, and I sure hope we'll have enough time to get ready. I want to take Willabelle to New Orleans for a month or so, and when we get home, I've promised her she can redecorate the house however she pleases."

Alex hadn't thought her heart could sink any lower, but it suddenly took another sharp dip. "What's Willabelle going to do, just haul all of Mama's pretty things outside and burn them?"

Frank spun around on his heel. "No, of course not. We'll just put them away for you. I do so want you to have a home and family of your own one day."

"This has always been my home," Alex countered, but she knew the argument was already lost.

"Well, sure it is, and I want you to come home with all the grandbabies whenever you can."

"It sounds as though you and Willabelle have my life all planned out for me. Have you picked me a husband?" Afraid he was about to provide a name, Alex held her breath and balled her hands into fists at her sides.

Frank laughed as though she had been joking. "The choice ought to be yours, Alex, but with all the people Willabelle and I intend to invite to the reception, you're sure to find someone you'll like."

"Anything is possible, I suppose," Alex mumbled, "but what if he doesn't like me?"

Frank came forward to squeeze her arm. "Don't you worry. If you'll just start dressing like a lady, the men will surely notice just how pretty you are."

Alex lowered her voice to a sultry whisper. "Maybe I ought to just cover myself in ostrich feathers."

Frank recoiled as though he had been slapped. "Don't

you dare mention those damn birds or their feathers in my presence ever again. You understand me, missy? Now I'm going into town to visit Willabelle, and I won't be coming home for supper."

Alex moved aside to let him pass, but in her view, he was already gone.

That night the old nightmare tore Clay from his bed. Drenched in cold sweat, he staggered to the window and opened it wide to let in the chilly night air. But his fever was one of the spirit, and couldn't be cooled down as easily as his shaking body.

He drank in the night in huge gulps and counted the stars overhead. It was still a long time until dawn, but he turned and sat slumped on the windowsill rather than return to bed. His heart was still pounding wildly, but he took it as a good sign he was still alive.

In the first few years after the Civil War, the bloody nightmare had often shredded his sleep, but now it only came when there was something weighing heavily on his mind. He had not had such a bad day, though, except for the brief time he had spent out at the Howard ranch. That had been its own kind of nightmare. With a quick shudder, Clay stood to twist and stretch, but his body still ached as though it had been tied in knots.

He bet Alex Howard always slept like a babe, and he could not help but admire the way she said precisely what was on her mind. Unlike some other women he knew, she did not hint, or tease, or cajole to get her way. She just looked him right in the eye, spoke her piece, and then silently dared him to contradict her. If he were so forthright, he would lose all his patients in a week and quickly decimate the ranks of his friends.

He wondered if Alex even had any close women friends.

As one of Fort Worth's most eligible bachelors, he was invited to all the elegant parties, but he had never seen Alex at any of them. He avoided such invitations whenever possible, but maybe Alex wasn't even on anyone's guest list.

It hurt him to think the spirited girl might not have had any choice about spending more time with her horse than suitable young men. As best man, he would have to make certain Alex had a good time at her father's wedding reception, but he sadly feared she was going to need a lot more than a pretty dress to receive the kind of attention from men she truly deserved.

Haunted by that thought as much as by the lingering effects of the recurring nightmare, Clay got no more sleep that night and very little in the nights that followed.

Chapter Two

The next time Alex saw Clay Burnett was Friday afternoon at the wedding rehearsal. Willabelle had brought along her three dearest friends, and as the wedding party assembled in the parlor, the ladies began to fuss over the good doctor as though he were the last available man in Fort Worth.

Clay just kept peeling their hands off his arms with an admirable restraint, but when he looked every bit as uncomfortable as Alex felt, she couldn't understand why Willabelle's pretty friends didn't see just how unwelcome their attentions truly were.

Unable to watch the silly trio paw Clay, Alex smoothed out the skirt of her new pale blue gown and hoped no one would notice she was still wearing her worn riding boots rather than the elegant new brocade slippers she had had made for tomorrow's ceremony. She just wished she could have worn one of her mother's gowns to the wedding; but she was nearly a head taller than her dear mother had been, and none of the precious gowns stored away in their heirloom trunk had fit her.

In the course of the last three weeks, Alex had become resigned to the inevitable changes in her life, but she was still struggling to gain control of her future. With Willabelle invading her home, she definitely wanted out, and finding a husband appeared to be her only option. She doubted it would take much to make a rancher happy, and then she would have plenty of time on her own to do just as she pleased.

That was why she had gone along with Willabelle's numerous suggestions for sprucing up her wardrobe. Clay had appeared rather startled to see her wearing a dress that afternoon, but none of the other men who were invited to the wedding would know her well enough to recognize it wasn't her usual attire. She made a mental note to search out the men who didn't seem to be too fussy about their own appearance, because then they would be unlikely to be too particular about hers.

"If you'll just stand right here, Miss Howard," James Adams, the Methodist minister, requested. "We're almost ready to begin."

Alex had been astonished when Willabelle asked her to be the maid of honor, but her father was so eager for her to accept, she had not had the heart to refuse. Now as she stood beside Willabelle, who had the good sense to remove her hat, Alex hoped she could get through the actual wedding as easily as this rehearsal.

Clay took his place beside Frank, but he found it difficult to concentrate on the minister's softly voiced instructions when he was so eager to get through the rehearsal and leave. He had been invited to stay for supper, but that would mean putting up with Willabelle's friends for the better part of the evening.

He glanced past Frank and Willabelle to Alex, and saw

by her distracted expression that she was paying no closer attention to the minister's words than he was. At least she wasn't fidgeting. He felt as though ants had gotten inside his clothes, and it was all he could do to stand still. After the way Alex had teased him the last time he had been out at the ranch, he had not been anxious to see her again, but now that Willabelle had introduced him to three of the most cloying women he had ever met, he believed that he owed Alex an apology.

At the conclusion of the brief rehearsal, Clay avoided Willabelle's friends, took Alex's arm, and ushered her out onto the central patio. "It seems ostriches neither quack nor cluck," he whispered. "Instead they twitter and giggle."

Pleased that he now understood her point, Alex moved across the smooth terra-cotta paving stones to the lily pond where she had splashed and floated small wooden boats as a child. She gathered up her skirts and sat down on the wide, low wall surrounding the water. "I did my best to warn you, doc. Which of Willabelle's friends do you suppose will be the first to arrive at your office with a mysterious complaint that can't even be diagnosed, let alone cured, in less than a dozen visits?"

Clay leaned down to scoop up a handful of water, and just as quickly flung it away. "The redhead," he answered with obvious distaste.

Startled, Alex first studied Clay's disgusted frown, and then responded with a low giggle. "You're worse off than I thought, doc. I'm the only woman here with red hair."

Certain she couldn't possibly be correct, Clay straightened up and glanced back toward the house, but to his immense relief, they weren't being observed from any of the windows. "Let's think a minute. The taller of the three was a brunette, wasn't she?"

"Yes, was that Phyllis?" Alex asked.

"No, Phyllis was the little blond," Clay answered. "Gertrude was the brunette."

"You're a lot better at names than I am," Alex murmured thoughtfully, "but as I recall, the little chubby one called herself Edna Mae, and her hair is light brown."

"Are you sure it isn't red?" Clay asked.

Alex rearranged her skirts to cover the scuffed toes of her boots. "Positive. I'm the only redhead here today, and I'm unlikely to turn up in your office anytime soon."

Clay found Alex's prediction oddly disappointing. He propped his boot on the edge of the pond and rested his arm across his knee. He peered down into the water as though he were searching for fish rather than for something intelligent to say. "I'm sorry. I hope I didn't offend you. I've always thought your hair was an especially beautiful shade of red."

Alex had heard more jokes than compliments about redheaded women, but Clay sounded sincere. "Thank you," she murmured, practicing her most ladylike behavior.

"You're welcome. Thank God I rode my horse rather than bring the buggy," Clay added, "or all three of Willabelle's friends would undoubtedly expect me to take them home."

Alex smoothed a stray curl back into the bow she had tied at her nape. "You don't relish being so popular?"

Clay just shuddered and shook his head.

After a long moment of a curiously companionable silence, Alex offered an apology of her own. "I've been seriously considering your suggestion that I'd make a good rancher's wife. I'm sorry about being so ungracious when you made it."

"No, on the contrary, it was presumptuous of me to offer an opinion on such a personal subject."

"Well, presumptuous or not," Alex replied, "I hope you were right, because this just won't seem like home once

Willabelle moves in, and I'd really like to have a ranch of my own."

Although Clay didn't move, his reflection blurred and rippled out over the water. "What are we talking about now, real estate or marriage?"

Alex thought he had made an attempt at humor and assumed she was laughing with him. "Marriage, of course, but real estate will certainly be involved. More than half the people coming to the reception tomorrow will be male, and quite a few of them will be ranchers."

Clay stepped back from the pond and began to pace back and forth in a slow oval. "I really don't believe you've thought this through. You'll be marrying a man, not simply assuming ownership of his property, so I sure hope you won't jump into something you might soon regret."

"What I regret is not understanding just how lonely my father has been. If I had, I would have had more time to plan for my own life rather than just being caught up in his and Willabelle's."

Clay paused in mid-stride. "Don't you like Willabelle at all?"

"I've not spent much time with her yet, but she's a lot nicer than I expected, even if she does have ridiculous taste in hats. It's just that she's not my mother, and it's difficult for me to see her and Papa together without feeling unbearably sad."

Afraid she had confided too much, Alex rose and nearly tripped over her skirt. "Damn it all," she exclaimed. "I'll be lucky if I don't fall on my face tomorrow."

"You should have extended your hand, and I'd have helped you to rise," Clay offered.

"That's the kind of thing I'm supposed to know, isn't it? But I've just not had any practice at acting helpless. Say, maybe we can stick close together tomorrow, and you can give me hints on etiquette, and I can help you fend off Willabelle's friends."

Her eyes appeared more blue than gray that day, and Clay had to look away before becoming lost in the lovely innocence of her gaze. Now horribly self-conscious, he cleared his throat noisily. "I'd be honored to assist you in whatever way I may, but I feel obligated to advise you to judge every man you meet on his own merits. There's a lot more to being a man's wife than you seem to realize."

The doctor was actually blushing. Alex stepped close and slipped her arm through his. "Anyone who's grown up on a ranch understands what goes on between males and females, and anything I might have missed, José Blanco explained in sufficient detail. Of course, there's always a chance he might have missed something. Maybe I ought to come down to your office, and we can just have ourselves a real illuminating little chat about marriage."

Appalled by that possibility, Clay patted her hand before pulling away. "I'm sure that's unnecessary, but speaking of my office, I really do have to get back into town. Please tell your father there were a couple of patients I still needed to see and offer my apologies to Willabelle and her friends for missing supper."

Alex watched Clay nearly sprint across the patio and slip out the back gate. She sure hoped the ranchers coming to the party tomorrow wouldn't all be as skittish about keeping company with women as the handsome physician. If they were, she was afraid she was going to end up as lonely as her father must have been.

The following afternoon, Frank rapped lightly on Alex's bedroom door. "Hurry up, Alex. It's time for the wedding."

"Just a minute, Papa," she called. The gown Willabelle

had helped her select was a pale lavender with so many ruffles and pleats Alex felt more like a princess than a rancher's daughter. She could barely breathe in the tightly laced corset, and with the train of her skirt supported by a crinolette, she doubted she would be able to sit down.

For the last ten minutes, she had been studying her reflection in the long mirror in the corner, and even to her critical eye she looked prettier than she had ever dreamed possible. That she was also miserably unhappy simply lent a soft glow to her gaze that she prayed would go unnoticed.

"I'm so sorry, Mama," she breathed out softly, and then gathering her courage, she went to join the rest of the wedding party in the parlor.

Clay had gotten very little sleep the previous night, and his head was pounding as a result. His dark gray suit was new, and the pearl gray brocade vest far fancier than anything he ever wore, but he had known Frank too long to look anything but his best for the wedding. He turned away to adjust the fit of his coat, and when he turned back around, Alex was standing in the doorway.

At least Clay thought it was Alex, but with such an elegant gown and a fashionably upswept hairstyle, she had surpassed her usual prettiness to become a great beauty. He jammed his hand into his coat pocket to make certain he still had the ring, but the gesture failed to still the slight tremble in his fingers. He could not recall if he had agreed to Alex's suggestion that they stay together during the reception, but now it would scarcely be a sacrifice.

Alex raised her skirt slightly and made her way to Willabelle's side with dainty, cautious steps. Willabelle was dressed in a creamy beige gown that very nearly matched her blond curls. She had chosen to wear a lacy ecru *mantilla* rather than a hat or veil, and looked very pretty, but Alex still had to force herself to smile.

Gertrude, Phyllis, and Edna Mae wore gowns in shades

of peach, pale apricot, and pink to complement Willabelle, but as on their last visit, they appeared to be more interested in capturing the interest of the best man than in assisting the bride.

A tiny gold cross dangled from Reverend Adams's watch fob, and Alex fixed her gaze upon it and refused to listen to the brief exchange of vows. It didn't matter to her that her parents' marriage had ended at her mother's death, and listening to her father pledge to love Willabelle was simply too painful to hear. All too quickly she heard the minister pronounce the couple man and wife. With a hasty kiss for them both, she crossed to the table where a bottle of chilled champagne sat ready to be opened.

Clay rushed to Alex's side. "Wait for me," he urged in a hoarse whisper. "We promised to stay together, remember?"

"I don't recall you agreeing, but it will be good to have you around, because this suffocating corset is liable to make me faint dead away before the day is over."

For a young woman to mention her undergarments was most inappropriate, but because she had linked the reference to her health, Clay forgave her and offered the only advice he could. "You're far too slender to need one," he assured her. "Why don't you just remove it right now?"

"Then I won't fit in this dress, and I promised my father I'd do my best to look like a lady."

"You look better than that," Clay responded easily.

Alex wasn't quite certain how to take his remark, but hoped he had meant it as a compliment. "Thanks, doc. You look real handsome yourself. Now, I do believe you're the one who's supposed to open this first bottle of champagne."

"Yes, of course." Clay managed the feat, and proposed a carefully rehearsed toast to the happy couple, but before he could taste more than a sip of the sparkling wine, the musicians and the first of the guests began to arrive. As

Alex left his side to greet them, he was surrounded by three eager females, and it was all he could do not to yell as though he had suddenly been attacked by Commanches.

Once the house became too crowded for comfortable conversation, the guests spilled out onto the patio, where the musicians were waiting and the dancing began. The musicians Frank had hired weren't particularly talented, but everyone regarded them as wonderfully entertaining. Willabelle and Frank danced alone at first; then the couple separated to bring Clay and Alex out to join them.

It had been years since Alex had danced with her father, but she managed not to step on his feet while they circled the patio in a graceful waltz. Frank was such an effortless dancer it was easy for Alex to follow his lead, but when the couples divided again, she found herself in the arms of a solidly built man who danced with all the charm of a locomotive chugging up a steep grade.

Before the last notes of the tune had faded away, Alex hurriedly escaped her partner and excused herself to get a drink of water. As she slipped through the couples moving out onto the patio to dance, Clay pressed close and followed. Alex recognized his presence even before she glanced over her shoulder to make certain it was he.

"You ought to be dancing, doc. There are going to be a lot of disappointed women if you don't."

Frank had made certain that in addition to the champagne that would be served later for toasts, there was also a variety of alcoholic drinks under the careful supervision of a bartender. For those who didn't care for spirits, there was a fragrant fruit punch, as well as cool water. The day held the pleasant warmth of spring, but amid the crush of the crowd the temperature was steadily rising.

Alex accepted a cup of water from one of the maids who usually worked in Willabelle's boardinghouse, gulped it down, and wiped her mouth on the back of her hand.

When she noted Clay's startled expression, she quickly offered him a cup, too.

He accepted a cup, but leaned close to whisper. "A lady sips her drinks, Alex; she doesn't toss them down her throat like a cowhand."

"I knew that," Alex replied, but she was embarrassed not to have remembered in time.

Then a gray-haired gentleman introduced himself as Vernon O'Nolan. He invited Alex to dance, and she went back out onto the patio with him. He held her as though he feared she might break, and made her so nervous she repeatedly stepped on his toes. She apologized, but he seemed more charmed than offended.

"You just need a little practice is all, darlin'," he replied, "and if I'd known Frank's baby girl was all grown up, I'd have come a calling long before this."

Vernon seemed nice enough, but Alex was so awkward in his arms that she broke away the moment the tune ended. Clay took her hand before anyone else could reach her, and she relaxed immediately in his embrace. "Before today, I'd not danced with anyone but Papa," she confided, "and I didn't realize just how difficult this would be."

"You're doing fine," Clay insisted, and easily guided her around the patio in time to the music. "O'Nolan owns a big spread the other side of Dallas, but he's too old for you."

Alex leaned back slightly to meet Clay's gaze. His dark eyes glowed with both intelligence and wit, but she could see he was serious. "You needn't worry. I wasn't actually considering him. Anyone else you'd care to warn me about?"

"Sure." Clay nodded toward a balding man dancing with Willabelle. "That's Cecil Henton. He's made a fortune in cattle, but gets mean when he drinks. He nearly killed a man last year in a saloon brawl up in Wichita."

"Sounds charming," Alex murmured, "but I don't like his looks anyway."

"That's good." Clay concentrated on his footwork for a moment, then pointed out the young man dancing with Gertrude. "That's John Robinson. He's closer to your age; but his father makes all the decisions on the family's ranch, and his mother is a busybody who wouldn't give you a minute's peace."

"I'll cross him right off my list," Alex promised.

"Do you actually have one?" Clay inquired.

"No. But it sure sounds as though I left too much to chance. It's a good thing you're so eager to help me."

Clay gazed around the colorful swarm of dancers and smiled at someone he recognized. "Your father insisted being nice to you was part of the best man's duties."

Alex didn't respond to Clay's comment, but it hurt to think that rather than enjoying her company, he was merely doing as he had been told. She slipped from his grasp before he could offer another insightful opinion, and danced next with Leonard Rispler, a green-eyed man with curly hair. He was so friendly Alex had no trouble conversing with him, and distracted, she wasn't nearly so clumsy; but at the end of that dance, her father quickly drew her aside.

"Rispler gambles," he confided softly. "I love playing poker with him because he always loses big, but I sure don't want you encouraging him."

"Thanks, Papa," Alex replied. "Is there anyone here you'd actually like to recommend?"

Frank waved to a friend who had just arrived, then frowned thoughtfully. "Well, Clay's nice enough, but he doesn't own even a scrap of land."

At the mention of Clay Burnett's name, Alex's smile wavered, but she was saved from having to reply when Willabelle appeared to introduce them to a salesman who lived in her boardinghouse. He was a short fellow with narrow shoulders and such a long, pointed nose Alex was instantly reminded of a rat. Then completely unable to concentrate on his conversation, she hurriedly excused herself to attend to the other guests.

The party was going even better than Alex had hoped. Everyone seemed to be having a good time either dancing or just talking and laughing with friends. The ranch hands had dug a pit the previous day to barbecue a whole side of beef so there would be plenty of meat along with Frank's favorite dish, a corn pudding laced with chiles, for anyone who got hungry before they served the cake.

Alex gave in to her own lingering sense of sorrow and stepped out the patio gate. Anxious to spend a few minutes alone, she leaned back against the cool whitewashed side of the house and closed her eyes. She drew in as deep a breath as her corset allowed, and tried not to dwell on just how little success she was having in meeting a respectable rancher in need of a wife. The hinges creaked as Clay came through the gate, and Alex opened her eyes to find him, hands rested lightly on his hips, observing her closely.

"I'm not used to being around so many people," Alex hastened to explain. "Wait just a minute please, and I'll give being an attentive hostess another try."

Clay nodded. "You're doing fine. I just followed you out here because there's something important I needed to say."

Instantly apprehensive, Alex licked her lips and pushed away from the wall. Clay looked different somehow, and it wasn't just the superb fit of his new clothes. Even without her father's comment, in the last couple of days she had grown more keenly aware of the physician as a man, but he sure didn't appear to be impressed with her. She wiped her palms on her skirt, then quickly regretted the careless gesture. She might be the only one there who felt as though she were attending a masquerade ball, but she sure didn't want Clay offering any more hints to improve her manners.

"Well, hurry up, doc," she urged. "Spit it out."

They had talked easily about other men, but it occurred to Alex that Clay might be searching for precisely the right words to confide something far more personal. He was the best-looking bachelor there, and at thirty-two, it was high time he took a wife. With that unsettling realization, Alex couldn't breathe at all, and this time she couldn't blame it on her corset.

"I'm not quite sure how to say this," Clay began hesitantly, "but Fred Tritle just got here. He owns a sizable ranch, and might impress you as a nice enough young man, but he's a womanizer through and through and will just make you miserable if you're stupid enough to become his wife."

Appalled that he wasn't speaking for himself after all, Alex responded with a startled gasp. "Now, stupid isn't usually a word used to describe me, doc, but I do appreciate the warning."

Alex brushed by him with a long, fluid stride that carried her through the gate and out onto the crowded patio before Clay had the presence of mind to notice that even without her spirited stallion, she had again left him choking on dust.

Chapter Three

Josiah Blaine was the next man to invite Alex to dance, but she was too preoccupied with Clay Burnett's unwanted advice to appreciate her partner's appealing smile.

"You're awful busy lookin' after everyone else, Miss Howard," he said. "What can I do to help you with the party?"

Alex resisted the impulse to beg him to loosen her corset laces, and instead asked him to make certain a horse had been hitched to the buggy her father and Willabelle planned to take into town. "I don't want them to wave goodbye as they go out the door, and then find the buggy isn't waiting."

"It will be my pleasure," Josiah replied. "I've heard you own a fine stallion. Perhaps you'd allow me to see him sometime soon."

"You can take a look at him today if you like. When you reach the barn, Daniel has the first stall on the right."

Josiah gave Alex's hand a fond squeeze as the music

ended. "Daniel. That's a fine name for a horse, but I'd rather wait until you have the time to show him."

Alex had to admire Josiah's persistence, even if she completely missed his meaning. "There's nothing to show, Mr. Blaine. I raised Daniel from a colt, and he won't ever be for sale."

"Perhaps not," Josiah replied, "but an interest in your horse will provide me with an excellent excuse to come see you again."

"Excuse?" Alex repeated with a puzzled frown. "Do you need one?"

"I don't know. Do I? Suppose you tell me."

Alex finally recognized his flirtatious question for what it was. She laughed in spite of herself, and grateful for his easy-going humor, she decided she did, indeed, want to see him again.

"No," Alex answered. "You'll be welcome here anytime. In fact, it will probably be real lonely here with my father away on his honeymoon."

"Then, I'll come calling tomorrow afternoon, but for now, I'll go check on that buggy for you, Miss Howard."

Alex thanked him, and hoped he didn't have some horrible fault that would preclude their becoming friends. She would have liked to follow him out to the barn right then and talk horses for the rest of the afternoon, but the patio was crowded with guests she dared not abandon.

When Fred Tritle approached with a peacock's supercilious strut, it was all she could do not to laugh. He wore his wavy black hair slicked back from his high forehead, and the fancy red vest that brightened his somber black suit would have made a gambler proud. Even without Clay's warning, Alex would have avoided the man, and she quickly introduced him to Phyllis, who seemed genuinely pleased to have met such a fine gentleman.

Relieved to be rid of Fred, Alex danced another time

with Josiah Blaine; but she wasn't used to any man regarding her with such a worshipful gaze, and she began to feel uneasy. She regretted inviting him to call on her the next day, but couldn't think of a polite way to tell him not to bother.

Alex drank nothing stronger than the fruit punch all afternoon, but Gertrude and Edna Mae got so tipsy that Clay had to help them out to their buggy. Phyllis, teary-eyed about having to leave the party early, drove them home. Clay was relieved to have the twittering trio gone. He had done his best to be cordial to all the women at the party, and danced with most, but those three had simply been a nuisance.

Despite the noisy fun swirling all around him, Clay still kept an eye on Alex, but he remained at a distance until Frank and Willabelle began making their final preparations to leave. Then he maneuvered his way through the crowd to her side. "This has been a really long day," he whispered in her ear.

The warmth of Clay's breath caressed Alex's cheek, but she was still too annoyed with him to enjoy having him stand so near. In the last couple of hours, she had seen him dancing with the ladies and talking with the men, but at no time had there been any real sparkle of amusement in his eyes, or hint of relaxed enjoyment in his posture. No wonder the day had seemed endless to him, she thought, when like her, he was pleasing everyone but himself.

"Why don't you ride on into town with Papa and Willabelle?" Alex suggested thoughtfully. "After all, once they leave here for the hotel, your responsibilities as best man will be over."

"That may be true, but I'll still feel responsible for you."

The crowd suddenly surged forward, and Alex very nearly had to shove Vernon O'Nolan aside in order to face

Clay. "Oh, Lord, did Papa pay you to look after me while he's gone? Because if he did, I'll pay you double just to leave me be."

Her face was flushed from the excitement of the party, giving her expression a charming glow. As Clay stared down at her, he was uncertain which would be worse, to confirm her suspicion that Frank doubted she could manage on her own, or to reveal the fact that the colonel had apparently forgotten about his daughter and hadn't mentioned her at all.

"A man doesn't have to pay a good friend to look after his kin," Clay argued, deftly sidestepping her question. "I won't mind stopping by now and then, but I was talking about tonight. You have guests who have had too much to drink, while those who are overly fond of cake will soon start complaining of stomach aches. Let's make certain the party cools down slowly, so no one falls from his horse on the ride home or has to stop along the road and be sick."

Alex had all but given up hope of finding a nice rancher. "Thank you," she responded. "I was so worried about getting the party rolling, I didn't give enough thought to how it would end."

Frank and Willabelle made one last circle of the patio to accept their guests' best wishes, then climbed up into the beribboned buggy and, still laughing happily together, left for town.

"They seem to be a real good match, don't they?" Vernon O'Nolan leaned close to ask.

Alex bit back her first response and simply nodded. Vernon's comment was echoed all around her, and she smiled as though she agreed, but her heart remained heavy. Taking Clay's advice, she asked the quartet to begin playing soothing rather than sprightly tunes, closed the bar, and urged everyone to have something to eat or to lie down for a brief nap if they cared to rest before going home. With her gentle coaxing, the conversation slowed to a hushed murmur, and gradually the guests began to depart.

After sending Willabelle's maid into town with the bartender and musicians, Alex hurried to her room and changed out of the beautiful gown, crinolette, and the wretched corset that had come close to squeezing the life out of her. While she would have preferred pants, with a few guests still remaining, she thought she ought to wear the pale blue dress she had worn for the wedding rehearsal. When she began straightening the furniture in the parlor, that was a sufficient hint to start the last of the guests toward the door.

"I trust that we'll be seeing each other again soon, Miss Howard," Fred Tritle exclaimed with a wide grin. "Quite frankly, I don't understand how we've missed knowing each other before this."

"Just luck, I guess," Alex replied.

"You mean bad luck, of course," Fred laughed, and believing that had been her intention, he bid her a good night.

Alex turned away from the door to find both Clay and Josiah Blaine observing her all too closely. "What?" she asked them. "If Tritle didn't understand I was being rude, does it still count as rude?"

Clay shook his head as though he thought her incorrigible. "Yes, Alexandra. It sure does."

"I don't think it's wrong to speak your mind in your own home," Josiah argued. "Besides, Tritle is a pompous ass, and I've never liked him either."

"That really isn't the issue," Clay insisted.

"Gentlemen, please." Alex opened the door. "I think you better go now, Mr. Blaine."

Josiah paused when he reached her. "It was a lovely

party, Miss Howard, and I'm looking forward to seeing you tomorrow.''

"Thank you. Good night.'' Alex would have prompted him with a quick nudge had he not left then on his own, and she sighed gratefully as she closed the heavy door behind him. "Is that the last of them?'' she asked Clay.

"I think so, but why is he coming back tomorrow?''

Clay looked as tired as Alex felt, and she wasn't up to arguing with him. "He wants to see Daniel.''

Clay's eyes widened in alarm. "Who the hell is Daniel?''

"My pinto stallion. You've seen him. But why are you so upset? Don't tell me there's something wrong with Josiah, too. Not that it matters. I don't like him all that much.''

"You don't?''

Alex leaned back against the door and crossed her arms over her bosom. "No. He's just a mite too eager to please, and that makes me nervous. I could see you didn't like him, though, and you must have a good reason.''

"None I'd care to state,'' Clay hedged, for Josiah was an honest young man, who did own a ranch, and no one had ever said a word against him. "Why don't you check the kitchen, and I'll look around and make certain no one's fallen asleep out on the patio.''

"Thanks. It might be days before I'd think to search in the bushes.'' Alex wandered out to the kitchen, but the women who cooked for the family and ranch hands had already cleaned up and gone home. There would be dozens of dishes and glasses to wash come morning, but those would wait.

Alex checked the bedrooms to make certain no one had actually taken a nap, but the beds were all undisturbed. After the noisy party, the house seemed almost too still, and not wanting to dwell on how empty it felt, or the hollow echo of her footsteps, she went on out to the patio. Clay had lit a lantern near the house, but in the gathering dusk, she couldn't locate him and had the sinking sensation that he had already left.

"Doc?" she called softly.

"I have a name," Clay answered, and strolled up behind her.

Startled, and yet enormously relieved that he was still with her, Alex remained where she stood. They were all alone in the large house, but she wasn't afraid of him, just keenly aware of his presence, as she had been earlier in the day.

"Clay Burnett," she whispered softly.

Clay savored the sound of her voice, then widened his stance, slid his arms around her waist, and pulled her back against his chest. "Clay is enough." He dipped his head, and rubbed his cheek against her temple. "I'm no good with words," he murmured against her ear.

Alex rested her hands on his. "No one would ever mistake me for a poet either, doc."

"Clay," he reminded her with a deep chuckle.

Alex tipped her head back, and Clay nuzzled her throat gently. "I wasn't certain you could laugh," she told him. "I hope you aren't laughing at me."

"No," Clay promised. "But I sure wish you'd stop poking fun at me."

"I'm sorry if I've been unkind." Alex relaxed in his arms, and yet leaned into him the way a cat presses against her master. "At least no one laughed at me today, or if they did, they were too polite to let me overhear."

Puzzled by that sorry opinion, Clay eased her around in his arms. The lantern's pale golden glow caressed her fair skin, but her long lashes made deep shadows on her cheeks. He lifted her chin with a fingertip.

"Look at me, Alex. Why would anyone have been laughing at you?"

"Well, I did my best to dress and act like a lady for

Papa's sake, but I'm afraid I might have looked as silly as I felt." She ran her hands up Clay's lapels with a distracted caress. "At least I didn't trip and fall, or step on too many toes. Although now that I think of it, men weren't exactly lining up to dance with me either."

"I should have danced with you more often," Clay wished aloud.

"No. You did your part." Alex could feel his heart thumping steadily beneath her palm. Standing in his arms in the darkened patio, it suddenly struck her as terribly sad that she had never had a beau. Her father had made her believe all she needed was a pretty dress, but that wasn't nearly enough to satisfy the sweet longing that made her chest ache with the threat of tears. It was all she could do to recall Clay was just completing his duties as best man when she felt so comfortable in his arms.

She tried to push away before making a complete fool of herself, but he tightened his hold on her. "I'm all right, doc. You can go on home."

Clay had only one compelling argument for remaining with her, and that was how desperately he wanted to stay. He wished he could put his heart's desire in words, but all that escaped his mouth was a low, hungry moan. He knew Alex wasn't the type to be swayed by pretty promises anyway, and so he just kissed her, as though it were the only way men and women ever made their needs known.

When Clay's lips first brushed hers, Alex drew back, but then he slid his fingers through her hair, tossed away her combs, sending her curls dancing over her shoulders, and easily lured her back to him. His mouth was warm, his taste as sweet as champagne, and without conscious thought, Alex opened her mouth to welcome a deeper kiss and raised her arms to encircle his neck. She felt a shudder course through him as well as the masculine strength he had coiled around her so tightly.

She slid her hands up under his frock coat, but his vest and shirt were still in her way. Without asking permission, or believing it was required, she slowly freed his shirttail from his trousers. Finally able to caress his bare skin, she splayed her fingers across his back, then slid her hand over his ribs.

Clay raised his mouth from hers to yank off his tie, and unwittingly gave Alex room to explore the flatness of his belly and the dark curls covering his chest. When she rolled a leathery nipple through her fingertips, he let out another low cry.

"Have I hurt you?" Alex asked fearfully.

Clay wrapped his hands around her wrists and held on tight. "No. Yes, but not nearly enough."

Alex reached up to kiss him. "You're not making any sense, Clay."

Clay fought simply to think, but his senses were too full of her. With a halo of flame red curls, she was the most beautiful woman he had ever seen, and so wild he knew he would never be able to hold her. Yet he couldn't bear to set her free.

"God, how I want you," he exhaled against her mouth.

His tongue slid over her lips, and Alex responded eagerly. She kissed him with a hunger that fed his own, until they were swaying in each other's arms, too lost in passion's dreams to fear they might fall. And still they wanted more.

It was Alex who took the first step toward the doorway. "My room," she offered between fevered kisses, and without an instant's hesitation, Clay followed her lead.

When they reached her bedroom, Alex didn't bother to light a lamp. She simply led Clay to the big brass bed and figured they had everything they needed right there. She peeled off his coat while he worked on the tiny buttons running down her bodice. He licked the delicate shell of her ear, sending her into a flurry of giggles, then impatiently brushed her hands away to unhook the chain on his pocket watch before unbuttoning his vest and shirt. He ripped them off together and tossed them over a chair.

He reached for Alex's dress, but then stilled his haste and slipped it off her shoulders with a surgeon's delicate touch. Beneath it she wore a soft linen camisole heavily trimmed with lace, and as he removed it, she leaned into his embrace as gracefully as a swan glides across still water. He pulled her close, and she ran her hands over his hard-muscled shoulders. He had admired her spirit, but it was the joyousness of her surrender that stole his heart.

Breaking away to catch her breath, Alex danced out of her slips and drawers, and then as Clay unbuckled his belt, she slid his trousers and fine woolen drawers down over his hips. They were laughing together now, and she backed him down on the side of the bed to pull off his boots and socks. Then freeing him from the rest of his clothes, she chucked them all aside.

Clay reached for Alex's hands and drew her down beside him on the bed. For a tall, slender woman, she had delightfully rounded breasts, and he bent his head to tease one nipple and then the other until it became a flushed bud. His desire had grown all day, and he wanted her badly; but he forced himself to move slowly, carefully, tenderly.

It had been years since Alex had been held, and she was shocked by her own hunger for the magic of Clay's touch. That he obviously craved hers as well made her heart soar. Even in the seductive darkness, she could see the warmth of his gaze. She trusted him completely, and not merely with her body, but also with her heart and soul.

Clay ran his hands down her body, memorizing every

curve and dip before exploring the sweet warmth between her legs. She was already wet, but he blazed a path between her feminine folds with exaggerated care.

Alex had assumed making love must be pleasant, or folks wouldn't be so eager to do it, but she had not dreamed anything could feel as glorious as Clay's increasingly intimate caress. She tilted her hips, inviting more, and at the same time began moving her hands over him. She knew how men were made, but not this particular man. As she wrapped her fingers around his arousal, he again moaned way back in his throat, and she quickly released him.

"Don't stop," he begged. "I want it all."

Alex wasn't exactly sure what all was, but enticed him lovingly with her own low, throaty moan. "All I want is you," she whispered.

Clay needed no further encouragement to move over her. He probed slowly, wanting to ease into her rather than causing her pain, but his need for her overwhelmed his self-restraint. He plunged then, sinking to her depths, and lost in her heat he gave way to pure sensation and prayed she would share the pleasure as deeply as he.

Alex tensed, for José Blanco had neglected to mention that losing her virginity would cause her such searing pain. That Clay hadn't warned her either struck her as cruel; but she clung to him, and gradually the pain began to fade. In its place came a delicious warmth, then the tender yearning she had merely glimpsed from the smooth tracings of his fingertips.

As Clay continued to move within her, she felt her heartbeat quicken to the frantic rhythm of his, but it was the taunting new sensation that swept her whole being spiraling down into her very soul. It throbbed and built, creating a desperate need she would gladly have died to assuage.

When its fiery splendor suddenly burst forth, she felt Clay shudder with the very same incredible joy. At peace in his arms, she was filled with a luscious weakness, and at last understood that they had, indeed, had it all. Clinging to the hope they would share it again, she saw the man she adored through a shower of stars that lingered long into her dreams.

Chapter Four

Sunday morning, Alex slowly awakened with a lazy stretch. She and Clay had made love again during the night, and she could not remember ever being so blissfully happy. For a long moment she lay still, just savoring her glorious memories, but then becoming lonesome for Clay, she yawned and opened her eyes. Her bedroom was awash in bright sunlight, and thinking she and Clay had slept unforgivably late, she turned toward his side of the bed.

But Clay wasn't cuddled against her as he had been all night. Instead, he sat across the room slumped in a chair beside the window. He was fully dressed, and had propped his boots on a small table that held one of the bouquets of fresh daisies and bluebonnets that had been placed throughout the house for the wedding. The flowers had barely begun to wilt, but Clay looked utterly wretched.

Alex was surprised to find him out of bed, let alone dressed, but the sadness of his expression frightened her.

She shoved her hair out of her eyes, sat up, and hugged the sheet to her bare breasts.

"What's wrong?" she asked him.

At the sound of her voice, Clay swung his head toward her, but his frown didn't lift. "I scarcely know where to begin."

Alex stared at him a long moment. "I swear if you say you're sorry you've been with me, you won't have to watch out for my papa. I'll shoot you myself."

A slow smile tugged at the corner of Clay's mouth. "I'm safe then, because I'm not in the least bit sorry."

"That's not how you look." Growing self-conscious, Alex gripped the sheet more tightly. "I didn't seem like such a big disappointment to you last night."

Clay glanced back out the window where hazy clumps of bluebonnets darkened the bright sea of prairie grass. He had watched the sun rise before getting dressed, but that had been several hours ago. Since then he had just been watching Alex sleep and searching for the words that refused to come clear in his mind.

"Your father and Willabelle planned on leaving Fort Worth early this morning for Galveston to catch the boat for New Orleans. I imagine they've already gone. Reverend Adams will be finished with church services around noon, and then he'll probably be invited somewhere for Sunday dinner. We ought to be able to find him back home around three."

Alex could think of only one reason why they would need the preacher. "Are you trying to propose to me, doc?"

"It's Clay, remember? And no, it's too late for some flowery proposal. We need to get married, and quick."

Alex had been so happy when she had awakened thinking he was still in her bed, but now she was beginning to feel sick. "I may have threatened to shoot you if you were sorry, but I sure as hell won't use a shotgun to prod you toward the altar. It's plain the very last thing you want is a wedding, so why don't you just go on home and forget last night ever happened?''

Clay pushed himself out of the chair and approached the bed. He had a razor in his medical bag, but hadn't felt up to shaving. A day's growth of beard shadowed the angular planes of his cheeks and hardened his already stern expression. "I can't forget last night, Alex, nor could I live with myself if I walked away from you."

He was thinking of her as a responsibility again, she just knew it. "Well, what I can't live with is the thought of getting up every morning and having you look at me as though I were the worst mistake of your life. No, thank you. I'd rather die an old maid."

She ducked her head and looked away, but Clay refused to allow her to ignore him. "Alex," he coaxed gently. "There's a chance we may have created a child. I won't let you bear that disgrace alone."

Alex fought to hang on to the tender lover he had been, but it seemed as though another man entirely was standing beside the bed where they had made such stirring love. "Are you trying to present me with a choice?" she asked. "Either I marry a man who clearly doesn't want me or live with the disgrace of having a child out of wedlock? Well, there's another choice as I see it. That's just to wait. Maybe we won't become parents after all, and we can forget we ever met."

"Is that what you want?" Clay asked.

There was a catch in his voice that snagged Alex's heart, but she was so confused she wasn't certain she had actually heard it. "What really happened last night? Were you just so full of champagne that any woman would have looked good to you?"

"I never get that drunk," Clay exclaimed, "and I didn't have much to drink yesterday."

Alex's eyes darkened to a smoky gray. "I understand. You were just lonely, and I was within easy reach."

"No. It wasn't that at all." Clay hadn't felt lonely until he had taken her in his arms. Then he had understood just how much he had missed, and the pain had been excruciating.

"It was just that you sounded as though you'd marry the first rancher who came through the door, and I knew that would be an awful mistake not only for you, but for me as well."

And yet he still looked so terribly sad Alex couldn't help but believe he had gotten exactly what he had wanted, and then found she wasn't what he wanted at all. He had shown her what love was meant to be, and now he was taking it away, and breaking her heart in the process. She thought she might cry for days, but not in front of him.

"Go on out to the kitchen," she suggested. "Maria will give you something for breakfast while I'm getting dressed. I think I might make a lot more sense with my clothes on."

Clay nodded, picked up his jacket, and closed the door quietly on his way out. He had left his medical bag in Frank's study, and retrieved it on his way to the kitchen. He doubted he could eat, but at least he could ask for hot water to clean up.

Alex buried her face in her hands, but even as tears stung her eyes, she willed herself not to cry. Something was dreadfully wrong, and she didn't believe Clay was telling her the truth. He was far too serious a man to lead a woman on, and he had done a great deal more than that with her. Still, it was plain he didn't want her.

Clay had thoughtfully hung the blue dress in the wardrobe, but Alex was in too dark a mood for ruffles and flounces. Instead, she pulled on her comfortably worn pants, a shirt that had faded to misty blue, and boots. Afraid it might take an hour to brush the tangles from her hair, she gave up, left her wild mane flying free, and went looking for Clay.

He was pacing the parlor, but had shaved, combed his hair neatly, and managed to pull clothes that had lain on the floor all night into presentable order. Alex was amazed.

"You look as handsome as ever," she swore. "No one will ever guess you had a difficult night." She shrugged at her own sloppy garb. "For some reason, I didn't feel up to wearing a dress today."

"If you want to get married in pants, or your nightgown for that matter, it's all right with me."

"I'm not getting married today, Clay." Alex hooked her thumbs in her belt loops and, standing with one hip jutting forward, silently dared him to contradict her.

As Clay took a step toward her, there was a loud knocking at the front door. "That must be Josiah Blaine. Shall I tell him you don't feel up to entertaining company and send him on his way?"

"Oh, good Lord," Alex breathed out in a desperate sigh. She reached for her hair and felt a mess of curls. Clay's offer tempted her to hide, for she was certain Josiah would need only a single glimpse to note the night had left her irrevocably changed, but she had never admired cowards. She squared her shoulders and strode to the door. As she pulled it open, she saw Josiah's eager smile freeze, then thaw with a nervous twitch, and slide into a startled grimace.

"You'll have to forgive my appearance, Mr. Blaine. I've been cleaning house."

"Obviously. Perhaps I ought to return another day." He was dressed as handsomely as he had been for the party, but now his shoulders drooped with disappointment.

"No. Please stay," Alex urged. "Daniel always enjoys company. Come on, let's go on out to the barn."

Alex tried to pull the door closed behind her; but Clay slipped around it, and Josiah nearly stumbled over his own feet when he saw that the physician intended to accompany them. "I didn't expect to see you here again, Dr. Burnett. You're not feeling sick are you, Miss Howard?"

In truth, Alex had never felt worse, but it was her spirit that ached. "Thank you for asking, but no. The day just got off to a poor start, but now that you're here, I'm sure I'll perk up." She led the way around the house with a long, restless stride, not once realizing how much the two young men trailing behind her enjoyed the view.

"Daniel's five years old," Alex explained proudly as they reached the barn, "so I figure he's yet to reach his prime. If you have several mares you'd like to breed, I'll cut you a deal on his stud fee."

Clay watched Josiah's mouth drop open and wondered if Alex had deliberately embarrassed the young rancher or truly believed he had come to discuss horses. "Alex is an excellent judge of horseflesh," Clay stated confidently. "Daniel is as fine a stallion as any I've ever seen."

Alex accepted Clay's praise with marked skepticism. "It's a shame you didn't specialize in veterinary medicine, doc."

"I'm seriously considering making a change," Clay responded agreeably. "I know I'd enjoy having patients who don't complain."

"Yeah, I just bet you would. Give me a minute, Josiah, and I'll bring Daniel out where you can get a good look at him."

As Alex entered the barn, Josiah turned his back to the doorway to speak to Clay. "Is something going on here?" he inquired in a forced whisper.

"I sure hope so." Clay added a knowing wink he was grateful Alex couldn't see.

Before Josiah could question Clay any further, Alex rode Daniel out of the barn bareback. She walked the stallion around the two men, then looked down at Josiah and smiled invitingly. "I didn't take note of your horse, Mr. Blaine. Can he give us a race?"

"Alexandra," Clay cautioned, "that's not a good idea."

"I'll say," Josiah readily agreed. "My mount's sound, but he isn't fast."

Clay had expected Alex to lead her horse from the barn, but as he grabbled for Daniel's bridle, he bit back an order and made a low request. "I don't want you riding."

Alex waited for him to add a compelling reason that would inspire her to slip from Daniel's back into his arms, but Clay continued to glare at her as though he had the right to tell her what to do. "Get out of my way, doc, or I'll gallop Daniel right over you."

Clay knew that was no idle threat. Alex was most definitely a challenge, but rather than engage in a battle of wills, he wanted her to obey him willingly. He had the physical strength to yank her off Daniel's back, but he dared not use it. He didn't want to break her spirit, but he longed to tame it.

Alex was about to tap her heels against Daniel's ribs, when José Blanco walked up beside her. "*Querida,*" he called softly. "You need to change your clothes to entertain your callers. Go on in the house and leave Daniel here with me."

Clay was certain the foreman had been eavesdropping again; but when after a heart-stopping pause, Alex jumped from Daniel's back and started walking back toward the house, he was too grateful for José's intervention to scold him. Clay's horse stood in the corral, and it wasn't until that very moment that he realized he had completely forgotten the animal.

"Thanks for looking after my horse," he told the foreman and released Daniel's bridle.

"I keep an eye on everything," José claimed proudly. He picked up Daniel's reins. "Why don't we stand here and pretend we are talking about horses while Miss Howard gets dressed?"

Josiah walked around Daniel and gave a low whistle. "I won't have to pretend. He's a beauty. I'll bet he's fast."

"Like the wind," José replied, but he was still regarding Clay with a suspicious glance. "His sire was a big black stallion the colonel rode during the war. I'll bet you remember Samson, Dr. Burnett. His dam was a Comanche pony. Don't try and ride him. Alex is the only one he'll tolerate on his back."

Clay understood that José was warning him away from Alex rather than the stallion, and while it was far too late for that, he nodded.

After Josiah had satisfied his curiosity about the stallion, he and Clay walked back toward the house. "Dr. Burnett," the young man began hesitantly. "While I might have caught a glimpse of Miss Howard in town a time or two, we hadn't actually met until yesterday. I'd certainly appreciate your advice where she's concerned, but if she's your girl, I wish you'd just come out and say so."

Alex wasn't there to dispute what Clay said, and he couldn't help but smile. "Yeah, you could say she's my girl. I've already proposed, and I expect we'll get married in the next week or so."

Josiah was absolutely flabbergasted. "That doesn't make any sense," he exclaimed. "Why didn't her father delay his honeymoon? Didn't he and his bride want to attend his daughter's wedding?"

Clay slid his hands into his pockets, found the combs he had retrieved from the patio, and gazed off toward the horizon. He was a physician, after all, not an attorney, and plausible excuses didn't come easily to him. When the silence was growing strained, he finally thought of one.

"Frank Howard was a widower for nearly ten years. When he decided to remarry, Alex didn't want to intrude on his happiness by mentioning our plans. It would have been like stealing his thunder, if you understand."

Clay's expression was so thoroughly convincing that Josiah believed him and started to back away. "Well, I sure wish she'd told me last night, then I wouldn't have gotten my hopes up where she's concerned. I don't mind telling you this is damned disappointing."

"I'm sure Alex didn't mean to mislead you," Clay promised. "She probably thought you were just interested in her stallion."

"Wait a minute," Josiah said. "I'm sure she mentioned something about being lonely. Why would she do that if she was about to marry you?"

Josiah had him there, and before Clay could fabricate another convenient lie, Alex opened the front door. She was wearing the new blue gown and had tied her hair back with a ribbon, but she still looked a mite frazzled. "Well, are you two going to stand out there and talk, or are you coming in for tea?"

"Before I come in," Josiah Blaine announced loudly, "I want to know if you're really planning on marrying Dr. Burnett. Because if you are, I'll bid you a good day and leave for home."

Alex was mortified to think Clay might be bragging about what had happened between them last night, and she could feel the heat of a bright blush creeping up her cheeks. Pinned by the inquisitive rancher's accusing gaze, she swallowed hard, but couldn't find her voice to either confirm or deny any wedding plans.

Clay watched Alex sway slightly and feared she might faint before admitting how seriously they were discussing marriage. He reached into his pocket and withdrew her tortoiseshell combs.

"Here you are, honey. I forgot to give these back to you last night."

Josiah Blaine swore under his breath and walked off. Alex reached out for the combs, but only because they had belonged to her mother. She waited until Josiah had mounted his horse and urged him toward the road at a canter; then she slammed the front door in Clay's face and threw the bolt.

Not a man to be so easily deterred, Clay circled the house and entered through the patio. Alex hadn't left the front door; she had simply slumped to the floor and sat sobbing with pitiful wails. He knelt down beside her and drew her into his arms.

"Alex, you mustn't carry on so, honey." He patted her back and spoke her name softly, but it took him a long while to settle her down. He then leaned back and offered his handkerchief.

"Is the thought of marrying me so awful?" he asked. "Or is it just not having any choice about it?"

Alex hadn't meant for him to see her cry, but she was so miserably unhappy, she couldn't have held in her tears another minute. "We do have a choice, remember?"

"To wait?"

Alex nodded, and again buried her face in her hands. "Go on home. Please."

"No," Clay replied. "I can't leave you like this." He sat down so he could lean back against the door and cuddled her in his arms.

Alex's tears dampened Clay's coat, and she mumbled an apology; but she knew he was staying with her simply out of a sense of duty. She was his responsibility after all, not his dearly beloved, and she was positive no woman ought to marry a man who had already broken her heart, because he would surely do it again and again.

Alex fell asleep sprawled across Clay's lap. He eased the ribbon from her hair and with a gentle touch combed out the snarls. He did love her gorgeous red hair. It was one of the reasons she was so pretty, although certainly not the only one.

Neither of them had gotten much sleep the previous night, and in the next hour, he caught himself dozing off a time or two. Fearing Alex might never allow him to hold her again, he didn't really want to let her go, but he had learned during the war that sometimes it was necessary to make a strategic retreat.

He rose with her still cradled in his arms, carried her into her bedroom, and laid her carefully upon the brass bed. She snuggled down into her pillow without waking up, and he leaned down to kiss her cheek tenderly. He lingered longer than he had intended, but after reminding himself this was merely a retreat rather than a defeat, he left with every intention of making a swift return.

Chapter Five

The next time Alex awoke, it was late afternoon, and she was greatly relieved to find Clay had gone. It was too late to go riding, which was all she really wished to do, so she simply sat out on the patio by the lily pond and trailed her fingers through the water. She wondered what had become of her little boats, and thought perhaps she ought to whittle some new ones.

"Young ladies do not whittle," she reminded herself absently. They passed their time fussing with their clothes or embroidering linens, reading poetry, practicing the piano, or singing sweet songs. They also spent an inordinate amount of time calling on each other to exchange gossip.

Alex did none of those tiresome things, nor did she even want to. Instead, she went looking for José Blanco. "Do we have any scraps of wood that would be good for whittling boats?" she asked him.

Alex had again changed into her riding clothes, but

there was nothing familiar in her gaze. She looked sad, and José thought what she needed was attentive company, not wood. He shrugged helplessly.

"*Querida,* I will ask the hands to whittle boats. What size do you want?"

Alex showed him with her hands. "Just little ones for the lily pond."

"Good. Maybe we can have a contest, and you can choose the winner. The men would like that."

Alex knew the hands enjoyed any type of competition, but she still needed something to do. "It's a shame we can't start the roundup before Papa gets home," she mused wistfully.

"I told your father he should not leave you here alone." José removed his broad-brimmed hat to wipe his forehead on his sleeve rather than spit in the dirt in front of Alex.

"Really? And how did he reply?"

"I do not believe he even heard me."

"Probably not," Alex agreed. "He was too lost in Willabelle."

"And you, *querida,* what is it that weighs so heavily on your mind?"

Alex had known José her whole life, so his question did not seem impertinent. "Dr. Burnett thinks we ought to get married."

José had not expected such an astounding announcement, but his face remained a mask of concern rather than dismay. "But you do not?"

Alex folded her hands behind her and leaned back against the rough side of the barn. "Let's just say I've gotten myself in something of a mess, José."

"You want another young man? The one who was here earlier?"

"No." Alex couldn't believe she had thought all she would have to do was line up the bachelors at the wedding reception and pick out the one who caught her fancy. How could she have been so incredibly naïve? "It's Clay I want," she admitted.

"If he wants you, and you want him, then where is the problem?" José inquired.

Alex licked her lips and instantly recalled Clay's luscious kiss. The problem, as it were, was so great she could hardly get her mind around it. "Well, let's just say the good doctor didn't propose in the most eloquent fashion, so I don't think his heart's really in it."

José grew very still. "He does not strike me as a man who would propose marriage and not mean it."

"No, he means it," Alex granted, but she was too ashamed to admit why Clay thought he had to make her his wife.

José rested his hands on his hips and stared at Alex a long moment. "I am going to tell you a secret, but you must never tell another soul."

Her interest piqued, Alex straightened up. "Do you know something about Clay? Tell me."

"It is not just about Burnett; it is about all men," José explained, and he took a step toward her and lowered his voice. "Men need to have their own way. But if a woman gives it to him, is it then his way, or hers?"

Alex mulled his advice over a moment and saw the wisdom in what some might mistake for a riddle. "Yes, I understand. Thank you, José. You've been very helpful, as always."

"It is my pleasure, *querida.*"

Alex strolled back toward the house, preoccupied by all that needed to be done. There were so many important decisions to be made, but she would have to begin with Clay. He would probably come out to the ranch in a day or two, but she knew she ought to approach him first. It was a frightening prospect, and yet wonderfully exhilarating.

Clay had meant to return to the Howard ranch Sunday night, but a youngster who had climbed up on his family's shed in an attempt to fly like an eagle had fallen and broken his arm. The bone had not been difficult to set, but the boy's parents had been so terrified by the accident that Clay had had to remain a while to reassure them.

He had then gotten back to his office too late to make the trip out to the ranch without it appearing as though he had planned his arrival to coincide with Alex's bedtime. While he definitely hoped to sleep with her again and soon, he didn't want her to think that's all he wanted, and so he remained in the apartment he kept above his office.

Monday morning he was greeted by a dozen patients, and in the afternoon, the grocer's wife went into labor. It was her third child and should have come into the world easily, but the babe wasn't born until dusk. She was a pretty little thing; but her mother was exhausted, so Clay tarried to make certain she would recover from her ordeal. But by the time he left, it was again too late to visit Alex.

On Tuesday, in addition to his regular patients, a couple of bullwackers overturned their wagon loaded with barrels of whiskey, and he had to sew up a deep cut and bandage an odd assortment of gashes, but by two o'clock his waiting room was clear. Finally able to leave for the Howard ranch, he cleaned up and changed his clothes. He had just hung the sign on his door stating he would be away for the afternoon, when he saw Alex coming down the wooden walkway toward him.

At least he thought it was Alex. She was dressed in another new gown made of a bright blue-and-green plaid. She was wearing dainty blue gloves and a small hat festooned with blue ribbons. She looked so adorable she took his breath away, but she was moving slowly along the row of shops and taking quick glances in the windows. Clay wondered if she was afraid of tripping on her skirt or simply searching for something.

She was so much fun to watch that he waited rather than call out to her. When she was a few steps away, she finally looked up and saw him. He doffed his hat, and smiled.

"Good day, Miss Howard."

Alex had been silently rehearsing what she wished to say and was startled to find Clay on the street. She read the sign on his office door, and her heart fell. When it had taken her half the day to dress up and come into town, she couldn't believe he was leaving.

"Good afternoon, Dr. Burnett. I seem to have come at a bad time."

"You mean this is a professional visit?" Clay was so badly disappointed he didn't know what to say, and then grateful for whatever reason had brought her to him, he quickly unlocked his door. "Please come in. I'll run my errand later." He left the sign in place and turned the bolt to assure their privacy.

He ushered Alex through the empty waiting room and seated her in his office rather than in one of the two rooms equipped to treat patients. He laid his hat aside, then leaned back against his desk and crossed his arms over his chest.

"You probably don't remember this; but you cut your knee rather badly once, and your father sent for me. You were all legs then, like a fawn."

Alex recalled the incident all too well and shifted nervously in her chair. She would never understand how other women were comfortable in so many layers of clothing, but she felt like an impostor swathed in an elaborate disguise. "I'm still all legs, doc."

Clay smiled knowingly. "Well, not entirely. Now, what brings you here?"

Alex swallowed hard and glanced toward the carafe of water on his desk. "Could I please have a glass of water?"

"Certainly." Clay quickly poured her a drink and refrained from being critical of her as she gulped it down. He replaced the glass on the desk. "Forgive me if I misunderstood, but this isn't a professional call after all, is it?"

Alex glanced down at her gloves and was surprised to find they weren't the scarred old pair she wore to ride. "No. I do remember when you sewed up my knee. There's only a thin scar, so you must have done a real fine job."

"Thank you." Clay had begun to think it was a good thing he had left the sign on his door, because at the rate Alex was progressing, they were going to need several hours. "Alexandra," he coaxed gently.

Alex raised her hand. "Just give me a minute, doc, Clay. I want to do what's right, and I appreciate that you do, too; but I don't want us to have to get married."

Gathering all her courage, she looked up at him. "I'd like us to marry all right, and this very afternoon if you're not too busy, but it has to be because it's what we both really, truly want, not because we think we must."

Clay had been marshaling his thoughts for another long argument, and it took him a moment to realize Alex was offering exactly what he thought was best. She was a beautiful, wild creature, one who would probably make him the worst of wives, but he had never even considered marrying another woman. Now that he had been with her, he never would.

Clay smiled easily. "It's what I really, truly want, and I doubt that you'd be here if it weren't exactly what you want as well."

All Alex knew was that she wanted him, but she nodded as though she were far more confident than she actually was. "You have a real handsome smile, Clay. You ought to use it more often."

"It's easy to smile when you've given me such a good reason. Where did you leave your buggy?"

José had sent a man into town for the buggy her father and Willabelle had taken to the hotel, but Alex had removed the ribbons before she had used it. "It's just up the street."

"Fine, let's go get it. There's a nice jewelry store on Main Street. Then we can pick up a marriage license and go on over to the Methodist church and speak with Reverend Adams."

Alex remembered to extend her hand, and Clay helped her from her chair; but then he pulled her into his arms and hugged her so tightly she was afraid she might swoon. "Hold on there, doc, or I won't have enough breath to say 'I do.' "

Clay relaxed and drew back. "You look positively ravishing today, Alexandra, and I couldn't help getting carried away. I can wait, though."

"I'll look forward to it," Alex promised with a sparkling laugh, and she blessed José for giving her such excellent advice.

As they crossed his waiting room, Clay hesitated. "Edna Mae came in here yesterday morning complaining of a strange tingling sensation in her right wrist. So even if she wasn't a redhead, she's the one who got here first."

"How does one treat such a peculiar ailment?" Alex inquired.

"Well, I wrapped a bandage around her wrist and told her not to do anything more strenuous than lift a teacup for several days."

"Will that cure it?"

"Nothing will help until she hears we've gotten married, and then her complaint will vanish instantly. I could probably have told her to stand on her head, and it wouldn't have done any harm; but I'm not the malicious sort."

"Wait a minute, doc." Alex rested her palm on his chest. "Our getting married might cost you a great many female patients."

Clay paused to kiss her lightly. "Probably, but I won't miss them one bit."

"I'm so relieved, but it's bound to hurt your income."

Clay had his hand on the door, and his first impulse was to rush her right through it and marry her before she changed her mind. But he couldn't bear to mislead her.

"Alex, doctors don't make much money. There are families who pay me in chickens, or whatever produce they can spare, and then I trade those things for what I need. We're not ever going to be rich, so if that's what you thought—"

Alex touched his lips with her fingertip. "I happen to be real fond of chicken dinners, doc, and my mother left me all the money we'll ever need. You can go ahead and treat sick folks for free if you like."

Clay had been well aware that Frank was wealthy, but he had had no idea Alex had money of her own.

"We'll work everything out in time," he promised, and he was grateful he had more than enough money on him to pay for a marriage license and buy Alex a nice wedding ring.

Forty-five minutes later they were seated and holding hands in Reverend Adams' study, attempting to sound as though they were a real sensible couple, when all they had to do was exchange a glance to remember that being sensible had nothing whatsoever to do with them being there. When the preacher appeared to be more dismayed than happy that they wished to wed, Alex squeezed Clay's hand and wondered if they shouldn't have gone looking for a judge.

"Do you have some serious objection?" she offered hesitantly.

"No, of course not," the minister assured her. "Dr.

Burnett, you're a responsible gentleman, and you're of age, Alexandra. I'm just puzzled as to why you're in such a rush to marry while your father's away on his honeymoon. Are you afraid that he might oppose it?"

"Good heavens, no," Alex exclaimed. "Why would he? Clay was his best man, so you know they're close friends."

"Yes, I do. Don't you two have your own friends you'd like to invite to your wedding?"

Clay had the worst feeling that if they weren't wed within the hour, Alex might again refuse to consider the match, and he couldn't bear to let her slip away. "I'm a man of modest means, Reverend," he confessed suddenly.

"If we marry while Frank and Willabelle are in New Orleans, we'll have our own honeymoon at the Howard ranch. They'll only be away a month to six weeks, so we don't have time to plan another lavish party before they return. Even if we did, coming so soon after the one for Frank and Willabelle, it would likely be a burden on the family as well as our friends."

Alex was astonished by Clay's fanciful reasoning, but slapped her free hand against his thigh as though what he had said made perfect sense. "You're a happily married man, Reverend, and must surely understand our desire to be alone together while we can to get our marriage off to a good start."

James Adams hadn't seen much of Frank Howard, nor Alexandra, after her mother had died. At the rehearsal for Frank and Willabelle's wedding, he had been stunned to find the skinny little red-haired girl he remembered had blossomed into such a beautiful young woman. He stared at the gloved hand she had left resting on Clay's thigh, and feared he had been remiss in not calling on the family and encouraging them to attend church regularly.

Uncomfortable with where that line of thinking led, he shoved himself out of his chair. "Do you wish to send for a couple of friends, or will our caretaker and organist do for the witnesses?"

Alex would have leaped out of her chair, but Clay kept a firm pressure on her hand to keep her in place. "They're already here, so please invite them to join us. May we wait here while you call them?"

"Certainly. Since it will be such a small service, perhaps you'd prefer to have the wedding here as well."

Alex frowned slightly, but in her mind the main sanctuary was better suited to the big, fancy weddings where family and friends overflowed the pews. The study smelled faintly of furniture polish, and bookshelves filled with leather-bound volumes lined the walls. Alex had always loved to read, and felt right at home.

"I miss my mother terribly," she confided softly. "Since she can't be with us, a small ceremony here in your study will be more than adequate."

When James Adams left the room, Clay ran his finger around the inside of his collar. "I hope you're telling the truth," he murmured.

"I always do," Alex assured him. "What are you worried about?"

"I just don't want you to regret not having a beautiful dress and half the town packed into the church for a spectacular wedding."

"I won't regret a thing," Alex replied confidently, "but if it's a crowd you want, we can just wait and invite everyone we know to the christening."

"Alex!" Clay cried, but he was so tickled by her offhand suggestion that he couldn't help but laugh. He was still chuckling to himself when Reverend Adams returned with the caretaker, who had been sweeping the front steps when they had arrived, and the organist, who had been in the sanctuary rehearsing the hymns for the following Sunday. Mrs. Adams also entered the study, accompanied by their two youngest children, a little girl, and a boy barely old enough to walk.

"I do hope you won't mind if we attend," she said.

The room was becoming a mite crowded, but Alex rather liked having another woman present. "Not at all, Mrs. Adams, do join us," she replied graciously.

It took a moment for everyone to move into the proper place, but as the brief service began, Alex straightened proudly. Her father and Willabelle's ceremony had passed in a blur, but she wanted to be able to recall every word of her own. Keenly alert, she anticipated each of Clay's promises and recited her own vows with a stunning composure. As Clay slipped the gold band on her finger, she made a silent promise never to remove it.

Clay had not expected Alex to go all teary-eyed on him, but as the minister pronounced them man and wife and he kissed his bride, her remarkable calm began to concern him. Then deciding he could not have coped with another flood of tears, he became anxious for them to be on their way.

There was the marriage certificate to sign, the minister to pay, and the witnesses to thank while they were all congratulating him and Alex heartily, but as soon as Clay possibly could, he led Alex from the study. When they stepped outside into the sunshine, he was amazed to find it was still hours before dark.

"It's too early to dine at the hotel, so I suppose we might as well go on out to the ranch."

Alex took his hand to climb up into the buggy, but could barely contain herself while Clay walked around to his side and got in. "You weren't actually serious about honeymooning at the ranch, were you?"

Clay eased back on the reins. There was a dapple gray mare hitched to the buggy, and he thought it was a damn good thing it wasn't Daniel, whom Alex might have quickly ridden away. "Did you think I was merely joking?" he asked.

"Not exactly. I just thought you were making up a convenient excuse for us to get married today. I don't want to go to the ranch, though. I want you to take me to your house." When Clay's dark eyes widened in surprise, Alex hurried on. "You do have a home, don't you?"

"There's an apartment above my office, but it's not much of a home."

"Well, it appears to be the only one we have at present, and I'd like to see it before sundown."

Clay always left his bed neatly made and kept his clothes in the wardrobe, but it wasn't the cleanliness of the apartment that worried him. It was the complete lack of the warmth and charm Alex was used to having at home. Because this seemed like a particularly poor time to have an argument, he sighed and gave in.

"Fine. We'll go back to my office, and you can take a look at the apartment; but you won't ever have to spend a night there if you don't want to."

Alex stayed his hand before he could turn the mare out into the road. "What did you plan to do, Clay? Have us live out at the ranch, but call it a honeymoon until my papa and Willabelle get back? Then we'd just all live there together as a family?"

She glanced away as though she were thoroughly disgusted with him, and it was all Clay could do not to remind her that when he had met her outside his office that afternoon, she had not given him any time to plan for their future.

"I was on my way to your ranch when we met today," he offered in as moderate a tone as he could manage. "I had expected us to talk for as long as it took to decide just what we wanted to do, and where, and when we'd do it.

Our living arrangements would certainly have come up before, rather than after, the wedding."

That Clay was almost shouting at her so soon after their wedding tried Alex's patience sorely, but she had taken so much time to dress like a lady, she forced herself to behave like one awhile longer. Again she laid her palm on his thigh, but this time felt him tense at her touch.

"Just take me home, Clay," she urged sweetly. "I promise not to make a worse scene there than I would here on the street."

"Now there's a comfort!" Clay replied with a furious snort, and he was shocked to find that he had already begun to sound exactly like his brand-new wife.

Chapter Six

The building where Clay rented space was built of brick, but the interior walls had been plastered and whitewashed. The antiseptic decor was appropriate for his office and treatment rooms, but bordered on the monastic in his living quarters. In addition to Clay's apartment upstairs, there was a second unit occupied by Burt Neubeck, who clerked in the dry goods store. He was a quiet fellow who had never created any problems, but sharing the second story meant Clay had only half the space.

As Clay unlocked the door and showed Alex inside, he held his breath and tried to see his place through her eyes. He had been unable to find a creative way to arrange the sparse furnishings to make the single room more attractive. Two windows allowed ample light during the day, and there were gas lamps for the evening; but that was not much of an advantage.

Clay doubted the plain pine wardrobe would hold Alex's gowns in addition to his suits and shirts. The matching dresser was small, and he had had to fold a tiny piece of cardboard into a square and jam it under one of the back legs to prevent it from tilting at such an angle that anything placed atop it would roll off.

There was a washstand painted a bright green, but at least the white porcelain pitcher and bowl were handsome. The mirror hanging above was new and clearly reflected the blank wall on the opposite side of the room. The iron bed was of a simple design befitting a bachelor's room, but the white paint was chipped and in dire need of a new coat. A worn brown carpet covered the center of the room, and pale muslin curtains hung limp at the windows.

Alex needed only a few seconds to survey Clay's pitiful quarters before she turned toward him. "We could use a couple of comfortable chairs and maybe some new curtains."

Clay was enormously relieved Alex hadn't simply turned up her nose and walked out on him. He drew her into his arms for a warm hug, and when he at last stepped back, her teasing smile was such a welcome sight that he embraced her again.

"I know it's awful, but all I do here is sleep. It's not a fit home for you," he explained.

Alex did her best to be diplomatic. "I'll grant that it looks as though we might be a bit crowded, but I still prefer it to sharing a house with Willabelle. That I absolutely will not do. It wouldn't be fair to her, or me."

Clay wanted to please Alex, but not really knowing how, he rested his forehead against hers. His hair brushed the cluster of ribbons on her hat, and the thought of her donning such a cute little bonnet provided an instant boost to his spirits.

"I'll find us a home somehow," he promised.

That Clay was such an earnest young man was one of the attributes Alex admired most about him, but she didn't want him worrying needlessly. "You were right," she offered. "We'll be better off at the ranch for a while, and we have at least a month to make other plans. You can always keep this place, though, for the times you need to remain in town with a patient."

Alex turned away from Clay to remove her hat and placed it atop the dresser. Next she peeled off her gloves. "I didn't see anyone tending your office," she remarked casually. Don't you employ a clerk to keep track of your patients?"

"Yes, Mrs. Gilroy, a widow who's gone to Dallas to visit her sister for a few days." Clay watched Alex pluck the combs from her hair and shake out the glorious red curls. "Alex? Just what is it you're doing?"

Alex doubted Clay was really so dense, but provided a broad hint in a sultry voice. "It's early yet, and I thought we ought to make good use of our time before leaving for the ranch." She sat down on the side of the bed and began to unbutton her shoes.

Clay could only dimly recall being thoroughly annoyed with her as they had left the church, and her provocative suggestion convinced him she also intended to forget that incident. He was uncertain what he had done right since then, but surely there would be time enough to analyze it later. For now, all he wanted was to be with her.

When Burt Neubeck began yelling Clay's name as he ran up the stairs with a loud, thudding clatter, the young physician's heart fell. "Just give me a minute. That sounds like my neighbor," Clay said and went to the door.

"Thank God I found you, Burnett," Burt blurted out, gulping for breath. "Mordecai Sloan just came into the store and keeled over in a faint. He needs you right away."

Still seated on the bed, Alex was far too colorful an addition to Clay's room to be overlooked. Once Burt's urgent message had been delivered, his eyes were instantly drawn to her, and his mouth fell agape.

"Gosh, Miss Howard, is that you?" he gasped.

Alex rose with all the grace she possessed and came toward the men. "I think it's a good thing we're married, doc, or my being here might cause a terrible scandal."

"May I present my wife," Clay announced proudly. "We've not had time to notify the *Star-Telegram*, but you may certainly tell whomever you like."

Burt had torn out of the dry goods store still wearing his apron, and when he wiped his hand on it prior to congratulating Clay, he suddenly recalled his errand. "We better hurry, or Mordecai's likely to be dead. It was nice seeing you Miss, Mrs. Burnett."

"Thank you." Alex ran her hand down Clay's back and urged him out the door. "I'll wait here," she promised, but she could see by his troubled frown just how little he wanted to go.

"I keep all my books downstairs in my office. Find yourself something to read," Clay encouraged.

"Good idea," Alex replied. "I've been meaning to study up on anatomy."

"I've other books, too," Clay shouted as he followed Burt down the stairs.

Alex and Clay had not been wed an hour, but as she closed the door and leaned back against it, she feared she had already been provided with an accurate glimpse of what their life together was likely to be. Clay was the most responsible of physicians, and his patients relied on him to be available at any hour of the day or night.

Clay might feel torn between them and his family, as she knew he must that afternoon, but his patients would have to come first. After all, a man could always find the time to make love to his wife, while people didn't choose when they fell ill, suffered some terrible accident, or, like Mordecai Sloan, simply keeled over.

Alex sought the windows, hoping for a comforting view, but the nearby buildings blocked the rolling prairie and provided no relief. At least she could gaze up at the sky, but the inviting blue only intensified her now aching sense of loneliness.

Determined not to cry on her wedding day, Alex marched herself downstairs to Clay's office and scanned the bookshelves for interesting titles. She had expected medical books; but apparently he also had a fondness for history, and there were a few novels. She debated a moment, then withdrew *Moby-Dick*. She had read it before, but at present, the adventure set on the open seas was especially appealing.

She climbed the stairs slowly, then this time succeeded in removing her shoes without being interrupted. After plumping up Clay's pillows, she climbed up on the bed and leaned back. Soon entertained by Melville's vivid prose, she could almost smell the sea breeze and thought it a shame women weren't welcome on board ships unless they were passengers on a cruise.

Reminded of her father and Willabelle, she hoped they reached Galveston safely, and then had a marvelous time aboard their ship and in New Orleans. Having made love with Clay, she now better understood her father's eagerness to remarry, but she still wished he had picked someone other than Willabelle.

When after reading several chapters Alex's glance drifted toward the windows, she was surprised to find the sky now streaked with a fiery red and gold sunset. The day had passed too quickly, but as she turned her gold wedding band on her finger, she began to think it hadn't passed nearly fast enough. She lit the lamps, but when she returned to the bed, she dozed off long before Burt Neubeck arrived with a bowl of chicken and dumplings from the Lone Star Cafe.

"Things aren't looking good," Burt explained. "Dr. Burnett believes Mordecai suffered a stroke, and he doesn't dare move him. He told me to tell you that it might be a long night, but he didn't want you to go hungry."

Alex quickly covered a wide yawn. "Thank you so much for bringing my supper, Burt, and please thank Clay for his thoughtfulness."

The clerk had brought along a linen napkin and utensils, and as soon as he had bid her a good night, Alex set her dinner atop the dresser. With no chair, she had to stand while she ate.

"We're going to need a table as well as chairs," she noted, and decided to begin making a list. It had taken her so long to get ready to come into town, she hadn't wanted to waste a second eating. Now she was ravenously hungry and used the last soggy lump of dumpling to wipe the bowl clean.

She was then at a loss for what to do. At home she spent so much time out-of-doors that remaining inside in the evening was a nice change. Here, with no more than a single room, she simply felt trapped and again went downstairs to Clay's office where she could at least sit in a chair while she read.

She had intended to wait up for Clay, but when she grew too sleepy to stay awake another minute, she returned to his apartment. She hung her beautiful gown and lacy undergarments in the wardrobe, and then believing her chemise would make a fine nightgown, she climbed into bed. Hours later, she felt Clay's arm tighten around her waist as he joined her in bed, but she simply smiled in her dreams.

Unfortunately, Clay's dreams weren't nearly so peaceful. With dawn still more than an hour away, he cried out in his sleep and awoke from the ghastly nightmare drenched in cold sweat. Not wanting to inflict his pain on Alex, he hurriedly left the bed and began to pull on the clothes he had discarded only a few hours earlier.

Badly startled, Alex sat up. The light in the room was a misty gray, but she could see her new husband clearly. "Clay, what's wrong? I thought I heard someone scream."

"It was just me. I'm sorry I woke you. I often have bad dreams." Anxious to get away, he grabbed his socks and boots and went to the door barefooted. "I'm going out for a walk. Go back to sleep."

Frightened first by his anguished cry, and then his intent to abandon her again, Alex called out to him. "No, wait. Do you often prowl the town before dawn?"

Clay paused only briefly at the door. "No, but then I've always been alone here."

As the door closed behind him, Alex rolled off the bed. In her view, Clay had sounded as though she was in his way there. Furiously angry with him, she went to the washstand and splashed cold water on her face to clear her head. She then opened a window and drank in the cool night air, but Clay's parting words continued to echo painfully in her mind.

She could understand that their sudden marriage might have interrupted his comfortable routine, but she could not comprehend how he could imagine that all a wife required was a hot supper.

As the sun rose, she was dressed as beautifully as she had been for their wedding, and certain their marriage was over before it had even begun, she startled the owner of the livery stable and drove her buggy home.

Clay had not expected to wake up screaming, but he would never use Alex's supple body to escape the dark horror of his memories. By the time he had walked far enough to cool down, he was so anxious to see her he had nearly run all the way home, only to find her gone. That she had not given him a chance to apologize or explain was so unfair that he again closed his office to come after her. Cursing her under his breath, he remounted his horse and rode out to the ranch.

José Blanco was at the corral, along with half a dozen hands who were laughing as one of their fellows attempted to ride a pinto pony that did not wish to be ridden.

"Where's my wife?" Clay called to the foreman.

José jumped down from the top rail of the corral and came ambling toward him. "I did not even know you had a wife; but how could you have misplaced her?"

"I'm in no mood for games, José. Where's Alex?"

José spread his arms wide. "She loves to ride. She could be anywhere."

Clay gazed past the men at the corral, who were now all straining to follow their conversation. The Howard ranch was so large, he feared he could search the prairie for days and not find a single trace of Alex. Certain she would eventually come home, he dismounted, and then just to make certain Alex wasn't hiding nearby, he checked Daniel's stall in the barn; but it was empty.

All the while, José was watching him with an amused smile. "You're not going to think this is nearly so funny when Alex gets home," Clay told him.

All trace of laughter left José's expression, and he lowered his voice to a threatening whisper. "Alex was laughing when she left here yesterday, but she did not return wearing a bride's shy smile. Instead, she was as unhappy as I have ever seen her. If you cannot make her happy for even one day, then I do not think you are man enough for her."

Clay stared down at José, but he took note as the hands drifted away from the corral to form a semicircle behind the foreman. "I have nothing to prove to you, or to Alex," he boasted confidently, and the darkness of his menacing scowl gave clear warning he would brook no interference.

Without taking his eyes off José, Clay peeled off his frock coat and tossed it over his horse's saddle. Then he began to roll up his sleeves. "I can tear you apart one at a time, or in a clump, whichever you prefer, but you'll have to find yourselves another doctor to stitch up your bloody wounds."

Returning from her ride, Alex was astonished to see Clay nearly surrounded by ranch hands. From his aggressive stance, it was plain that he was mere seconds away from a brutal confrontation. With an angry shout, she urged Daniel to a gallop and sped toward the corral. At the last instant, she pulled the spirited horse to an abrupt sliding halt to form a defensive barrier between Clay and the hands.

Alex was disgusted to find José providing so little in the way of leadership in what appeared to be a deeply troubling situation. But before she could question his actions, Clay reached up to drag her off Daniel's back and sent her hat flying. Had he hefted her over his shoulder, she would have beaten her fists on his back, and probably bitten him, too. But cradled in his arms her knees were pressed close to her chest, severely limiting her options.

She had a clear view of the tense muscles along Clay's jaw and the harsh set of his mouth, but had no idea why he was so furious with her. After all, he was the one who had walked out. Unwilling to make a scene in front of the hands, she relaxed rather than fight Clay's confining hold. She heard José laugh at her plight, but knew she could count on his help should she really need it.

Clay carried Alex through the back gate and across the patio. Although tempted to drop her into the pond, he found the control to skirt it and strode on into the house.

When he reached her bedroom, he kicked the door open wide and reached her brass bed in two long strides. Then, none too gently, he dropped her in the middle.

"What's it going to take to keep you off that horse?" he asked. "Can't you understand that I want babies with your beautiful red hair and my brown eyes? Is that too much to ask?"

Alex did not appreciate being bounced on the bed like a stack of laundry, but the fire in Clay's dark eyes warned her to stay put. No one had ever been as angry with her as he obviously was, but armed with a quick wit, and her own righteous anger, she had a ready retort.

"What I wanted was to spend my wedding night with my husband, but obviously, that was way too much to ask."

Alex was leaning back on her hands, but her expression was as challenging as her words. Clay stared at her a long moment, and then ripped his gold watch from the pocket in his vest. He noted the time, and then carefully laid the watch on the edge of the washstand.

"We've not been married a day yet," he told her, and he sat down on the side of the bed and yanked off his boots. "Now, I'm real sorry the night didn't go as we'd hoped, but that's no reason to say it's over."

Alex's eyes widened as Clay stood to remove his vest and shirt. When he looked up, his expression had softened, but he still didn't appear pleased. She had been so disappointed to be left all alone, not once, but twice, and yet now that Clay was with her, she still felt sad. Tears blurred her vision, and she didn't raise a hand to wipe them away.

Clay could have handled Alex's sarcastic anger, but he couldn't cope with her tears. He had known they were a poor match, and God help him, he had married her anyway. Somehow he was going to have to find the strength to make it work.

He sat down beside Alex and pulled her into his arms.

"I want us to have a happy marriage, honey. I really do, but you're not ever going to be able to obey me, are you?"

Alex remembered her wedding vows clearly, but now realized she hadn't really appreciated what the promise to obey her husband had meant. "I can't obey a man who isn't there," she murmured against his chest, but she was fully aware she hadn't answered his question.

Clay cupped her chin to force her to meet his gaze. "I was a sharpshooter during the war, and your father would tell me to find a tree, or high ground, where I could pick off Yankee officers in the distance. I never saw the faces of the men I killed, but I saw plenty of our own men who were mortally wounded.

"I had no medical training then, and there was nothing I could do to ease their pain except remain with them until they drew their last breath. It was because of that horror that I became a doctor, and I still won't let anyone die alone. I just can't. Not even on my wedding night when I wanted to be with you."

In the morning's confusion, Alex had completely forgotten Mordecai. "You lost Mr. Sloan?"

Clay nodded. "He'd had a stroke and never regained consciousness. He had no family, no one to even call the undertaker except me."

Alex had had such noble thoughts yesterday, and she tried to summon them now. She pulled away to sit up straight and yanked off her gloves to wipe her eyes. "I understand. You have to be a doctor first."

Surprised by her comment, Clay took a firm hold on her shoulders. "No. You don't understand anything. You'll always come first with me, even if we can't be together."

Alex heard the heartfelt edge to his deep voice, as well as his words, and met his kiss with a welcoming tremor. Now easily lured down onto the bed, she kissed him until they were both so breathless they had to stop. She combed his hair from his eyes.

"I know I can ride Daniel and still make babies. I'm sure I can. I didn't ride him at a gallop today until I saw the trouble you were in."

Clay propped himself up on his elbow. "Did you really believe I was in such desperate need of rescue?"

"Well, yes. Weren't you? I swear I'll fire that whole lot if they were disrespectful to you."

Clay eased over her and tried not to laugh. "I'm a lot tougher than I look, Mrs. Burnett, and I would have tied them in knots and left them jerking about in the dirt."

Alex licked her lips invitingly. "Now, that would really be something to see, but I'll not risk your being hurt."

Still amazed she would be so protective, Clay whispered, "Kiss me."

When Alex arched her neck to reach up for him, her eager passion matched his own. It warmed him clear through to discover there was at least one area in which she would obey his command. Taking every advantage of that delightful show of cooperation, he skimmed off her clothes before removing the rest of his own. Then, with an imaginative devotion, he kept his adoring wife in bed until sundown.

Chapter Seven

Frank and Willabelle Howard did not return to Fort Worth until the end of May. They had sent a telegram, so Alex and Clay were expecting their arrival, but that did not mean the young couple was truly prepared. After living together in the spacious ranch house, Alex dreaded the move into Clay's small apartment, but she had packed her belongings and was ready to go.

Clay checked his pocket watch. "They should be here soon, and I wish you looked happier about it. I sure hope that you're not ashamed of me," he teased.

"Too late for that," Alex teased in return, and too anxious to sit still, she paced the parlor in a most unladylike rhythm. She had begun wearing softly feminine dresses when Clay was home, but none that required a corset or crinolette. She preferred her old boots to her new shoes, and usually made a conscious effort not to clump through the house, but that afternoon, she was simply too nervous to mind her step.

Clay went to the window and looked out. "No sign of them yet. Maybe they decided to spend an extra day in Galveston."

"Papa said they'd be home today, and they surely will." Alex raised her hands to smooth her curls off her face. "If they don't get here soon, though, I swear I'm going to be sick."

"Come here," Clay coaxed, and he caught her hand and pulled her down on his lap in her father's favorite chair. "You don't have to tell them about the baby today. It's best to wait a couple of months to be sure."

Alex resisted his embrace only a moment, and then relaxed against him. Clay had been so certain that she had gotten pregnant the first time they had been together that she hadn't really been surprised when it proved to be true. She had not once been bothered by morning sickness, but she sure felt nauseous now.

"I wish I knew how much money Mama left me," she murmured fretfully. "I hope it's enough to buy a few acres and build a house."

"And a barn," Clay added. "My horse wouldn't mind a lean-to out back; but we can't have your magnificent stallion only partially protected from the elements, and I absolutely refuse to share the house with him."

"Guess we'll have to build the barn first, then," Alex replied.

Amused, Clay tightened his embrace. He was continually amazed by how bright Alex was, and enormously pleased with the logic of her reasoning. "Good thinking, but I could live in a haystack with you."

"Do you mind setting your sights a mite higher?" Alex was laughing, though, because she thought she might also prefer a haystack to his apartment. She had come to care for Clay more deeply every day, but while they often exchanged such affectionate banter, neither had ever spoken of love. Alex thought the man was supposed to be the first to give voice to his feelings. She frowned slightly as she wondered if maybe Clay wasn't waiting for her to speak of love.

Clay ran his fingertip across her lower lip to erase her slight pout. "What are you thinking?"

Unwilling to beg for the words he did not seem inclined to speak willingly, Alex kissed him instead. "What I'm always thinking," she confided softly. "Of you."

Clay sincerely doubted that, but as long as her delicious kisses were more intoxicating than champagne, he dared not call her a liar. He wound his fingers in her hair and kissed her so long and hard neither of them heard the carriage arrive, nor the front door swing open. Lost in each other, it wasn't until Frank cleared his throat loudly that they realized they were no longer alone.

Willabelle's purple hat was adorned with a tightly curled ostrich feather that bobbed like a bouncing spring when she laughed. "Your papa was so worried about you, Alexandra, but it looks as though Dr. Burnett has kept you from growing bored."

"He's done a lot more than that," Alex revealed playfully. She slid off Clay's lap and dipped her head to hide her smile as she shook out her skirt.

Taken aback by his daughter's provocative comment, Frank sucked in a deep breath. Alex struck him as different somehow, and he suspected it wasn't simply because of her pretty clothes. "Damn it all, Clay, maybe you better tell me exactly what's been going on here."

Clay unfolded out of the chair, but immediately slid his arm around Alex's waist to draw her near. "Alex and I were married the Tuesday following your wedding," he announced proudly. "I'm not ashamed to be caught kissing my wife, and I don't believe she minds being seen with me either."

"You two are married?" Frank could barely speak the word.

"Oh, this is wonderful!" Willabelle exclaimed. She clapped her hands and rushed forward to embrace the newlyweds, while Frank hung back and continued to regard Clay with an incredulous frown.

Alex was pleased with how confidently Clay had revealed their marriage, but while she appreciated Willabelle's enthusiasm, she didn't know what to make of her father's startled reaction.

"Papa, aren't you happy for us?" she asked.

Frank gestured helplessly. "This is so unexpected; I don't know what to say."

"Just congratulate Clay, dear," Willabelle prompted sweetly, "and send for someone to help the carriage driver unload our trunks."

"Yes, of course. We ought not to forget our luggage," Frank replied, and relieved to have the errand, he hurried out the door without speaking to Clay.

Dismayed that Frank hadn't taken the news of their marriage with more grace, Clay gave Alex a reassuring hug. "Your father's simply surprised. I'll go and have a talk with him."

Alex stifled the impulse to follow her husband, or to at least peer out the window to watch his exchange with her father, but she had a sinking feeling things weren't going nearly as well as they should have. She hugged her arms as though chilled.

"Did you have a nice trip?" she remembered to ask Willabelle.

Willabelle's smile slid dangerously close to a triumphant smirk. "It was delightful from beginning to end, although I'm sure I don't need to tell you how charming a man your father is."

Fearful he might not be using charm on Clay, Alex had to swallow hard. "Yes. He certainly can be."

"Now that we're home, do you and Clay have plans for a honeymoon?" Willabelle slowly removed her hat and patted her creamy puffed hair.

Alex observed her new stepmother's glance flit around the parlor, and wondered if she hadn't already bought new furniture in New Orleans. "Clay and I don't need to leave town to be happy together."

"Well, no, of course not, but once you've taken on the responsibility of a home, and you'll surely want children, it's very difficult to get away. Go now while you still can, dear. I promise that you'll not regret it."

Willabelle sat down in a dainty rosewood chair, removed her gloves, and began to comb the ostrich plume on her hat with daintily manicured nails. "I did so want children, but neither of my previous marriages produced any," she confided wistfully. "Now it's probably too late for me to become a mother."

"You mean this is your third marriage?" Alex asked too quickly.

"Why, yes. I was widowed during the war, and then lost my second husband two years ago. Does three husbands seem like a great many to you?"

"I can barely contend with one," Alex marveled, but she could not bear to think of ever losing Clay.

Amused by Alex's response, Willabelle raised a hand to hush a sparkling laugh. "I only had one husband at a time, dear."

Outside, there was no hint of laughter. Clay had known he would have to face Frank eventually, but he had repeatedly put off considering how his former commanding officer might react to having him as a son-in-law. He waited impatiently while Frank sent the carriage driver around to the kitchen for something to eat, but the hunched set of Frank's shoulders kept him wary.

When Frank suddenly spun on his heel and swung at him, Clay was ready to block the blow. Using his greater height to every advantage, he grabbed hold of Frank's arm, twisted it behind his back, and forced it up between his shoulder blades.

"Settle down," Clay ordered in a hoarse whisper. "Try and act like the fine gentleman Alex and your new bride believe you to be. Even if I'm not your choice for Alex, I'm hers, and you'll have to get used to it."

"You must have taken advantage of her," Frank growled, "or the two of you would never have been in such an awful hurry to get married."

While there was an element of truth in Frank's accusation, when Clay and Alex shared such a passionate attraction, he preferred to see their marriage as inevitable rather than scandalously quick. Disgusted he had not been welcomed into the Howard family, he released his father-in-law and brushed off his hands.

"Now you've insulted us both," Clay declared.

"I doubt it," Frank swore, and yanked his coat back into place. "You never came to call on Alex, and I didn't notice the two of you spending any time together at our reception. Did you even dance with her more than once?"

"Yes," Clay assured him. "But then you were too busy celebrating with your friends to notice what Alex and I were doing." That was indeed a stretch, Clay thought, but he would not admit it aloud.

"What you're forgetting," Clay insisted darkly, "is that I was there when you did your best to humiliate Alex because she'd not received any marriage proposals. I'm sorry I didn't object in stronger terms, but it was plain you hadn't cared whether or not she had had any suitors until you decided to marry Willabelle. Then you wanted Alex out of your way. That's the only disgrace here, Frank, and you're the one who ought to be ashamed. Now I'm taking my wife and going home."

Clay stomped back into the house, went straight to Alex, and took her hand. "Come on, we're leaving."

"Oh, Clay, won't you folks stay for supper?" Willabelle invited. She set her hat aside and rose to accept the role of gracious hostess before even being home half an hour.

Clay shook his head. "Thank you, Willabelle, but no."

Over the last six weeks, Alex had had the opportunity to study every nuance of Clay's expressions and mannerisms. She knew how he tilted his head slightly to the right when he offered thoughtful observations or how he leaned back when he had grown skeptical. She loved the predatory grin he often wore when he joined her in bed and how hard he would fight to keep his infrequent chuckles from rolling right into deep laughter.

She also recognized how tightly he clenched the muscles along his jaw when he was angry. While Willabelle might believe Clay was merely determined to get back into town early, Alex could see he was not simply in a rush, but livid. She pressed his hand firmly.

"In a minute, my darling," she coaxed soothingly. "I need to speak with Papa." She had never used any endearments and hoped Clay would realize how important it was for her to stay awhile longer. When he released her as though he had been scalded, she knew he had not understood at all.

Still, she turned to her father, who had followed Clay inside but hung back. "Could we go into your study for a few minutes, Papa?"

Frank jammed his hands into his pants pockets. "That's not necessary, missy. I don't keep secrets from Willabelle."

"I don't keep secrets from Clay either," Alex countered,

"but I thought you'd prefer to discuss the money Mama left me in private."

Frank shot Clay a disgusted glance. "It's not all that much, and you're not to have access to it until your twenty-first birthday. Your mother didn't want anyone marrying you for your money."

"Damn." The word slipped out before Alex could catch it, but Willabelle's horrified expression struck her as absurd. "You must have heard that word before, Willabelle. I was hoping to have my money now to buy us some land for a house."

Willabelle's mouth drew into a tiny moue, and her voice rose to a childlike whine. "Don't you have a home, Clay?"

"Oh, Christ," Clay muttered under his breath. "Yes. I have a home of sorts, but the two of us need something larger."

Seized by a sudden inspiration, Willabelle reached out to touch Clay's sleeve. "What about my boardinghouse? The tenants all know I planned to sell the place when I returned from my honeymoon and should have found other lodgings by now. It's a pretty house and wouldn't need more than a little paint to make a fine home for you two. Wouldn't it, Frank?"

"What Alex wants is a ranch, Willabelle, not a home in town, although that would obviously be best for the doctor."

Alex was far too perceptive to believe her father was merely having trouble accepting her marriage, and she didn't appreciate his moody response one bit. Badly embarrassed for Clay, and despite the stiffness of his pose, she slid her arm through his.

"Thank you for your suggestion, Willabelle," Alex offered with far more enthusiasm than she felt. "We'll talk it over and let you know what we decide. Now we really do need to be going, and we might as well take your carriage back to the livery stable."

With Clay and Frank unwilling to even look at each other, Alex easily arranged for their departure. A couple of the hands had already unloaded Frank and Willabelle's luggage and quickly stowed Alex's belongings. The driver had barely had time to eat a chicken leg, but Alex promised to tip him when they reached town. Clay tethered his gelding behind the carriage, and they got under way in a hurry.

When Clay ignored Alex to gaze out the window, she refused to allow him to sulk, slid along the bench, and cuddled up beside him. "I'm so sorry," she began. "I've no idea why my father was rude to you, but it was completely uncalled for. I would have told him so had we been able to speak privately."

"I don't need you to defend me," Clay responded grudgingly.

"Perhaps not, but I expect you to speak up for me whenever it's necessary, which, unfortunately, will probably be often."

"Nonsense," Clay argued unconvincingly. "But first off, there's no reason for us to discuss the boardinghouse when I can't afford to buy it."

"I was merely being polite. I don't want to live there," Alex assured him. She waited for him to offer an alternative, but he remained maddeningly remote. She rested her head on his shoulder.

"I don't recall my parents ever arguing about anything. Did yours?"

Clay had succeeded in distracting her with affection during her previous attempts to inquire into his background, but the afternoon had gone so poorly he didn't mind admitting he had damn little to tell. "My mother died when I was small, and it was my father who raised me. We just sort of drifted from town to town. He'd usually bar tend, or sometimes clerk in a store. But before we ever got comfortable anywhere, he'd say it was time to move on."

Clay's attention was still focused on the passing landscape; but at least he was talking to her, and Alex continued her efforts to draw him out. "He never remarried?"

"No. He'd get drunk every once in a while and sob my mother's name. I don't think he ever stopped loving her. He died a couple of months before the war began, and I was one of the first to enlist. I was just a stupid kid then, and thought fighting the Yankees would be a great adventure."

"I'll bet a lot of men believed the same thing."

Clay covered her hand with his. "Well, they didn't for long."

Clay now seemed merely sad rather than annoyed with her, and Alex recalled one of her few memories of the war. "My mother used to read me my father's letters. I'm sure he must have written wonderfully romantic things to her, but there was always a part she could read to me about the beauty of the countryside, or something amusing someone had done in camp."

"He really loved your mother," Clay murmured softly, "and now I think you're even prettier than she was."

"Oh, no, Clay. She was perfect."

"No one's perfect, Alexandra." But reconsidering her remark, he began to think aloud. "You do resemble her, and now I can't help but wonder if maybe every time your papa looks at you, he doesn't feel guilty for wanting Willabelle. That would explain why he was suddenly so anxious for you to find a husband and leave home."

Hurt that her father might see her mother whenever he looked her way, Alex needed a long moment to mull over that unsettling prospect. "Yes, I suppose a constant reminder of Mama would upset him, but I always thought he loved me, too. Besides, if he really wanted me gone, why wasn't he grateful rather than so surly to you?"

Uncertain how she would react, Clay drew in a deep breath and exhaled slowly. "He accused me of taking advantage of you."

"Really?" Alex closed her eyes and conjured up the vivid memory of the evening of the reception when she had gone out to the patio shortly after dusk. "The day he was married, I recall being so awfully tired and feeling terribly alone. Then you walked up behind me. Hmm," she murmured softly.

Clay laced her fingers in his and drew her hand to his lips. "Is a 'hmm,' good?"

"Oh, yes. That whole night was heaven, Clay, but perhaps I'm the one who took advantage of you."

Clay couldn't help but laugh at the innocence of her candor. "When I wanted you so badly, that would have been impossible."

They rode along in companionable silence until Alex sat up suddenly. "Clay, if my mother left me only a modest sum, why would she have feared anyone would have married me for my money?"

Equally intrigued, Clay also sat straighter. "When you put it that way, it doesn't make much sense. Perhaps your father was simply too upset with us to be reasonable. But let's stop worrying about money. I put myself through medical school playing poker, and while I'd not thought about playing cards again, I could do it."

"A respected physician can't hang around saloons posing as a card sharp," Alex insisted emphatically. "Besides, it won't damage anyone's reputation if we race Daniel and keep the winnings."

Clay swore a particularly colorful oath he hadn't used since his army days. "You are not riding Daniel, is that clear?"

More amazed by his creative use of profanity than insulted by his demand, Alex again snuggled close. "José can ride him. I'll simply place an ad in the paper describing Daniel as the fastest horse in Texas. I'll list his stud fee, as though that were all I intended, and let other men challenge us to a race."

Clay shook his head, but it was more in wonder than refusal. "I can't help but admire the way you think, but I want your solemn promise that you're not going to ride Daniel until after the baby's born."

Alex raised her right hand. "You have my word on it."

Clay still appeared decidedly skeptical. "José told me no one rides Daniel but you."

"That's true, but I'll speak with him."

"With José?"

"No, silly, with Daniel."

When Alex got around him so easily, Clay could readily imagine her convincing a horse to do her bidding. "Maybe we ought to take those little boats the men carved for you and race them on the river. We'd be sure to win a lot of money staging a miniature regatta."

Alex shoved away from him. "Are you making fun of me, doc?"

"Of course not. It's just difficult for me to keep up with your schemes."

"Well, I have to do something to keep myself occupied."

Clay hadn't seen that tear-brightened look of hurt in her eyes for weeks and hated himself for causing it. At the same time, her words pierced his heart like a knife because he knew she ought to have her own home where she would never run out of rooms to decorate, gardens to plant, or delicious meals to plan.

He drew her back down into his arms and hoped the gentle rocking of the carriage would prove as soothing as his embrace. There wasn't anything he wouldn't do to provide a ranch where he prayed her restless spirit would at last be content. He wouldn't have to play poker in saloons, either, because Frank often got together with other wealthy men who enjoyed a friendly game of cards at the same fine hotel where Frank and Willabelle had begun their honeymoon.

It had been a while since Clay had been invited to join them, but as Frank's son-in-law, it wouldn't be too difficult to arrange, once Frank got over being mad at him. News of the baby would probably accomplish that, and with what Daniel would surely win in the races Alex would stage, he would have the stake to play.

He still possessed the steely nerves to win, as long as Alex didn't take up playing cards and distract him so horribly he couldn't tell if he was holding jacks or threes. Of course, she would probably distract the other men, too, so maybe it wasn't such a bad pastime to encourage. But for now, he would keep this scheme to himself and count on Daniel to go along with hers.

Chapter Eight

Alex felt Clay come awake with a start and roll away from her to sit on the side of the bed. She reached out to caress his back. "Another awful dream?"

"Yes. I didn't mean to wake you."

Wanting him to remain with her, Alex raised up and knelt behind him. Using a sure, yet light touch, she began to knead the tension from his shoulders. She loved the feel of his sleek, muscular body, and when he leaned into her hands rather than shrink away, she grew more bold.

"Tell me about the dream," she coaxed in a seductive whisper.

"Never!"

Alex increased the pressure of her slow massage to trace widening circles, but she longed to ease Clay's troubled spirit as well as his aching body. "What do you believe happened to the souls of the men who were killed during the war?"

Clay shrugged and rolled his shoulders beneath her touch. "What do you mean?"

"Do you believe their souls are still wandering the battle-fields?"

"Probably. I can still hear them scream."

Alex raised up slightly to kiss the soft spot behind his ear. "I believe angels came for the soldiers, beautiful angels with flowing robes and whisper-soft wings."

Clay responded with a disgusted grunt. "I never saw any angels amid all the smoke and noise."

"Of course not. Only spirits can see angels. I'm sure your friends saw them when they died, and they floated up to heaven in the angels' arms."

"It's more likely they all went straight to hell."

"I don't believe in hell," Alex breathed out against his ear. "A God who forgives endlessly would not damn anyone to eternal torment."

"When did you become such an expert on the afterlife?"

"My mother told me all about heaven when I was a child. She's an angel now. I'm sure of it."

Clay pressed his chin against his chest as Alex's hands played down his spine. He considered her childlike view of heaven charming, but it was ample proof of the gap that existed between the girl who had lost her mother and the young woman she was today. She had been reading his anatomy texts and merely for amusement was memoriz-ing the bones in the body with a speed and accuracy that would have placed her at the top of his class in medical school.

In so many ways she was a treasure, and if she wished to believe in the angels her mother had described, he would not fault her for it. "I can't remember anything at all about my mother," he murmured softly.

"Imagine her, then. Perhaps she and my mother are

great friends, and together they dance around heaven sprinkling stardust on the clouds."

"That's a pretty image, but I doubt my mother was the type of woman who'd be welcomed into heaven as graciously as your dear mother."

"She must have been, or you'd not have grown up to be such a wonderful man."

Clay caught Alex's hand as he turned. "Thank you, but now I think you're the one who's dreaming."

"It's a very nice dream, then." Alex leaned forward to meet Clay's kiss and easily lured him back down onto the bed. She had intended to distract him so thoroughly his nightmares would no longer haunt him, and she was surprised by how quickly she had succeeded. She really didn't care what fanciful tale she had to spin; she couldn't bear to let him suffer for deaths he had not caused, nor could have done anything to prevent.

"You truly are a good man," she insisted when he gave her a moment to breathe between kisses, and consumed with a fierce yearning for more of her, he couldn't argue.

Clay frequently took Alex to dinner at the Lone Star Cafe, and while he made it a rule never to discuss his patients, he had good reason for an exception that evening. He lowered his voice to make certain he would not be overheard.

"Willabelle came to see me this afternoon," he revealed softly.

Alex had gone for a long walk and had been out most of the afternoon, but couldn't help but wonder if Willabelle had not also stopped by to see her. Clay had found a couple of chairs for their apartment, but Alex still felt poorly equipped to entertain guests.

"Was she hoping we wanted to buy her boardinghouse?"

Clay cast a hasty glance toward the two men dining at a nearby table, and once assured they were wholly involved in their own conversation, he continued. "No, although I did tell her we'd decided against it."

"She hasn't taken ill, I hope."

"On the contrary, she's in perfect health. She simply wanted my help in conceiving a child."

Alex had just taken a bite of bread, and nearly chocked. "My God. Did she actually ask you to father her babe?"

Clay had not meant to confuse Alex, but that she would leap to such a scandalous conclusion struck him as so ridiculous he could not help but laugh out loud.

"No," he replied. "She's relying on your father to fulfill that role. She merely wanted medical advice because she's been unable to conceive in the past."

Alex was embarrassed not to have understood something so obvious on her own. "I'm sorry. I should have known that, and as long as you don't intend to be directly involved, I hope you were helpful."

Clay found Alex's deep blush delightful, but didn't want to see her so mortified in the future and made a mental note to make his part in such personal topics clear from the beginning. "I offered what help I could, but that's not really what concerns me."

Now afraid she would offer another incredibly stupid comment, Alex waited silently for Clay to explain. She hadn't had much appetite that evening, and now she had even less; but she toyed with her ham as though her dinner held at least some appeal.

Clay leaned forward slightly. "Willabelle's main concern is that she won't have a child, but if she does give birth, and to a son, she fears you'll hate your half brother for inheriting the ranch you've grown up believing will be yours."

Alex blotted her mouth on her napkin while she sought

an intelligent response to that convoluted possibility. "I hope you told her that you and I intend to have a fine ranch of our own, and that we won't be needing Papa's."

Before Clay could reply to her optimistic plan, Fred Tritle entered the cafe and, sighting them, headed their way. Clay watched him approach and hoped the man had the good sense not to expect to be invited to join them. Alex, however, didn't notice Fred until he spoke her name.

"Alexandra, it's good to see you again, but I don't know which is more surprising, your marriage to Dr. Burnett or your outrageous boast of owning the fastest horse in Texas."

Pleased Fred had taken her bait so quickly, Alex slid the toe of her boot up Clay's calf in a teasing caress before she replied. "I should think it must be our marriage, as Daniel's speed is well-known."

"By whom?" Fred scoffed.

"Why, experts on horseflesh, of course," Alex responded proudly.

Fred shook his head. "I'm positive my stallion, Lancelot, has greater speed."

"Believe whatever you wish. My only interest is in stud fees. Obviously you own what you believe to be a fine stallion, so I'll earn nothing from you. I'd really rather enjoy a piece of chocolate cake than argue, so I'll bid you a good night. Will you order dessert for me, dearest?" Clearly dismissing Fred, Alex took a tiny bite of ham and chewed carefully.

When Fred did not immediately move on, Clay offered his own prompt. "You're interrupting our meal, Mr. Tritle, and because I never know when I'll be called out on an emergency, I regard every minute I'm able to spend with my wife as precious. Let's have this debate another time so we can enjoy our supper in peace."

Fred's expression darkened, and he lowered his voice

to utter a threatening challenge. "This is no debate, Burnett. I demand a race to prove who owns the better horse."

Alex frowned slightly. "That's really not a good idea. Daniel would surely outrace Lancelot by several lengths, and your friends would make fun of you for weeks. Wouldn't you rather avoid such a needless humiliation?"

Because she was a lady, Fred choked back the obscene response her taunt deserved. "Despite your obstinate opinion, the results of the race are by no means a foregone conclusion. You're a reasonable man, Burnett. Can't you talk some sense into her?"

"I regard my wife as an extremely sensible woman. After all, she had the good sense to marry me," Clay added with a ready grin.

Disgusted that the couple was too lost in fond glances to focus on the issue at hand, Fred spoke in a voice loud enough to catch the interest of everyone in the popular cafe. "I'm challenging you to a race this coming Saturday, and the humiliation will be entirely yours if you fail to appear."

Clay shrugged. "Well, it might provide an amusing experience, but you'd have to make it worth our while."

"You expect me to pay for the privilege of racing you?" Fred nearly shouted.

"Please, Mr. Tritle," Alex scolded. "We were having such a pleasant evening until you appeared. I do believe my husband was referring to a small wager. Weren't you, dear?"

"That I was, and it's not a fit topic for the supper table."

Alex continued to toy with her food as Clay quickly arranged how bets might be placed. "Oh, by the way," she then remarked absently. "Because you've challenged us, the race will take place at my father's ranch."

"Absolutely not. I want it right here in town."

Alex leaned back in her chair. "No. That's much too

dangerous. A child might dart out into the street and be trampled. I simply couldn't bear being a party to such a terrible tragedy."

"Neither could I," Clay agreed firmly. "Invite whomever you wish to attend, and we'll see you at the Howard ranch at ten o'clock on Saturday."

"You may be sure that I'll invite the whole damn town," Fred swore as he turned away.

Alex didn't dare look at Clay, but it was plain Fred Tritle was so insulted he would bring everyone he knew and the amount wagered was bound to be considerable. "That was much too easy," she whispered once Fred had walked right on out of the cafe.

"Only if Daniel is as fast as you claim," Clay pointed out.

Alex licked her lips. "Order the chocolate cake, and we'll begin celebrating our victory now."

While Clay doubted that was wise, as always he admired Alex's confidence where Daniel was concerned. He almost wished she could ride her stallion in the race, and then was greatly relieved that she would not. "Cake it is, and after Daniel's won the race, let's tell your father and Willabelle about the baby."

Fear veiled the bright sparkle in her eyes, and while she quickly averted her glance, Clay had seen the sudden change. "Alex, what's wrong? Aren't you happy about the baby?"

Alex now had to force the smile that had come so easily a minute earlier. "Yes, I'm happy. The idea of becoming a mother is rather daunting."

Clay reached across the table to take her hand. "Please don't be frightened. I'll take such good care of you. I promise."

Alex nodded, but she wasn't worried about giving birth. Women had been doing that since Eve. What frightened her more each day was the prospect of raising a child when she had none of her mother's expertise. Because Clay hadn't raised any brothers or sisters either, she doubted he knew anything more than what he had read in his medical books. She would not insult him by saying so, however.

"Let's skip the cake," she begged.

Clay was dismayed by how rapidly Alex's mood had swung from elation to despair, but hoping to raise her spirits when they reached home, he was as eager to leave as she. He took her hand as they left the cafe and hoped that while it was still early, she would not mind going to bed now—since he had no intention of letting her sleep. He was now desperately sorry he had laughed at her while describing Willabelle's visit, but it simply served to confirm his sorry opinion of himself where words were concerned.

Saturday dawned bright and clear with a shimmering promise of real heat by early afternoon. Alex was wearing her pale blue dress and a broad-brimmed straw hat, but Clay was still worried about her getting too much sun.

"If you feel even the slightest bit of discomfort, please tell me immediately, and I'll take you inside the house to rest," he offered.

"I'm fine, doc. I'd be riding Daniel myself today if not for you."

They had left town early and with ample time to spare, Clay yanked on his horse's reins to bring their buggy to a halt in the middle of the road. "What bothers you most, that I extracted that promise or that I made it necessary in the first place?"

Alex had been concentrating on the race, but the hurt in Clay's voice instantly dissolved the colorful images in her mind's eye. "Neither. I understand why you're concerned, and I don't blame you for anything," she insisted. "Now let's go. We mustn't be late."

Even knowing the race was vital to their future, Clay found it impossible to believe it was more important than giving thoughtful consideration to his question. When they had wed, Alex had been slender, but now she was simply thin. She enjoyed going on long walks each day, and he hated to forbid that activity, too; but clearly she wasn't thriving. It wasn't merely because he was a physician that he felt responsible for his bride's health either.

His voice was low. "I'm serious, Alex."

"Well, so am I," she replied and glanced away.

She hadn't thought about how her father would react to the race until he had come striding out to the barn when she had first gone home to speak with José. Once informed of her purpose, both men had been eager to help, but her father's advice had been strictly professional rather than wildly enthusiastic.

Frank had made no further comment on her marriage to Clay, but she could not help but feel he had evaded the topic rather than truly accepted it. He would surely be pleased when Daniel won the race, but she had been unable to force herself to contemplate how he might respond to the news that she and Clay were expecting his first grandchild. That he and Willabelle had apparently had no success in their efforts to become parents would only make things that much worse.

Alex didn't want Clay to suspect he was the cause of the dread that hovered on the edge of her excitement, however. She turned back toward him and laid her hand on his thigh. "I hope we have a dozen babies, but right now, let's just concentrate on the race.

"Papa pointed out that while Fred only rides his stallion into town occasionally to show him off, Daniel is a working quarter horse and has not only far more speed, but the greater endurance as a result. José is going to give Daniel his head, let him get way out in front, and Daniel will do his best to stay there. Before Fred Tritle knows what happened, we'll have won every penny he's wagered, and a lot more as well.''

Clay had bet his life savings, which was a pitifully small sum, but if Daniel lost, he would lose not only that money, but his hopes of playing high stakes poker to bring their ranch that much closer to reality. That ghastly prospect had him on edge; but he was equally worried about Alex's health, and he would take no gamble there.

When Clay's frown didn't lift, Alex wanted to throw her arms around his neck, hug him tight, and assure him everything would turn out exactly as they had planned, but his expression was so darkly forbidding she did not dare.

"What's the worst that could happen?" she asked instead. "Daniel might not run well for José and lose. If that happens, I'll start working him with the other hands until we find someone he likes. Fred will have to give us a rematch or risk being called a coward, and we're bound to win then. Please don't worry so.''

Clay knew she sincerely believed every word she said, but he was still nervous and refused to explain why. "Fine," he exclaimed with far more confidence than he felt. "Daniel will win and that's all there is to it.''

Alex looped her arm through his. "I'm glad you finally understand. There will be some who'll laugh and call Daniel an Indian pony, but don't listen to them. That's precisely why he's so fast and strong, and those who believe it a flaw will be flat broke before noon.''

Clay wished she had as much faith in him as her stallion; but all Daniel had to do was be the fine horse he was, and Clay had taken on a hell of a lot more responsibility. He clucked to his faithful gelding to get them under way again.

Alex was relieved they were at least traveling in the right direction, but Clay still looked so apprehensive she tightened her grasp on his arm before voicing a sudden suspicion. "You didn't want to ride Daniel yourself, did you?"

Clay had not even considered it and shook off her question with an amused chuckle. "Of course not. José's no heavier than a spider, and he's the far better choice."

Comforted he was not simply pouting, Alex pointed out the beauty of the wildflowers as they made their way along the familiar road, but Clay could not help but recall the day he had ridden out to the Howard ranch expecting no more than a fine meal with an old friend. That afternoon had been a disaster, but now, his first exasperating encounter with Alex had taken on the glow of a fond memory. If only the luck that had brought her to him would hold awhile longer, everything would be fine.

While Alex and Clay had expected to be among the first to arrive at the ranch, a half dozen of Frank's friends had already joined him out at the barn. The men waved, but continued their conversation. José had Daniel saddled, and the pinto stallion snickered softly as Alex left the buggy and approached him. She ran her hand over his glossy hide and whispered loving encouragement only he could hear.

Then Alex turned to Clay and spoke just as softly. "Try and look nervous," she advised. "Then more bets will be placed on Fred's horse."

With Frank staring at him, Clay was striving too hard to appear confident to follow Alex's suggestion, but he nodded as though he would try. There had been plenty of talk in town, so he had known Fred Tritle wasn't the only one eagerly anticipating the race, but he was still surprised by the growing swell of spectators now coming down the road. Nearly two hundred had gathered before Fred, all dressed in black, finally appeared astride Lancelot.

The horse was such an inky black his hide caught the sun with the iridescence of a raven's wing. His flowing tail brushed the ground, and his mane caressed his proudly arched neck with a silken splendor. He pranced alongside the crowd, clearly as pleased with himself as his owner was.

Clay turned to look at Daniel and, even without Alex's warning, knew what comparisons people would draw. Daniel was as magnificent a stallion as Fred's any day, but with his spotted hide, the beauty of his conformation was not equally clear. Catching each other's scent, the stallions began exchanging challenging neighs and dancing in place, which kept the enthusiastic crowd from pressing in too close around them.

"Lancelot is all show," Alex whispered. "Just like Fred."

A slow smile curved across Clay's lips as Alex slid her hand into his. "I can see that," he replied, and he had to fight not to allow his grin to grow too wide.

The men taking bets moved through the still growing throng and jotted down the hastily voiced wagers. Other men merely shouted colorful boasts, which were promptly countered with equally boisterous jests, but it soon became apparent that Lancelot was the favorite.

Willabelle had dressed for the event in one of her most peculiar hats, a huge cream puff of beige tulle with ostrich feathers spouting right out of the top. Alex recognized her easily as she made her way toward them through the crowd. "Please don't make me laugh," she begged Clay, "or I'll never stop."

"An hysterical shriek might be a more appropriate response," Clay replied, but he waved to Willabelle and managed a pleasant greeting.

"Isn't this fun?" Willabelle nearly chirped. "Please promise you'll stay for dinner after the race. We've prepared all your favorites, Alex, and yours, too, Clay."

Even with Willabelle's urging, on each of Alex's trips

out to the ranch, she had remained only long enough to sip a single cup of tea before returning to town. Now her stepmother appeared almost pathetically eager to have them stay much longer, and Alex at last realized how quiet and lonely the ranch must seem for a woman used to the constant activity and company she had known in town. They were both out of their element it seemed, and discovering a kinship she had not expected, Alex forced down her earlier fears.

"We'll look forward to it," Alex assured her. "Now we really ought to find a place near the finish line. I want Daniel to see me leave and believe he's coming to me."

"It's too far to walk," Clay pointed out, and after tipping his hat to Willabelle, he took a firm hold on Alex's arm to help her back up into the buggy.

Alex thought she could probably run the three-quarters of a mile distance herself, but climbed up without protest. She waved to Willabelle and her father, but blew only Daniel a kiss. The hands had measured the distance and marked it with stakes topped with red streamers, but as Clay and Alex rode to the finish line, they heard more whistles and jeers from those betting on Lancelot than shouts of encouragement.

"Don't let them bother you," Clay urged, but the warmth of Alex's smile assured him that she didn't.

They parked the buggy away from the road and moved to their rightful places at the finish line. Clay slid his arm around Alex's waist and eased her back against him. With as much as he needed at stake, he hoped Daniel would win for Alex's sake alone. She was so dear to him, and he did not want her to suffer even the slightest disappointment.

"Better hang on to your hat, doc," Alex warned. "It's almost time."

Clay was intent upon hanging on to her, but they both

jumped as a loud crack of a pistol signaled the start of the race. The young couple then swayed against the surging crowd as everyone leaned forward for a better view. For a brief instant, a swirling cloud of dust obscured the track; but rivals on sight, the stallions soon tore down the road, and the hammering beat of their hooves echoed with the mighty roar of thunder.

Clay did, indeed, have to grab for his hat, but it was only to wave it in the air as José and Daniel flew by in a checkered blur a full two lengths ahead of Fred Tritle on Lancelot.

"My God," Clay breathed out in a triumphant shout. "Daniel can nearly fly!"

Alex leaped into Clay's arms, but seeing him so happy was almost better than watching Daniel win. Now, if there were only some way to put such a satisfied smile on her father's face, the day would be absolutely perfect.

Chapter Nine

It was nearly sundown by the time Alex and Clay finally headed for home, and exhausted, she had to rest her head on his shoulder. Her father and Willabelle had been so thrilled by Daniel's easy win over Lancelot that the small dinner party Willabelle had planned for the family had grown to a gathering of friends nearly the size of their wedding reception in April. The rollicking celebration had lasted all afternoon, and while Alex had certainly enjoyed talking about Daniel and the enthusiastic speculation on his future races, she knew it wasn't the way Clay had intended the day to end.

"I'm sorry to have disappointed you," she murmured before covering a wide yawn. "But I just couldn't tell that whole crowd about the baby, and we had no chance to speak with Papa and Willabelle alone."

In truth, she was simply relieved to be able to keep the secret awhile longer. She still harbored the faint hope her father's opinion of Clay would improve without the bribe of a grandchild. There was also a purely selfish desire to be spared the attention that would surely be showered on her when they finally announced she was expecting. She doubted other women felt the same way; but she had never done anything the way other women did, and that was becoming an increasingly difficult problem.

Clay would have liked to have stood on the wall surrounding the lily pond and shouted the news of their baby, but he had regretfully respected his wife's wishes. However, the only thing that kept him from feeling totally frustrated was the knowledge Alex couldn't keep their child a secret indefinitely. He hadn't wanted to spoil such an exciting day by arguing about it either.

"Don't worry," he assured her. "While we were sitting out in the patio today, what disappointed me most was that although we had met when you were a beautiful child, I lacked the good sense to keep track of you over the years."

Enormously flattered, Alex straightened. Clay looked as tired as she felt, but his smile was relaxed and happy. "Why, Clay, that's such a sweet thing to say, but you didn't miss much."

"Well, let's hope not," Clay responded, and Alex brushed his lips with a light kiss before she again rested her head on his shoulder.

They had won far more money than Clay had anticipated and would be able to start looking for land. Because Fred Tritle fancied himself an expert at cards, Clay intended to find an opportunity to play poker with him before Fred got over his furious anger at Lancelot's loss. Angry men could never concentrate on their cards, and beating Fred at the poker table as easily as they had in today's race held an incredible appeal. Clay chuckled softly to himself, but Alex had already fallen asleep and didn't hear.

* * *

Because Alex's time was entirely her own, there was no need for an excuse to go out each day, but she enjoyed having at least a pretense of an errand. Once Mrs. Gilroy had returned from Dallas and recovered from her initial astonishment at finding Clay had married a young woman he had not once mentioned within her hearing, she had resumed keeping such meticulous care of his patient schedule that Alex did not dare interrupt him to say goodbye. Each time she left, she simply went down the stairs and out the back door.

That day she needed only a couple of spools of thread to do some mending, but rather than walk a half block to the dry goods store where their neighbor Burt Neubeck worked, she instead chose a route that would take her all around town with the intention of completing her shopping on the way home. Her head down to protect her hat from a gust of wind, she would have run right into Josiah Blaine had he not reached out to catch her.

Startled, Alex laughed rather than scold him for not merely stepping aside. "Good morning, Mr. Blaine. I've not seen you in a while. How have you been?"

Josiah stepped back to affect a slight bow. "Do you really care, Mrs. Burnett, or are you merely being friendly in hopes of attracting more patients for your husband's practice?"

"I was simply being polite," Alex admitted freely, "which is more than I can say for you, and if you intend to continue asking such impertinent questions, I'll be on my way."

Before Alex could push past him, Josiah wrapped his hand around her upper arm to detain her. "I'm so sorry. That was very rude of me. I saw the race last Saturday and should have offered my congratulations then."

Alex hadn't noticed him in the crowd, and after the way

they had parted in April, she wasn't surprised he hadn't come up to the house. "Mr. Blaine, I'm afraid I'm the one who owes you an apology. The night we met, I'd no idea how fond of me Clay truly was. When you called on me the next day, everything had changed between us. Obviously you were hurt, and I'm so very sorry."

While Alex was dressed in a muslin gown sprinkled with violets rather than lavender silk, she was every bit as pretty as she had been at her father's wedding. Captivated anew, Josiah strove to make amends. "No, please, the fault was entirely mine. I've no excuse for my behavior other than to plead for forgiveness on the grounds I was taken with you. I do hope that you're content with your choice."

It took Alex several seconds to realize Josiah was referring to Clay. Then she could barely contain her smile. "Oh, yes, indeed I am. We hope to begin looking for land to build a home. I intend to raise horses, though, rather than cattle."

"With what I saw of your Daniel on Saturday, you're already off to a fine start. Have you considered the old Collins place? It's on the river, and would have sold long before this were it larger."

"Thank you for the suggestion, Mr. Blaine. I'll ask my husband to pursue it."

Pleased they were conversing so easily, Josiah grew more bold. "It's a lovely day, and I have my buggy. Why don't we go out there now, and then you'll be better able to describe the property to Dr. Burnett this evening."

Alex doubted that was wise, but with the whole day stretched out before her with little other than tiresome mending to do, she was sorely tempted. "That's very thoughtful of you, but don't you have more important things to occupy your time?"

Josiah laughed at the absurdity of that notion. "Fortunately, no, my herd's already on its way north with an able contractor in charge of my crew, so I've nothing but time on my hands. Besides, if you aren't interested in the Collins property, perhaps I'll give some serious thought to purchasing it myself."

"Really? Does it border your ranch?" Alex asked.

"Near the river it does, and it's very pretty land. Come see for yourself. We'll be back by mid-afternoon, and you have my word as a gentleman that I'll not give your husband any cause to be jealous."

Alex briefly debated the invitation, and then because she was positive she would give her husband no cause for jealousy, she agreed. It wasn't until that evening when she began to explain how she had spent her day that she realized what a poor choice she had made.

"You did what?" Clay always washed up downstairs in the room they used for bathing before taking his wife out to supper, but that night rather than escort her to one of their favorite cafes, he turned and blocked their door. With his feet planted wide, his stance as well as his expression gave clear evidence of the volatility of his mood.

When Alex appeared too bewildered to reply, Clay rephrased his question. "I didn't mean to shout at you," he apologized with forced calm. "Perhaps I misunderstood you. Please begin again where you met Josiah Blaine on the street."

It wasn't so much Clay's threatening tone of voice as his narrowed gaze that frightened Alex. She had never felt truly comfortable in their small quarters; but the heat of Clay's anger seared the air, and barely able to breathe, she cast an anxious glance toward the west window.

"Where did I lose you?" she asked fretfully. "When I mentioned the Collins property, or that I'd gone to see it with Josiah Blaine?"

Clay attempted to count to ten, but didn't get past seven before a sarcastic rebuke burst from his mouth. "Josiah

Blaine, or any handsome bachelor for that matter, is no fit companion for a married woman; or did the fact that you are married to me conveniently slip your mind? I promised to check on available land. Didn't you trust me to do it?"

"Well, yes, of course I did; but you were busy with patients today, and Josiah was kind enough to take me out there. His behavior was beyond reproach, by the way, and I absolutely refuse to vouch for my own. Aren't you at all interested in my opinion of the Collins place?"

"No, as a matter of fact, I'm not. Reuben Collins was a patient of mine, and I'm well-acquainted with the property. It's a long way from town for one thing, and not nearly large enough for what we have planned for another."

Alex laced her hands behind her back rather than wring them pathetically. "I see."

It had been so nice to have something worthwhile to do, and Josiah had provided unexpectedly nice company; but she knew better than to admit that to Clay, ever. Clearly he thought she had no business looking at property on her own, and that hurt worse than his low opinion of her choice of companion.

"Because it has upset you so, I'd rather not discuss my day any further. As for supper, I'm too tired to be hungry," she insisted honestly, for Clay had ruined her appetite. "But why don't you go out and get yourself something to eat?"

Clay opened the door, then came back to slide his arm around Alex's shoulders. "No. I insist that you join me. You're much too thin, and I need your charming company as much as you need the nourishment."

He swept her through the door before Alex could offer a protest. She had loved the Collins place and was bitterly disappointed Clay would not even consider it. She ordered only a bowl of split pea soup for supper and did not once look up at her husband while she sipped it. When he chose to take a walk rather than go to bed with her, she took it as another insult and refused to wait up for him.

Clay was so furiously angry with Josiah Blaine he would have torn off his head and kicked it down the street had he met him in town; but the rancher had gone home, and Clay was left to walk as he once had to escape his nightmares. At nine o'clock, he wandered into the hotel to have a brandy and was soon invited to join a friendly game of poker.

Fred Tritle wasn't at the table, but Clay recalled how he had planned to use the man's anger against him and was able to channel his own rage into winning every dime wagered. When he finally arrived home, he was extremely proud of the way the night had ended, but took care not to disturb Alex's dreams.

Clay awakened Alex before he left the next morning and dropped a handful of ten-dollar gold pieces on the bed. "I should have taken you on a real honeymoon even if we went no farther than Dallas. Perhaps then you'd feel more like my wife than a willful girl who does whatever she pleases. Use the money to buy something for the house I intend us to have real soon."

Alex had a difficult time hanging on to her temper as she pulled herself upright. Apparently Clay would rather insult her anew than apologize, but because she had slept poorly, she chose to ignore his obnoxiously condescending tone.

"Where did you get all these?" she asked.

"A grateful patient," Clay lied smoothly. "Now, try and stay out of trouble today."

"I'm your wife, Clay, not your child."

"I'm thrilled you remember. Try and behave like it, then."

He was gone before Alex could hurl the coins at his back, but she was beginning to believe her real mistake had been in telling him she had gone out to the Collins place without him. As for staying out of trouble, she had no intention of being anything other than herself.

She planned to furnish their house with her mother's things and tucked away the coins in her lingerie drawer in the dresser rather than shop for something she didn't need. Eager to distance herself from Clay, she chose the one place she could go without risking more criticism, her father's ranch. In no mood to wear a fancy dress, she pulled on the pants she usually wore for riding, but when she couldn't button the waistband, her eyes flooded with tears.

She wasn't ready for her pregnancy to show, and while it wouldn't be noticeable to anyone else, she was desperate to hide her expanding waistline and so wore her shirttail out. She yanked on her boots and within half an hour of waking was on her way out to the ranch in Clay's buggy.

When she met Josiah Blaine on the road, he appeared astonished to see her dressed in her old clothes. She greeted him warmly, but didn't admit how badly Clay had reacted to her report on their excursion.

"I'm hoping to race Daniel again soon," Alex called as her buggy rolled past Josiah's. "This time please come on up to the house and take part in the victory celebration."

She clucked to her horse to keep him moving on down the road and trusted Josiah to understand that she did not want to be followed. She waited a full five minutes before glancing back over her shoulder and was relieved when all she saw of the attentive Mr. Blaine was a speck of dust in the distance.

When she reached the ranch, she found Daniel out in the corral. He neighed a greeting and trotted toward her.

As eager to see him, Alex climbed the wooden slats to sit on the corral's top rail. "I miss you," she swore and ran her hands over Daniel's velvety muzzle. His coat shone with a healthy glow, and he looked eager to race again that very day.

Willabelle had been watering the plants in the patio when Alex had driven by in the buggy, and when Alex did not immediately come to the house to say hello, she went out to find her. "Won't you come in for some breakfast?" she asked. "Your father's working on his accounts, but he'll lay his ledger aside to visit with you."

They had gotten along fine as long as everyone was celebrating Daniel's victory, but Alex didn't trust her father not to turn critical that day. Already unhappy with Clay, she wanted to avoid any further trouble with the other man in her life.

"Thanks, but I'd rather not bother Papa."

"You're no bother," Willabelle insisted, but Alex remained seated on the top rail, her shoulders hunched forward in a dejected slump.

"Thank you." Alex wished her stepmother would just leave her be, but Willabelle remained where she stood. Alex would have liked to ride Daniel across the prairie where no one could intrude on her private thoughts, but such a blissful journey was no longer possible.

"Alex? Is something bothering you, honey?" Willabelle had always been persistent, and to lessen the distance between them, she grabbed hold of the handy post and stepped up on the corral's bottom rail.

Alex caught herself before taking out her frustration on Willabelle, but just barely, and her tone continued to be cool. "I'm anxious for us to have our own ranch," she replied, which was at least part of the truth if not all of it.

Grateful for that tiny break in Alex's aloof façade, Willa-belle offered her best advice. "A house isn't nearly as important as having the right man, and anyone can see by the way you and Clay look at each other that you've made a fine match.''

Dismayed by Willabelle's unexpected observation, Alex finally glanced down at her. ''Just what is it you imagine you see?''

Willabelle licked her lips as she composed her words and then smiled thoughtfully. ''There's a tenderness in your glance that's like a caress. It's a silent connection, but still a tether that links your hearts. You're very good for each other. Clay no longer seems haunted by the past, and you, my dear, are a lovely young woman at last.''

Alex had seen the same remarkable change in Clay, but because she didn't feel any different herself, she assumed Willabelle had been misled by her more feminine manner of dress. Fine clothes might give her the appearance of a lady; but she didn't always act like one, and she had a horrible suspicion yesterday's argument was only the first of many. She doubted she could hold on to her temper the next time Clay lost his, and then there would be hell to pay.

''I'm not much of a wife,'' Alex admitted without realizing she had spoken outloud.

Because Alex did not look as though she would ever come down, Willabelle climbed up to the next rail and hung on tight. ''I'll agree that marriage does take some getting used to, and I certainly ought to know, but as long as you love Clay and make him aware of it often, you'll be the very best of wives.

''Clay reminds me a bit of my first husband, Paul Nesbitt. Now there was a man,'' she recalled wistfully. ''Not that I don't love your father, as Lord knows I do, but no woman ever forgets her first love.''

Alex was still pondering Willabelle's comment on being a wife and scarcely heard her compliments for Paul. "What about your second husband," she asked just to keep the woman lost in her own memories and too busy to pester her.

"Well, now, Lowell Dupré was a fine man in many ways, and the security he provided was greatly appreciated; but there was no grand passion between us, and I missed that terribly. I feel blessed to have found it again with your father. I do hope I'm not embarrassing you, dear, but now that you're married to Clay, you do understand what I mean, don't you?"

"Oh, yes," Alex agreed easily. "Indeed I do." Passion was the one thing she and Clay shared in abundance.

"Then, why are you worried about being a good wife? All any man truly wants is a woman who adores him. If she's as pretty as you in the bargain, so much the better."

Alex pulled her lower lip through her teeth. "Is that all a woman needs, too, Willabelle, just a man who adores her?"

Considering the question almost too obvious to merit a reply, Willabelle couldn't help but giggle. "It has to be mutual, of course, but yes, it's the most important thing. Clay is so attentive, though, I imagine he must say that he loves you morning, noon, and night as well as prove it often with that long, lean body of his."

Alex wasn't about to admit the word love had never passed Clay's lips, but then she had never spoken of her feelings for him either. On the verge of tears, she had to turn away. Daniel nudged her knee, and she reached out to scratch his ears.

"I really envy you and Clay having your whole lives ahead of you," Willabelle swore softly. "I don't know why your father hasn't given you the land to build a home. He's certainly got plenty, and it will all belong to you one day anyway.''

Anxious to hide her distress, Alex wiped her eyes on her sleeve. "You might have children.''

"We might, but I really believe if I were meant to be a mother, Paul and I would have been blessed with a child before he was killed. But that was so long ago, and we ought to concentrate on today. Why don't we go on inside and talk to your father about land for your house right now?''

"No. Clay is much too proud to accept such an enormous gift. We'll have a house when we can afford it ourselves, and not before.''

José Blanco waved as he came toward them, and Alex was relieved to be able to turn the discussion to Daniel. She quickly lost herself in plans for winning races and raising stud fees and hoped Clay wouldn't greet her harshly when she returned home.

Mid-morning, Clay stitched up a gash in a little boy's knee, and the memory of the sultry afternoon when he had sewn up a similar wound for Alex was so vivid his hands shook as he tied the last knot and snipped the suture. As soon as the tearful young mother had taken her darling boy home, Clay stepped out into the waiting room. Finding it empty, he called to Mrs. Gilroy, who was seated at a small desk near the door.

"I'm going upstairs to speak with my wife, but I'll only be gone a moment. Should anyone come in, please ask them to wait.''

"As you wish,'' she replied, and quickly busied herself with his appointment calendar.

Virginia Gilroy had worked for Clay for several years. She was neat in her appearance, pleasant to his patients, and adept at collecting the proper fees. She was not, however, skilled in keeping her opinions to herself, and Clay easily read a silent censure in her tightly pursed lips.

He took a step toward her. "You don't approve of my wife, do you?"

Appalled that he would make such an embarrassing inquiry, Mrs. Gilroy kept her eyes firmly focused on her desk. "It's not my place to pass judgment on her, Doctor."

"I agree, but should anyone ask for one, I expect yours to be highly favorable. Is that understood?"

Mrs. Gilroy was fairly bristling with suppressed indignation now. "Of course, sir, for it's plain you hold her in high regard."

"Yes, I most certainly do." Clay left without further comment, but he thought it was a damn good thing Virginia Gilroy had never overheard any of his and Alex's arguments.

Even before he opened their door, the silence warned Clay the apartment was empty. The room was no longer the stark retreat it had once been. A vase of fresh flowers sat on the new table, and beside the chair Alex favored rested a growing heap of books she was either engrossed in or intended to read.

A curl of white lace dangled from the top dresser drawer, and a subtle hint of lavender sachet flavored the air. The wardrobe doors weren't closed tight, allowing a glimpse of the muslin dress Alex had worn the previous day. Clay crossed the threadbare rug to the washstand and picked up the soap Alex had brought from the ranch. It was creamy smooth and when lathered gave off the enticing fragrance of vanilla pudding.

Assailed by his wife's presence even when she was away,

Clay dropped the soap and sat down in his chair. The crowded apartment was home, but without Alex, he felt more alone than he ever had as a bachelor. When he had been alone his entire life, why had he never felt lonely until now? he wondered.

He had never understood how his father could continue to grieve for a woman so long dead, but in a day burdened by memory he could almost hear his father's heart-wrenching sobs. They had frightened him badly as a child, then begun to embarrass him as he grew older. But now, with a long-delayed burst of painful sympathy, he felt the very same aching sense of loss his father had known.

There had been no photograph of his mother, but his father had cherished a small pencil sketch drawn shortly before they were married. It had shown a dark-eyed young woman with a flirtatious smile, and Clay had buried his father with it tucked in his breast pocket so it would rest over his heart for eternity.

It had been a sentimental gesture on Clay's part; but he had feared he had failed his father as greatly as the man had failed him, and it was all he could do to set things right. That he had no such beloved token of Alex struck him as even more desperately sad.

"What a pair we are," he mused. They were both so damn independent and stubborn it was a wonder they made it through any day without cursing each other. He was going to have to remember that she had been raised as a son whose companions had too often been *vaqueros* and cowboys not known for possessing gentlemanly ways.

"And some gentleman you are, Dr. Burnett." He had a veneer of manners thinner than an onion skin, and being older, and therefore supposedly wiser, he knew he ought to be a better husband if he wanted a better wife.

That decided, he returned to his office where he found three elderly sisters waiting to see him. They always came together, each with her own particular complaint, and while he treated them tenderly, that he could not imagine Alex growing even another year older sent a chill clear through him that no amount of good intentions could shake.

Chapter Ten

Clay grew increasingly anxious as the day progressed and Alex failed to return, but he refused to give Mrs. Gilroy the satisfaction of seeing him worry and checked their apartment at frequent intervals without making any such announcement. It wasn't until he had finished for the day, however, that he finally found his errant wife sprawled across their bed sound asleep.

Feeling worn-out himself, he kicked off his boots and stretched out beside her. Alex didn't wear her pants in town, so he assumed she had gone out to the Howard ranch; but he wished she had told him where she was bound. Not that he had given her any such opportunity that morning, he recalled.

As so often happened, it was far easier for him to justify her actions than his own, and giving in to a numbing weariness, he closed his eyes and dozed off. Nearly an hour passed before Alex shifted position and woke him. He turned on his side, slid his arm around her waist, and pressed his whole body against the length of hers.

Her hair smelled of sunshine, and sensing she was awake, Clay nuzzled her thick curls. "I've missed you."

All day, Alex's thoughts had been filled with Clay, but she couldn't describe doubt tumbled with regret as missing him. Consumed with a new worry, she laced her fingers in his and inquired softly, "Clay, what if I lose the baby?"

Jolted right out of his amorous mood, Clay rose up and grasped her shoulder to turn her toward him. "Do you have any warning symptoms, a backache or cramps?"

Alex hadn't meant to frighten him and ran her hand up his arm in a soothing caress. "No. I feel fine," she assured him, but then rushed on before she lost her courage. "I was just wondering if you'd leave me."

Clay was so insulted his first impulse was to shake her, but when her thinking was so addled, he feared it would take the force of an earthquake to slam some sense into her. "How could you even ask me such a stupid thing?"

When Alex responded with a sad stare, her eyes the misty blue-gray of soft rain, he had his answer. "All right, I'll agree last night wasn't the best one we've ever shared, but that doesn't mean I'd ever leave you. My God, are you hoping for an excuse to leave me?"

Clay was staring at her so intently Alex felt as though she were some peculiar medical specimen being studied under a microscope. Horribly self-conscious, she glanced away. "No. It was just a question. I didn't mean to make you angry again. That's all I'm truly good at it seems."

"Nonsense." Clay raked his hair out of his eyes, but he couldn't see anything more clearly, least of all his lovely wife's wildly careening train of thought. Thoroughly confused, he lowered his voice to an enticing whisper. "Did you worry this incessantly before we were married?" he asked.

"I had no reason to worry then," Alex replied truthfully.

"Alex!" Clay burst into laughter; he just couldn't help himself. In the space of a minute, Alex had provoked such a wide range of emotions he doubted his heart would beat steadily before dawn. And yet he had missed her terribly. That realization made him wonder which of them truly made the least sense.

"What am I going to do with you?" he asked before scooping her up into his arms. He hugged her tight and took a deep breath in the faint hope of gaining control of his own emotions, if not hers. Then he pulled her down on the bed with him.

"Let's go back to your first question and begin again. If we lost this baby, it would break my heart as well as yours; but you're a young woman, and in a few months you'd be strong enough for us to try to make another baby. We're already a family, though, aren't we?" he asked.

Alex heard the faint hesitation in his voice and was ashamed that he couldn't predict her answers any better than he could understand the confusion that prompted her questions. Pressing close, she slid her leg between his and ran her hand across his broad chest.

"I want very much to be your family, Clay, and you are already the most important member of mine."

Knowing Alex always spoke the truth, Clay gave in to the fierce yearning he had fought all day. As he moved to strip away her clothing, he strove to possess not merely her supple body, but to touch her elusive soul. As always she shared her gift of affection with a generosity that stunned him, but his heart still yearned for the tender promises of love he could still not bring himself to speak.

A long while later, Clay drew Alex's fingertips into his mouth and sucked lightly. When she laughed way back in her throat, he kissed her thumb before releasing her hand.

"I am sorry about last night," he confessed in a husky sigh. "You know more about ranching than I ever will, and I should have paid close attention to your thoughts on the Collins' place rather than refuse to hear them. Please tell me now."

Alex was afraid he was consumed with guilt rather than curiosity. "You made it plain you weren't interested in my opinion."

Clay shrugged. "It was a regrettable error in judgment on my part. You're an intelligent woman with the experience to render an expert opinion. Now, let's hear it," he insisted more emphatically.

Alex propped herself on her elbow, and while Clay's expression was the serious one he so often wore, the warmth in his dark eyes inspired trust. Hoping to avoid yet another argument, she chose her words with care.

"The ranch didn't strike me as being too far from town, but then you're the one who'll be traveling back and forth, not me. As for the size, I'll grant you it's smaller than most, but it's plenty big enough for us, Daniel, and a dozen mares. Besides, it might be a real good idea to begin with something small rather than take on more than we can handle alone.

"The house is on a rise and has one of the prettiest views of the river I've ever seen. Maybe someday when nobody falls off a ladder or becomes desperately ill, you'll have the time to go out there with me."

"I'd like that." Clay laced his fingers in her curls to ease her back down into a fond embrace. It had already occurred to him that with a smaller spread he wouldn't have nearly as difficult a time keeping track of her. Then again, he had only himself to blame for ever giving Alex a reason to run from him. That night, however, he was confident they were getting along just fine.

* * *

Vernon O'Nolan owned a dapple-gray stallion named Smokestack, and he was the next man to challenge Daniel to a race. Like Fred Tritle, he agreed to race at the Howard ranch, but insisted the distance be increased to a mile. Confident his beautiful horse would win, he wagered even more heavily than Fred and encouraged his wealthy friends to do the same.

Alex had sworn Daniel would use the additional distance to beat Smokestack by an even wider margin than he had beaten Lancelot, but Clay was not truly convinced until the day of the race when Daniel blazed past them in a commanding lead. Her prize stallion again the winner, Alex leaped into Clay's arms, and as he spun her around, he was convinced she was the one who had brought him good luck, and a whole lot more money, rather than her big spotted horse.

This time Frank Howard had hired musicians, and the second victory party lasted well into the afternoon, but when Alex began to yawn, Clay sent her to her former bedroom for a nap rather than take her home. After all the other guests had left the ranch, he woke her and escorted her into the parlor where her father and Willabelle were waiting.

"We have some news," Clay announced proudly, but he had to hang on to Alex's hand to prevent her from shrinking away. "I've bought the Collins ranch," he then told them. "So Alex and I finally have a real home."

Astonished, Alex grabbed hold of Clay's arm. "Why didn't you tell me?" she exclaimed.

Clay broke into a wide grin. "I just did. Yesterday I spoke with the attorney who's handling Reuben's estate, and we made the deal. There wasn't time for us to go out there together last week, but I imagine we can make the time to move in.''

Frank rolled out of his chair to come forward and shake Clay's hand. "I know I've been cool to you, but I sincerely doubted you could provide for Alex. Obviously her faith in you was justified, and I apologize for not being enthusiastic about your marriage from the beginning.''

Clay didn't dare look down at Alex as he accepted her father's tardy congratulations, but he knew she had to be as relieved as he was. He felt her hand on his back in a gentle caress, but kept still about their other good news.

Alex felt certain Clay had bought the Collins ranch more to please her than in a shrewd business move, and with her father and Willabelle as happy as she was, it was suddenly easy to confide the secret she had fought to keep. "While we're celebrating,'' she began with an enchanting smile, "there's something even better you ought to know. We're expecting a baby after the first of the year.''

"You don't mean it!'' Willabelle cried. "Oh, Frank, we'll be grandparents! Isn't that wonderful?''

For a brief instant, a suspicious gleam filled Frank's eyes, but he laughed it away and congratulated Clay for the second time.

Clay did not want Alex becoming overtired, and now able to offer the appropriate excuse, he hurried her on out to their buggy and started for home. As soon as she had stopped waving goodbye, he kissed her. "Telling them wasn't so difficult, was it?''

"No. But I'm not sorry I waited.'' She looped her arm through his. "I wish it wasn't too late to go by our new ranch. I want to put up a big sign over the gate at the entrance so people won't keep calling it the Collins place now that it's ours.''

Clay could not recall ever hearing Alex sound so happy,

but he could not help but wish some of her joy had been centered on him.

Later that night she pressed his hand to her belly and asked if he could feel their baby move. He felt the slight flutter that could have been a tiny foot, and a rush of pure bliss brought tears to his eyes.

He quickly cleared his throat and tried his best to be thoroughly professional. "Yes, that's the baby. What's it feel like to you, a girl or a boy?"

Alex considered the choice a long moment, and then laughed. "I'm hoping for a houseful of girls to help me handle you."

Clay leaned down to kiss her long and hard. "I'd say you've done a real fine job of that all by yourself, Mrs. Burnett, but I'll look forward to our having lots of beautiful red-haired daughters."

Alex snuggled close and prayed they would always be this happy in their house by the river. There were repairs to be made, and the house would have to be painted inside and out, but she hoped by the time their baby was born, their home would be perfect.

"What do you want to call the ranch, Clay?"

Clay had actually pondered the question through several poker hands. "With Alex and Clay Burnett, we could put the Burnett in the middle and call it the ABC, but with all the money we've won on Daniel, it might be more appropriate to name it for him and call it the Flying D."

"Yes, I like that," Alex mused thoughtfully. "Then we could have a D with wings for our brand. Thank you for giving me such a wonderful surprise. It's the best gift I could ever receive."

Desperate for a stronger link than mere gratitude, Clay smothered her murmured words of thanks with deep kisses and kept her locked in his arms long after she had fallen asleep.

It took longer than they had anticipated to renovate their new house, and more money than Clay had thought possible; but Daniel won another three races, and Clay's luck with cards held, so their financial situation continued to improve. By the time they finally moved out to the ranch, Alex was six months pregnant, and her belly was nicely rounded. She was no less restless, however, and in Clay's view, still far too active for an expectant mother.

The autumn evenings grew chilly, and as they sat by the fire reviewing the day, Alex's gaze would sometimes drift away. Clay would admire the sweetness of her smile and wish he were privy to her innermost thoughts. Then he silently cursed himself for not being satisfied with all they did share. It was a battle he frequently fought within himself, but one he carefully hid from Alex.

There were nights when Clay lingered in town for the high stakes poker games he was now invited to join. He still played with the necessary detachment to win, but after Fred Tritle had conceded that Daniel was, indeed, the fastest horse in Texas, Clay had taken no pleasure in beating him again at cards.

One night in December, he had won so easily that he had gotten drunk merely to shake off his disdain for the lack of challenge a game of cards now presented. Too ashamed to ride home in such a disgraceful state, he had slept in the apartment above his office. He had awakened early the next morning and, unable to wait an entire day to see Alex, had ridden out to the ranch to eat breakfast with her and change his clothes.

When Alex had assumed he had been up all night with a patient and greeted him warmly, he couldn't bring him-

self to tell a convenient lie, but he didn't disabuse her of
the idea either. He was too bright not to see where such
rotten behavior would lead, and as he rode back into town,
he swore off the fleeting comfort of liquor for good.

But even with all the good luck he had had, he felt as
though a big chunk of himself was missing. He didn't know
how much longer he could pretend to Alex that he didn't
ache for her love, but he was far too proud a man to ever
make such a pathetic confession.

Later that same day, Alex sat down to go over her Christmas list, but she couldn't seem to find a comfortable pose.
She had not felt like eating anything at noon, so she
couldn't blame her discomfort on indigestion, but when
her back really began to hurt, she grew alarmed.

They had a woman who cooked and cleaned for them,
but she had gone home for the day. They had hired two
men to care for Daniel and the brood mares they had
purchased, but both had gone into town for supplies and
wouldn't be back for several hours.

Alex stood and paced the parlor in a slow oval, but
exercise failed to lessen the pain; and while she had never
minded being alone on the ranch, today the solitude mag-
nified her fears. Clay would not be home again for hours,
and she dared not wait for him on the off chance he might
have to stay in town again.

She had studied the portion of Clay's medical books
devoted to pregnancy and childbirth, so she understood
how the natural process should progress, but she had never
considered she might have to endure it alone. When the
pain in her back wrapped itself around her belly in a
sudden burst of agony, she knew whatever choice she made
would have to be made soon.

She thought she could probably give birth alone—after
all, Clay had calmly described the delivery sequence even
more clearly than his books—but she certainly didn't want

to experience such a momentous event without him. What was best for the baby? she agonized. Suffering through a wild ride into town, or remaining there and dealing with the horrible risk that without help she and the babe might both die?

Her worst fear was that Clay would arrive home and find them dead, and she couldn't bear to leave him in such a tragic way. She had only her pride to blame for not telling him how much she loved him, and pride had absolutely no value now. Without another thought as to the consequences, she hurried out to the barn, urged Daniel into his bridle, and rode him as slowly as she dared into town.

Clay had had an unusually busy morning and was relieved to find his waiting room empty by mid-afternoon. He was standing beside Mrs. Gilroy's desk scanning the next day's appointments when Alex rode Daniel right up to the door. Certain his contrary wife would have only one reason for riding the stallion into town, he nearly tore the door off the hinges getting to her.

Tears were rolling down Alex's cheeks. "I know I'm not supposed to be riding, but—"

Alex got no further before Clay pulled her down off the horse and carried her into his office. "Put the closed sign on the door, then get someone from the livery stable to come for Daniel," he called over his shoulder, and as he strode into the first treatment room, Mrs. Gilroy rushed to carry out his orders.

Clay could feel the strength of the contractions through the thick folds of Alex's dress and placed her on the examining table with great care. "Why didn't you send someone for me the instant your pains began?"

"There was no one to send. It's too soon, though. What are we going to do, Clay? It's too soon."

Clay had planned to take time off to stay home with Alex when her time drew near; but those good intentions were meaningless now, and he blamed himself that his dear Alexandra had had to ride into town in what had to be the worst agony imaginable. He had chloroform to relieve her pain, but he feared there would be no time to use it.

Nearly hysterical himself, he forced himself to concentrate on procedure rather than the identity of his patient. He quickly removed her boots and stockings.

"It's just a few weeks early, Alex, so the baby will be fine. Your contractions are coming so quickly that we don't have much time. Go ahead and scream if you like. I won't take it as a criticism of my ability as a physician."

Alex had been so desperate to reach him that she had refused to give in to the pain, and she did no more than wince and cry softly now. "Wait a minute, Clay, there's something I must tell you."

Clay was too nervous to laugh, but he managed a hoarse chuckle as he removed her lace-trimmed chemise. "The baby's the one who won't wait, my dear, but go ahead, I'm listening."

Alex had to wait for a contraction to subside before she could respond, but as soon as she had drawn a deep breath, she hurried to finish before another pain caught her. "I've loved you for so long, but I thought you should be the one to say the words first. That seems absurd now, utterly stupid. It doesn't matter if you never love me. You're the best of husbands, and I'll never love anyone but you."

When Clay didn't respond immediately, Alex feared she had simply embarrassed him. She wasn't a bit sorry she hadn't kept her feelings to herself, though. The next contraction tore through her insides with a savage rip, but she had no breath to scream; and while Clay issued an urgent command to push, his voice seemed to come from very far away. She tried, but her strength ebbed away before she heard a baby's faint cry.

Alex awakened in bed upstairs. It was already dark, and the gaslights were lit. She was more tired than she had ever been, but she remembered where she was. She ran her hands over her stomach, but rather than merely flat, it was sunken slightly. After months of sharing her body with a baby, it felt hollow. The other side of the bed was empty, and Alex was certain that if she had given birth to a healthy child, the babe would be wrapped in a blanket beside her.

Huge tears filled her eyes, but she recognized Clay as he approached the bed. "I'm so sorry," she moaned. "Was the baby a boy or a girl?"

Clay leaned down to kiss her. "You needn't apologize. You did fine. Our son's asleep in the cradle I'd planned to bring home at Christmas. Would you like to see him?"

Alex was so sleepy she could barely raise her hand to cover a yawn. "We have a little boy?"

"Yes, and he's a handsome lad even if he does appear to have my dark hair and your blue eyes. We'll just have to try again for those red-haired daughters." Clay reached into the handsome cherrywood crib he had placed next to the bed and presented his wife with a sleeping infant wrapped in a soft blue blanket.

Alex's hands shook as she combed her son's sparse hair with her fingertips. "Is he too small to survive more than a day or two?"

Clay sat down on the edge of the bed. "No. He'd weigh a little more if he had been born next month; but he's perfectly healthy, and you needn't worry so. We can talk about names later, but first there's something I need to say."

The strain in his voice warned Alex his remarks weren't going to be good, so she concentrated on their beautiful baby. He had such a sweet little face, but Alex couldn't tell which of them he resembled. His hair was definitely dark brown, though, and asleep, she had to accept Clay's word on the color of his eyes.

"I'm not sure where to begin," Clay sighed unhappily.

"Maybe it should be left unsaid," Alex offered softly.

"No, that's been the whole problem. While it's a pitiful excuse, I've been sitting here thinking the reason I'm no good with words of love is because I never heard any. I truly expected to lead as solitary a life as my father had after my mother's death. And quite honestly, I actually thought I was content until the day I discovered you'd grown up."

Alex wanted to interrupt him right there, but held her tongue and listened with growing awe as Clay described how much he had wanted her from the instant she had walked out on her father's announcement of his plans to marry Willabelle. He recalled how the sunlight had turned her hair to fiery gold.

There was so much he remembered fondly, and it broke Alex's heart to hear the very same longing in his voice that she had hushed in her own. He described incidents she had forgotten, and some that she wished he would have; but they were all flavored with the love he could no longer contain, and she was uncertain which of them was the greater fool.

Clay handed Alex his handkerchief to wipe away her tears. "I didn't mean to upset you. You've already been through far too much for one day."

"I'm not upset with you, Clay. I'm just happy."

"Well, you probably won't be nearly so pleased after I tell you that there have been times I let you believe I'd stayed in town with a patient when actually I'd been playing poker. But damn it, I'm awfully good at cards, and I didn't want all the money in our bank account to come from Daniel."

"And that's what you were doing last night?" Alex inquired hesitantly.

Clay nodded. "Yeah, and I got drunk, too. It didn't seem like such a terrible risk to me then, but now, well, if you'd gone into labor . . ."

"Yes, that is a terrifying thought, isn't it? But it didn't happen, and perhaps we ought to concentrate on today and making tomorrow even better, rather than agonizing over all the mistakes we've made."

"You'll forgive me, then?" Clay asked in an anguished whisper.

"For what? For being as stubborn and proud as I am? I can scarcely criticize you for those faults. Now, let's talk about names for our son. We really should have thought of some names for boys as well as girls."

As Clay saw it, he had just given her a good reason to yell at him for weeks, and she had disregarded his stupidity with a shrug. "One of the things I love most about you, Alex, is that you don't harbor a grudge. I'm afraid that's a trait that's going to become increasingly valuable over the years."

"Nonsense, as you always say. With but a few rare exceptions, you have always behaved as a gentleman, but that's not the only reason I love you. Now, please help me find a name for our little boy."

"I already have one," Clay admitted with a ready grin. "I want to call him Alex for you, but from now on, I'm going to call you Alexandra. You're a beautiful woman, and you deserve a woman's name."

A fresh burst of tears stung Alex's eyes. "That's so sweet, Clay, but I won't agree unless we call him Alexander Clayton Burnett so that he's named for both of us."

Clay laughed and shook his head. "You are going to fight me every step of the way our whole lives, aren't you?"

Alex licked her lips. "I'm not fighting you, which I realize might be grounds for an argument right there, but think how much fun we always have making up.''

Clay stood up to walk around the bed, and then stretched out beside his wife and child. He reached out to coil one of Alex's glorious red curls around his finger. ''Yes, we do, and your passionate nature is another trait I adore. I guess it's just been difficult for me to get used to being happy. All the bad dreams are gone, and you and this dear little boy are all the angels I'll ever need.''

As Alex leaned over to kiss him, she could have sworn she heard the faint rustle of an angel's wings, and she whispered, ''Let's name the first of our little girls for our mothers.''

''I can't wait,'' Clay murmured against her lips, but he already had paradise in his arms.

NOTE TO READERS

I began "Texas Lullaby" with every intention of writing a love story in which Alexandra faced the many challenges resulting from her swift transition from free-roaming rancher's daughter to a staid physician's wife and darling infant's mother. Her real challenge, however, proved to be in winning Clay's heart just as his was to capture hers.

The story of how two such proud and independent characters succeed in becoming a family was a joy to write, and I hope you had as much fun as I did sharing Alex and Clay's lives. I welcome your comments through Kensington's Web site: www.Kensingtonbooks.com, or by mail in care of Zebra Books, 850 Third Avenue, New York, NY 10022. Please include a legal-size SASE for a reply, bookmarks, and a newsletter.

SNOWFLAKES AND KISSES

Victoria Dark

Chapter One

"Be a good boy, now." Olivia Knowles stroked Pootie's head, then scratched him under the chin. The little pug bore the coddling with a resigned set to the wrinkles in his face, looking up at his mistress with one baleful eye. His other eye was angled away, gazing somewhere down the narrow, crowded London street. "Take care of your business while I'm in the solicitor's office facing the ogre."

Pootie wheezed, as if in agreement, the little dog's breath boiling out into the cold air in puffs of steam. Olivia set Pootie on the sidewalk and handed his leash to her young companion.

"Don't worry, mum. I'll see that he has a good walk around." Luther wound the leash around his hand. In his livery of green and silver, complete with oversized tricorn hat, the eleven-year-old swaggered as he followed the dog.

Olivia smiled to herself as she noticed Luther had discarded the warm coat she had found him in a second-hand clothing store, the better to show off his new finery.

Since she had found him on the streets of London and taken him with her when she had gone to Auntie O's to live, the boy had put on nearly a stone in weight. Still, the livery was too big.

Pausing, Pootie sniffed a clump of half-melted snow, gray with coal soot, at the base of a lamp post, then snorted and disdainfully headed on.

The sky was gray; the street was gray; the people hurrying along it, their heads bent against the wind, were also gray. Looking over the scene, Olivia shuddered. She had forgotten how very oppressive London could be, especially in winter. And the business that had brought her back to town was more oppressive still.

Reluctant to enter the solicitor's office, she glanced at Marvin, who sat atop the box of the ancient traveling coach. The equipage which had transported them from Sussex to Town drew curious stares from passersby. But whether it was the four horses, each a different color, or the faded crest on its weathered door, or the giant of a man on the box that captured people's attention, Olivia could not have said. All were equally remarkable.

Marvin met her gaze. In answer to her unvoiced question, he nodded, assuring Olivia he would watch both boy and dog.

There was nothing for it, then. Unable to put off her meeting with Sir Derrick Blackwell any longer, Olivia tangled her reticule strings around her gloved fingers, gathered up her courage, and faced the door to his solicitor's office.

Inside awaited the man she had once been engaged to.

That was before she had thrown him over by eloping to Gretna Green with his nephew, Peter—an insult a man like Sir Derrick Blackwell wasn't likely to forgive or forget.

Well, what couldn't be changed must be endured, as Auntie O was wont to say. Sir Derrick had no power over her life, she reminded herself. Since she was widowed, she was her own woman.

She only wished the fact made her less apprehensive.

Olivia drew in a deep breath and, stiffening her spine, opened the door. On her entrance, a clerk rose from behind a small corner desk like a marionette pulled straight up by a string attached to his bald pate.

"I'm sorry, madam. We do not receive unescorted females—"

"You would do well to ascertain to whom you are being rude before proceeding." Olivia stilled the man with a haughty look she had learned from Auntie O during her lessons in "how to get on." It involved raising one brow and raking one's intended victim with a rather acid gaze from head to toe, then staring unblinkingly into the offender's right eye.

To Olivia's amazement, the man's mouth opened and closed very much like a goldfish's; then he quailed visibly— despite how disreputably faded and worn she knew her black mourning dress and woolen cloak must appear.

She would have to remember the maneuver. She wondered wistfully if it would work on Sir Derrick.

Probably not. One would have to possess an ounce of human frailty to be vulnerable to the tactic. And Sir Derrick possessed about as much human frailty and warmth as a marble statue.

"I'm certain I'm sorry, m-madam," the clerk stammered at last. "It is m-my employer's policy, you understand. I—"

"I understand," Olivia cut him off, looking into her reticule to keep from taking pity on the poor man and smiling. She produced her card, her last one, carefully edged in black ink by her own hand. There wasn't any money to have more printed, but that hardly signified now that she was living in disgrace with Auntie O in the country—and enjoying every moment of it.

"You may announce me. I'm certain Sir Derrick Blackwell is awaiting me with great impatience since he has been here"—she glanced at the clock high on the wall—"some thirteen minutes."

The clerk did his goldfish impression again as he gazed from the clock to Olivia and back. "Why, Sir Derrick arrived exactly as the clock struck eleven, how—"

Collecting himself, the fellow's mouth snapped shut. He bowed and disappeared through a door.

Olivia could have told him she knew when Sir Derrick arrived because she knew his type all too well, a stickler for details, always punctual to the minute. His letter had stated eleven as their meeting time. Derrick Blackwell would have crossed the solicitor's threshold at eleven o'clock, precisely.

Moments later, the clerk reappeared. His expression was properly bland as he showed her into an inner office and announced her, then exited.

A somberly dressed man stood behind a massive desk. Bowing, he said, "Mrs. Knowles, I am Mr. Brown. Sir Derrick's solicitor."

She inclined her head slightly, all too aware of Sir Derrick, himself, standing beside the small fireplace. Dressed in a cut-away coat of forest green broadcloth that was tailored to fit his wide shoulders perfectly and taupe unmentionables sheathing his long legs, he was the epitome of a proper gentleman of the *ton*.

And as handsome as Lucifer.

Well, she had certainly never objected to his looks. It was his personality, or rather lack of one. His stony expression reminded her very much of the marble statue she had mentally compared him to just moments before.

A hard man. She had grown up under the thumb of just such a man, her stepfather. She hadn't been able to face a lifetime with another.

Oh, what a narrow escape she had had! Though Peter had been less than perfect—far less, alas, or she would not be here—if he hadn't convinced her to elope with him, she would have been wed to this glowering stone of a man.

And if life and society were fair, she would not have had to have this meeting at all. In trying to manage her affairs by herself, she had quickly discovered a woman was accorded no respect in what was viewed as a man's domain, the buying and selling of property. It still rankled that she had been thwarted at every turn in trying to handle so simple a matter.

Winding her reticule's strings about her fingers, she felt herself shrinking beneath Sir Derrick's stare, until she remembered Auntie O's training and lifted her chin. Auntie O's rule number one was to never let your opponent see your unease.

Sir Derrick bowed slightly. "Olivia." He spoke her name quickly, as if begrudging having to speak it at all. His cool attitude enveloped her like her cloak.

"Sir Derrick." *He has no power over me,* she reminded herself again.

"I trust you've been keeping well." His tone was as dry as two vellum sheets rubbing together.

Oh, but this was too much for her sense of the ridiculous. "I doubt that very much."

He stilled for an instant, allowing his surprise to show. A human trait? No, surely not. An aberration, she was certain. Or, perhaps, indigestion.

Then Sir Derrick seemed to wrap the mantle of a superior being about himself again as his black gaze bore into hers, his eyes gleaming like coals. "To the contrary. Why should I wish you ill?"

His sarcasm was in the words, not his tone. Wonder of wonder, had the man blood in his veins after all? Well, by throwing him over in that manner, she had embarrassed him royally. She had trounced his pride. Even cold, pompous paragons, she allowed, did not like their pride trounced.

And she was the offender, Olivia reminded herself. She should not be cheeky.

Mr. Brown looked from her to his employer, rather at a loss. After clearing his throat, he said, "Please, be seated, Mrs. Knowles. Allow me to take your cloak." He started around his desk.

"Thank you, no." Holding up a hand, she stopped him. Auntie O's rule number three: always stand when in an adversarial situation. Olivia knew being seated while Sir Derrick towered above her would make her feel at even more of an emotional disadvantage. Heavens, he already towered over her with them both standing, and she felt disadvantaged enough.

"You both are wondering why I asked for this meeting," Olivia said, anxious to get her business done with and escape.

"If you'd come to the point of it, I'd be grateful." Derrick placed his hands behind him.

"Yes, well." She wet her lips. His eyes were still dark coals, staring at her unblinkingly. Under the intensity of the look, Olivia felt something skitter through her. Unable to help herself, she looked away for an instant and gathered her courage before again meeting his gaze. "I understand that you have paid all Peter's debts."

"That is true. As the head of the family, his creditors presented his accounts to me to be settled with his estate."

"Only there was no estate. All Peter left to mark that he'd ever trod the world were his mountainous debts and my beautiful baby daughter," Olivia said softly, grieved that her husband's life had been so futile. Even the way he had died had been a waste. On a bet, he had tried to jump his mare over a fence that was too high.

Sir Derrick's gaze moved to her hands, and she quickly untangled her fingers from her reticule strings. *Old habits,* she thought, regretting she had given away her discomfort.

"I see," Derrick said slowly. Ah, he had wondered why she was so unfashionably dressed—if she was really in such dire straits. The black bombazine he glimpsed under her cloak was faded by streaks, the hem frayed.

The tip of one finger on her black gloves was darned. Even her black bonnet had a look of age about it, beneath the black gauze veil and long, curling rooster feathers, which were probably new. She was set on playing on his sympathies.

The show hadn't been necessary. Indeed, he had long been prepared to see that Olivia and Peter's daughter received an allowance. It was his duty, as head of the family.

However, considering the past, Derrick thought he could be forgiven for letting Olivia dangle in the breeze for a while after Peter's death. Until she came to him.

But perhaps that had not been wise.

Her thick-lashed green eyes gleamed as they caught and reflected the firelight. Dark brown curls framing her oval face looked so silky, he wanted to touch one, to see how it would feel between his fingers. . . .

He pushed the thought roughly aside. She had made it clear what she thought of him when she ran away with his nephew.

As anger surged in his chest, Derrick turned to the fire and stared into the flames, refusing to give in to his desire to toss dignity aside and rail at her for what she had done.

Drawing in a deep breath, he expelled it slowly. Better just to end this farce. "I collect you are here because you find yourself in need of funds."

"Not at all."

"I have made provisions—what did you say?" Derrick turned back, certain he had not heard aright.

Olivia lifted her chin a notch higher. Those green eyes gleamed. "I am here, Sir Derrick, because I do not wish to be in your debt."

"I don't understand."

She loosened the strings of her reticule and drew out a folded parchment sheet. "This is the deed to a small manor and lands my maternal grandmother left to me recently. It is in Northumberland." She had tried to sell it to settle Peter's debts, but had discovered that all men seemed to think women incapable of good judgment when it came to business. And were therefore fair game. "I wish to sign it over to you, so I might repay you." Olivia held the parchment out to him.

Derrick looked at it, frowning. "What am I suppose to do with this . . . manor?"

"I think it is worth more than Peter's debts. You may give me whatever difference you find between its value and the amount Peter owed. Or you may sell the property, taking whatever money is due you and giving me the remainder."

Derrick still made no move to take the deed. Olivia's hand trembled slightly as she placed it on his solicitor's desk.

Brown looked at his employer with raised brows, as if asking what he should do.

"Leave us."

Derrick's soft command was instantly obeyed. As the door closed behind the solicitor, the fire crackled and popped. Sir Derrick's expression grew impossibly colder.

Olivia almost quailed before his stare. *He has no authority over me, he has no authority*—it became a chant. She was a free woman. Why did he make her feel like a little girl being chastised by her stepfather for some willfulness?

The very fact that he could make her feel that way made her angry. Straightening her shoulders, Olivia met his stare. "It's no good your trying to intimidate me with your dark looks. I've no notion why you're angry, anyway. I'm trying to repay you." She was proud of herself. Her voice did not crack.

"I'm not angry," he snapped, though he knew he lied. "I am trying to figure out your game, Olivia."

"Game?" She blinked up at him, the picture of confused innocence.

Damn, he thought, *but she should be on stage.* "Yes, *game.*" He motioned at her person. "You come in here, dressed as you are—"

"My clothes are perfectly respectable."

"—undoubtedly to illicit sympathy."

"That is the last thing I was thinking of."

"And you think to cozen me into believing this"—Derrick made a sweeping motion with his hand at the deed— "mythical manor is worth more than Peter's debts and have me give you money for the difference."

Her green eyes blazed with more than the reflected firelight. Olivia drew herself up. "And why on earth would I do that?"

"The way Peter gambled, you must find yourself at a loss."

"If I'd wanted your money, Derrick, I would have married you."

The words were softly spoken, but Derrick felt the verbal slap more potently than if she had smacked him with the palm of her hand.

As Derrick's face lost all expression, Olivia put her fingers to her lips. Oh, God, had she really said that?

He clasped his hands behind him again, looking more like stone than ever. With wonder, Olivia realized it was a nervous habit, like her tangling her fingers in the strings of a shawl or a reticule.

Sir Derrick became a marble statue to hide his feelings— feelings beyond pride and anger. He was flesh and bone beneath that pomposity.

And she had hurt him when she eloped with Peter, in a way she had not realized before.

Remorse washed through her. "I'm sorry. I tried to tell you at our engagement party that I did not wish to marry, but you resisted my every effort to get you alone," Olivia said, rushing her speech into the sudden quiet.

"Yes. You did. I didn't understand why you whispered as we danced that you wished to meet with me alone on the balcony. I thought it was girlish whimsy." Vain fool, he had thought she wanted to hold him and taste his lips as much as he had wanted to taste hers.

"It wouldn't have been proper to do so," Derrick went on. "Why didn't you just say what you felt when we were together at dinner? I would have released you from the engagement if you had only asked."

"While I waited on the balcony for you, my stepfather found me and warned me against just such an action." Olivia's tone was bitter. "I know you were told I was anxious for the match, but I was never given a choice in the matter. Lord Stodgeforth saw you as a man who would go far in government. He was anxious to set you up in a position inside the foreign office where he would have counted you as an ally to his policies.

Derrick stoically absorbed the blow. It was only his pride that smarted, he told himself. Her elopement, which had quickly become the *on dit* of the *ton,* had certainly been a major embarrassment. So much so, he had chosen to turn down the appointment to the Foreign Office he had actively been seeking. It had come at the behest of Olivia's stepfather, who was an assistant minister, and Derrick was certain Herman Stodgeforth had set the wheels in motion before Olivia's elopement.

Olivia shook her head, her green eyes serious. "I wronged you, Derrick. For that, I am truly sorry. Auntie O says I should have faced my problems head on and should not have used Peter to escape. But, I can't regret that I did. Because of my marriage to him, I have my daughter."

Her daughter. Something tightened in his chest at the knowledge Olivia was a caring mother—he had imagined she would be when he had made his offer of marriage. He had planned things he would do with his children, all the love and attention he would give them. Most of all, he planned to be nothing like his own father, who had cared little about his offspring.

Giving himself a mental shake, Derrick refused to grieve for all he and Olivia might have had together. "I trust your daughter is well," he said at length.

"Well and happy and, I think, exceptionally bright." A dimple appeared in one cheek as she smiled.

Derrick looked from the dimple, to her lips, then forced his gaze to the parchment on the desk. "You mentioned an 'Auntie O.' Is she the baby's nurse?"

"No. I take care of Charisse myself. Well, most of the time." Olivia had left her in Ivaniva's capable hands today. "Auntie O is my great, great aunt Olivia—for whom I was named. The Dowager Duchess of Orwell. My daughter and I are living with her in Sussex.

"Anyway, since I cannot change the past, I need to repay your generosity. As a matter of honor, you see. Whatever difference there is, I plan to put at interest and invest, and hope it pays enough to keep Charisse and me."

He stiffened. "Ah, I see now."

"See what?" Olivia blinked at him.

"I almost believed you. Until you mentioned 'honor.' I don't know what game you're playing—"

"Very well." She whirled and grasped the door handle.

Without thinking, Derrick crossed the short distance and caught her arm, spinning her around to face him.

And forgot what he had been about to say.

As her blazing gaze met his, an unexpected heat pooled in his groin. He did have one regret over the whole matter. He had never kissed those coral lips. Not properly. Not as he had wanted to do. There had just been a chaste peck after she had accepted his offer of marriage.

Staring at her lips, without thinking he drew her to him until her skirts brushed his legs, their bodies almost touching. He was suddenly aware of the faint scent of lavender that clung to her, the flawless ivory of her skin, and the tiny gold flecks in her thick-lashed green eyes.

Chapter Two

As sensual awareness arced between them, like lightning sizzling through the sky in a summer storm, Olivia caught her breath. Staring up into Derrick's dark eyes, she knew he felt it, too, by the surprise crossing his features.

Then his lids drooped as his gaze moved to her mouth. *Can he be thinking of kissing me?* She didn't know what made her more angry—the realization he might be thinking of it, or the fact that she wanted him to.

Suddenly, he released her arm and stepped away. His face once again became expressionless, save for a slight contemptuous lift to one dark brow. Looking at him, Olivia realized her mistake. Had she really expected Sir Derrick Blackwell to lose control? Hardly.

"A matter of honor? Forgive me if I misjudged you, Olivia. After you ran off in the night with my nephew, breaking your promise of betrothal to me, I should have realized honor comes first with you."

Derrick had no idea why he had said that. Insanity! This woman made a shambles of his self-control.

Her anger flashed again, which was very much preferable to the strange, insane feelings that had possessed her an instant before.

Straightening her cloak, she lifted her chin. "The first time I saw you, Derrick, I thought how very handsome you would be if only there was a drop of blood, or an iota of human emotion, in your body. I know now I was wrong. There are human emotions—possessiveness, arrogance, vindictiveness. All the worst of human traits. Good day."

Though she closed the door softly, as Derrick stared at it, the room seemed to reverberate with the sound.

Outside, Olivia drew a deep breath of the chill air and clasped her hands together to still their shaking. Well, she had done what she had come for. Oh, but she had been right to dread the encounter. Now, to get Luther and Pootie and shake the dust of this place from her shoes.

Up the street, Pootie lifted his leg beside the wheel of an elegant curricle, which Olivia knew instinctively must belong to Sir Derrick. The footman minding the equipage shouted at Luther, half spooking the matched blacks in the traces. As the footman was forced to calm them, Luther tugged Pootie's leash, urging a fast getaway.

Bending down, Olivia clapped her hands, and Pootie rushed to her, with Luther running behind.

As Olivia scooped up the pug and hugged him, tears blurred her vision.

"He had a good walk, mum. Did everything he was supposed to." The boy resettled the too big tricorn on his head and frowned. "Mum, what's wrong?"

"Nothing."

Glancing at the old coach, Olivia found Marvin had wound the reins around the brake handle and was climbing down from the box, the big man's movements brisk and purposeful. She had long ceased to wonder how he simply knew things without being told.

"No, Marvin!" Tilting her head so her bonnet brim shielded her face from Luther's inquisitive gaze, Olivia went on, "Please, just let us get home. If we start now, we might make it by nightfall."

"Did someone hurt you, mum?" Luther asked, pushing an oversized sleeve up past his skinny elbow and making a fist.

"No. No, Luther." Olivia caught the boy's shoulder and hugged him briefly—as briefly was all he allowed before he tore away. "I miss Charisse. I want to go home," she said, without really lying.

A fortnight later, Sir Derrick glowered at the big man standing with arms folded across his massive chest before the closed, rusty, and locked gate of Camden Hall.

The massive gatekeeper looked him in the eye without blinking.

"What?" If his tone was less than amenable, Derrick thought he could be forgiven. For the last twenty minutes the giant had stood just so, despite Sir Derrick's blandishments, attempted bribery, slander, muttered threats, and a damned cold wind howling out of the northeast.

Derrick was at a loss. It was a long way back to London. And cold. The sky was a smooth blue-gray of impending snow. He didn't know the area—if there were any inns nearby, or even a village, for that matter.

He doubted it. This was a wild, isolated section to be stranded in. Even though it was about to snow, the gatekeeper to the only residence Derrick had seen for the last thirty miles refused to unlock the gate and let him through to shelter—or even talk and tell him why he was being kept out.

Blowing on his gloved hands, he had a strong urge to clip the fellow on the chin.

For no reason that Derrick could fathom, the man's eyebrows lifted, and a hint of a smile played about his lips. Spreading his hobnailed boots in a wider stance, the giant posed before the gate as if daring Derrick to throw a punch.

Pushing aside the urge to do violence—he wasn't in the habit of accosting men who were about their jobs—Derrick tried again. "If you will not let me through, at least take a message to the dowager or Mrs. Knowles. Give either of them my card."

The man's expression changed not a whit. A snowflake sailed through the air, landing on the earth between them.

Derrick wanted to curse. Good God, he had written to the dowager duchess that he had business with Olivia and would be paying her a call today. He frowned and folded his arms across his chest to try and keep the fingers of cold from prying between the many capes of his greatcoat. His low-crowned beaver hat did little to protect his ears.

Could Olivia or the dowager have instructed the fellow to lock him out? Derrick rolled the possibility around in his mind, then discounted it. What had either of them to gain? He was here to settle money matters between him and Olivia. Judging from the state of her dress at their last encounter, she would want to see him. He knew now she had not been trying to cozen him. The Northumberland property was worth a great deal.

Reining in his temper, Derrick said, "What will it take to convince you? I've explained that the dowager and Mrs. Knowles are expecting me. Are you in the habit of detaining their visitors at your whim?"

The gatekeeper never moved so much as a finger. More snowflakes sailed through the air between them. Small and round, bouncing as they struck, the flakes were really more like pellets of ice. Already, the brown-leaf litter at Derrick's booted feet was speckled with white and on its way to being completely covered. A cold blast of wind snatched at his hat.

"I *am* a baronet!"

Obviously unimpressed, the big man stood like a stone.

Through the overgrown yews and rhododendrons of the unkempt garden, Derrick could just see a corner of the red brick manor house. Wood smoke rolling from the chimney teased him with the warmth to be had within. And perhaps a hot cup of tea. And biscuits and cheese.

His team of blacks fidgeted in their traces, rocking the curricle, even though the brake was set.

"You *do* understand. *I am expected.* You *must* open the gate." Derrick spoke slowly and clearly, as though talking to a small child.

"Marvin, he ain't dumb, sir. He just don't talk." A pint-sized footman in an ill-fitting tricorn appeared from behind the yew hedge, a pug dog straining against the leash in the lad's hand. Snow became steady white streaks slicing the frigid air.

Gazing at the lad, Derrick felt he had spied a cork life ring in a storm-tossed sea. Swallowing his exasperation, he asked the boy, "Perhaps you could tell me why—Marvin, is it?—refuses to open the gate."

The lad shrugged. "He don't want to."

"He don't—doesn't. . . . I see." Sighing, Derrick fished beneath the multiple layers of his clothing for his purse. "In that case, would you mind telling the duchess, or Mrs. Knowles, that I am waiting at the gate?"

"Not if Marvin won't let you in."

"What?"

Again, the boy shrugged his thin shoulders.

Purse in hand, Derrick drew out a shilling in the hope that all was not yet lost.

"Not if Marvin objects." The lad eyed the shiny coin,

unmoved. The pug snorted and tugged against his leash, wanting to be off amid the yews.

"Why?" The single syllable gushed from deep within Derrick's chest.

The lad gestured at the gatekeeper. "If Marvin's decided against you, sir, it ain't wise to go against him."

Derrick felt defeat seep into every fiber of his being. Cold and remorse and defeat.

He had lost his last opportunity to see Olivia.

He need not have come out here to the wilds of the country, himself. He could have sent his man of business to apprise Olivia of the money due her regarding the Northumberland property and the actions Derrick had taken on her behalf concerning it.

God's blood, it would have been far easier not to see Olivia again. Not to look into those sparkling green eyes and remember how thoroughly she had hated the thought of being wed to him. Not to see that dimple in her cheek when she smiled and to wish, in spite of his better judgment, just one of her smiles would be for him. Hadn't he long ago learned the futility of wishing for warmth and affection from people who had none to give him?

Gazing back at the manor, Derrick shook his head, admitting the truth to himself. The property was just the excuse that had brought him. He had had to come. He had said things he should not have said. That he had done so out of hurt and pride meant nothing. He was here because Olivia deserved to hear his apology from his own lips.

Derrick flipped the coin to the boy. "Then, there's nothing for it but to leave." Defeated. Olivia had no wish to see him again. What had he expected after that debacle in his solicitor's office? "If Marvin wouldn't mind, please inform the duchess and Mrs. Knowles I was here to see them." Snow caught in his lashes, melting into his eyes.

"Also, I'd be grateful if you could tell me where to find the nearest inn."

Unexpectedly, the gatekeeper moved. The man went to the lock, produced a key and opened it. After lifting it from the hasp, he began walking the gate open.

"What is he doing?" Derrick saw, but he didn't believe.

The lad stepped back out of the way as the big man swung the gate wide. "He's letting you in, sir."

"Why?"

Why? Derrick thought, after keeping him standing there until his blood was frozen in his veins. After standing like a militant stone for the better part of a half hour. Why now was the gatekeeper opening the bloody gate?

"He wants to, sir."

The lad allowed the pug his head and followed him back the way they had come.

"Who?" No, Olivia thought, surely she could not have heard aright.

Seated in her favorite chair in Auntie O's private sitting room as she nursed Charisse, Olivia looked at her aunt incredulously. Snow struck the bay window, collecting outside on the sill.

Why would anyone be about on a day like this? Especially the stuffily proper baronet?

"I said, Sir Derrick Blackwell is here to see you. Has playing at wet nurse made you hard of hearing?" Auntie O raised a derisive brow. Standing just inside the door, her aunt had a distinctive curl to her lightly rouged lip as she observed the baby at Olivia's breast.

The rouge was pointed up by a small black patch on Auntie O's rice-powdered cheek. Indeed, in her white velvet gown with pannier sides and petticoat quilted in gold thread, she was dressed in a manner fashionable more than thirty years before. The outfit was completed by an enormous white wig in the style made popular by Madame Pompadour.

"I wish I had known Sir Derrick was coming." Olivia would have persuaded Auntie O to wear something more appropriate . . . if anyone could prevail upon the dowager to do anything in keeping with traditional behavior.

But her aunt's independent nature and eccentricity, Olivia knew, were exactly why she so admired the octogenarian.

From the north sitting room, which had been converted into a studio, came snatches of rapid speech in French as her aunt's newest artist-in-residence worked on the background to a portrait Auntie O had commissioned him to paint—after finding him starving on the streets of Bath.

From his passionate words and tone, he seemed to be coaxing a lover. At intervals, rather strident notes from a violin erupted up from the music room on the floor below. Aldolfo, another of Auntie O's protegees, worked on a violin composition.

In counterpoint to it all, every few minutes came "Now—" *Bomp!* "Now—" *Bomp!* "Now—" *Bomp!* "Now!" *Bomp, bomp!* Nikoli and Ivaniva, who traveled with the circus in warmer weather, were practicing their knife-throwing act in the long hall outside the sitting room.

"Which room have you put Sir Derrick in?" Olivia placed Charisse on her shoulder and straightened the soft blankets. As the little girl fussed at having her meal interrupted, Olivia patted her daughter's back.

"All those with fires laid were occupied, except for your bedchamber."

"You didn't have him put in my bedchamber?" Olivia looked askance at her aunt.

"Of course not. I told Luther to show him in here." Auntie O smoothed a snow-white ringlet over her shoulder.

"Here?" The notes of the violin grew more strident.

"Really, Olivia, this habit of questioning all I say grows quite tedious."

Leaping to her feet, Olivia thrust Charisse into her aunt's hands.

Brows riding up on her forehead, the older woman held the child as if not quite certain what it was. "What shall I do with her?"

"Hold her." Olivia frantically tied the strings to her camisole, covering her breasts. "It is beyond enough the man has shown up without warning. But I can't believe you sent for him to come in here while I was feeding Charisse."

"I've told you time and again, you should hire a wet nurse. I can be forgiven for momentarily forgetting your peasant leanings."

"I've told you, I want to nurture my daughter." Olivia turned her attention to the buttons on the front of her dress. She had had little enough nurturing in her own life. She was determined to give her child every ounce of love and care she could.

"That is most commendable. Truly," Auntie O said, her arched brow indicating just the opposite. "I only wish children should come into the world a bit more . . . mature. Eating solid food, perhaps. Walking and taking care of their own toilets. Like a five- or six-year-old."

"That is because you never gave birth." Olivia finished the last button, appalled as she imagined producing an offspring of the size of a five-year-old.

After taking Charisse back from her aunt, who was more than willing to let her go, Olivia retrieved the blankets that had fallen to the floor and swaddled her daughter against drafts.

As Charisse caught Olivia's finger and tried to draw it

to her mouth, "Now—" *Bomp!* "Now—" "Good God!"
Bomp! Bomp! Bomp! Bomp! erupted in the hall outside.

"That *must* be Sir Derrick." The duchess clasped her
hands together.

Chapter Three

Muttered words followed. Olivia thought that indeed, unfortunately, it *must* be Sir Derrick.

Auntie O opened the door a crack. "I suppose I should have told Nikoli to have a care with his knives, that company was expected," she mused.

"I'm certain Sir Derrick would agree about now." As Olivia resumed her seat, Charisse caught a grosgrain ribbon adorning her mother's lacy widow's cap. Cooing with interest, she tried to bring the ribbon to her mouth.

"No, you must not eat my headwear." Olivia rescued the ribbon and made a silly face at her daughter. Charisse laughed and settled for gnawing her fist.

A knock sounded at the door.

"Enter," the duchess called, moving to the settee.

Stately in his manner, Luther swung the door wide. Bowing rather smartly, he announced, "Sir Derrick Blackwell, my lady."

Standing aside, Luther waited as Sir Derrick entered the

sitting room. "He had a close call with the knife thrower," Luther added, his rust-colored brows rising on his forehead. To Sir Derrick, he said, "I'll see your horses are brought to the stable and cared for."

"Thank you." Derrick nodded, and the boy exited, closing the door behind him.

Ice-encrusted and looking a bit pale beneath his tan, Derrick paused for an instant. Then he moved back a half step as he took in the dowager duchess's exotic mode of dress. Frowning, he darted a glance at Olivia.

Keeping her expression bland, though she wanted to laugh, Olivia continued to pat Charisse's back.

At length, good breeding won out. Bowing, Derrick said somberly, "Lady Orwell, I trust you are well." Turning to Olivia and inclining his head, he added, "Mrs. Knowles, you also."

"Perfectly well, thank you." The duchess smiled. "Sir Derrick, how good of you to come in this foul weather." All graciousness, Auntie O moved across the room and extended her hand, the whalebone panniers and steel cage supporting her sweeping skirts creaking with each step.

As he bowed over her beringed fingers, there came the distinctive, "Now—" *Bomp*. "Now—" *Bomp*. "Now—" *Bomp, bomp*.

Derrick straightened, scowling. "That . . . that fellow in the hall." He drew in a deep breath as though collecting his dignity.

Olivia hid her laughter behind a cough.

"Yes?" the duchess asked politely.

"He *threw* a knife at me."

"Nonsense." The duchess caught his elbow, leading him farther into the room. "Do come by the fire. You look a bit pale. Must be terribly cold out." Auntie O went to the bellpull and tugged thrice, indicating to Horice in the kitchen there were three for tea. "You'll feel better after a nice cup of tea to warm you. Now, let me take your coat and hat.''

Plainly taken aback, Derrick drew himself up to his full, rather impressive height. "I said, *the fellow threw a knife at me.*" He glared at the duchess as if daring her to dismiss the charge a second time.

"Was it a man wearing high bucket-topped boots?" Auntie O asked. "That would be Nikoli," she said, not waiting for a reply. "A distant cousin of mine, on the Russian side of my family. No, he did not throw a knife at you, I can assure you of it. Now, your coat and hat, Sir Derrick."

As the duchess waited, Derrick raised a dark brow and looked askance at his hostess.

Increasing her pats on Charisse's back, Olivia hid behind the baby's blankets. So, he did not like to have his word questioned. Well, it would do him good to learn how it felt! No doubt, this was the first time anyone had dared show such audacity to the paragon, Sir Derrick Blackwell.

"Your things are encrusted with ice," Auntie O added patiently, as though speaking to a small child or a half-wit. "It will melt and soak you through. That is your business, of course; but it should also soak my Persian carpet, and while it is old and a bit worn, I am very fond of it. So, Sir Derrick, I must insist you have a care to remove your things."

Olivia recognized Auntie O's rule number seven: talk down to anyone who isn't complying with a request.

Derrick looked helplessly at Olivia. After a second, the quality of his gaze changed, his eyes becoming impossibly darker, his face softening. His gaze moved to Charisse; then he looked away. Squaring his shoulders, he gave Auntie O his muffler.

As she draped the muffler over a lyre-backed chair, Sir

Derrick removed his hat. "Madam, I'm loath to disagree with you; however, the fellow *did* throw a knife at me."

"Pish." The dowager took the curly-brimmed beaver from his hands.

Looking as though she had slapped him, Derrick said stiffly, "If you or your niece did not want me to come here, you needed only to post a reply to my letter discouraging me. There was no need to have your gatekeeper bar me from entry. And when I didn't go away, and he finally let me in, to have someone fling knives at me."

"Are you accusing us of conspiring to harm you? We didn't know you were coming," Olivia protested. She knew it. He could not be agreeable and civil. It was beyond the man's inflated sense of self-importance.

"Well, yes, I did know, Olivia," Auntie O owned, tapping ice from Sir Derrick's hat so that it fell into the fireplace.

"You *knew?*" Olivia felt warmth seep into her cheeks at having just dealt Sir Derrick such a set-down, when indeed he had been expected. Just not by her. "Why didn't you tell me?" She could have certainly used some warning, to steel herself, if nothing else.

Snuggled against her shoulder, Charisse made a cooing sound and drooled, then blinked her thick-lashed, dark eyes and thrust a chubby finger back into her mouth.

"I had forgotten it was today or I should have spoken with Marvin to make certain he would let Sir Derrick pass. And I would certainly have told Nikoli to be more aware as he and Ivaniva practiced their act."

"Their *act?*" Derrick frowned.

"He and his wife are circus performers. You might not have noticed Ivaniva. She would have been at the end of the hall with knives sticking around her. But, I tell you again, there was really no danger to you." The duchess shot what might have been an apologetic glance at Derrick.

Shaking her head, her white ringlets wiggling, she

turned to Olivia. "And I did *try* to tell you Sir Derrick was coming, dear. Is it my fault that every time I so much as mentioned his name, you flew into the boughs? No discussion of his visit was possible."

As Derrick stared at Olivia, she thought of pulling Charisse's blankets over her head.

Instead, she stiffened her spine and ignored the increasing warmth in her cheeks. "You must own you did provoke me awfully at our last meeting, Derrick."

He was quiet for a space, then nodded. "And most unfairly. When I had the property you gave me the deed to appraised, I was made aware of how unfair I was. That is why I felt I must come myself to conclude our business— to set things right about money due you and also to make my apologies."

There was no expression on his chiseled features. No hint of regret to match the words. Olivia wondered if it was simply a sense of duty mishandled that had propelled him here? Or had the man true feelings of remorse for his harsh judgment and words?

Then his dark gaze met hers, and she saw the regret therein. He truly was remorseful.

And she didn't like knowing it one bit.

It was much more comfortable to think of him as only interested in his own feelings, she admitted to herself.

"Marvin kept you out at first, you say?" Auntie O asked Derrick.

His attention was drawn back to the dowager. "He kept the gate locked a full half hour."

"How odd," Auntie O mused.

"Indeed, I thought so, given the inclement weather and that I had written that I was coming."

"No, I don't mean that." The duchess dismissed what he said with an elegant flip of her blue-veined fingers. "You see, once Marvin has decided against someone, he doesn't usually relent. I can't recall his ever having done so before."

Sir Derrick blinked. "He doesn't usually . . . and then there was a knife *flung* at my head."

The dowager duchess fixed him with an indignant gaze, one fat ringlet trembling as it lay on her narrow shoulder. "I told you, Sir Derrick, I know for a fact that Nikoli *did not* fling a knife at you."

"Madam," Derrick's tone was low and controlled, "I beg to differ—"

"Because if Nikoli *had* thrown a knife at you, you would now be bleeding. He is very *good* at throwing knives," Auntie O added decisively.

Though Olivia tried to subdue it, a snort of laughter escaped her at Derrick's expression. His attention was drawn to her again. She hid her face against Charisse and patted the baby's back.

Charisse burped loudly and with, Olivia thought, exquisite timing.

When Olivia dared a peep past the baby's blankets, Derrick looked all at sea, as if he had wandered into Bedlam. No doubt, a woman like Auntie O was outside his experience. The older lady did not play by his narrow precepts where men ruled and women rushed to agree with all they said.

Turning back to the fire, he said, "I see."

Plainly, he hadn't a clue.

"Sir Derrick, you *are* dripping." Auntie O tapped his hat briskly, and the rest of the ice atop it fell onto the hearth.

Slipping off his greatcoat, Derrick followed her lead and shook it over the hearth stones. Steam rose from where the ice pellets and snow struck. He draped the coat across the chair where his muffler rested, stripped off his gloves and added them to the stack, then placed his hands behind his back, standing stiffly.

Auntie O added the hat atop the mound. Then awkward stillness settled over the room. For once even Auntie O seemed at a loss as to how to go on.

Charisse had no such problem. She turned around and cooed, looking straight at Derrick, a string of drool slipping past the finger still thrust in her Cupid's bow mouth.

Olivia caught the drool with a clean nappy she kept on her shoulder for such accidents. Glancing up, she saw Derrick's features soften again as he gazed at the child.

Auntie O said, "Please, do be seated, Sir Derrick, and let's not let a bad start ruin our visit." The grande dame was all graciousness as she indicated a wing chair on the opposite side of the fireplace from where Olivia held Charisse.

"Thank you, Lady Orwell." Holding his hands out to the fire, he said, "But if Olivia wouldn't mind, I'd rather hold the baby."

As if understanding every word, Charisse lurched toward him, squealing with delight.

After rubbing his hands briskly before the flames, Derrick took the child, deftly catching blankets and all.

Olivia reluctantly let go of her daughter, though she knew the child was in no danger.

Derrick sat in the chair Auntie O had indicated, placing Charisse on his knee and making certain the blankets were tucked properly about her. The child looked up at him with interest, smiling around the finger in her mouth and reaching for his cravat with her free hand.

To Olivia's amazement, Derrick smiled back, never flinching as Charisse tugged his cravat, destroying the elegantly folded lines of the neck cloth.

"She is plump and healthy. You've done well by her, Olivia." Derrick bounced Charisse, to her giggling delight.

Feeling pride swell in her breast, Olivia said, "She is already pulling up on the furniture and taking steps as she holds on."

"And gnawing each piece worse than Pootie when he was a pup," Auntie O inserted.

"Taking steps? Eight months is remarkably young for that, isn't it? She must be a very bright child." He continued to bounce Charisse.

Surprised that Derrick remembered how old Charisse was, Olivia said, "She babbles and tries to talk, too. I think she is developing faster than most children."

"Has she always been so alert and interested in what is happening around her?" Derrick asked.

Auntie O looked from one to the other of the adults, then rolled her eyes heavenward. The violin music became particularly harsh.

Charisse cooed as if answering Derrick, and he seemed not the least offended when a drop of drool found his knee.

"I would advise you to have a care, Sir Derrick. She leaks. Copiously, and from both ends," said the dowager drily.

"Charisse *has* always seemed unusually alert." Olivia reached across the space between them and wiped drool from Charisse's chin with the nappy.

"*Charisse,* a lovely name for a lovely child." Derrick's gaze found Olivia's.

Leaning back, tangling her fingers in the fringe of her shawl, Olivia murmured, "Thank you."

"I think I'll go check on our tea." The dowager rose gracefully for a woman of her years and placed a hand on Derrick's shoulder, restraining him when he would have gained his feet, as manners dictated. "Pray, be still while you have the baby. The child erupts more violently than Vesuvius when jostled too much. Remember my rug.''

The door closed softly behind Auntie O. Olivia watched as Derrick continued to play with her daughter. Unlike the proper countenance he showed to the world, with the child, Derrick was relaxed, giving her his finger and having a playful tug of war as he kept her from bringing it to her mouth.

It seemed so odd. Olivia had thought him a cold, bloodless paragon concerned only with his own importance. Learning he truly regretted his rudeness in London had shaken that view. Now, finding that he possessed a far gentler side than she ever could have imagined, Olivia wondered if she could have misjudged him in other ways.

It didn't matter. It was far too late for second thoughts. Anyway, Olivia knew she was better off than if she had gone through with the marriage. She would have smothered. Or become like her mother.

Olivia had spent a lifetime living beneath a man's thumb, first her stepfather's, then her husband's—though Peter had been much less demanding. Still, her independence was a sweet wine, indeed.

And when she had the money from the sale of the Northumberland manor, there would be no reason to ever subjugate herself to any man again.

But she did owe Derrick an apology, for having misjudged him so badly.

Just as she gathered the words together to make one, Derrick spoke: ''She is as beautiful as her mother.'' He met Olivia's gaze over the top of Charisse's white frilly cap.

Olivia's mouth snapped closed. Warmth erupting in her chest, she dropped her gaze and pulled her shawl strings so tightly around her fingers that they grew white with loss of circulation. ''Thank you,'' was all she could think of to say in the face of the unexpected compliment.

Silence again settled over the room, broken by Charisse's cooing and laughter as Derrick continued to play with her.

Thankfully, moments later, Auntie O preceded Horice, the cook, and the tea tray into the room. Then Horice carried Derrick's things to the kitchen to be hung up before the big fireplace there.

"I don't trust myself to handle a teacup and the baby." He returned Charisse to her mother, reluctantly it seemed.

As Olivia's fingers brushed his during the exchange, it was as though champagne had been uncorked beneath her diaphram. She caught her breath at the unexpected sensation.

Charisse resented being returned. The child frowned and threw herself back toward Derrick. Olivia was obliged to hold on tightly as Charisse wailed her disapprobation.

Derrick felt a pull in the region of his heartstrings. The baby's eyes were liquid black and the curls escaping her cap a lighter brown than her mother's hair, but otherwise her face was a perfect miniature of Olivia's. Charisse might have been his child. . . .

"Perhaps you would like me to fetch her nurse?" he asked Olivia.

The dowager snorted. "I wish someone would."

Lifting a winged brow, Olivia looked askance at her aunt, then explained to Derrick, "Charisse hasn't a nurse."

"I remember now. You told me that in London." Derrick looked like he approved, putting Olivia at ease.

Auntie O said, "I have tried to tell Olivia that people of breeding have proper servants to take care of their infants and do not take total care and feeding upon themselves. What is the point of rank and privilege if one behaves like a peasant? It is just not the way things are done."

Coming from somewhere deep in the bowels of the house, impassioned French love words filtered through the yellowing, flocked wallpaper. The violinist paused. A

small dog barked. From outside in the hall, came "Now—"
Bomp! "Now—" *Bomp!* "Now!" *Bomp! Bomp! Bomp!*

Titling her bewigged head, the dowager said, "It sounds
as though Nikoli is getting his timing worked out." The
old lady lifted the teapot and poured. "Cream and sugar,
Sir Derrick?"

"One sugar, please." His gaze sweeping the older lady's
mode of dress, Derrick wondered how anyone attired so
absurdly could appear so totally dignified.

As if reading his look, Olivia sat Charisse on her lap and
said, "Auntie O should have explained that she is dressed
as she is because she is having her portrait painted. She
thinks today's fashions are only pale shades to the glory
of the dress in her younger days, so she has been posing
in this white velvet creation."

The duchess bent a disapproving eye on Olivia. "Pray
don't make excuses for me, young lady." To Derrick, she
said, "She isn't telling you that I dress how I wish, even
when I'm not having my portrait painted." The dowager
shrugged elegantly. "I feel I've reached an age when some
eccentricities are expected."

Thinking the old lady had reached the outer limits of
eccentric, he didn't say so as he accepted a bone china
cup and saucer. There were golden scones and a honey
pot on the tray. He had no wish to say anything displeasing
to his hostess.

However, word of the old lady's odd behavior had
reached him in London. Now that he saw for himself what
an inappropriate place Camden Hall was for a young lady
to bring up a child—*God's blood, a circus knife thrower!*—he
would tell Olivia he would make other arrangements for
her and Charisse as soon as possible. They obviously
couldn't remain here.

He blamed himself. He should have set aside his pride
and made certain Peter's widow was taken care of. It had

been his duty. But he had had no idea that Olivia's step-father had broken off all association with her when she had defied him and eloped with Peter. In effect, she had been left on the street when Peter died. Olivia must have had no choice but to seek shelter with the dowager.

Derrick had been unaware of her need. But that was hardly an excuse. He failed in his duty. Before she inherited the Northumberland property when her maternal grand-mother died, she must have been in dire straights.

The shame was his.

The violinist began torturing his instrument again, as if in accompaniment to Derrick's thoughts. Then the French-man began speaking as if coaxing a recalcitrant lover, turn-ing Derrick's thoughts to another vein.

"That is the artist, de la Croix, working on his painting of me. The background, I believe. He talks to his canvas," the dowager said, explaining the French love words. "Would you like honey on your scones, Sir Derrick?"

"Please."

Setting his teacup aside, he accepted a dainty dish with two honey-drenched pastries. As he took a bite, his stomach growled gratefully. Derrick hoped the violin might mask the rude noise.

The dowager passed a cup and saucer to Olivia. Both were careful to keep it out of Charisse's interested reach. Olivia set it on the tea table at her side, away from the baby. Turning to the side so Charisse couldn't grasp the cup, Olivia sipped her tea. After the shock of Sir Derrick's arrival, then his compliment, she needed a restorative.

But hadn't she guessed that he was attracted to her? Olivia thought about the fleeting sensation when he had grasped her arm in London and the fancy that he wanted to kiss her. And how much—just for that mad, mad instant—she had wanted him to.

Feeling her cheeks take flame yet again as she remembered the sensations his dark gaze sent rioting in her chest, Olivia sipped her tea, keeping her face averted.

"So, Sir Derrick," Auntie O began in the manner of one making idle conversation, "my niece tells me when she saw you in London, you were a perfect ass."

Chapter Four

Olivia choked as she swallowed her tea. Hastily, she set the cup aside and leaped to her feet. Charisse laughed as she was jostled on her mother's hip.

Snatching a napkin off the tea tray, Olivia coughed into the linen, trying to regain her breath. *Of all the . . . why would Auntie O say such a thing!* She looked at her aunt, tears streaming from her eyes as she coughed.

Rising quickly, Derrick took the child, settling the baby on his own hip. He then thumped Olivia on the back.

As the spasm passed, Olivia held up her hand signaling him to stop. Eyes watering still, napkin pressed to her mouth, she met Derrick's dark gaze.

"Are you all right, dear?" Auntie O arched one painted brow in mild concern.

Was she all right? Giving her aunt a sardonic look, Olivia tried to say just what she thought of the question. But she was beset by another bout of coughing as she drew in breath to speak. This time the spasms were less severe.

As the fit subsided, Charisse was quiet as she looked at her mother thoughtfully, as though trying to understand what game she played.

"Thank you." Olivia reached out and took Charisse from Derrick.

Auntie O, having made that outrageous statement, sipped her tea daintily.

As Olivia fussed with the baby, Derrick mused ruefully, "I don't think I should have used the word 'perfect.' But I did treat you wrongly. As I said before, I came here today to tender my sincere apologies and hope that you will forgive my lapse in manners."

His dark gaze was hooded. Was that what was important to him, that he had a lapse in manners? Olivia wondered. Not that he had hurt her with his vile words and accusations?

Perhaps she had been right in the first place, after all. He was mainly concerned with his own consequence, that he had had a lapse in manners, not with her feelings. And the impression he had almost kissed her had nothing to do with his feelings. To men, she had learned during her marriage, intimacies were a casual thing.

Auntie O cleared her throat meaningfully, making Olivia aware she was staring at Derrick. Diverting her gaze to Charisse, instead, Olivia smoothed the curls which had escaped from the child's bonnet.

The dowager set her cup aside and dithered over the scones. "Now that you say that, Sir Derrick, I don't think Olivia *did* call you 'a perfect ass.' I believe her exact words were 'a monstrous great roaring ass'—was that it, dear?" The last was directed to Olivia.

The fire crackled merrily in the silence following the question.

Olivia had no need of its warmth. Her embarrassment

provided all the heat she required and, quite possibly, she suspected, would continue to do so for the entire winter.

"I must put Charisse to bed for her nap," Olivia managed to say at length.

At a loss as to how to go on, how to stop her, Derrick stood and watched as Olivia opened the door and left the sitting room with the darling little girl.

As she did, the pug he had seen the boy Luther walking earlier rushed inside and ran straight to the dowager. The old lady lifted the dog onto her lap—it being far too fat to make the jump.

"There's my good boy. Where have you been? Did you have a nice walk with Luther?" she asked as though expecting an answer.

Looking up at Derrick, she said shrewdly, "Olivia might need assistance with the child. I fear we are rather short-staffed here. You might offer her your help—if it isn't beneath your dignity."

As the sitting room door closed behind Sir Derrick Blackwell, the dowager scratched the pug beneath the chin. "Oh, dear, Pootie. I fear my joys in life have dwindled to stirring the pot and watching for the results."

She sighed and broke off a bit of scone and gave it to the dog. He snapped it up, licked his mouth, and whined for more.

"I suppose I *ought* to have told Olivia that Sir Derrick was coming here. She cut up so stiff, however, at the mere mention of his name, she'd likely have run for the hills if she had known.

"And, you know, such passion as Olivia displayed after her meeting with Sir Derrick could hardly have been induced by simple business."

The old lady shook her bewigged head. "But I suppose I am wrong to meddle."

Looking up at the dowager with one eye, the other

angled toward the fire, Pootie licked his flat nose and wisely offered no opinion.

Gaining her bedroom, Olivia drew in a deep breath and expelled it slowly. *What was Auntie O thinking?* Had her aunt gone senile to make such an outlandish statement?

Well, Olivia owned, she had said something very like those words on her return from London. But she certainly never meant for them to be repeated to Derrick. She wouldn't willingly have insulted him. Not to his face, anyway.

"Not after having ill-used him so, by eloping with Peter," she told Charisse.

Charisse frowned. *"Ga."*

"But there was no choice but eloping, was there?" Olivia asked the child. "I could not bear the thought of being wed to a man who reminded me so much of my stepfather, a man more a dignified stone than flesh and blood."

Only she had found that Derrick was more than stone, hadn't she?

"It doesn't signify," she told Charisse firmly. Sitting on the edge of the bed, she hugged her daughter and rocked her back and forth. "I promise you, sweet, that you shall never feel trapped by having all your choices made for you. That you will be allowed to be your own person, and when you are all grown up, you will have autonomy over your life. And *I* shall certainly never willingly become a man's chattel again," Olivia added with feeling.

The little girl smiled up at her and yawned. Warmth filling her, Olivia hummed softly until her daughter yawned again and closed her eyes.

As Olivia placed Charisse in the center of the bed and tucked the covers around her, there came a soft knock at the door, which she had left open.

Derrick stood there, the look on his face unreadable.

Hiding her surprise, she placed her finger to her lips, glancing at the sleeping child. Derrick nodded to show he understood.

"I need to speak with you alone," he said softly as Olivia drew near.

Olivia tangled her fingers in the fringe of her shawl. Had he been listening to what she said?

"Sir Derrick, you must know that is quite improper—"

"The hell with propriety," Derrick growled. Pulling her against his hard length with one hand, he held the back of her head with the other. Looking down into her face, he studied it as though he wanted to memorize it. "From what you tell me, if I had been less concerned with propriety, we'd now be wed."

"No, we wouldn't. What are you doing?" *Silly question!* As his gaze moved to her lips, Olivia knew exactly what he was doing.

What surprised her was the warmth surging inside her at the anticipation that look filled her with. Suddenly, her limbs felt weak; she wanted to lean against him. And as she looked into his thick-lashed, dark eyes, her breath caught in her throat.

How could I have once thought this man passionless?

"I've wanted to kiss you since the first time I saw you. It was at Almack's, remember? I'd only gone to please the patronesses. Just as I expected, there was the usual herd of debutantes, all alike in their pastels, all very proper, eager to please, and totally insipid creatures.

"But then I saw you. You were vibrant. You didn't like being there. It flashed in your eyes whenever you thought no one was looking. You refused all requests to dance."

"I felt like a slave on an auction block."

"But you accepted my request."

"My stepfather was scowling at me. I dared not refuse

you.'' Her breasts tingled where they were flattened against his hard chest, and the warmth growing inside her pooled low in her abdomen. She was no innocent. She understood the hard bar of male heat pressing against her softness all too well.

She had felt passion before, with Peter. But never this suddenly. Never with this breath-taking expectancy.

Derrick murmured, ''Ah, so that's it. Fool that I was . . .'' He shrugged. ''But I think now I am going to have that kiss.''

To his surprise, Olivia moistened her lips with the tip of her tongue. Conscious or not, it was a heady invitation. Groaning deep in his throat, Derrick slanted his mouth across hers. Her lips were as sweet as he had known they would be, her body as soft as she pressed against him.

And, she was pressing against him.

She wanted him, too.

He felt like shouting in triumph. Instead, he held himself in check, afraid to rush this. For this would surely be the only time he held Olivia close, except perhaps in his dreams.

Cupping her face, savoring the feel of her against him, he kissed the corners of her mouth, her temple, her closed eyelids. When she made no move to pull back, Derrick removed her widow's cap. Hiding her glorious hair was a crime.

Not content to just uncover it, he found the pins and removed them, loosening the rich chocolate brown tresses and spreading them to fall over her shoulders. Flames from the logs in the fireplace cast flickering light over the waves. He lifted a curl, inhaling the light scent of lavender, then brought it to his lips.

She gazed up at him in wonder, her eyes moss green pools with golden flecks. Derrick trailed a finger over her bottom lip, and as her pupils grew wider, the golden flecks disappeared completely.

"Kiss me again," Olivia whispered. She had never felt such wonder. Would it happen again?

Derrick obeyed, the kiss deep and long and hard, his tongue slipping inside her mouth. Her tongue met his in a mating dance as old as time, as new as this moment. Her enthusiasm made him throb with need. And showed him a little glimpse of the heaven that might have been his.

Olivia wound her arms around his neck and pressed closer, amazed at how much she wanted to stay in his arms, wanted this kiss never to end.

But it had to. This could go nowhere.

Frightened by the intensity he evoked so easily inside her, Olivia pulled back as far as his arms would allow, which wasn't far.

Derrick moved to nuzzle her ear. Shivers raced along her spine. Hot need coiled inside her.

Catching his shoulders, she pushed him back. "You were listening as I talked to Charisse. To myself, really. You know why I would never marry you." Her voice came out so husky, she barely recognized it as her own. Her breasts throbbed with the need to be pressed against his wide chest once more.

"I'm kissing you. Not marrying you." And why not? She was a widow, not a virgin. It was expected that widows would have discreet liaisons. Knowing now how she felt about marriage and her freedom, he was forewarned. And it would be better, really, not to expect anything. Then he would never be disappointed.

He need only keep his guard up and not let himself care too much.

As he pulled her against him once more, Olivia realized that at this moment in time in his arms was the only place she wanted to be. There would be time for logical thought later. Time to savor and regret that these wondrous feelings he ignited inside her wouldn't last.

And to wonder what it was about this man that was so powerfully appealing.

She didn't want to analyze anything just then. To do so, a part of her knew instinctively, would be to admit what folly this was.

Then his mouth claimed hers once again. And all thought spun away.

Chapter Five

Sounds outside in the hallway suggested the knife-throwing act had started practicing again. The violinist had stopped torturing his instrument and was coaxing Mozart's sonata from it.

Without letting go of her completely, Derrick broke off his sensual assault long enough to close the door. Then he bent his head to place kisses at her temple, at the pulse beating beneath her jaw.

Without knowing quite how it happened, Olivia found the back of her knees pressed against the chaise lounge at the foot of her bed.

"Derrick?" She glanced at the chaise.

Derrick changed places with her, sitting down and pulling her onto his lap. He groaned again as her soft bottom pressed against his erection.

Splaying his fingers into her hair, he kissed her—long, slow, sensuous kisses that filled her with the taste of him. Cupping his cheeks, she marveled at the slightly rough texture of his day's growth of beard, the clean smell of soap still clinging about him.

Deftly, he undid the top button of her dress, his dark gaze watching her for her reaction. "You like what I'm doing."

It wasn't a question.

"I feel . . ." Words failed her, and shyness closed her lips.

"You want me to go on?" This was a question, though Derrick wasn't at all certain how he would manage if she told him to stop.

Olivia nodded. Her tongue darted out and wet her lips in a way that set his blood flaming anew. His fingers trembled on the next button. When a few more were released, he untied her camisole and pressed kisses to the swells of her breasts.

Sighing, Olivia arched against his mouth, inviting him to even greater intimacies. "When you touch me, you seem to consider my enjoyment above your own," she said wonderingly. "Peter seemed to think only of his own pleasure. I told him how unsatisfied I felt, as if there was something more, but he . . ."

In the act of easing her camisole lower, Derrick stilled, his dark head bent. Olivia knew she had said the wrong thing.

As though waking from a dream and finding herself at the edge of a precipice, Olivia stood abruptly, straightening her clothes. What had she been thinking?

She had *not* been thinking—that was the problem!

She had allowed her feelings control. Wonderful, enchanting feelings. But only feelings, nonetheless.

Still, she admitted to herself, if Derrick had made love to her like this when they were engaged, she might find herself married to him now. Then she hadn't known that for a man making love had little to do with the finer emotions. "Auntie O says passion is as natural for a woman as for a man." Olivia felt she was babbling. She couldn't stop. "But, since Peter died, I have never . . . I am not in the habit . . . That is to say, I don't usually allow . . ."

She expelled a harsh breath. "How bloody ridiculous! I need not explain myself to you." Clenching her fists, she added, "You'd better go."

Derrick stood. "Yes, I'd better." But truth be told, he didn't want to. With a glance at the child, still sleeping peacefully, he left the room.

What was between Olivia and himself was far from finished. If he could not have her hand in marriage, her body had betrayed that it would be his. With some coaxing.

Lost in thought, he walked between Nikoli and his target once again.

"Now—" *Bomp!* "Now—" *Bomp!* "God's blood!" *Bomp! Bomp! Bomp!*

Feeling the need to cool his heated blood, Derrick donned his almost dry greatcoat and gloves, intent on finding the stables and checking his horses.

A mouse scurried into a hole beside the tradesman's door. Everywhere Derrick looked were signs of lack of funds and neglect. The kitchen was bare of the cured hams and foodstuffs that would generally have hung on the rafters. Still, the large Dutch oven in the huge fireplace produced succulent smells that reminded him he had not had a proper tea.

Outside, the snow was falling thicker. That was okay. He wanted this trip outside to cool off. A gust of cold and snow followed him into the stables as a glowing lantern alerted him to someone else's presence.

The gatekeeper turned, a pitchfork in his hand, as Derrick rounded the hay mow.

After studying him a moment, the big man nodded, then went back to pitching hay to Derrick's black carriage horses.

Two pails of water were set outside the stalls. Picking up the first one, Derrick poured it into the bucket nailed onto the inside corner of the stall for the horse to drink from. He then poured the second pail for the next horse. There were four more horses yet to be tended. After leading out the first one, Derrick found a rake and began mucking out the stall, disregarding the shine on his Hessians.

The hard work felt good. It required no thought, and it released the pent-up tension in his muscles. Energy he might have put to more pleasurable use. . . . Moss green eyes and coral lips hovered at the edge of his thoughts.

Looking up, he found the gatekeeper eyeing him oddly.

Bending back to his task, Derrick doubled his efforts, banishing all thoughts of Olivia. At least, for a while.

"I put your valise and trunk in the blue room, sir," Luther said as Derrick came back inside the kitchen door. The winter sun had dipped below the horizon, and still snow fell, driven into drifts by an icy wind off the North Sea.

"Thank you."

"There's a fire laid to take the chill off, and I can fetch warm water if you'd like to freshen up before supper. It's served at seven." The lad eyed Derrick's tall black Hessians with a lifted brow. "You stepped in it, right enough, I'm afraid."

Looking down, Derrick agreed. Though he had scraped off what he could on the boot board by the back door, the once shiny footwear was still a mess.

It had been worth it. He was exhausted. He might even manage to sit across from Olivia at dinner and not make a fool of himself over her. Again.

"A right mess," Derrick told the boy. "A shilling if you can have them cleaned before morning."

"Right enough, sir." The lad gave him a toothy smile. "I'll have 'em spit polished and gleaming like a diamond stickpin in the neck cloth of a Rotten Row dandy."

"And what would you know about a Rotten Row dandy?" Derrick wasn't surprised that the lad hailed from the city. He detected a hint of London in the boy's careful speech.

"What wouldn't I know, sir? I picked enough of 'ems pockets. That's before Mrs. Knowles took me in and give me an honest trade."

Supper was a strange affair. The thing Derrick couldn't fathom was why he was surprised. It could be nothing else, considering the strange household.

The dowager duchess sat at the head of the table, the painter and composer on either side. Tonight she wore a more modern black velvet gown with long sleeves, and a black wig to match. The outfit was perhaps only twenty years out of style. She held court as the two artists argued the merits of various sculptors, disparaging many.

Nikoli and Ivaniva—Derrick had never learned the family's last name—and five children were spread liberally along either side of the long table. A sixth, smaller than Charisse, was held in Ivaniva's lap.

Clapping Derrick heartily on the back in welcome as he had appeared in the dining room, the knife thrower seemed to hold no animosity toward him for having walked between Nikoli and his target, twice.

Derrick was placed at the foot of the table. A place of honor in regard to his rank, or just the chair usually left vacant, he didn't know which. But he suspected the latter.

Despite their different backgrounds and the carefully patched evening wear of some, this was a gathering of friends. The hum of jovial conversation buzzed about the table. Derrick felt left out until Olivia came into the room, carrying Charisse, and smiled shyly at him.

She looked radiant in a forest green velvet dress. A matching ribbon was threaded through her wonderful hair, piled atop her head in an elegant fashion. A white silk shawl completed the outfit. Charisse sat astride her mother's hip.

All the gentlemen leaped to their feet. Derrick helped Olivia to be seated, pulling out the chair to the right of his seat.

After she was seated, Charisse firmly trapped on her lap, the little girl banged the flat of both hands on the table and laughed up at Derrick, showing four perfect teeth.

"You look lovely this evening."

"Thank you." Pink tinting her cheeks, Olivia fussed with Charisse's blankets. Horice served her plate from a steaming tureen of turnips, cooked in some manner that left them a creamy caramel brown.

Olivia blew on a spoon of mashed turnips to cool it, then fed it to Charisse. The child smacked and reached for more.

Watching the mother and child, Derrick felt a smile tug at his lips. It died when he tried to remember his own mother even visiting him and his siblings in the nursery.

"She likes everything, that little one," Ivaniva said, speaking to Olivia with an accent Derrick could not identify. Smiling, she looked down at her own daughter, who was much more interested in watching her older brother make faces at her than in food. "Theresa is still hard to please. But, then, she is young and should not eat too much solid food anyway."

Charisse lunged forward, grabbing the edge of her mother's plate. Olivia caught her hand before the little girl touched the hot food. She managed to trap one of Charisse's arms behind her back and hold the other as she continued to feed her daughter.

"I fear you'll find this common fare, Derrick," Olivia said as Charisse smacked a bite.

Olivia acted as though she had been beset by shyness and was searching about for some topic of conversation. Derrick smiled inwardly. He could tell from the looks she darted his way, she was as aware of him as he was of her.

His gaze rested on her lips a moment; then realizing it was a mistake to be thinking of what had happened this afternoon when silk knee breeches left nothing to doubt, he turned his attention to his plate. "It smells delicious," he said honestly—though neither turnips nor the roast rabbit, on the platter which Luther carried around now, were among Derrick's favorite foods.

Taking a bite, he was surprised. "It is not common at all. This is wonderful."

"Horice is a wonder in the kitchen. He can turn anything edible into a feast. I understand he was once head chef at the Savoy," Olivia said. Pink tinged her cheeks as she looked at Derrick. Her gaze went back to her plate.

"But that was before he was thrown into prison for poisoning the maitre d'," said Nikoli's oldest son, a boy of about fourteen.

"Alexi!" Ivaniva scolded. "You will hurt Horice's feelings!"

"It's all right, mum." The cook raised a disapproving brow at the boy. "The lad did right nice with his snares to fetch us the rabbits, so I will take no mind of him this time." Horice pointed his serving spoon in the boy's direction.

"Next time, there'll be some 'ot besides honey on those scones you like to nick when you think I'm not looking." With a wicked smile, Horice left the dining room.

A second of silence followed his departure.

"Horice isn't a poisoner," Olivia hurried to assure Derrick. "The man whom Alexi is talking about became ill after eating some prawns and *swore* he saw Horice sprinkling them with something. Horice says it was merely salt. But he was convicted of attempted poisoning and went to prison. However, the next time the maitre d' ate prawns, he died. A doctor declared it a severe allergic reaction, and Horice was set free."

The painter said, "The chef, he told me that he could no longer find work. Although he was proven innocent, tales clung about him, and no one would hire him, even though as a cook, he is *tres excellent*." He gave a Gaelic shrug. "For an Englishman."

There was a general murmuring about the injustice of it.

"I think there has only been one death here at the table since Horice became my cook, and that has been quite some years ago." The dowager dismissed the deceased with a wave of her hand.

Looking a little green, Alexi asked, "Someone died?"

"Apoplexy," the duchess supplied. "Quite ruined my appetite, and Horice had prepared that most wonderful trifle for dessert."

"As it seems to have ruined Alexi's." The violinist laughed.

As chuckles followed the remark, then general chatter resumed, Derrick took another bite. He liked these people. They seemed content to embrace the moment, never giving a thought to propriety or their own consequence—or lack of it. Seeing the carefully darned elbows on dinner jackets and frayed cuffs, he thought the entire group was likely inches away from the workhouse. If not for the dowager's kindness.

But the dowager seemed little better off, judging from

her lack of proper servants and the way the manor was falling into disrepair.

Chewing another bite of rabbit, Derrick made up his mind to talk to Olivia about her finances immediately after supper. It would certainly be a relief to her to know he had taken care of her future needs, he thought, admiring the brave face she must often have to put on.

Even if the cook had been wrongly convicted, even if circus performers did not endanger anyone entering the halls, the place was crumbling about everyone's ears. Putting a meal on the table seemed to be a challenge. No, this was not the proper atmosphere in which to bring up Charisse. The sooner Olivia and the baby were away, the better.

Olivia would be happy to hear she now had the means to provide a better home for her child, he thought.

"You did *what?*" Fists clenched at her sides, Olivia glared at Derrick.

He clasped his hands behind him and looked at her in the damned superior manner he had, as if *she* was being dense.

"I said I had the Northumberland property evaluated by three agents. I took the highest evaluation and subtracted what Peter's debt came to—"

"Yes, yes, I understood that part." Olivia strove to keep her voice level; still it seemed excessively strident, ricocheting around the parlor, now empty except for the two of them. Everyone was to bed, and she had no wish to disturb them.

When Derrick had asked Olivia to stay after everyone had begun to retire for the evening, a financial discussion was not what she had expected. With a wink, Ivaniva had offered to put Charisse, who was fussy and yawning, to bed with her own baby, freeing Olivia to linger.

After what they had shared that afternoon, Olivia expected him to take her into his arms. To be honest, that's where she wanted to be, to find out if she would experience the same wondrous feelings. In Derrick's arms, she felt more than she had thought possible, more than she ever had with Peter.

She wondered, now, if it had meant anything at all to Derrick.

His winged brows drawing together, he continued, "I took the remainder and divided it, placing part of it at interest to provide you and Charisse with a quarterly income. The rest I invested for you in diverse ways. The country and commerce are changing rapidly. The use of steam engines, for one thing, is changing industry, and I suspect soon will change transportation. I have the figures written down here if you want to see—"

As Olivia took the paper Derrick produced from his jacket, her fingers trembled. "You had no right," she said quietly.

He drew himself up stiffly, the planes and angles of his face seeming to grow harder until he reminded her of the bloodless statue she had once compared him to. "I don't understand what you mean."

"And *that*, Derrick, is what is so very sad."

Chapter Six

As he frowned down at her, Olivia silently thanked God for reminding her why she had run away in the night rather than be married to Derrick Blackwell. He would have always held her reins, controlling every aspect of her life.

She would have felt as smothered as she had in her stepfather's house. Perhaps, she would even have ended up like her mother, content to exist in a drugged fog.

Derrick could not help it. As a man, he had been trained from birth that it was his duty to dominate.

"I assure you, I was very careful in my choices," he said. "Furthermore, I have some experience in choosing wise investments. Olivia, you told me in London that you hoped what was left after Peter's debts were accounted for was enough to keep you and Charisse. I have tried to make it go as far as possible in yielding an income now, as well as growth for the future."

Tangling her fingers in the fringe of her shawl, Olivia sighed. "I have no doubt of it. When he informed me that

I would be married to you, my stepfather touted the fact that it's rumored you have doubled the fortune you inherited by your wise investments. And I *would* have asked for your advice about how to invest the money. But you took it on yourself to handle my finances without even so much as consulting my wishes!" Her voice rose, though she strove to keep it even.

After a lifetime of having every aspect of her life decided for her, first by her stepfather, then by Peter, handling her own funds was to have been her mark of independence. It would have proven to Olivia that she could meet her own needs and those of her daughter.

His winged brows drawing downward, Derrick said, "If you think I've cheated you—"

"As to money, no," she assured him, placing her fingers on his lapel. "I wouldn't insult you like that. You are much too honorable to take anything not yours. You probably wrestled with your conscience before allowing me to repay Peter's debt."

Derrick clasped his hands more tightly behind his back, and she guessed she had hit the mark.

"You may even have been generous in your estimates and rather overvalued the property, to prevent my repaying you in full." Olivia pressed on as his frown deepened, "Or *vastly* overvalued it, to thwart any repayment at all."

"Olivia, be sensible—"

"That's what you did! How dare you!" Olivia stared up at him.

"After insulting you as I did, accusing you of—I felt it only fitting that I make it up to you for my words."

"You cheated me of my right to repay my husband's debts." It was an accusation. "And you did it because you think I am a lesser mortal. Women aren't to be held as accountable, is that it? Then you cheated me of the freedom to make my own choices about the money I expected."

Derrick was at a loss. It wasn't that he couldn't see her points, but such aspects had never occurred to him before. "I had only your best interests at heart—"

"You felt you had the right to decide for me," she accused.

Catching her hand where it still rested against his chest and pressing more tightly against it, he said softly, "I am more qualified than you to handle your financial affairs. What do you know of the schemes to separate people from their money? They're spread out everywhere in the financial world, like rabbit snares."

Her hand was soft and small beneath his. Surely, she could feel his heart beat. He knew it was as close as he could ever come to giving her his heart. She had not wanted it before. Certainly, she wouldn't want it now that he had just shown her how little he understood her.

Again.

"I know very little about the financial world, and that is why I would have sought advice from you, or someone who did know." Her eyes became overbright. "But you took my choices away, like I was no more than a toddling child."

As she looked up at him, twin tears trailed down her cheeks. He pulled her against his length and stroked her back, soothing her as he might a child.

Unresisting, she let him, sighing as she felt his strength surround her. Leaning against him, she enjoyed the sheltered feeling he gave her. However, one part of her mind rebelled, telling her it was better to stand alone. His strength was the trap she must avoid.

"You don't know what it is to be powerless," Olivia said, her words muffled by his evening coat. "Or how frightening power is when it comes and you've never tasted it before. I confess it feels good to know that I don't have the responsibility of making decisions about the money, when my and Charisse's whole futures ride on it. It feels seductively good." She bit her lip. It took a great deal to admit how afraid she was.

"I have taken care of the money. Why should you need to know anything more?" He wanted her trust, he found, if he could not have her love.

"Because to be independent, I must be able to make wise decisions! I must learn to handle my own affairs and get over my fears. And if I don't learn, I am certain to fall prey to one of the rabbit snares you spoke of." Olivia sighed. Derrick didn't understand what it was like to feel powerless over one's own life. To be powerless.

"If I did wrong, I apologize," he murmured against her hair. "It was for the best of reasons."

The deep timbre of his voice vibrated through his chest and into hers, making warm feelings riot there. Derrick would never willingly hurt her, or Charisse. She understood that now. But he would always dominate. It was his nature, what he had been trained to do since birth, Olivia reminded herself, even as she pressed closer to his hard male length.

Tilting her chin up with his finger, Derrick said, "I don't think I've ever wanted a woman more. Is it only because you want nothing of me?"

As Olivia moistened her lips, his gaze moved to her mouth, and the sensation of butterflies rioting in her stomach increased tenfold. "I would not say that I want nothing of you." Her voice was disturbingly husky to her own ears. Her cheeks warmed at her own temerity.

He smiled. "Never be embarrassed by honesty—though, when your cheeks grow pink, it does add sparkle to your green eyes." He brushed the damp trails of her tears from her cheeks with his thumb.

The knowledge that she wanted him was bittersweet. Even as it fired his blood, Derrick thought of the many women he had wanted in just the way Olivia wanted him, the many women he had dallied with without ever wanting more than a few nights of pleasure in their arms.

Now, Fate had dealt him the same hand.

But he wouldn't let Olivia know. He would take as much as she would willingly give and ask no more. He had his pride, he thought, as he bent to kiss her.

Her lips were incredibly sweet and soft. Her mouth opened, and she wound her arms around his neck, drawing him closer.

With a groan, Derrick deepened the kiss, delving into the sweet recesses of her mouth, seeking out the secret places. Her tongue took up the challenge, finding his and dueling with it, making him want to lay her down right there by the fire and explore the wonders of her body. Take what she offered and not let her know he wished for more. More than she was capable of giving.

Olivia pressed closer still. As her breasts flattened against his chest, she yearned for more than kisses. Heavy warmth pooled low in her abdomen. Unable to bear the sensations he was causing, she broke free of his kiss and gasped for air.

Derrick kissed the side of her neck, her throat. And moved downward. His teeth grazed her breast through the velvet of her dress, and she arched, moaning with delight and surprise.

He straightened. "We could go up to my room." His voice was a harsh rasp.

"It wouldn't be very wise, would it?" She wet her lips, knowing that she wanted all of him, no matter how unwise.

Splaying his fingers over her lower back, he pulled her softness tightly against his erection. Closing his eyes, Derrick confessed, "Definitely, not wise."

Moving suddenly, he caught her behind the knees and lifted her.

Twining her arms around his neck, a riot of anticipation chased through Olivia as Derrick crossed the room carrying her. Shifting Olivia's weight, Derrick swung the parlor doors open.

And found Marvin standing in the hall. Derrick's trunk was on his shoulder, and Derrick's valise and a lantern sat on the floor beside the big man. Marvin thrust Derrick's greatcoat out to him.

Chapter Seven

Olivia squirmed, and Derrick set her down, but kept his arm around her shoulders. Taking the heavy woolen coat from the gatekeeper, Derrick frowned. "That is my luggage."

Marvin looked from Derrick to Olivia, then picked up Derrick's valise and the lantern in one hand and, balancing the trunk on one brawny shoulder, turned and started walking away.

"Marvin, what are you about?" Olivia called. "Derrick is our guest!"

The gatekeeper kept walking, disappearing around the corner as he turned toward the front of the house.

"Marvin!" Olivia looked at Derrick at a loss.

"I don't think he approves of us being together." Derrick kissed the tip of her nose, aching to scoop her up and continue on upstairs. "I had better rescue my things."

As Derrick's footsteps died away, Olivia touched her lips, fevered and bruised from his kisses, and the realization of what she had almost done sobered her. What was she thinking?

She wasn't thinking! She had thrown all good sense to the wind as desire had stolen her powers of reason.

Going back to the fireplace, she took the poker from the rack at the side of the marble hearth and pulled the ends of the burned logs together; then using the ash shovel, she carefully covered the embers, banking the fire until the morning.

But the fire within her was another matter. She sensed what she had experienced with Peter had only been a start. Derrick's kisses set her aflame, and she wanted more. To know the full measure of the pleasure to be found in his arms. To experience all that he might teach her about passion.

But if she allowed Derrick to rekindle the fires he had started, would that fire consume her and all her hopes for the future? Or was she strong enough to remain her own person, preserve her independence, even in his arms?

Silly goose. Olivia shook her head. What was she worried about? He had not offered her marriage again. Only a night in his bed.

Unfamiliar with the house, Derrick followed the light of Marvin's lantern and the sound of his footsteps, muttering oaths when he barked his shin on low tables or stumbled on a carpet edge.

He was certain of one thing—Marvin had much to answer for. And answer he would, as soon as Derrick caught up with him. Derrick thought of Olivia as he had left her, her thick-lashed eyes heavy-lidded with arousal, her lips parted and inviting.

Yes, Marvin had much to answer for!

As Derrick gained the great hall, Marvin opened the

entrance doors and went out into the night, carrying the trunk and valise.

Pausing in the entryway, snow floating in on winter's cold breath, Derrick put on the greatcoat, preparing to follow the big man outside. Though he yearned, instead, to turn back to Olivia, he needed his luggage and to set Marvin straight. What did the beggar think he was about, anyway?

Derrick closed the door and trudged through the snow, hurrying to catch up. The night was abysmally dark. The only light was the beckoning lantern, now disappearing around a bend in the carriage sweep.

Snow struck Derrick's cheeks and found its way between the high points of his starched collar and his neck, melting against his skin. Since it began that afternoon, it had accumulated well past his ankles, reminding Derrick sharply that he still wore his knee pants and dress slippers, not his sturdy Hessian boots.

Through the yaw branches, he saw the lantern light still. Rounding the curve, Derrick found Marvin waiting for him to catch up.

"You'll sleep in the gate house," Marvin said in a crisp Oxford accent. "It's snug. Much more comfortable than the grand bedrooms in the manor, if the truth be told."

"You speak." For an instant, Derrick stood stock-still, forgetting his anger.

With Derrick's trunk on one wide shoulder, Marvin shrugged the other one. "I speak."

"Then, *why* haven't you before now?"

"Not speaking saves arguments." The gatekeeper turned and started on toward the gate house. "She's vulnerable," he said over his shoulder, as if in answer to a question. "She thinks she can make herself into the duchess, needing no one and doing as she pleases, but she's not cut of the same cloth, you know."

"Who are you to decide?" Derrick felt his anger flare again. But as the cold night air cooled his ardor and his mind cleared, he realized he was the one most likely to be hurt if he had taken her up to his bedroom. He had only sparked Olivia's passion, but being with her might revive the feelings he had once had for her.

Vain feelings, he knew.

"There's that, too," Marvin said, going into the back door of the gate house.

"What?" Derrick followed him. The tiny kitchen was cheery and warm. A fire burned brightly in the fireplace. Several pots were hung above the stonework mantel, and a checkered tablecloth covered a small eating table. A worktable and pump were in the corner.

"The reason I let you in the gate is you care deeply about Mrs. Knowles, though you've told yourself you don't." After he set the lantern down on the table, one corner of which was stacked with books, the big man swung the trunk off his shoulder, depositing it on the floor.

The truth of the statement hit Derrick. His feelings didn't need to be revived. God help him. He cared about her, still. And what he felt had deepened since he had seen Olivia with her daughter. It made him realize all they might have had if only he had shown her his heart, instead of his impeccable manners.

Going back to the door, Derrick stepped over the threshold and stomped the snow from his evening shoes. How had he fooled himself into thinking he didn't care? That he could be with her without it tearing him apart when he left?

He drew in a deep breath of the cold air and wondered at the capacity of the human heart to fool itself.

Subdued, Derrick came back inside and closed the door. "Are you a mind reader?"

Marvin snorted. "They called me a mind reader, but it's

really hearts I see. I feel what people around me are feeling, but it's not by choice." The big man picked up a rolled paper from the table.

Derrick took it and unfurled the poster. It touted the powers of *Marvin the Marvelous,* who knew all, saw all.

"You were in the circus?" Derrick rolled the poster back up and set it aside.

"Aye. But it was too much." Marvin closed and opened his hands, looking down at them as if he had never really noticed them before. "I needed to get away from people, so I came here with the Romanoffs—Nikoli and his family—a few years ago. I stay out here in the gate house because keeping away from people helps."

His gaze met Derrick's unwaveringly. "The question you should be asking yourself, I'm thinking, is what are you going to do about how you feel?"

The question caught Derrick off guard. And it was a question to which he had no answer.

"Sir Derrick, there you are! Do have some breakfast before it grows cold. Horice has outdone himself this morning. These stewed apples are divine." The duchess motioned for him to be seated, the curls of her elaborate red wig trembling. Her navy blue day dress had a military motif, complete with gold-fringed epaulets.

Derrick remembered his mother wearing a similar dress when she and his father brought him to Eaton for the first time. "Thank you, Lady Orwell."

"Just 'Lady O,' please."

"Lady O," he said.

As Derrick took a seat, the dowager went on, "When Luther reported you weren't in the blue room, I feared you had decided to go back to London in that most inclement weather last night. And I dare say, the roads are no more passable this morning."

"Marvin decided I would be more comfortable spending the night in the gate house," Derrick said drily.

"How odd." The dowager raised her brows.

Derrick offered nothing else. Placing his napkin across his lap, he said, "I trust you rested well, Lady O?"

"At my age it doesn't do to sleep too soundly," she returned drily, spearing a kippered herring with her fork.

"I find you very vital."

The dowager added, "For someone who is old enough to have attended Methuselah's birth." With a small smile, she said, "I don't mind being old. Either one gets older, or one doesn't, after all. Getting older is preferable, I suppose, given a choice."

"You have a point," Derrick agreed and poured himself coffee from the tarnished silver pot.

She laid down her fork and steepled her thin fingers, looking thoughtful. "So, since you spent the night in the gate house, I take it that you haven't convinced my niece to trust you with her future happiness."

His cup touching his lips, Derrick paused, thankful he had not yet taken a sip. If he had, he surely would have sprayed the table at that remark. It was his turn to raise his brows.

Lady O waved an airy hand. "Plain speaking is another privilege of age. So, you've not made progress with your suit?"

"Your niece made plain what she thought of my suit when she eloped with Peter," Derrick said stiffly, choosing to overlook what had happened between him and Olivia the night before. That had been passion, after all. Not love.

"Well, you can lick that wound and keep it raw, or you can get on about the business of convincing her." The dowager lifted her fork again.

He started to deny that he wanted to convince Olivia of anything. But the glint in the old lady's eyes forestalled such a useless gesture. Were his feelings so transparent? Derrick wondered. He had certainly managed to lie to himself about them.

Derrick said, "I find your niece hard to convince of anything. She wants to be like a certain great, great aunt of hers, who is completely independent and indifferent to what the world and society think."

"Pish. Olivia is nothing like me. She needs a dozen youngsters at her knee and a husband to dote on. But she is so terrified of becoming her mother, she will not see the truth of it."

Derrick remembered meeting Olivia's mother at the party to announce his and Olivia's ill-fated engagement. Dark circles rimmed Lady Stodgeforth's eyes, and her hands trembled. She pleaded a headache shortly after the engagement was announced and excused herself from the proceedings.

"Olivia's mother is ill a great deal, I understand." He had heard rumors of a nervous disorder.

"My mother is an opium addict."

Shoulders squared as though prepared to do battle, Olivia stood in the doorway. Blinking big dark eyes, Charisse sat on Olivia's hip, swaddled in multiple blankets against the drafts in the old house.

Derrick rose as she entered the room. A feeling of unease skittered through him as she fussed with the baby's blankets, avoiding meeting his gaze. As he helped Olivia be seated, Charisse looked up at him and cooed prettily.

Sadness shadowing her eyes, Olivia gazed at her daughter as she went on, "I am not excusing it, but it is Mother's escape from being constantly under my stepfather's thumb."

She finally looked at Derrick, and instead of the warmth that had been in her gaze the night before, there was a wariness.

"And that is why you did not wish to marry me. Ogre that I am, I remind you of Herman Stodgeforth." He kept his words light, but the truth of them stabbed his heart. All his life, proper manners and deportment had been his refuge. To Olivia, he must have appeared very much like the staid Lord Stodgeforth.

Olivia said nothing.

"I'm sorry. Your mother's problem must be very painful for you." Derrick touched the baby's cheek, understanding the change in Olivia. Without passion as an opiate, she had had time to realize just what a risk they had been about to take.

Charisse laughed and threw herself toward Derrick. As Olivia held on tightly, Derrick caught the child, also. Their fingers overlapped around the baby, and Olivia gasped, wide-eyed, as she looked at him.

So, she wasn't as immune to his presence as she would have him think. The knowledge gave him hope.

He let go, and then regretted it. Hadn't he been letting go of what he really wanted all of his life? First, he let go of the vain hope that his parents might demonstrate love for him. Then he had let go of the hope Olivia would bring her light and laughter into his life.

She still saw him as a man like Herman Stodgeforth—a man like his own father had been. But inside of him, there surged a tidal wave of warm feelings for her.

Marvin's question of the night before came back to Derrick: *What are you going to do about how you feel?*

"Do try the stewed apples, dear. I'm certain my great, great, great niece will enjoy them," said the dowager duchess.

"Charisse has had her breakfast." However, Olivia absently dipped stewed apples onto her plate.

His own plate forgotten, Derrick's gaze went from the bright-eyed child to Olivia's bosom.

Olivia said, "I've been thinking, Derrick, in regard to what we spoke about last evening."

"Which time are you referring to?" he asked, deliberately looking at Olivia's mouth. As faint pink touched her cheeks, Derrick felt a smile tug at his own lips.

She lifted her chin. "The money. What you've arranged is quite satisfactory. Except for that matter of money due you, of course. That can be satisfied from the funds at interest. I'll sign whatever paper is necessary, if you would be so kind as to draw it up."

"You will? But I thought you wanted to decide where the money would be placed."

"I have decided to accept your choices," she said, exasperation coloring her voice. "So, you'll be free to return to London. Today, if you'd like."

He shrugged. "I have no plans to return."

"Mamamama," Charisse babbled, then laughed as Derrick made a face at her.

"Really, Olivia, there is a foot of snow on the ground. The roads will be quite impassable. Will be for a fortnight, I shouldn't wonder. Kippered herring, dear?" The dowager's hand hovered above the platter.

"No, thank you, Auntie O." Olivia looked at Derrick warily. "You'll expire of boredom here in the country, I'm certain."

"Not at all. I find ... much to entertain me here."

Ignoring her mother's dark look, Derrick gave Charisse his finger.

The child tried to bring it to her mouth, then looking straight at Derrick, said, *"Dadada."*

Derrick felt as though his heart doubled in size.

Chapter Eight

"My word, did you hear that?" Auntie O looked at Olivia. "The child thinks Derrick is her father."

"It's just accidental. Charisse can't know what she's saying," Olivia said, staring into Derrick's eyes.

"Let me take her while you have your breakfast." He rose and held out his hands. Charisse leaned toward him, gurgling happily. Not waiting for her mother's consent, Derrick took the child and swaddled the blankets carefully around her.

Frowning, Olivia watched as Derrick opened the double doors and went into the adjoining parlor, Charisse securely on his hip. He stood at the bay window talking to the child in low tones, pointing at the new-fallen snow, then at the sparrows that hopped about.

"*Gagagaga,*" Charisse said, waving wildly at the birds.

"Olivia, you need not look so apprehensive." Auntie O touched her napkin to her lips. "Derrick seems to have a natural way with her. She's perfectly happy to let him mind her while you eat."

"I'm not apprehensive." Olivia poured herself a cup of coffee, then drew her shawl more tightly about her shoulders. "I am . . . amazed."

Derrick returned to the dining room moments later, a bemused expression on his face. "I fear she objected to the style in which I tied my neck cloth."

The neck cloth was in his hand. He used it to dab a bit of ejected milk from Charisse's chin.

"I warned you that she erupts." The dowager raised one gray brow.

"Here. I'll take her now." Olivia half rose, reaching for her daughter. Why she felt so uneasy as he carried Charisse about, Olivia had no idea. It wasn't that she didn't trust Derrick to be careful with the child.

"Pray, finish your breakfast. I'll not expire from a little mishap," Derrick said. "I came back in here because I thought it too cold in the parlor. The fire laid there is very small."

He smiled at Charisse, who frowned and caught his nose with wet fingers.

Laughing as he pulled free, Derrick glanced at the dining room hearth. "I see there is little more of a blaze in here. If you'd like, Lady O, after Olivia has finished her breakfast, I'll give Charisse back to her and build up the fires. Where is the wood kept?"

"I would like that very much." The dowager steepled her fingers. "However, I fear wood is in short supply, Sir Derrick. I find myself having outrun the carpenter this quarter. And the woodcutter needs payment on delivery— he has a family of twelve to feed, and I do worry that they are getting enough, at that."

"Auntie O?" Olivia questioned, then remembered Derrick. Embarrassed to have Derrick overhear her aunt's lack of funds, Olivia asked, "How could you be out of money?"

"Quite easily. I spent it." Lady O sighed. "I didn't expect so very much cold weather. This isn't usual for us this far south, you know. And it will soon be Christmas, so I have had extra expenses." Raising her brows, she looked at Olivia meaningfully. "Anyway, it's only a few days until the end of this quarter and the new year, so I'm certain we shall scrape by until then."

"I see." Olivia tangled her fingers in her shawl. Her aunt was generous to a fault. Whatever use the money had been put to, Olivia had no doubt it was well spent. That, however, would not keep them warm.

The dowager turned back to Derrick. "I was thinking of having Marvin chop up an armoire. My husband's grandmother brought it with her from France as a bride. It is in the style of Louis XIV—a monstrous big thing, ornate to the extreme." She frowned. "I've never cared overmuch for the style."

"I'm certain that won't be necessary," Derrick said slowly, shooting a glance at Olivia as if to ask if her aunt was serious. "There are a great many trees on the parkland. If Marvin knows where there is an ax or a bow saw, I'll see that wood is cut."

"You know how to cut wood?" Lady O looked impressed. "One of your many hidden facets, I think."

Touching her napkin to her lips, Olivia said, "I've finished. I'll take Charisse so you may go find Marvin." She held out her hands, and Derrick gave Charisse to her.

After Derrick had donned his greatcoat and left the dining room, Olivia thrust Charisse into Lady O's lap. "Just for a moment. I . . . I've thought of something I need to ask Derrick."

"But she leaks!" the dowager called after Olivia's disappearing form.

She watched until Olivia was out of sight. After peering this way and that to be certain no one else was lurking about, Lady O jiggled the little girl and made a funny face. "I'm going to get all that sweetness." She smooched one plump cheek, sending Charisse into fits of giggles. "And I'm going to get all that sweetness over here." She smooched the other cheek, to the baby's delight.

Sitting back, Lady O looked at the little girl, who stared back with raised brows, thoughtfully gnawing her knuckle.

"Oh, my, you are something. Did you know that? You're going to break hearts and be a law unto yourself, exactly like your great, great, great aunt."

"*Ga.*" Charisse took her finger from her mouth and grasped the dowager's nose.

"Wait!" Olivia hurried after Derrick. She caught up to him just before he stepped into the main hallway, which connected the wing with the rest of the house.

"Yes?" Derrick paused. His ebony eyes grew impossibly darker as he gazed at her face.

Looking into the ebony depths, she forgot what she had hurried after him to say. "I'll walk with you," Olivia said, looking down at the strings of her shawl, tangled through her fingers. She would never remember what she needed to ask if he continued to look at her like that.

"Certainly."

As they started forward, he placed his hand lightly on her shoulder. Completely aware of his touch, she felt as cloth-headed as when he had been staring into her eyes.

As they stepped into the long hallway, there came an ominous "Now—" *Bomp, bomp!*

"Watch out!" Derrick shoved Olivia behind him.

Nikoli, dressed in his thigh-high boots and holding several large, shining knives, stood at one end of the hallway. The target, on which was drawn an outline of a person, was farther down. Sighing, Nikoli crossed his arms, knives in hand, as he waited for them to move.

It took Derrick an instant to realize three more *bomps* reverberated, five in all, though Nikoli had not thrown a single blade.

Carrying a wooden mallet, Alexi appeared from behind the large corkboard target and gave each knife sticking in it a tap. Each disappeared into the board in turn.

"Ah, my new friend," Nikoli said, walking to where Derrick still shielded Olivia. "I thought we would be less disturbed here, so I moved the target from the hallway upstairs."

"It was a logical choice," Derrick said, frowning as he watched Alexi.

"I see a look of wondering on your face. It is not that I, Nikoli Romanoff, am not the greatest knife thrower in all the world."

Olivia realized how close Derrick held her. She moved away from his warmth.

Nikoli said something in what sounded like Russian, and Alexi rushed behind the corkboard. Faster than Olivia could take in his movements, Nikoli threw the blades he was holding. Five knives sticking in the corkboard vibrated with the force of their impact. They formed a straight line from a foot above the floor to the top of the board, and each looked exactly a foot apart.

"We do the act as we do because my Ivaniva stands before the board as I throw. Although I am an expert, she is my wife." He shook his head. "One should not tempt fate."

Shrugging, he looked at Derrick. "You will, of course, keep my secrets. This act is how we feed our children."

"Of course."

As they moved on to the great hall, so Nikoli and Alexi could continue, Derrick raised his brows. "So, when Lady O said there was no danger . . ."

"There really was no danger. They practice the timing, so it looks like Nikoli is throwing the knives, when he actually drops them into his tall boot, and Alexi, of course, taps the fake ones through from the opposite side of the board."

Olivia could not prevent a smile at Derrick's look of ill-usage. "I'm sorry. Auntie O and I could not tell. The secret was not ours to share, after all."

"You minx. You enjoyed my discomfort." Derrick smiled and caught a curl of dark brown silk. He said softly, "I'm happy you didn't wear that hideous widow's cap today."

Dropping her gaze to the toes of her shoes, Olivia stepped away. She pulled her shawl more tightly about her shoulders against the chill permeating the old house and remembered Auntie O's rule number fourteen: when doing business, be businesslike.

Squaring her shoulders, she said briskly, "I followed you because I needed to ask you, now that I have money, how can I draw upon it? Charisse and I have been living here for some time, and I haven't contributed to the household."

"I have some banknotes in my wallet—" He held up a hand to forestall her protest. "You can take them and write me a draft against your account, thereby maintaining your independence."

"Good. Then I'll send Luther to the woodcutter's house and order wood. Though I know Auntie O wouldn't want it, I want to c-c-carry some of the bur-r-rden." Her chattering teeth gave her speech a hint of a burr.

Derrick caught her shoulders, rubbing his hands up and down her arms. Olivia wondered if there was a rule for when one wanted to be held by the person with whom one was doing business.

"Go back to where it's warm. Do what you think best about the wood. I think Marvin and I can manage something for today." He paused. As if pulled by a loadstone, Olivia moved nearer still, until their bodies were touching, and Derrick wrapped her into the folds of his greatcoat.

It was wonderfully warmed by his body's heat and smelled of his cologne. She wanted him to kiss her. Now that they had settled matters between them, now that he knew she would remain independent, surely she could enjoy the mysterious allure of his embrace without chancing her future. What was it that attracted her to this man, when she knew he was all that was wrong for her?

Olivia bit her lip. "I never asked you. Why did Marvin have your luggage last night? What did he do with it?"

"He asked me to stay in the gate house," Derrick said wryly. "He seemed to think there was some danger in us remaining under the same roof."

Derrick smoothed his hands down her back, pulling her closer to his wonderful warmth. How could anything that felt so wonderful hold a trap? Olivia thought, bemused.

"Marvin doesn't speak. How could he ask you to stay at the gate house?" She locked her hands around Derrick's waist, thinking she would explode if he didn't kiss her soon.

Derrick smiled. At last, in this house where nothing was quite what it seemed, he knew something Olivia didn't. Not only did Marvin speak, but once the pump was primed, the flow was nearly impossible to stem. He had kept Derrick awake the better part of the night.

Brushing her bottom lip with his thumb, Derrick leaned close. Olivia caught her breath in anticipation.

"I'd better go." Derrick disengaged her arms and was whistling a Scottish air as he gained the front doors.

Chapter Nine

Staring at the door Derrick had just gone through, Olivia stamped her foot. How dare he play such games with her! She crossed her arms against the chill she felt now that she was no longer warmed by his body heat and coat.

It wasn't that she cared a fig for Derrick Blackwell. Well, no more than any other of her acquaintances. He was still staid, overbearing, and far too aware of his own consequence for her to have truly tender feelings for him.

However, he intrigued her on a purely physical level, she admitted reluctantly. The feelings Derrick stirred in her with just a kiss were more tumultuous than anything she had ever known before.

He had known she wanted him to kiss her just now. She had all but stood on tiptoe and pressed her lips to his. And he had turned away, laughing at her.

Now, Hades would freeze over before she again let him near!

Turning on her heel as her teeth started to chatter once more, she went in search of Luther.

She found him in the kitchen, peeling vegetables. Olga and Ludmilla, Ivaniva and Nikoli's older daughters, were helping. Identical except in size, one being a year older, they darted shy glances at Luther, handsome in his too-big livery.

"Aye, mum. I used most of the wood stack when I laid the fires this morning. Except what I figured Horice would need for cooking, that is." Luther placed a peeled potato into a bowl with several others.

Spreading her hands before the kitchen hearth, Olivia said, "As soon as Horice can spare you, I'd like you to go to the woodcutter's and tell him we need all the wood he can bring."

"Pardon me, Mrs. Knowles." Horice stood by the other side of the tall fireplace as he turned a haunch of beef on a spit over the coals. "But yesterday morn, when I went into the village greengrocer's, I noticed the woodcutter's house, and it didn't have much wood stacked up beside it." The cook shrugged. "I noticed because I seen we were gettin' low. No doubt, with the cold weather, people have bought him out. It may take some time for him to cut more for you."

Olivia tangled her fingers in the fringe of her shawl. "Sir Derrick is going to help Marvin chop down a tree from the parkland to tide us over. Perhaps they will need to cut more than they planned."

"Marvin?" Luther and Horice said in unison, disbelief in their voices.

"Why not Marvin?" Olivia asked. A feeling of foreboding skittered through her as the two exchanged an uneasy glance.

"Marvin'll do his best, no doubt," Horice said. "He's good enough at tendin' the horses—he learned that much in the circus. But I doubt he knows which end of an ax to cut with." He focused his attention on his roast. "I wouldn't be no better, mind you. I grew up in great house on the Thames, where my father was the chef. I don't even like walking through the woods. There's . . . things." He shuddered expressively.

"Mum, it ain't a job for someone what don't know what they're doing. I saw a man hauled into a doctor's office in King's Street once. Bleeding from the mouth, he was. One of the gaffers carrying the stretcher said a tree fell on him." Luther paled at the memory.

"It would have been better to ask Father," Ludmilla, the older of the two girls, said. "He cuts the firewood when we are traveling with the circus."

"Yes, I should have thought of Nikoli," Olivia agreed, tangling her fingers more tightly.

"Good thing Sir Derrick knows what he's about. He'll keep Marvin from harm, he will," Luther said stoutly.

"But why would Derrick know . . ." Wood cutting was surely outside a gentleman's training. No doubt, he was thinking Marvin would know how to fell a tree.

Horice snorted. "Marvin taught at Oxford before he was with the circus. Ancient languages, or something as useless." Looking abashed, he said, "But I wasn't supposed to tell no one. It's his business, Mrs. Knowles. Please don't say nothing."

Olivia blinked. "But how could he teach? He doesn't speak."

"He can speak right enough when he wants. Talk the head off a rusty nail. But I shouldn't a said anything about that either. How a man goes on is his own business, I say." Horice turned the roast on the spit.

Olivia didn't have time to wonder at the revelation. If neither Marvin nor Derrick knew what they were doing, one or both could suffer. "I have to find them before one of them gets hurt. But how can I know where to look? There's ten acres of parkland surrounding the manor."

"Should be easy enough in the new snow," Luther pointed out. "The footprints will lead you right to them."

"You are a genius!" Olivia gave the lad a smacking kiss on the forehead.

Luther turned red between his freckles as the girls giggled.

Picking the front edge of her skirts up, Olivia left the kitchen at an unseemly run.

After what seemed an eternity of trudging through foot-deep snow, Olivia recognized Marvin's red muffler through the trees. Even in the thick woodlands, as Luther had predicted, she had encountered little trouble following the footprints of two men and a horse in the fresh snow. The sounds of an ax being wielded had died a few minutes before. Now the two were talking excitedly. She only hoped it wasn't because one or both of them had done themselves an injury.

The snowy wood was beautiful, with patches of azure blue sky visible through mostly bare winter limbs. The few evergreen trees were magnificent under their mantles of white. Her breath rolling out in steamy puffs, Olivia thought she might have enjoyed the excursion if not for her growing concern.

Rounding a holly, heavy with snow which powdered her skirt as she brushed past, Olivia saw Derrick seated on the back of a horse, an ax raised awkwardly above his head.

Heavens, she was just in time! Even she knew one couldn't cut a tree down on horseback.

As he took aim at a limb in an oak, the horse snorted and fidgeted. Holding its halter, Marvin stroked its nose soothingly. Just as Derrick drew back again, the horse side-stepped once more.

"No!" Olivia shouted. Derrick swung. Though the tree was bare of leaves, every branch and twig held snow. As the limb vibrated, powdery white crystals rained down on her. A glob hit squarely atop her stocking cap, and the frigid mess shifted down her collar.

"Olivia? What are you doing here?" Derrick swung gracefully off the horse's bare back. As he passed behind the horse, he lightly swung the ax, sticking it firmly into a log.

"You can't chop down a tree atop a horse." The snow beneath her collar melted, trickling icy water down her back. "It's a good thing I came to see what the two of you were about!" she snapped.

Derrick glanced at Marvin, then grinned at Olivia. "It is?"

"Yes!" Wishing she had taken time to find her muffler, she pulled at her collar. Her actions allowed the snow water to run farther down her dress. "Oh, *blast,* that's cold!"

"I wasn't chopping down a tree." He motioned at the log in the snow. A chain connected it to the horse's harness. "Marvin knew where there was a small oak blown over by a storm last summer. The dry wood will burn better than green wood, even if it will be harder to split."

Olivia glared at him, in no mood to find she had suffered ice down her collar for nothing. "If you weren't atop that horse trying to cut the limb off the tree, what were you doing?"

Derrick didn't answer. Moving nearer, he brushed off the top of Olivia's stocking cap, then her shoulders. "Because it is so near Christmas, I thought you might wish to start decorating." Suddenly, he held a green sprig above her head.

Olivia looked up. "Mistletoe?" He had been getting mistletoe out of the tree. Reading the expression in his dark eyes, Olivia shook her head. *"Don't you—"*

Before she could finish, Derrick kissed her soundly on the cheek.

"Oh!" How dare he! In no mood to be playful, Olivia took an indignant step backward—right into the thick holly bush, which pricked her even through coat and clothes. Losing her balance, she fell, sitting on her bottom amid the prickly branches. Snow avalanched from the limbs, covering her.

Olivia stared at the mound of snow in her lap. Everything was perfectly still and silent for a second, as though the woodland was holding its breath not to laugh.

"Olivia, I'm sorry." Derrick grasped her arms and hauled her out.

"You should be." She hid her tears by vigorously brushing snow from her clothes. More was melting down her neck, and she shivered. "I j-just came because I was afr-r-raid one of you would b-b-be hurt."

Derrick looked at her wonderingly. "Why would you think that?"

"Because I thought neither of you could use an ax," Olivia sniffed.

"Thank you for caring," Derrick said, helping her dust the ice crystals away.

"And I thank you, Mrs. Knowles," Marvin added. "I truly appreciate your concern."

As Olivia gaped at him—he *did* speak!—Marvin nodded to Derrick. "You help Mrs. Knowles." With that, he started back toward the manor, guiding the horse and log through the woods.

"You're soaked through, or soon will be. We have to get you to where it's warm." He pulled off his greatcoat and put it around her shoulders, then wrapped a protective arm about her and helped her walk.

Stumbling along beside him, Olivia couldn't control her shivering. "Now you'll g-g-get chilled."

"I'll be fine." Derrick scooped her up in his arms and started on down the path of footprints.

"You can't carry me all the way back," Olivia protested.

"Then, I'll carry you as far as I can."

"No. Put me down. I can walk."

He shook his head. "I caused your discomfort. Let me help make things better."

"Derrick—"

"Olivia." He shook his head, his dark gaze holding hers for an instant before he started forward again. "You don't have to be independent all the time, you know."

Chapter Ten

"What are we doing here?" Olivia asked as Derrick put her down outside the gatekeeper's cottage.

He kept his arm wrapped around her shoulders, reluctant to let go when she was trembling so with cold. The exertion of carrying her had warmed him, except for his fingers and feet. Those had lost feeling.

"It should be warm inside. I built up a roaring fire in here this morning, not knowing the manor was without wood." Derrick swung open the door, and she hurried in before him.

After stomping the snow off his Hessians, he followed and found her with her mittens already off, her fingers stretched toward the still-hot embers in the fireplace.

Derrick knelt and added several small logs to the andirons from a small stack by the hearth. Olivia shivered, despite the warmth of the glowing coals.

"You need to get out of those wet things." After checking the kettle for water, he hung it on a hook over the fire.

"Oh, a cup of tea would be lovely!" Olivia breathed, still shivering. She took off her damp stocking cap and tossed it onto the hearth beside her mittens.

Derrick pulled a bench from the side of the table and positioned it in front of the fire. "Sit here."

"Thank you."

After Olivia was seated, he knelt and lifted first one foot and then the other, pulling her boots off. Frowning, he said, "These are wet inside. Your stockings are soaked through, and your feet are like ice."

"The snow was deeper than the boots are tall." Olivia bit her lip against the pain as Derrick set her foot down.

"And still you trudged through the drifts because you were afraid for me," he said softly.

"I was afraid for Marvin, too." She kept her gaze trained on the flames, which were starting to lick between the wood.

"Of course." Derrick sat back on his heels. "You need to get out of those wet things. More than a foot of the hem of your dress is soaked." He rose and left the kitchen. In a moment, he returned with a blanket. Taking his great-coat from her shoulders, he wrapped the blanket securely about her.

"I'll go find Ivaniva and tell her what has happened. She can find what you need in your room and bring it to you."

He lingered for a moment, wanting to tell her how much her concern meant to him. Her trudging through the snow to save him from harm had given him a warm feeling. But, no doubt, as Olivia had said, she had been just as concerned for Marvin.

This realization, that she would have done the same for anyone, took a little of the warm glow away. Well, what did he expect? She had not run away with Peter because she had any feelings for him. It was only passion Derrick had been able to ignite inside her the last couple of days, and he knew that quite surprised her.

Going out of the door, Derrick told himself not to be a fool. He hadn't lived two-and-thirty years with knowing passion and love were, indeed, separate things.

But, perhaps, with time . . . and if he kept stoking the fires inside her, Olivia might grow to care for him. Just a little.

Surprised at the direction of his thoughts, futile thoughts, Derrick shook his head and hoped the cold would clear it.

After the door had closed behind Derrick, Olivia stared into the flames. "Liar," she said aloud. She had scarce given poor Marvin a thought. Instead, she had pictured Derrick crushed and lifeless—the thought had been almost more than she could bear.

And so she had made a grand cake of herself!

She should have known a man like Derrick was up to any challenge. That was one of the things she found so unfair about the world. Men were taught everything. Women were taught to humbly obey men.

But Derrick had never asked for her obedience, she remembered.

No doubt, he would have taken it for granted, her other self argued.

Still, when she looked up into his dark eyes, he calmed her uncertainties and made her feel secure, as though whatever happened, he would never let her down. Hadn't she felt that way when he had told her he would provide wood for the day? It was only later when she talked with Horice and Luther that she became concerned.

She should have listened to her first instincts, that Derrick was a man one could count on. He would do whatever he said he would do, and do it well.

And that was the trap! Counting on him, allowing herself to come to depend on him, meant never learning to count on herself. Depend on herself.

It meant giving up all hope of independence.

And while Derrick would always assume he knew what was best for her, just like with her money, he would dominate and smother her at every turn.

She remembered the way her stepfather had dominated her mother, criticizing the color of her gowns, or the way she wore her hair, and everything else about her, no matter how hard her mother had tried to please him. Eventually, she was afraid to make the smallest decision without his approval. Finally, she preferred to drift in an opium haze to facing life.

Her mother's last letter had been almost completely incoherent. As tears formed in her eyes, Olivia felt powerless.

Dashing the moisture away, she concentrated on getting out of her wet things and hanging them to dry as best she could.

When the knock at the door came, she called, "Come in." Stripped but for her camisole and drawers, Olivia had her back to the door as she hung her dress on a peg on the wall near the fire.

"I am sorry." It was Derrick's voice.

Turning around, Olivia was totally nonplussed at his being in the room—even when she found him with his back to her.

Grabbing the blanket she had discarded, she wrapped it around her from chin to ankles. "I'm covered." She felt warmth surge into her cheeks.

Derrick turned. "Ivaniva couldn't come. She was nursing both Charisse and her own babe," he said apologetically.

"Your aunt gathered some things from your room, but she suggested there was nothing for it but for me to bring your dry clothes, as she would not go out into the cold and risk her health."

"I see," murmured Olivia, eyeing a lacy camisole atop the stack he held. Auntie O knew she wore her practical muslin garments now that she was nursing Charisse.

At the thought of nursing, her breasts throbbed. No wonder Ivaniva had been obliged to feed Charisse. It was well past time.

Derrick set the clothing on the bench. "I'll wait outside." He turned toward the door.

"No, wait." Olivia looked down at the stack and silently berated her aunt's lack of foresight. She had sent out a lovely red merino dress that hooked up the back. And the hooks were impossible for Olivia to fasten and unfasten without help. "I need you—I mean your help." She tried to make her voice sound matter-of-fact, but felt her cheeks warm. "And besides, it's cold out and you've not fully thawed out yourself."

"My feet feel frozen," he admitted.

"If you would just turn your back . . ."

"No, I should wait outside—"

"*Why* must you always dictate how things will be?" Olivia stamped her foot. She sucked in her breath as a pins-and-needles sensation shot through it. Tears sprang to her eyes. When Derrick's brows drew down in concern, she snapped, "Just turn around, please!"

"No." Derrick helped her hobble to the bench and forced her to sit. Frowning, he reexamined her feet, handling each like delicate egg-shell porcelain.

Even his gentlest touch was painful as sensation returned. Olivia bit her lip, holding a cry of pain inside. But she was moved by the concern she saw on his chiseled features.

"Just sit still," Derrick said gently. He took a wash basin from a peg on the wall. In a short time, he had added water to it, then a splash of the hot water from the kettle. After removing his gloves, he tested it by dripping a little on his forearm.

He pulled his greatcoat and hat off and tossed them onto a chair; then he knelt at her feet again. "I'm sorry. This will feel like you are being scalded, but I promise you this water is only lukewarm."

He gently placed her feet in the basin, holding them firmly as Olivia cried out.

Grasping the edge of the bench, she fought back tears. It did, indeed, feel like the water was boiling hot.

Derrick busied himself rinsing the teapot and putting fresh tea leaves to steep.

After a few minutes, Olivia said, "My feet are getting better. They hardly hurt at all."

Derrick took a cloth from a folded stack on the work-table, and he knelt before her again, lifting one foot and inspecting it critically.

"This one is fine." Derrick dried it carefully, noting that her foot was no longer than his hand. There was something about the high arch he found wildly erotic. He imagined pressing his lips to the hollow of it.

Bemused, he placed it on the floor and took the other out of the water.

"What are you looking for?" Olivia leaned forward.

Glancing up, he tried very hard not to notice the length of bare leg visible where the blanket had parted. Looking back at her foot, Derrick cleared his throat. "White splotches of skin."

"My feet were just wet and cold. Surely, they shall be perfectly fine."

"I'll just make certain." He tried to subdue his urge to

stroke her foot more than was necessary to dry it. "This one feels fine, also."

"Feels fine?" Olivia blinked at him as he stood.

"I meant *is* fine."

With the blanket wrapped up to her chin, Olivia stood also. "Well then, off with your boots."

"My boots? Why?"

"I saw you wince as you stood. Your feet must have been nearly frozen—you were out longer than I was. Use the bootjack beside the door and pull them off, then put your feet in the basin," she ordered like a dragoon captain.

His feet were not the reason he had winced, but rather than explaining the nature of the pressure he felt, he obeyed, applying his boot heel to the wedge of the jack.

While his back was turned, Olivia tried in vain to get all the length of the blanket closed. "I was certainly wrong about your ability to handle an ax." *Keep the conversation directed away from anything intimate,* she told herself.

Derrick slid his foot from his boot, then removed the boot from the jack. "My father owned a hunting lodge in the north country. When I was about twelve, he took me up there for the grouse hunting." His tone was unemotional. "Father thought young men should be educated in many basic areas, like chopping wood."

"You didn't like it at the lodge, alone with your father?" Olivia guessed.

Derrick wedged his other heel into the jack. "On the contrary, I lapped it up like your pug dog at a bowl of cream," he said, still without emotion. "Looking back, I think it was the only time I really spent alone with him."

"So, he taught you to chop wood and hunt," said Olivia, sensing she had stumbled on an old hurt. "Good. You have your boots off. While you soak your feet, *facing the fire,*" she said meaningfully, "I shall dress."

Olivia waited until his feet were in the basin, his back

turned to her, before quickly dropping her blanket and getting into her dry underthings. "It must have been a special time for you, just you and your father," she said over her shoulder as she wriggled into the dress. As she feared, she couldn't do up the hooks.

"Indeed. He showed me the manly arts of fishing a fly and hunting and building a proper fire . . ." His voice trailed away.

"And?" Sensing a deep hurt inside him he couldn't or wouldn't let out, Olivia came up behind him and placed her hands on his shoulders.

When Derrick stiffened, she thought he would brush her hands away. Then he shook his head and sighed. "It was special. To me." The words were softly spoken.

"I'm certain it was special to him also. He made the trip with you alone. He must have wanted to spend time with you."

Beneath her kneading fingers, the muscles of his shoulders tensed. The fire crackled. Her memories of her own father were warm and filled with love. He had made her feel special, though he had died when she was only a child of nine.

She sensed Derrick hadn't been as fortunate.

"I thought that if I could just get everything right, just master his every instruction, it would make us closer." Derrick added softly, "I could have his respect, if not his love."

"And did you?"

"He criticized my every effort." Derrick shrugged, as though brushing the memory away.

"How awful for you." Impulsively, she hugged him, aching for the little boy who had needed love and found only disappointment.

"Well, that was just the way of it." He caught her hand and pressed a kiss on the back of it. In a day, he had seen her lavish more love and affection on Charisse than his father or mother had given him his whole life. And he was grateful Charisse had such a loving parent.

Releasing Olivia's hand, he took his feet from the water and bent to dry them.

"Just one moment!" Olivia went around the bench and knelt before him, lifting his foot—much the same as he had done to hers.

As she took the cloth and dried it, inspecting it carefully, Derrick smiled. She did the same with the other, drying it and looking over every inch before setting it down.

Then Olivia surprised him by crossing her forearms on his knees and looking up into his eyes.

"If you would tell me the rest of it, the part that feels too painful to speak of, it might help," she said softly, her green gaze filled with caring and concern.

Feeling she had reached inside him, Derrick sucked in a harsh breath. Indifference he had dealt with all his life. How could he have guessed that caring was harder to bear? The caring in Olivia's green eyes stripped his soul bare.

Gazing past her into the fire, he said, "As we left, I told him how much I enjoyed our time together at the lodge, and I hoped I wouldn't disappoint him next time." Derrick paused. "My father looked at me as if I'd sprouted a second head. He said that there would be no need for another trip. He'd done his duty by me in teaching me things a man of my station should know. He added that he hoped I'd always carry on in a manner befitting my birth."

His father had known Derrick was reaching out to him. As Derrick thought about it now, he felt the sting of his sire's words despite the years. And he felt angry.

Olivia understood a little of Derrick's hurt. After her mother had remarried, Olivia's stepfather belittled her at every turn.

But she had had the memory of her real father's love to sustain her.

Tears blurred her vision for the little boy he had been, so alone. "How awful for you, to never have known approval, or love."

"I think it was then I decided it was better to never need anyone. To simply maintain dignity and not risk rejection." He lowered his voice, searching her face. "But then I met a woman with moss green eyes and a zest for life that made me want more—"

Realizing he was confessing more than was wise, Derrick lifted Olivia to her knees, then smoothed his hands down her torso.

Her eyes darkening, she wrapped her arms about his neck. "Made you want more what?"

He kissed her forehead, certain what he was feeling was unwise. "Did you know, a room seems to light up when you walk into it?" Bending to her, he kissed the tip of her nose.

"Not truly."

"Yes." Spreading his knees, he fitted her between his thighs. "Even when you are on your high ropes—"

"I beg your pardon. When have I ever gotten on my high ropes with you?" A smile twitched her lips.

Derrick looked past her, into the fire. Though he still held her around her midriff, Olivia felt he was far away.

"I was always a little jealous of Peter," he confessed, surprising her. "After his father's death of consumption, my sister coddled Peter terribly, spoiling him. But having grown up with indifferent parents, I thought it had to be better for Peter than no attention at all. I never tried to intervene.

"I saw too late how irresponsible he was. All I could do was deny him money and hope he would learn his lesson."

Derrick's ebony gaze found hers. "Then he snatched you from under my nose."

Olivia wet her lips. "Peter confessed he'd only married me because he was angry that you wouldn't give him money for his gaming debts." She dropped her gaze to his open collar and the strong column of his neck. "I realized how foolish I had been, especially when I found out how much he was in debt."

Olivia again met Derrick's gaze. "Forgive me for hurting you."

"How can I not?" But he wondered if he would be able to forgive her for the next time she hurt him.

Unable to resist, Derrick kissed her long and deep. Then kissed her again. No, the feelings she engendered in him definitely weren't wise.

Chapter Eleven

He broke off the kiss. "We have to go."

"Why?" As though disoriented in a thick fog, Olivia wondered why he had spoken at all. Why he hadn't just kept kissing her.

"It isn't that I wish to leave." Derrick touched her cheek.

Olivia caught her breath. That gentle brush of his fingertips was by far the most intimate touch she had ever felt. It was as though their souls met where his fingers traced her skin. And from the darkening look in his eyes, he was affected just as strongly.

She caught his hand and pressed a kiss onto the palm.

He sighed. "I am only flesh and bone, Olivia."

"This feels so right."

He grasped her face between his hands and pressed a quick kiss on her lips. "But we must go. Marvin will be at the door any second."

"Why do you think that?" She blinked.

A brisk knock sounded, and Derrick smiled ruefully.

"Because Marvin thinks you are vulnerable and must be protected from me. That is why he dragged me out here last night."

It was truly the other way around, he knew. Olivia had never had gentle feelings for him, though he had begun to hope the passion that flared between them might engender more. With all his being, he hoped for more. And that made him the one who was vulnerable.

As another knock sounded, Olivia rose on shaky legs. "Just one moment, please." Her voice sounded husky to her own ears. She put her fingers to her lips. They felt hot and bruised. Turning, cool air slipped down her back, and she remembered the undone hooks.

"Derrick, my dress," she hissed, turning around so he could do it up.

When Derrick opened the door and Marvin entered a few moments later, his gaze went from Derrick to Olivia, who pretended an interest in her still-wet boots on the hearth.

Marvin set a pair of her sturdy country half boots on the bench.

Frowning, Olivia picked one up. "How did you know I needed shoes?" Shaking her head, she said, "Never mind. Thank you for bringing them."

Slipping into his greatcoat, Derrick said, "Marvin, what say you, being we have such a nice big trunk on that oak, I saw a length off to fit into the fireplace in the main parlor. If you can help me get it in there, we will have a proper Yule log."

"Oh, Derrick, I'd forgotten that it is Christmas Eve." Olivia clasped her hands, remembering happy Christmases before her father died, when he would with great ceremony light the Yule log. Afterward, her mother, smiling and lively, would play carols on the pianoforte. "Perhaps, Horice has the ingredients for wassail and egg nog."

"The holiday has never been important to me. But I think we can manage a few festive touches for the children. Maybe, Luther and the Romanoff boys would want to gather ivy for festoons." He added, innocently enough but for a dark twinkle in his eyes, "And, they might go retrieve the mistletoe I knocked down."

"A wonderful idea . . . for the children," Olivia agreed, feeling her cheeks warm.

The afternoon sun streamed through the bay window, warming Olivia as she looked out, Ivaniva's baby astride her hip. Charisse was happily babbling to herself as she lay on a quilt Olivia had placed in a spot of sun on the floor.

Bundled against the cold, the older children played in the glistening snow—even Luther, whose lofty dignity as a footman did not often let him bend enough to join in games. Having great fun, Pootie chased after them and barked as, holding hands, they all skipped in a circle and chanted: *Christmas is a'coming. The goose is getting fat! Please put a penny in the old man's hat. . . .*

Olivia was carried back to her happy childhood in the Cotswolds. She had played in the snow and chanted the same old rhyme.

At the end, all the children fell down in the snow, laughing. The girls started to swing their arms and make snow angels. Olivia had often done the very same thing.

Ivaniva appeared under the portico and clapped her hands, calling everyone inside to help with the decorations.

Jiggling Theresa, who was fussy, Olivia turned away from the window, and spotted Charisse on hands and knees, taking off across the floor.

"Oh, no, you don't!" Quickly placing the younger and

less-mobile Theresa on the quilt, Olivia chased after her daughter.

Laughing, Charisse made it to a lyre-backed chair and pulled up, then looked at her mother and babbled, as if explaining that she had had a plan to use the chair to stand all along.

Though it was cooler on this side of the room, away from the dying fire, Olivia decided to let Charisse have her way. While Theresa seemed content to play with the toes of her booties, Charisse plopped down flat on the floor, then pulled up again and repeated the process.

Watching her daughter, Olivia couldn't remember feeling so content. Not since she was a child herself, at any rate. Last year, her grief for Peter had been fresh. Though she had not loved him, could never have loved him in the deep, abiding way she had once hoped would grow between them, she had felt an affection for him. His loss had hurt.

This Christmas, she was past that. She was a woman of independent means, which meant she was free to live life as she chose.

If she got past her infatuation with Derrick.

A little of her good spirits faded. Though she couldn't deny he had made her desire him, neither would she be so foolish as to believe what was between them was made of the stuff that lasted and nurtured.

But desire him she did. She never imagined just thinking of someone, just the memory of being in his arms, could stir such feelings as rioted inside her right now. The fire that leaped to life between them was powerful and special, even if it held no promise of forever. Forever wasn't what she wanted, anyway.

As if conjured by her thoughts, the parlor door swung open, and Derrick backed his way in, slowly, taking short, strained steps. He held one end of thick log. Marvin followed, hefting the other end.

"Put it down. Easy now," Derrick said, his voice strained. They placed it directly before the fireplace and straightened.

Olivia smiled. "It will be perfect for our Yule log."

Taking off his hat and tossing it onto a chair, Derrick nodded. "Except for one thing. We shan't get this log over the top of those andirons."

Frowning, Marvin pulled off his stocking cap and scratched his forelock.

"Turn the things around," Olivia said. "When the log is in place, chock it with old horseshoes or something to make certain it doesn't roll out."

"Beautiful and brilliant!" Derrick smiled at her and grasped the poker.

Olivia felt ridiculously pleased at his praise.

Theresa began to fuss again. After picking her up and wrapping her blankets around her, in case she was cold, Olivia watched as Derrick worked, dragging first one heavy iron out, then the other. He showed as much enthusiasm for the project as a youngster might, and his high spirits were contagious. She found herself smiling as she patted Theresa's back.

How could she ever have thought him emotionless? Could she have been so wrong about his character?

No. This was not the real man. Derrick was light-hearted and open here at Camden Hall, simply because he felt no need to maintain his dignity in such an undignified atmosphere. Back in London among those he considered his peers, he would revert to type quickly enough. He might feel emotion, but he would not show it.

As her smile faded, Marvin shot her a curious glance.

The andirons were soon turned backward, and the huge

log was in place. Marvin left to find something of iron to chock it with.

"Wooo, wooo." Pulling up on the chair again, Charisse stared curiously at the log, then looked up at Derrick.

"Hello, princess. Do you want to come here?" Squatting down, Derrick removed his gloves and clapped his hands.

Charisse frowned, as though considering.

"I don't think she is ready to walk, yet." The words had barely left Olivia's lips when Charisse squealed and toddled toward Derrick. She made several shaky steps before faltering. He caught her as she would have sat on her bottom.

"Those were her first steps?" Derrick asked, looking amazed.

"Her very first." Olivia managed a smile. But somehow she felt cheated.

"What a big girl you are!" Derrick picked up Charisse. "What a very big girl!"

The child laughed, catching his nose.

The older children swarmed into the parlor a few seconds later and showed off the holly and evergreen garlands and red bows they had tied. Soon, the parlor was transformed with decorative festoons and laughter.

The duchess appeared, looking very grand in her panniered white velvet and the enormous white wig. She lit the Yule log with great ceremony, then thanked Marvin and Derrick for providing it, as well as enough split firewood to warm the house until the woodcutter provided more.

To the children's delight, for tea time Horice served special treats of cinnamon rolls sticky with sweet icing, and they had hot chocolate to drink. Pootie made a pest of himself begging from first one child, then the next. At Olivia's suggestion, Luther carried the pug to the kitchen. She laughed as she heard Luther promising the dog his own special Christmas bone, which Horice had saved.

As the painter made a quick charcoal sketch of each

child and presented it to them for a present, the composer played Christmas carols on his violin. Everyone joined in the old songs. Nikoli pulled Ivaniva back against him and circled her shoulders with his arms. Ivaniva smiled contentedly. They stood at the edge of the circle around the fire, watching their children enjoy their treats.

Still holding Theresa, now sleeping, Olivia stood beside the pair. She was struck by the affection the two showed for each other, even though they had been married many years. They were a team in every way.

Doubting she would ever find the man she could trust so completely with her happiness, Olivia lost a little of the joy she was feeling. Years alone stretched out before her. True, she would have Charisse. But already Charisse was growing and changing. Soon, the little girl wouldn't need her mother's constant attention.

Derrick moved beside Olivia, Charisse on his hip. His gaze was dark and filled with warmth when Olivia looked up and met it. It warmed her far more than the heat from the blazing Yule log and, at the same time, intensified the small ache that had begun near her heart.

She wished things could be different between them. That he could truly be the person he seemed right now.

Charisse yawned, giving Olivia the excuse she wanted to get away from the festivities for a time. "She wouldn't nap earlier. I'd better take her. I need to feed her before she goes to sleep."

Alone in the parlor, Derrick swirled the last of his brandy in the snifter he cradled in his palm and contemplated taking his leave the next morning. After a wonderful supper of roast beef and Yorkshire pudding, and the festivities wound down and children were ushered off to bed, Lady O had produced the bottle of hundred-year-old brandy and shared it liberally. Eventually, the adults had begun to yawn and take their leaves.

Every time he had met Olivia's gaze during the evening, she had looked away. Her actions said plainly enough that she wanted no part of him.

He downed the brandy, enjoying the mellow fire it spread in its wake.

Marvin appeared in the dining room doorway, a rolled mattress on his shoulder. He placed it back a bit from the fireplace and unrolled it.

"What are you doing?" Derrick asked.

"This fire will likely burn through the night, and there's no screen. I don't think it should be left unattended." Lowering himself to the mattress, Marvin sat on the edge and pulled off his boots.

Looking at the blazing fire through the empty bowl of his glass, Derrick said, "I think I'll be leaving in the morning. You will make my goodbyes for me?"

"That is the wisest course." Marvin stretched out, turning his face to the fire. After a moment, he added, "She needs you, though she won't admit it. Not even to herself, I think."

Setting his empty glass aside, Derrick rose and left. Remembering his greatcoat on a peg in the kitchen, he passed through the dark house and retrieved it.

Pootie had been sleeping beside the kitchen hearth. Pausing, Derrick scratched the dog behind the ear. "Take care of her for me."

The dog thumped its stub of a tail in answer.

At the gate house, Derrick dropped his greatcoat over the back of a chair and lit a candle from the banked embers in the hearth. He then used the bootjack to remove his Hessians. No one had bothered to dress for supper that evening as the festivities, which started at tea time, carried on through dinner.

Smiling to himself, he remembered the jovial atmosphere and the excitement of the children. Even Charisse, who was too young to understand, seemed to catch the spirit of the occasion. It was by far the most enjoyable Christmas Eve he had ever known. Far better than the staid affairs in his family home.

And the best part of it all had been being near Olivia in her festive red dress, even if she had been cool to him.

Shaking his head for a fool, Derrick took the candle and went into the bedroom. And found the object of his thoughts sitting on the bed, her wonderful hair unbound and haloed by the moonlight streaming in through a high window.

After placing the candle in a holder, Derrick turned and looked again, unable to quite believe Olivia was really there. She was. She looked up at him, her green eyes sparkling with the reflected candlelight.

Dropping her gaze, Olivia tangled her fingers in the fringe of her shawl. "I took off my shoes and stockings." She gestured toward a chair in the corner. "I would have been undressed and waiting in bed for you, but I need help with these damned hooks," she confessed, a little breathlessly.

Derrick stood her up and turned her about, thinking she must hear the pounding of his heart. "You're certain this is what you want?"

"I'm certain." She pulled her hair aside to give him free access to the hooks.

He undid the fastenings, glad Olivia couldn't see how badly his fingers were shaking. As he pressed his lips to the side of her neck, she sucked in a deep breath.

Her reaction fired his blood. But he paused. "I have to ask, why? Tonight, you wouldn't look at me."

"I was trying to tell myself I really didn't want this."

"What happened to change your mind?"

Still facing away, Olivia said softly, "I couldn't convince myself of the lie. I do want this. I want to know what it will be like . . . between us."

Derrick opened the remaining hooks and smoothed the dress from her shoulders. It formed a red puddle at her feet.

"You are beautiful," Derrick breathed as she turned in his arms. Her ivory skin was smooth, flawless. The mounds of her breasts rose above her camisole, their dark centers clearly visible through the fine lawn material.

Cupping one, he tested its weight. Olivia closed her eyes, pressing closer to his hand. Watching her reaction, Derrick brushed her nipple with his thumb. She caught her breath as it hardened. He brushed it again, and she moaned.

"I want to see all of you." He stripped the remainder of her clothing from her, and she stood shyly before him. Smoothing his hands down her torso to the flare of her hips, Derrick whispered, "You are perfect."

"Not perfect. My tummy stayed rounded even after I had Charisse," she protested.

Placing his hand on her stomach, he found only the slightest roundness. "It's perfect."

"I've these little marks. Ivaniva says they are where my breasts grew too fast as they filled with milk."

Bending, Derrick kissed each tiny mark he saw. "Your breasts are perfect."

"My legs have always been too long."

Olivia shivered as he slid his hand up the inside of her thigh, just brushing the chocolate brown curls at the apex.

"Legs can never be too long," he said huskily, wanting to lay her on the bed and sink himself inside her.

Still, he wanted more to draw their lovemaking out, to give them both the most pleasure possible. Tilting her chin up with his finger, he kissed her, swift and hard. "You're getting chilled. Get into bed."

Derrick quickly shed his clothing, tossing it haphazardly over the rope frame on the room's other bed, which was presently without a mattress.

Sliding beneath the blankets, he pulled her body along his length. Skin to skin.

Though Olivia had been married, she found she didn't know what to expect. From the hardness pressed against her thigh, Derrick seemed more than ready for her. Still he took an exquisite amount of time, stroking every inch of her skin, then pressing his lips where his fingers had traveled. By the time he moved to kiss her breasts, nipping the taut tips, Olivia writhed with the need to have all of him. Raking her fingernails over his wide shoulders, she pleaded with him to stop the torture and, in the same breath, begged that it would never end.

Holding himself above her, Derrick kissed her deep and long. Then watching her eyes darken, he slowly eased into her moist center until he was fully sheathed. He felt his entire body go rigid as her muscles contracted, holding him.

"I've never felt anything so right."

"Nor I," Olivia breathed.

He wanted to shout in triumph. Then she moved beneath him, and he almost lost control.

After a moment, Derrick moved slowly. Olivia rose to meet him on each thrust. Soon he was beyond thinking. Beyond anything but the wonder of being one with this woman whom he had loved from the first time he had seen her.

Olivia gasped as she felt liquid heat exploding in her, and the explosions kept building, growing more intense. Clinging to Derrick's wide shoulders, she was carried upward into the starry night and shattered there into a thousand glowing fragments.

Feeling her begin to convulse around him, Derrick

found his own release. Afterward, he collapsed beside her and gathered her to him, kissing her bruised lips.

"Is it always supposed to be like this?" she asked breathlessly.

"Yes." *With the right person,* Derrick added silently. Kissing her nose, he cradled her head on his shoulder.

Olivia opened her eyes to find Derrick propped on one elbow, watching her. He smiled a lazy, self-contented smile. A dark stubble of beard shadowed his jaw, and she couldn't resist running her fingers over it, feeling the rough texture.

He captured her fingers and kissed them. "I would never have guessed that you are a screamer."

It took a second for his meaning to sink in. "I did not!" She pulled her fingers free from his grasp.

"And the moaning . . ." He dipped his head to nibble at her ear.

Pulling as far away as the narrow bed would allow, she said indignantly, "I never . . . moaned." Her cheeks warmed at the outright lie.

Derrick captured her before she could get out of bed, kissing her until she stopped struggling and was kissing him back. He broke off the contact with her lips and kissed the tip of her nose. "Marry me?"

Chapter Twelve

He knew the instant the words left his lips, he had said the wrong thing.

Olivia's green eyes widened; then she struggled again to get free. This time, he let her go.

Getting quickly to her feet, Olivia kept the covers wrapped about her—until she saw the action left Derrick propped on his elbow, his long length quite naked. With his wide shoulders, narrow hips, and a lightly furred chest, he was magnificent.

Blushing, she divided the blankets, keeping one and holding the other out to him.

"A little late for modesty," he said drily, but took it. Wrapping it about his waist, he sat on the edge of the bed.

"About marrying you, you can't be serious?" Struggling with an urge to bolt, Olivia instead sat down beside him.

It was on his lips to deny he had meant it, to make some glib comment to salvage his pride. To hide his feelings behind a mask as he had always done.

No, not this time. Though he suspected whatever he said would make no difference, he would say it. "Is that so hard to believe?" Derrick chose his words carefully. "You are a beautiful, desirable young woman."

"Beauty and youth fade."

"I love your gentleness. Your warmth and courage," he whispered. He took her hand and kissed the back. "Your soul."

"Don't." Her vision blurred as she placed her fingers over his lips.

He kissed her palm. "I know. You feel nothing for me— not in the way I care for you."

She stood and glared at him. "I wish that was true! If only that was true!" Beginning to pace, she tightened the blanket about her. "I was a fool to let myself believe what I felt was only carnal, when from the first time I saw you, I was attracted to you in a deeper way."

Derrick felt as though his heart stopped beating, then resumed, slowly and painfully thudding along. If Olivia cared for him. . . .

"It makes no difference what I feel." She turned and glared at him again. "You are still . . . *you*."

"I see." His words fell coldly between them.

"Oh, no. I didn't mean . . ." She had hurt him. Kneeling before him, she cupped his face. "I meant, being free has been my dream, my only dream, for such a long time. I haven't even thought about what I wish to do. How I wish to live my life. I have what I've always wanted, don't you see? You are a wonderful man, Derrick—"

"There's no need to balm my injured pride." He rose.

"When you let your guard down," she finished, standing also. "But I know what will be required of the wife you choose. She must be accepted by society, a hostess whose invitations are sought after by the *ton*. She must be politically minded to further your career when you enter the foreign service. As my stepfather pointed out, a man of your talents is bound to be of great service to the country and build a stunning career. I do not wish to be that woman. I couldn't. My mother tried, and has fallen apart under the stress.''

The blanket wrapped loosely about his shoulders, he moved and looked out the tiny window. He had already refused the invitation to enter government service, an invitation set in motion by Lord Stodgeforth.

Olivia found a loose string on her blanket and wound it about her fingers when he made no comment. "And, well . . .''

"Pray, get it all said.'' He continued to look out on the breaking day.

She rushed on, "In London, you *will* change back.''

"What?'' Frowning, he turned and faced her.

"Here, in this place you think little better than a madhouse, you have been open and warm. You've cast your dignity aside and joined us inmates, so to speak. Back in London, you will again be what is expected of you. What you've been all your life.''

"Never would I—''

"You can do no less!'' she cut him off. "It is who you are.'' Tears trailed down her cheeks.

"I see.'' God's blood, didn't she know the real Derrick Blackwell had been staying at Camden Hall? The London gentleman was the sham, the hollow shell.

No. And he knew with certainty that there were no words to convince her. She preferred to believe him like her stepfather, instead of trusting her heart.

Olivia twined the string more tightly around her fingers. Drawing a deep breath, she squared her shoulders. "I wish you would leave. Return to London.''

* * *

"Will this fog never lift?" Olivia sighed and stared through the window in Auntie O's private sitting room. The snow of two weeks before had melted, leaving mire. She missed the sun, hidden in a gray sky. All was shrouded by the white mist swirling before the window.

Astride her mother's hip, Charisse gnawed her knuckle. Teething, she was irritable and insisted on being held.

"I'm happy my portrait is nearly finished. I've written a friend who owns a very reputable London gallery and invited him to come for a visit." Using a cloth and wood spirits, Auntie O worked at a spot on her white velvet gown where a paint tail had flown from de la Croix's brush. "When he sees the painting, I think Jean's career will be launched."

"That's nice." Olivia jiggled Charisse as the baby started to fuss.

The dowager said, "If you are going to stare out the window waiting for him to return, you should not have sent him away. Or you should read the letters that come every day. The ones you so cavalierly tell Luther to use for kindling."

"I am not waiting for him to return." *That's the problem,* she added to herself. Olivia turned and met Auntie O's arch stare.

"Rule number forty-seven: never lie to oneself, my dear." Auntie O returned her attention to the stain.

"I would be miserable married to Derrick."

"Tall and handsome and caring as he is, I can see where it would be hell." Her aunt sighed. "Ah, if I was but forty years younger . . ."

"He's not really that way."

"But you do care for him," Auntie O said, shrewdly.

"Yes," Olivia said at length. Moving to the wing chair she had sat in the afternoon Derrick arrived, Olivia wondered that it had taken her so long to admit it. She had not really realized it until the morning after their lovemaking. Then the realization had stunned her to the roots of her being. She could see herself shriveling away, as her mother had done, trying to live up to impossible standards.

But now that she saw it clearly, Olivia admitted to herself that she had felt drawn to Derrick the first time they had danced at Almack's. She still remembered the glint in his ebony eyes and the way it made her feel shy and so self-conscious, she had missed a step.

Perhaps, that was why his suit had scared her into running away with Peter, whom she had seen at many parties during the season, and who had paid her flowery compliments, never standing on his dignity. With Derrick, she had been afraid not only of being trapped by the marriage laws, but by her own heart.

"Do you really think you could love him if he was the bloodless, unfeeling monster you've made him in your mind to be? Or if he didn't prize honor?" With a shake of white ringlets, Auntie O answered her own question, "I think not."

"He is a proper gentleman of the *ton*, with political aspirations. He needs a wife who can be a proper society hostess." Olivia placed Charisse on her shoulder as the little girl started crying and rocked back and forth, patting her bottom through her blankets. "He will come to realize I did a kindness for him when I turned him down."

"What if that is not what he wants? I suspect he was happier during his brief stay here than he's ever been in his staid and proper years in London. What if he truly just wants to marry you and live happily-ever-after, as in the fairy tales."

Olivia frowned at her aunt, wondering if the old lady

had finally succumbed to senility. "How could you 'suspect' something that outrageous?"

"That's what he wrote in atrocious verse in his last letter to you."

Olivia blinked. "You read my mail?"

"You seemed not to care about it over much." With a shake of her head, her aunt stoppered the bottle of wood spirits. "The stain is there to stay, I fear."

"You had no right, Auntie O." Olivia stared at her aunt.

"Yes, I know, and I am sorry." Her expression showed not a wit of remorse. "But I grew quite fond of Derrick during his brief stay, and I wanted to know something of the way he was feeling, before I wrote him to say you were *not* reading his letters."

Olivia frowned. "He wrote in *verse*?"

"He's decided to become a poet, you see. In order to express how he feels from now on."

Olivia felt all at sea. A poet? She had pictured him slipping back into the unsmiling paragon he had been before. Leading a brilliant career in some post in government, like her stepfather and other unsmiling paragons did. Not writing verse.

Her aunt went on, "He wrote that he's gotten great encouragement for his efforts from his friends at some coffeehouse where artists and writers gather. Shall I ring for our tea?"

"Please." Olivia felt in need of a restorative.

A short time later, his eyes darting this way and that, never quite settling on Olivia's face, Luther brought in the tea cart and the post. After depositing a stack of letters and a newspaper on the silver tray beside the dowager, he held up a missive and asked Olivia, "Should I use it for kindling, mum?"

"No. I think I ought to see what Sir Derrick has to say if he's going to be persistent and continue writing." Olivia steadfastly refused to look at her aunt, who she suspected would be smirking.

Giving her the cream vellum, Luther brightened. "I like Sir Derrick. He's a right 'un."

Olivia raised her brows at the London slang. "Now that the twelve days of Christmas have passed and we have had our holiday, I think it time to resume lessons for you and Ivaniva's children. You can tell them to be in the main parlor tomorrow at our usual time."

Luther's grin widened. "Yes, mum. I like reading. I've decided I'll be a butler one day, and butlers must read good." He frowned. "*Well*, I mean."

Smiling, Olivia nodded. "Very good." And teaching the children again would take her mind off Derrick. For a time.

Still rocking Charisse, she broke the wax seal and unfolded the letter.

> *Olivia,*
> *I doubt that you shall read this, but I must write it anyway.*
> *You've tore my heart asunder, and tossed it by the way. . . .*

She put the letter down.

"You look pale, dear." The dowager glanced over the front page of the newspaper. "Bad news?"

"It is a poem."

"I see. That's awful."

"No." Olivia felt compelled to defend Derrick's literary efforts. "Not awful. It rhymes a great deal. And . . . and the meter is perfect."

The dowager shook her head. "I fear this one is no better."

Realizing Charisse had fallen asleep, Olivia stopped rocking. "What are you talking about."

Taking the newspaper the dowager held out, Olivia was horrified to see a inch-tall caption:

To Olivia of the Green, Green Eyes

> *What is dignity, without your love?*
> *Position, without your smile?*
> *I throw it all to the winds above,*
> *And hope you'll see that I am sincere.*
> *Marry me, Olivia of the green, green eyes?*

"He almost completed the rhyme," the dowager allowed.

"He's run mad." Olivia shook her head, but a smile twitched her lips. "To place this in the *Times* for all to see . . ."

"I suppose he is trying to show you that his consequence is of no import to him. That your love would make him far happier." Her aunt shrugged.

"Why would he do that?" Olivia blinked, wanting to believe Derrick really cared more for her than his own social position. Most of all, that he wouldn't regret giving up his social position.

"Because that is what your aunt suggested, to find some way of showing I'd thrown my consequence to the wind." Derrick stood in the doorway, still wearing his curly-brimmed beaver and many-caped greatcoat as though he had just arrived. "A very wise woman, your Auntie O. Her rule number twenty-nine is, when something is of soul-deep importance, never give up and never give in."

"Derrick?" Olivia's vision blurred, and she blinked.

"You should have guessed he brought the newspaper. I do not subscribe to the *Times*." The dowager rose from the settee. "Put my great, great, great niece down here to finish her nap, and I shall watch her. I suspect the two of you have things to say to each other."

Once in the hall, Derrick closed the door behind them. "You're wearing black again."

"I felt I was in mourning."

"For Peter?" he said, looking grim.

"No. I grieved for the man I sent away, nobly saving him from marriage to a flighty creature who could not bear the thought of existence in the censorious London society he lived in."

"You were never flighty. You're wise. You saw through the pomp and circumstance of society to the empty existence beneath." He touched her cheek. "You were meant to touch people's lives, lifting them up, like the dowager."

Swallowing the lump in her throat, Olivia gazed at him. "Thank you. To be compared with Auntie O is a wonderful compliment."

Derrick smiled. "Christmas Eve, she asked me about financial advice in setting up her estate in trust, so her charities would be taken care of even after she can no longer hold the reins." He shook his head. "I would never have guessed she has more than five hundred pounds a quarter and supports two orphanages and a magdalene house."

"In addition to us strays, whom she's taken in." Olivia smiled. "Auntie O sees the orphans not only given clothes and meals, but schooled, and when old enough, given a proper apprenticeship so they may learn a trade. She does her best for her unwed mothers, also." Olivia knew she was avoiding talking about the one thing she wanted to speak of. How very much she loved him.

Tangling her fingers in her shawl fringe, she said, "So, being compared to her is *almost* the greatest compliment anyone has ever paid me."

"Almost?"

"A certain poem in the *Times* was the greatest. And the answer is y-y-yes." She shivered out the last word, whether from the cold in the hallway, or nerves, she couldn't guess.

"Yes? You mean, you'll marry me?" Derrick grasped her shoulders.

"Y-y-yes."

"You're chilled." Quickly undoing the buttons of his greatcoat, he enveloped her inside it with him.

Wrapping her arms about his waist, she melted against his warmth.

"Olivia, I am the happiest man alive! Never will I let you regret it. Never will I revert to that bloodless paragon you feared." He kissed her cheek.

"That was never really you. Anyway, you couldn't. After publishing that poem, you'll never be taken seriously again."

"You're right, of course. Though, I thought it rather good," Derrick said.

Looking up at him, Olivia felt her brows rise. Then she noticed his collar was open, and in true Bohemian style, he wore a flowing tie. Disabusing him of the notion the verse was literate became less important than kissing the vee of chest exposed.

Then his lips were on hers, and the world spun away. After a small eternity, she broke the kiss. "We could go to my room. But Nikoli and Ivaniva's room is next to it. We would have to . . . talk quietly." She blushed at her own temerity.

"The house does seem strangely silent. Just when one would want a mad painter making love to his canvas and a knife-throwing act practicing fervently."

"The painter has finished the portrait and is waiting for it to dry so he can varnish it. And while the children are visiting with cousins—Gypsies, who camp on the edge of the parkland at this time each year—Nikoli and Ivaniva are taking some time to themselves.''

"Then, they will be too busy to notice us.''

She blushed. "You said I scream.''

Derrick ran his hands down her back, cupping her buttocks and pulling her against his growing arousal. "Where is Aldolfo? We could ask him to work on his violin concerto.''

Olivia caught her breath as hot need surged through her. "Aldolfo has declared the world will never understand or appreciate his genius.''

"I fear that's true.'' Derrick sighed. "So he's given up composing?''

"Yes. But he's turned the main parlor into a workshop. It seems he has a fabulous talent for making violins.''

Derrick raised his brows. "Indeed? I am delighted to hear that.'' The shell of her ear caught his attention, just peeping out beneath her cap, and he had to taste it.

Olivia pressed closer. "Oh, Derrick, I love you.''

"Say it again,'' he breathed against her ear.

"I love you. And I want you. But there's nowhere to go to be alone.''

"A-hem.'' Marvin stood holding an armload of wood for the sitting room fire.

Blushing, Olivia would have pulled away, but Derrick would not allow it. Keeping her close, he moved to one side and opened the door.

"Thank you.'' Marvin nodded. "I put your team in the stable. Should take me a couple of hours to hay and feed them and muck out the other stalls.''

As what he was saying dawned on her, Olivia broke away from Derrick and kissed Marvin's cheek, inspiring a fiery blush to sweep over the gatekeeper's lantern jaw.

"Thank you,'' Olivia said, remembering the woodbox in the sitting room was nowhere near empty.

Saying nothing further, Marvin carried his burden of wood through the door.

"How soon shall we be married?" Derrick shed his great-coat and wrapped her in it. "As soon as the bans can be read, I think. Whatever money is yours will stay yours to do with as you like. We will live where ever you like—though, I think we should stay right here."

"Oh, Derrick!" Her eyes misted, and she could say no more for a moment.

"If you like, we could invite your mother to visit us. And perhaps while she's here, we can prevail upon her to fight her addiction. I know a doctor who works with people with problems like your mother's. He has an estate near Bath where his patients go for treatment."

Olivia read the concern on his face and wondered how she could ever have thought him unfeeling. "I think we ought to get a special license and be married as soon as possible, since we've decided to toss convention to the winds. But first," she lowered her voice shyly, "I think we should make certain that the gate house fire is safely banked."

"I'm almost certain it isn't." Derrick kissed her long and deep, pausing only to sweep her up into his arms.

Twining hers about his neck, Olivia continued to kiss him as he carried her down the hall.

Put a Little Romance in Your Life With
Fern Michaels

__**Dear Emily**	0-8217-5676-1	$6.99US/$8.50CAN
__**Sara's Song**	0-8217-5856-X	$6.99US/$8.50CAN
__**Wish List**	0-8217-5228-6	$6.99US/$7.99CAN
__**Vegas Rich**	0-8217-5594-3	$6.99US/$8.50CAN
__**Vegas Heat**	0-8217-5758-X	$6.99US/$8.50CAN
__**Vegas Sunrise**	1-55817-5983-3	$6.99US/$8.50CAN
__**Whitefire**	0-8217-5638-9	$6.99US/$8.50CAN

Merlin's Legacy

A Series From
Quinn Taylor Evans

Put a Little Romance in Your Life With
Rosanne Bittner